The Ancient Book of Magic

Lumen Series Book 2

Matt Sprunt

Living Room Adventures

ISBN: 978-0-692-79945-1

ISBN: 0692799451
Library of Congress Control Number: 2016918126
PRINTED IN THE UNITED STATES OF AMERICA

Table of Contents

Chapter 1

Cohar

Snap! Scott froze, cursing himself for not being more careful. One more mistake like that and he might as well scream out his location. He stood still as a deer, watching for any sign that he'd been discovered, but no other sound came. Still, he knew better than to start moving too soon. He waited for another five minutes straining his ears for any sign of life. Finally, he picked up a rock and hurled it high into the air as far away as he could. He heard the faint sound of it landing in the brush. Pop! Pop! Pop! The sound of gunfire exploded in the silence about fifty yards away.

"Hah! Sucker," Scott whispered to himself, "I've got you now." He crept along the trees as quietly as one can in the dark. He figured he had about fifteen to twenty minutes before the sun began to rise. He also knew if he could make it into position before then, Buzz would be a sitting duck.

Scott attended a military school where a competition, called the War Games, was held at the end of each year among the students. It was an exciting, but very competitive event where the students split up by division, and using high powered paint ball guns, tried to capture the other team's flag. For the past week, while Scott was attending summer school, he and Buzz, the school's military instructor, had been playing their own little version of war games each morning before dawn. Buzz had beaten him two out of the last three times. Today was Scott's turn to even up the score and he had Buzz right where he wanted him, or so he thought.

Suppose Buzz purposely fired to give away his location, Scott pondered. Maybe he wants me to think he's over there and now he's doubling back. Scott played each possibility over in his mind. He had been debating the possibilities for about five minutes when he heard a sound behind him.

He quickly ducked down, pointed his rifle in the direction of the sound and waited. With his heart hammering in his chest, he reminded himself to remain calm and stay quiet. With any luck, Buzz had not seen him. Another five minutes went by and all was quiet. Scott was beginning to think it had been his imagination when another twig snapped, only this time it was much closer.

"Come to Papa," he whispered to himself. As he waited, he noticed the sun beginning to rise over the mountaintops. Relief flooded over him, as he knew this would make it easier for him to spot Buzz. He heard another crack, quickly followed by another, but he still couldn't make out any shape.

"Be patient," he whispered to himself. Again, there was a resounding snap, followed by another one. Then a form emerged ahead in the woods for just a second before it disappeared again behind a tree. Scott aimed his rifle in the direction where he had last seen the figure. His finger lay on the trigger, tense and ready to pull. He didn't have to wait long. A minute later the figure reappeared and Scott fired his gun. Pop! Pop! Pop! The figure hit the ground and Scott leaped to his feet. He sprinted over to where Buzz lay.

"I got you, sucker! You walked right into my trap. Ha ha! Now we're even. Tomorrow determines the winner and I…" Scott stopped in midsentence and froze. Fear gripped his heart. He sucked in a shallow breath. He tried to take in more air, but it wouldn't come. A terrible pain arose in his chest, catching him in mid stride. Dread filled his whole being as he recognized the all-encompassing pain he had felt once before about a year ago. It had been on Lumen when he encountered an unfriendly Magus in the middle of the night. It was the death grip he so greatly feared. The death grip was a magic spell that constricted the lungs so a person couldn't breathe, eventually killing them if it was done long enough. The figure lying in front of him rose to his feet and Scott realized it wasn't Buzz at all, but Cohar. Scott would have gasped if he could have. His eyes grew wide.

It was Cohar who had put a curse on the dragons and forced them to kidnap Azinine in order to ransom her for the golden sword. It was Cohar who killed the high king, and it was Cohar who was leading the secret rebellion against the magi council. Scott had hoped Magus Cohar had been killed when he had destroyed the large crystal which powered the magus' magic.

"Nice to see you again, Scott," Cohar said with a smile on his face, but with venom on his tongue. "Are you surprised to see me? I'm sure you thought you put an end to my plans on Lumen. Didn't you? But, no, you only delayed them."

"So…what…are you…doing…here…on earth?" Scott choked out.

"I've come to get something I believe you have."

Scott was pretty sure he didn't have anything Cohar wanted, and also knew Cohar wouldn't believe him when he told him so. It was a lose-lose situation and Scott was sure Cohar was going to kill him regardless. In any case, he didn't reply. He was concentrating all his efforts on breathing. It wasn't nearly as painful as when he had felt it on Lumen and Scott guessed that was because he was on Earth, coupled with the fact that he was also a fair distance away from the castle. The magilume, the light that made magic possible on Lumen, was stronger near the castle because of its link to Lumen, but weaker the farther a person moved away from the castle.

Gathering every ounce of strength he could muster, Scott lifted his gun and pulled the trigger. He meant to aim for Cohar's face, but the pain coursing through his body had been too much and he wasn't able to fully lift his rifle. Instead, the bullet hit the hand Cohar was using to hold his staff. Cohar instinctively let go of the staff and it fell to the ground, immediately releasing the death grip. Drawing in a deep breath, and despite the pain he felt, Scott scrambled to his feet and shot off a few more bullets.

Using his cape as a shield, Cohar easily eluded the effects of the paint-balls and once again picked up the staff. Realizing the paintballs weren't effective, but knowing it was the only weapon he had, Scott continued to shoot. Suddenly, a blinding flash of light shot towards him from the tip of Cohar's staff, causing him to temporarily lose his sight. He felt the gun being ripped from his hands and once again the chest-crushing feeling enveloped him.

"You won't get away so easily this time," he heard Cohar threaten. Then, the sound of more bullets rang out from somewhere behind Cohar. Cohar whirled around looking for his assailant. The distraction once again released the spell and Scott took this opportunity to race back to the castle for help. The castle was still some distance away, but getting to Magus McDougal was the only thing he could think of. The task seemed impossible considering the distance and the pain he was feeling. Magus Cohar was sure to catch him before he could get anywhere near the castle. He had only run a few yards when another thought occurred to him and he quickly changed directions and took off in the direction away from the castle.

It was now light enough for Scott to see that Cohar had trapped Buzz in a glass holding cell, a spell Magus Cohar had mastered and used often to trap his victims. He turned his attention back toward Scott. With all the strength he could muster, Scott ran as fast as he could away from the castle. He could hear Cohar pursuing him from behind. Once again, he felt the death grip taking hold, making it harder for him to run. The pain was still there, but he knew he had to keep going or he was a dead man. With each step it was getting harder and harder for him to breathe and he was quickly slowing down.

"Give it up, Scott! You can't escape. You'll only make things worse by struggling." From the sound of Cohar's voice, Scott could tell he was still a ways behind him, but catching up quickly. He continued to struggle on as best he could until finally he fell to the ground clutching his chest.

"Perhaps we could make a deal. I'll spare your life in exchange for the Eigenholle," Magus Cohar said as he approached. Scott was having a hard time understanding him. For a second his words were clear and then they became garbled and then clear again and then garbled. Like a radio getting bad reception.

"What...is...an...Eigenholle?" Scott gasped out.

"Don't play games with me!" Cohar bellowed as his face contorted with rage. "You have the Eigenholle and I want it."

"Even...if...I...had...this...Eigenholle," Scott replied gasping for breath, "I wouldn't...give it...to scum... like you."

Cohar also noticed the strange speech, and asked, "Why are you talking so funny?" It suddenly dawned on Scott that he was far enough away, that the magilume, which allowed him to speak Lumen, was becoming very weak. When Scott did not answer, Cohar said with a malicious smile, "Very well. I hope you've had a good life." He raised his staff and began the death grip once again.

The run, along with the effects of the death grip, left Scott breathless and he desperately filled his lungs with air, feeling only a slight discomfort as he did. Relief flooded over him as he realized that the lack of magilume also made it impossible for the death grip to have any real effect on him; only a slight pain in his chest. Scott took in a few more deep breaths, all the while keeping his eyes on Magus Cohar who was still performing the death grip or so he thought. Scott's chest was still burning slightly, but he managed to get to his feet, anger flooding over him. His combat training took over, and without any warning, he slammed a foot into Cohar's chest, sending him hard to the ground. Cohar hit the grassy forest floor with a grunt. Scott jumped on top of him. He pulled the staff out of Cohar's grasp and then pinned the older man down. This didn't take too much effort, considering Cohar was about a foot shorter than Scott and weighed about thirty pounds less.

"Did you really think a simple magus like yourself could hurt me?" Scott menacingly whispered in his ear. "I have greater powers than you'll ever have. I ought to finish you now." He paused for several seconds for effect, but also because he needed to catch his breath. Then in a more cheerful voice he continued, "But I'm a compassionate person so I think I'll take you back to the castle and feed you to the lions."

"Why are you talking like that?" Cohar shouted. "I can hardly understand what you're saying."

"Ugh!" Scott breathed out. He couldn't understand Cohar very well either. He got off Cohar and started dragging him by one of his legs closer to the castle. Even though he had Cohar's staff, he was still a little worried Cohar would try something when the magilume got stronger, but he couldn't stand not being able to communicate with him.

"Let go of me!" Cohar shouted and tried to wiggle out of Scott's grasp. The humiliation of being dragged through the forest by a boy was more the he could bear.

"Just a little further," replied Scott holding tight to Cohar's leg. Cohar continued to struggle and yell, but Scott ignored him. Once he felt he was close enough to the castle, he let go and spoke again.

"Make one move and I'll blast you," Scott said holding Cohar's staff in his hand.

Cohar's expression was filled with unbelief. "I...I don't believe it," he stammered. "How could you possibly counter spell the death grip? You...you had no staff!"

"My magic is ancient," Scott replied confidently, knowing full well he hadn't used any magic at all. But nonetheless, he was determined to convince Cohar he was, indeed, powerful.

"As I said, make another move, and you'll be sorry. Now get on your stomach!" Scott ordered.

"I will not," Cohar protested and began to stand up, but Scott knocked him back to the ground with his foot.

"I said, get on your stomach!" Scott yelled, threatening Cohar with the staff.

Cohar reluctantly rolled over onto his stomach. Scott used his belt to tie Cohar's hands. Next, he took off his jacket and wrapped it around Cohar backwards, and then proceeded to tighten it up with the sleeves of the jacket to constrain his arms.

The trick now was getting Cohar back to the castle without the magus pulling any more tricks out of his sleeve. Even though he no longer had the use of his staff, Scott wasn't sure that would stop Cohar from using magic. After all, Azinine had used magic without a staff when she had turned his hair black the time they played tag in the clouds. She had also created the illusion of a spider on the wall when he had met her in the council room, and she hadn't used a staff then either. Scott knew the closer Cohar got to the castle, the stronger his magic would become. Hopefully Cohar had believed him about his own magic being ancient and wouldn't think of trying anything.

He lifted Cohar to his feet and then picked up the staff. "All right, let's go," he commanded. "If you try anything, I'll crush you like a bug." Scott, of course, was bluffing, but his bluffs had worked before.

"If you're so powerful then why tie me up? Why not just constrain me with magic?"

"That…that…that would be a waste of good magic," Scott blurted out before he realized how stupid it sounded.

Cohar looked deep into Scott's eyes before speaking again. "You may be powerful. Where you got your training I'm not sure, but we're going to get you, Scott Frontier. Mark my words, we will get you. You will never become king. You will never live long enough to even get the chance."

"Who's we?" Scott asked, a chill running down his spine. "I thought you were the leader of this rebellion."

"Ha! Me? You think I'm the leader? You are sorely mistaken. I am just one pawn among many. And now we know where you live, and where your mother lives and more importantly, who your mother is."

Scott looked at him incredulously. "I don't want to be your king! All I want to do is visit Lumen and be left alone," he snarled. Then, pointing a finger at Cohar, he continued, "And leave my mother out of this!"

"You're lying!" he spat back.

"I am not lying."

Cohar paused for a few seconds. "It doesn't matter if you want to be king or not. If the amulet chooses you, then you will be king, and we can't let that happen."

"They already tried the amulet on me and it didn't work," Scott blurted out.

Cohar stared at him, surprised at this bit of news. Then his face went from a look of astonishment to one of laughter and cunning. "Nice try. If the amulet had been tried on you, we would have heard about it. No, you are the son of Valar. If anyone has a right to the throne, it's you, and we can't let that happen."

"I told you I don't want to be KING!" Scott yelled as if that would some-how talk some sense into Cohar. Scott was fuming. Was he destined to die at a young age, just because these lunatic magi thought he might be the chosen king, even though he wasn't?

Just then a noise came from the woods, and relief washed over him when he spotted Buzz and Headmaster McDougal approaching. "You're a dead man," Cohar whispered to Scott before he turned to face the headmaster and Buzz.

Chapter 2

Visitors

A st first the men just glared at each other. There was definitely no love-loss between the two Magi. Finally Magus McDougal spoke, "Magus Cohar, how nice to see you again. It's been a very long time. You should have at least told me you were coming," he said sarcastically. "I would have given you a much warmer welcome." Then turning to Scott, he said, "Shame on you, Scott! Picking on an old man like this. Please release him."

"But…" Scott started to say, but was quickly interrupted.

"Be a good sport and do as I say."

Reluctantly, Scott removed the jacket and untied Cohar's hands. The moment Cohar was free, Headmaster McDougal raised his own staff and spoke a spell, but only a weak blast of light left his staff. Cohar faltered for only a second and then was able to move again. Headmaster McDougal tried again, but with the same result.

"A bit rusty, are we?" Cohar chuckled.

"Uh, Headmaster, we're too far away," Scott said trying to say it so only Headmaster McDougal could hear, but he wasn't successful. Magus Cohar's face took on a look of confusion, but Scott could see the light bulb in his head slowly coming on.

"Of course," Cohar muttered to himself. "We're too far away from the castle for magic to work properly. That's why I was having a hard time understanding Scott and that's why the death grip didn't work."

Scott shoved Magus Cohar in the back with his staff. "Start walking," he ordered as he pushed Cohar in the direction of the castle. Once they got a little closer, Headmaster McDougal was finally able to subdue Cohar with magic.

While Headmaster McDougal took Magus Cohar back to the castle, Scott and Buzz returned to the equipment shed to hang up their gear. Scott was fairly shaken up by the whole incident and his lungs still burned slightly. But after thinking about what had just happened his spirits began to soar as a new thought entered his mind. Now that Magus Cohar was captured, it would be safe for him to go back to Lumen, and he couldn't think of anything he'd rather do more than go visit Azinine and spend some more time with her. Azinine was the girl who had introduced Scott to Lumen. At the end of his adventures on Lumen he had discovered she was his roommate's sister. She was quite beautiful, and though Scott wouldn't admit it, he was quite taken with her.

Thinking back on his conversation with Cohar, Scott recalled what the magus had said to him about the others coming after him. *Was he just bluffing?* he wondered. He toyed with the idea of telling Headmaster McDougal about his conversation with Cohar, but he knew with that information, the headmaster would never let him go back to Lumen. Besides, if what Cohar had said was true, he wasn't even safe on earth. In fact, he reasoned, he was probably safer on Lumen.

"What will happen to Magus Cohar?" Scott asked Buzz, breaking the silence.

"I'm not sure. They might execute him, but most likely he'll be sent to the Black Abyss."

"The Black Abyss?" Scott asked curiously.

"It's a place where criminals are sent. It's a planet that gets very little light, so it's always dark and very cold. It's kind of like a prison, but a whole lot worse."

"How do you know this?" Scott asked. "Are you Lumen?"

"No," Buzz chuckled. "But I lived on Lumen for several years when I was much younger.

"Really?" Scott said in surprise. "Why?"

"It's a story I'm not proud of and don't really like to talk about, but let's just say I needed a place to hide out for a while and Headmaster McDougal helped me out. Now, enough questions. You need to get to class." Scott wanted to continue their conversation, but could tell Buzz wasn't comfortable talking about it, so he left it alone.

A week passed since Cohar had been taken back to Lumen to stand trial. Scott received word from Buzz that Cohar had been convicted and just as he had predicted the magus had, indeed, been sentenced to the Black Abyss. He also told Scott that Headmaster McDougal would remain on Lumen for another week. As a result, Scott was surprised when, just a few days later, he ran into the headmaster out on the field where drill was held.

"Headmaster McDougal, you're back." Scott said surprised.

"Yes. I was able to tie things up quicker than I had originally thought," he replied with a smile. He then continued, "Scott, there are some things we need to talk about. Do you have a moment?"

"Of course," Scott replied, a little puzzled by the look on the headmaster's face.

"How are you feeling?" he asked.

Scott shrugged. "If you're referring to the incident with Cohar, I was a little shaken up, but I'm doing fine now. You'd think after everything I've been through, this kind of stuff would be easy. But I guess you never get used to such things."

"I have to admit," Headmaster McDougal said, with a touch of admiration in his voice, "I was impressed with your ability to think so quickly. Most students would have run toward the castle. Instead, you ran away from it. That showed incredible presence of mind. Had the amulet selected you, I think you would have made a fine king."

"Ha! After everything that's happened to me here at school, I'm surprised to hear you say that. But thanks for the vote of confidence," Scott replied.

"It's true that your temper sometimes gets you in trouble, but you have more courage than most kids your age and you have a good heart. Those are important characteristics for a leader."

"I guess so," Scott shrugged.

"Scott," the headmaster continued, looking him directly in the eye. "Now that Magus Cohar has been captured, the magi council believes many of his followers will back down. Lumen should be a much safer place. But," he added when he noticed the smile spreading across Scott's face, "we still need to be careful."

"Sure, I understand. Will I be able to visit Lumen?" Scott asked hopefully.

Headmaster McDougal gave him a sly wink and said, "Azinine has been asking if you could visit her."

"She did?" Scott asked excitedly.

"She did. However, I told her no." Then seeing the crestfallen look on Scott's face, he quickly went on to explain, "It's still too soon to know if the danger is gone."

"But…" Scott tried to argue, but was cut off by the headmaster's next words.

"But…I have invited her to stay here for a while, along with Ned."

"Really?" Scott said, feeling like he was on an emotional roller coaster. "When are they coming?"

"They should be here sometime today."

Deciding to push his luck, Scott asked, "Can I have some time off school to be with them?"

"No," the headmaster said with a smile. "However, since summer school doesn't carry a full schedule, you should still have plenty of time to spend with them after your classes."

"Thank you, sir. I really appreciate that," Scott said with a huge grin on his face.

"You deserve it. But remember," Headmaster McDougal admonished, with one last warning, "we don't know if the danger is really over so please stay here on earth." From what Cohar had told him, Scott knew the danger wasn't over, but he wasn't about to tell Headmaster McDougal that.

Chapter 3

A Surprise

Azinine and Ned arrived at CastleOne late that night so there wasn't much time to do anything but go to bed. The next morning the group sat down to breakfast, eager to get the day started.

"So, what should we do today?" Ned asked.

"I have class for the first couple of hours," Scott replied. "But then I have a surprise for you and Azinine."

"A surprise?" Azinine asked, raising her eyebrows.

"Yep! Something I'm sure you'll enjoy."

"What is it?"

"If I told you, it wouldn't be a surprise. Would it?"

"How about a hint?" she continued to push.

"10:30 at the front entrance," Scott said smugly.

"That's not much of a hint," pouted Azinine.

"Sorry! I gotta get to class. Meet me at the entrance at 10:30."

"Okay," said Azinine, with a little pout still on her face.

Ned shrugged, "We'll be there."

Scott walked away, leaving Azinine and Ned sitting at the table. Azinine turned back to Ned. "What do you think it is?"

"I don't know," he said musing. "With Scott, it could be anything. He told us to meet him at the front entrance," Ned said slowly shaking his head.

"What's at the front entrance?" she asked.

"I don't know. That's what has me stumped." Suddenly a light bulb went on in Ned's head. "He wouldn't," he muttered to himself.

"He wouldn't what?" Azinine asked.

"I guess it's okay," Ned said again to himself, ignoring Azinine's question.

"What's okay?" she asked again, exasperated.

Ned looked back at his sister. "Oh, sorry. I was thinking the only reason for meeting him out front is if he planned on leaving the castle. I'm just not sure how he plans on doing this."

Azinine's eyes lit up. "Now that would be a good surprise. I've never been anywhere else on earth except for this castle."

When 10:30 arrived, Scott found Ned and Azinine out front waiting for him. He glanced down the long driveway of the castle, but there was no sign of his surprise in sight. "Hey there," he said putting his arms around the two of them. "The surprise isn't here yet, so we'll just have to wait." He sat down on the front steps and motioned for the two of them to join him.

"What are we waiting for?" Azinine asked as she settled in beside him.

"I'm not telling, so there's no use in you pestering me about it. Now," Scott said trying to change the subject, "tell me what's been happening on Lumen."

Ned and Azinine filled him in on what they knew about the happenings on their world. There wasn't really any information that Scott hadn't already heard from Headmaster McDougal and Buzz. After a few moments of catching up, Scott noticed his family's car heading up the driveway. "There," he pointed triumphantly as it pulled up.

"An automobile!" Azinine exclaimed. "Do we get to ride in it?"

"Absolutely! And not only that, we're going to tour a large city not too far from here. It's called Munich, or as the Germans call it, Muenchen."

"Ooooh, I can't wait," Azinine said, her eyes dancing with excitement. "Ned has told me so much about your cities. I've dreamed about visiting them for so long."

Mrs. Frontier parked the car and climbed out with Scott's little brother Josh close on her heels. He had a huge grin on his face, leading Scott to believe he was up to something.

"Scott," his mother said after giving him a hug, "I'm going in to say hello to Headmaster McDougal. I'll be right back and then we'll be on our way."

"Okay, Mom. We'll wait out here. Hey, runt," he said, turning to Josh, "it's good to see you again."

"Yeah, you too," Josh replied. "You don't mind if I tag along, do you? Mom felt she needed someone to help chaperone you guys."

"Right. More likely she brought you along so you could be watched," Scott retorted, playfully slugging him on the arm.

"Wow," Josh whistled, as his eyes traveled over his brother's shoulder. "Is that your smokin' hot girlfriend?" he asked in a much louder voice than Scott would have liked.

"She's sick!" Josh said out loud as a he approached her.

"I beg your pardon!" she replied indignantly. "I am not sick."

He looked over his shoulder at Scott. "And humble too."

Scott gave Azinine an apologetic look. "Sick is just a slang word that means he thinks you're quite nice to look at." Then he turned to Josh, "This is my *friend* Azinine. Yes, she happens to be a girl, and she is my friend, but she is not my girlfriend," he said, stressing the word. Then nodding towards Ned he continued with the introductions. "And this over here is Ned."

"Sure, we met last year," Josh replied still looking at Azinine. He walked over and stood next to her. "Hi," he said, putting his arm around her shoulder. "I'm Josh, Scott's older, better-looking brother. Why don't you sit in back with me. Then when we get to town, I'll show you around."

Azinine hesitated, taken off guard by Josh's forwardness. She turned to Scott for help.

"Playing hard to get, huh?" Josh piped in before Scott could reply. "Okay, maybe I'm not his older brother, but I do have more money." He reached behind Azinine's ear and pulled out a silver dollar.

Listening to this little interchange between Azinine and Josh, Ned turned to look at Scott with surprise in his eyes. If Azinine picked up on the signal, she didn't let on.

"Pretty good trick," she said, now recovered from her initial shock at the brashness of this young man. "May I see the coin?" she asked.

"Sure," Josh replied, handing her the coin.

She looked it over for several seconds and then gave it back. "Oh, look!" she burst out. "You have one also." She put her hand behind his ear and pulled out a coin. She then closed her hand around the coin, opened it again, and the coin was gone. "Oops! I lost it," she said in dismay. "Oh well! Easy come, easy go." And then putting her hand behind his ear again, she cried out, "Oh, there it is!" But this time she pulled not only one coin, but two from behind his ear. She then proceeded to pull coin after coin from behind his ear, and then made each one disappear.

"Azinine!" Ned spoke up firmly. "We have rules around here."

She threw him a nasty look, but nevertheless, stopped with the coin trick. Ned turned to Scott and whispered, "Scott, can I speak with you privately for a second?"

"Sure," Scott answered, wondering why his friend was so agitated.

The two of them walked a few yards off. They could hear Josh begging Azinine to show him how she had done that incredible trick, but to Ned's immense relief, she refused.

"Scott," Ned whispered, "do you know what this means?"

"Yeah," Scott said as though he were plotting something. "It means Josh is lingual too."

"Yes, I had hoped he would be. But that's not what I'm talking about."

"What *are* you talking about?" Scott asked.

"Are you sure you want to go into the city?" Ned uttered with dismay.

"Of course! Why wouldn't I?"

"Azinine will no longer understand you or Josh."

"Ooooh. I hadn't thought about that," Scott said. "But she'll be heartbroken if we don't take her."

"We could possibly get away with it if Josh weren't here. But what are we going to tell him? Sorry Josh, but Azinine has some strange disease where she talks with you for a little bit and then five minutes later, she can't understand a word you say?"

"Ha, that would be kind of funny!" Scott chuckled. "He's going to find out sometime. Besides, as soon as Headmaster McDougal finds out he's lingual, you two will drag him into his office and try to wrap that amulet around his neck. Maybe we should just tell him now."

"We'd better run that past your mother first," Ned cautioned. Scott agreed, so the two of them waited for Scott's mother to return. When she did, they explained the situation to her.

"Josh already knows," Mrs. Frontier reassured them. "After everything that's happened to you, and after our discussion during Christmas vacation, I thought it best to tell him. However, he doesn't know everything. I specifically left out the part about magic spells. It would drive him crazy! Not to mention, he would then drive me crazy!"

"That's cool," Scott said to his mother. "But I guess this means you and Ned will have to translate. It will be strange not being able to talk with her. Does she know all this?" Scott asked, turning to Ned.

"I think she understands in concept, but I don't think she has realized it in regards to this trip. She does speak some English, just not very well."

"Okay then. We had better discuss it with her so we all understand what is going on," Scott replied.

Once they were all in the car, Mrs. Frontier explained things to both Josh and Azinine. Azinine accepted the situation just fine, but Josh was quite bothered. He was still trying to get Azinine to show him the secret to her coin trick. Not being able to communicate with her would certainly put a damper on his efforts.

It was a bit awkward at times, and some things had to be repeated twice, but between Mrs. Frontier and Ned translating and the little bit of English that Azinine knew, they all had a great time. Azinine was fascinated by the food, the cars and the shops. She especially loved the trains and was intrigued by the beautiful buildings, such as the Palace Nymphenburg and the Palace Schleissheim. As they were touring the castle Schleissheim, Azinine spotted a man dressed in every day clothing typical of earth, but she was sure it was a man that was closely associated with Magus Mordi.

"Ned," Azinine said tapping her brother on the shoulder, "do you recognize that man?"

Ned looked over his shoulder to see who she was talking about. The man ducked behind a wall, but not before Ned got a good look at him. "I saw him at the Palace Nymphenburg and thought he looked familiar also. But I can't think of how I would know him."

"I could swear I've seen him on Lumen with Magus Mordi."

"Do you think he's following us?" Ned asked.

"I don't know. In any case, we had better let Valar know." They found Scott's mom, who was known as Valar on Lumen, and explained what they saw. She became concerned and decided it would be wise to cut their trip short and get back to the castle.

"Mom," Scott asked, "how did they find us? I haven't told anyone about this excursion, not even Headmaster McDougal."

"Hmm," his mother mused. After a minute of thinking, she said, "It's possible they're not trailing you at all, but me."

"You? "Scott questioned, remembering his discussion with Cohar. "But how do they even know you're here?" he asked.

"Well, "she replied, "they have many ears and eyes, and when I visited you on Lumen a couple of months ago, I may have given myself away. We knew it was a risk, but it was a risk we were willing to take."

"Why would they be after you?"

"Well," she began, but then hesitated. "Actually, I'm not sure," she finally said. Scott got the feeling she wasn't telling him everything. In fact, he was pretty sure she did know why they might be after her, but just didn't want to say.

When they returned to the school, Josh once again took up his quest to convince Azinine to reveal her secret coin trick. She still refused to tell him, but she did give him some hope after indicating that perhaps someday she might show him. After Josh and Mrs. Frontier left, the three friends spent the rest of the night talking about Lumen and reminiscing on the things they had done while visiting there.

Ned was delighted to know that Azinine had shown Scott how to play tag in the clouds and the forest, although he was a bit perturbed she hadn't asked him first if they could use his winged boots.

"Hey, Scott," Ned said, when a new thought occurred to him. "I don't mean to change the subject, but what was in that package your mother gave you the night of the celebration dinner?"

Scott thought about his friend's question for a second. "Actually, I'm not sure to tell you the truth. I had forgotten all about it. Let's open it and find out."

The three of them trudged up the stairs and plopped down on the beds. Technically, Azinine wasn't allowed in the boy's dorm, but since there were only a few students attending summer school, they figured it wasn't a big deal this one time.

Scott opened the drawer to his dresser and pulled out the package. Eagerly he ripped open the brown wrapping and opened the box. Inside, there were two objects. One was a stick that was about a foot long. On one end there was a small clear stone embedded in the wood. The other thing looked like a wooden jewelry box. Scott tried to lift the lid but it wouldn't budge. They all took turns trying to get it open, but none of them could figure out how to do it. After a while, they turned their attention back to the stick.

"The stick, as you called it," explained Ned, "is a Shalle, or a training wand. It's used for training magicians and witches. It allows you to cast spells and stuff, but very simple ones and most of the time they are only temporary. The box, on the other hand, I've never seen before and have no idea how to open it." He turned to his sister. "Do you have any ideas?"

Azinine was staring so intently at the box, that she didn't hear his question.

"Azinine!" Ned called louder.

She popped out of her trance and looked at Ned. "What?"

"Do you know what this box is?"

"Well," she answered slowly, "the writings on it are very old. I can't read them, but I recognize them from some of the books in father's ancient book collection. The box must be very old. I'd love to know what's inside, but I'm not sure how it opens either."

Scott wasn't paying any attention to his friends' conversation about the interesting box. He was too fascinated with the Shalle, and the idea of learning how to do magic. "I think it's time you guys taught me how to do some magic. After all," he reasoned, "why else would my mom give me the Shalle? She obviously wants me to learn."

"That makes sense," Ned replied. "But we'd have to do it on Lumen, we're not allowed to do it here."

"Now that Cohar is gone, that shouldn't be a problem, right?" Scott questioned. Even as he said the words, he felt a twinge of guilt as he remembered his conversation with Cohar and Headmaster McDougal's words of caution about going back to Lumen. However, the thought of learning magic was just too hard to resist. "Besides," he argued, "it's safe now. Headmaster McDougal is just being overly cautious. We'll be fine."

"I agree. I think it's a great idea," Azinine chimed in.

"I don't know, guys. Headmaster McDougal asked us to stay here," Ned reminded them.

"Ned, it's only for a little while," pleaded Azinine, wanting a bit of adventure. "If it makes you feel better, I'll disguise him so no one knows it's him."

"Oh, okay," Ned replied dubiously. "I guess we could as long as we're careful and don't stay too long."

"Then it's settled," Scott said triumphantly. "First thing in the morning we head to Lumen."

Chapter 4

Magic

When morning finally arrived, Scott was the first one up. He was looking forward to the day ahead and didn't want to waste it by sleeping. He pulled out the bracelet Azinine had given him months ago to signal each other, and sent a signal to her, letting her know he was awake. There was no guarantee she was awake and would see it, but it was his only option, seeing as how she didn't have a cell phone. He waited for several minutes, but nothing happened. He shrugged, and started pulling on his pants when the other stone on the bracelet lit up.

Sweet, she's awake. So far so good, he thought to himself.

Satisfied she was up and getting ready for their big day, he turned to wake up Ned. Just as he was about to nudge his friend's shoulder, he had another brilliant idea. He reset his alarm to go off Three minutes later. Then he ran to the bathroom and filled a cup with lukewarm water.

Hurrying back to his room he muttered, "I may live to regret this." He crept over to Ned's bed, carefully lifted the blanket and slowly poured the water onto the bed, making sure the water didn't directly touch Ned. He figured it would only take a few seconds before the water eventually soaked into his pajamas. He then scrambled into his own bed, just seconds before his alarm rang. Trying hard to hide his grin, Scott yawned loudly and sat up.

"Get up, Ned!" he said, looking out the window. "It's morning and what a glorious morning it is."

Ned opened his eyes and looked outside. Groaning a little, he proceeded to get up, but immediately brought his covers back down around him, his face showing astonishment. Scott almost burst out laughing when he noticed the disbelieving, but curious look wash over Ned's face.

"What's wrong?" he asked trying to stifle a chuckle. "You look like you wet the bed or something."

"Ugh! YOU did this! I'm going to kill you!" Ned said jumping up. Scott quickly grabbed his towel and headed for the showers before Ned could reach him. Ned got up, removed his sheets from the bed, and grabbed his own towel.

"I won't say a word to anyone at school, I promise," Scott said as Ned entered the bathroom. Then giving him a sly grin, he added, "But maybe you shouldn't drink so much before you go to bed."

"Ha, ha," Ned said. "You just wait."

Scott finished getting ready before Ned did, so he told him he was going downstairs to wait with Azinine. When Ned finally came downstairs he found Scott and Azinine sitting on a bench laughing hysterically.

"Ned, I'm so very sorry," Azinine said as sincerely as she could. "Scott told me about your bed wetting problem. I thought mother's spell cured that."

"Very funny," Ned retorted. "You know darn well your Romeo over there poured water on my bed as a joke."

"What? Do you really think I would do something like that?" Scott mockingly asked.

"As the infamous Bugs Bunny once said, 'I hope you know this means war!'"

"Ha! You're a good sport, Neddy boy," Scott said still laughing.

"Yeah, well, let's hope you're as good a sport when I get even. Now let's eat breakfast. I'm starved."

"Sounds good, but I'd suggest you hold off on the fluids," Scott jibed, sending Azinine and himself into another fit of laughter.

"Ha, ha, you are soooo funny," Ned replied.

Once they were on Lumen, the three of them located the MOC Ned and Azinine had left at Cylindhall, and flew to the Great Forest where Azinine and Scott had played tag.

Scott jumped off the MOC and whipped out the Shalle. "Halt! Or I'll blast you to…to…to the Black Abyss, or whatever it's called."

"Put that thing down before you hurt yourself!" Azinine ordered with a laugh.

"Maybe we shouldn't do this," Ned said, having second thoughts.

"Why not?" Scott asked.

"Look at you. You're a loaded cannon just waiting to accidentally go off."

"I am not. I was just goofing around. What's the big deal?" Scott asked.

Ned sighed. "Scott, magic isn't performed by just anyone who feels like it. A person isn't allowed to own, or even hold a staff, until he or she has been trained and certified. Doing magic can be very dangerous and it needs to be controlled. You wouldn't let a plumber perform surgery on you, would you?"

"No."

"If your car was broken, you wouldn't take it to a lawyer would you?"

"Not unless he knew what he was doing."

"Exactly," Ned said, feeling as though his point was getting across. "He might do more damage than when you brought it in. Sure, he could do a few simple repairs like changing a tire. But certainly you wouldn't trust him to overhaul your engine unless he had been trained. The same principle applies to magic. We could get in a lot of trouble for teaching you. Especially if you did something harmful or irresponsible."

Seeing the sense in Ned's argument, Scott conceded, "Okay. Then just teach me how to 'change a tire' for now."

"Okay," Ned replied, feeling much better about that. "We'll start simple and then go from there. We'll see how you're doing and maybe later we'll teach you more. Agreed?"

"Agreed."

"Azinine?"

"Agreed," she replied.

"Okay then," Ned said, clapping his hand together. "First, you need to understand that if you're to obtain the proper training, as Azinine and I have, you would have to spend years in the classroom."

"Years?" Azinine asked, raising her eyebrows.

"Okay, maybe I haven't spent years in the classroom like you, but I still know quite a bit," Ned replied.

"Just want to make sure you get your facts straight," she commented.

"Whatever. In any case, magic reacts differently depending on what you are trying to do, what you are trying to do it to, and how you go about doing it. There are so many rules that it would take us months to explain. It's kind of like learning a new language. You have to learn a whole new vocabulary and new rules of grammar. So, as you can see, we could spend months explaining how magic works.

"Second, magic is more of an art than a science. The effect and strength of magic depends not only on the magical words used, but the amount of emotion and concentration they are said with. Words, even in your world, can be very powerful depending on how they are used. For example, if you approached your mother saying something like, 'I like you,' that would have a positive impact on her. However, the impact would be much greater if you said, 'I love you.' Also, the degree of impact depends on the amount of emotion with which you say the word. For example, you…"

"I get the point, Ned," Scott said getting impatient.

"Fine." Ned said, "Let's start by teaching you how to change the color of something. This trick is easy enough and can be done with a simple magical command. In fact, you don't even need a shalle or a staff. The magical command is 'vechs' plus the name of the object, plus the name of the color. For example, see this stone in my hand. If you want to change its color to red, you would say, 'vechs ruen.' See? The stone is now red," he said as he held it out for Scott to see.

"Yeah, but you didn't say the name of the object," Scott pointed out.

"True, I guess I should have mentioned why that works before I did the trick," Ned said, patting him on the back. "There is a rule that if you are touching the object, you don't have to say the name. On the other hand, if you're not touching the object, then you would need the shalle and you'd have to say the object's name. You use the shalle by simply pointing it at whatever you are working with."

"What if I miss?" asked Scott.

"The shalle only has to be pointed at the object. To hit the object you have to concentrate on it. If for some reason you miss and hit something other than the named object, the magic won't work. It takes some practice and that's why we use the shalle. Okay, it's your turn."

Scott picked up a stone and said, "vechs ruen." To his utter delight, the stone turned red. "Vechs felb," he continued and the stone turned yellow. He looked over at Ned and Azinine and smiled. "Piece of cake."

"How did you know the color yellow?" Azinine asked.

"Azinine," Ned interrupted, "Scott can't really speak Lumen or understand any of the magical commands. When we say 'vechs ruen' he simply hears the translation in English. He's lucky. All he has to do is speak the command in English and it will translate.

"That's not exactly true," Scott countered.

"Really? What do you mean?" Ned asked.

"When you speak normal Lumen that's how it works. But I actually heard you say the word 'vechs,' and instantly I knew it was the magical word for 'change.' When I thought about the color yellow, I instantly just knew it was 'felb.' The only thing I can figure, is in order for me to perform magic, I really do need to say the magical command. However, being lingual, I don't have to memorize them, because I somehow already know them. They just come to my mind. I know that sounds strange, and I don't really understand *how* it actually works, but that's what happened."

"That's great! This means you won't have to memorize any vocabulary. You'll just need to learn how to use them," Ned replied. "Now for the real test. Try it using the shalle."

Scott tossed the yellow rock a few yards away. He pointed the shalle at it and said "vechs sharts skein," which literally translates into 'change black rock.' A tiny twinkle of light trickled out from the tip of the wand, but the rock lying on the ground was still as yellow as a canary. Scott looked at Ned for help.

"No, you said the words in the wrong order. You have to say 'vechs skein sharts' and hold the shalle like you mean it. Imagine if you were holding a pistol about to pull the trigger and speak the words with more conviction."

"Okay. Vechs skein sharts!" Scott said, this time with conviction. A small blast of light surged from the tip of the shalle and several rocks, including the one that was yellow, now lay pitch black. Azinine let out a giggle. "Well, at least I did it!" Scott said defending himself.

"Yeah, but I distinctly remember saying *pistol*, not *shotgun*," Ned joked. "Try it again, but get a little closer this time and concentrate only on that one rock."

Scott stepped closer and pointed the shalle. "Vechs skein ruen." Once again, a tiny blast of light left the shalle. However, this time he was successful. The rock he had been aiming at was the only one that turned red.

"Good job!" Azinine yelled clapping her hands together.

"Very good," Ned said taking the shalle from Scott. "Now you need to learn how to undo the damage you've done. The word is 'yederharstal.' You can either restore them one at a time, or use the 'shot gun' method you used earlier."

It took Scott a few tries, but eventually he restored all the rocks back to their natural state.

"Could I undo any spell, including someone else's, using that command?" Scott asked.

"Sure," Ned answered. "As long as the spell is temporary. There is a command for making a spell permanent. The permanent ones can still be undone, but it gets complicated."

"Okay then," Scott said, rubbing his hands together. "What's next?"

"Let's teach him illusions," Azinine suggested.

"Illusions are too complicated," Ned replied.

"Maybe. But they're also harmless. It could be quite entertaining."

"Ha, ha. That's all you like me for, isn't it? Entertainment!" joked Scott.

"Well, you're not good for much else," Azinine replied, winking at him.

"Watch it! I'm armed and dangerous," Scott replied holding up the shalle.

"What are you going to do? Turn me purple?" Azinine asked, giggling some more.

"Good idea," Scott said while pointing the shalle at Azinine.

"Scott, no!" Ned called out, but he was too late.

"Vechs yemp posa!" Scott yelled and a blast of light left the shalle. Azinine screamed and jumped out of the way. The shot of light missed her and hit Ned square in the chest. Ned looked down to see his shirt a bright pink. Scott and Azinine fell into a fit of laughter.

Azinine put her hand on Ned's head, and choked out, "Vechs ruen," through her giggles. His hair was now a flaming red.

Scott pointed the shalle at his friend's pants, and said, "Vechs nohsa grin," turning his pants a bright green. Scott and Azinine were now laughing so uncontrollably, they had tears streaming down their cheeks.

Chapter 5

The Magic Fair

They wiped the tears from off their cheeks, while Ned just shook his head. "You guys are hopeless. Yederharstal," Ned spoke and immediately he was back to normal. "I think we've had enough magic lessons for the day. What do you say we go to the fair?"

"Oh, that's a great idea," Azinine exclaimed. "Why didn't I think of that?"

"Then it's settled. We'll pick this up another day." Ned put his arms around both of them. And as he did so, he placed his hand on Scott's hair and whispered, "Vechs blaou," turning Scott's hair a bright blue. Of course, on Lumen, that wasn't really all that bad since blue hair was quite popular. Glancing over at him, Azinine noticed, but only smiled.

"Wait a second," Scott said, "I tried to turn Azinine's shirt pink, but she ducked and it hit you. I thought you said it wouldn't work if I hit something else?"

"I said it wouldn't work if it hit something other than the named object. The named object was shirt, and that's what it hit…my shirt. Now had you been concentrating more on Azinine and not shirt, the result would have probably been different."

"Hmm. I see. Good to know," Scott replied.

The fair was amazing. Scott had never seen anything like it. There were animals he had never even imagined existed, booths with various potions said to do all sorts of wonders, magic games, jousting contests on flying discs, thrill seeking rides, magician tournaments, and much, much more. As they walked, Scott paused to watch the jousting contest. Knowing this was all new to Scott, Ned and Azinine stopped to let him watch.

There were two men in a jousting ring. Their jousting poles weren't sharp on one end like the ones medieval knights used. Instead they were round and bulbous on each end so as not to skewer the opponent, but to knock them off their disc. Their discs were about three to four feet in diameter. One was yellow and the other was red. They rode them similar to how Scott would ride a skate board, except these discs hovered above the ground.

The two men circled each other flying about five feet in the air. The discs seemed to do whatever the jouster wanted them to do and Scott couldn't quite figure out how that worked. Suddenly the yellow jouster charged the other, dropping down to about a foot off the ground. Covering the ground were some sort of bubbles or clear balls. Scott guessed these were used to cushion the fall of the jousters if they fell. The attacking jouster swung hard at his opponent's legs, hoping to trip him up. His opponent jumped, narrowly avoiding the swing as his attacker zipped past him.

The red jouster quickly turned and pursued the yellow jouster. Someone from the crowd yelled out, warning him of his pursuer. The yellow jouster made a slight fake to the left and then turned sharply to the right. It was enough to throw his pursuer off and the two jousters circled around in opposite directions and began to circle each other again. It was then that Azinine found the eyes of two men in the crowd looking at them with more than just causal curiosity.

"I think we had better be moving on," she said to both Ned and Scott.

"Hold on, I want to see who's going to win," Scott replied, fascinated by the event.

"Scott, there are men looking at you, and I'm not sure the blue hair is fooling them."

Scott turned to her. "Blue hair?" he asked reaching a hand up and feeling his hair as if that would confirm his question.

Azinine gave him a guilty smile. "Yes. Ned's doing, not mine. Come on. We need to get out of here," she urged, grabbing him by the arm and pulling him away from the crowd. Scott let her lead him away, but he continued to look back as he walked, fascinated by the whole event. Azinine looked back to where the two men had been, concerned to find they were gone. She looked around trying to find any sight of them, but they had vanished.

Scott was so enthralled by the joust, that he didn't notice the looming beast bounding towards him until it was only a few yards away. Whatever the animal was, it was as large as a horse, and it was leaping through the air right at him. With his military training from school kicking in, Scott immediately dove to the ground hoping to get under the beast and escape being mauled. As he landed, he quickly jumped up and whirled around expecting to see the hound coming at him again, but it was nowhere to be seen. It was then that he noticed the crowd, including Ned and Azinine, laughing at him. Embarrassed and confused, he wasn't sure what had just happened, but from the looks of things, the joke was obviously on him.

"That was great! He got you good," Ned chuckled to Scott as they melted back into the crowd.

"What was that thing?" Scott asked, still a little shaken.

"It was a terror hound, or at least an illusion of one."

"Are you telling me that such a beast actually exists?" Scott asked incredulously.

"Yes, but I've never seen one in the wild. They have one in the Animal Showplace."

"The Showplace! We've got to take you to the Showplace," Azinine cried out. "They have some incredible exhibits."

"What is an Animal Showplace?" Scott asked, a little wary after his experience with the terror hound.

"It's basically a zoo," Ned replied.

"Oh? Sounds cool, but let's do that tomorrow. There's still a lot here I'd like to see."

Ned and Azinine nodded in agreement and steered Scott over to a potions booth. They could hear people gathered around laughing hysterically, but Scott couldn't see what was so amusing.

"Wonder potions is my guess," commented Azinine.

"What's a wonder potion?" Scott asked.

"There's no label on the potion so you wonder what it will do to you."

"Isn't that dangerous?" Scott asked.

"I guess they could be," she replied. "But the potions are only temporary and I've never heard of someone getting hurt by them. People take them all the time."

Just then a scream went up from the crowd followed by a loud roar. As Scott peered over the heads in front of him he discovered a creature that stood approximately seven feet high. The only thing he could think to compare it to was a large ape man or a kind of sasquatch.

"Is that a person?" he asked.

"I sure hope so," Ned replied. "If you watch carefully he should return to normal in just a minute."

"People can actually change shapes?"

"Sort of," Ned answered. "No one has been able to change shape for any long duration of time. I think the record is a day, but four or five hours is easily done."

"Can you teach me how to do that?"

"Not really. As far as I know, only potions can change someone into something else and neither Azinine nor I have studied potions much."

"Too bad," breathed Scott.

They watched as the ape-man-like creature slowly morphed back into the person who drank the potion. As the fur from the creature disappeared bit by bit, it was replaced by a silver suit on a slim girl. She ducked into a changing booth and shortly returned wearing her own clothes. She then handed the silver suit to the man operating the booth. Scott noticed several others wearing the same kind of suit.

"What is that suit they're wearing?" Scott asked.

"Some potions, like the one that girl just drank, make you larger than your clothes will tolerate, and would rip them if you left your clothes on. The silver suit stretches to almost any length and form. It also takes on the qualities of the form the potion created, so you can't tell a person is wearing it while under the influence of the potion. Only when they return to their normal selves can you tell they are wearing the suit. They are specially made just for potions."

"Wow, that's amazing. Do you have to wear one of those suits each time you take a potion?" Scott asked.

"Only if you think there's a chance you might ruin your clothes by taking it," Ned replied.

Others were beginning to drink their potions and Scott wanted a better look so the three of them made their way through the crowd up to the front. It was the most fascinating thing he had ever seen. There were potions that altered a person's ears and eyes. There were others that made you taller or smaller. One potion made a woman look exactly like the last person she had looked at before she drank it.

Scott wanted to try one, but Azinine didn't dare risk it. They were already taking a chance just having him on Lumen. She didn't want to bring any more attention to themselves than was needed. Instead, she suggested they go to the dreaming pond.

"What's the dreaming pond?" Scott asked.

Relieved he was so easily distracted, Azinine answered, "Oh, you'll love the dreaming pond. It's basically a pond where you share the same dream with other people." At Scott's confused expression, she laughed and explained, "You jump in with a few other people and let yourself sink. You continue to sink until you take in a breath of liquid. Once you've done that, you immediately fall out the bottom of the pond and land in the same dream as everybody else who jumped in with you. Because it's just a dream, you can take any shape you want. But just to warn you, it feels extremely real. Usually the dream is a sort of competition with everybody against everybody else. The goal is to outdo the others and to be the last one remaining. If you're beaten, your dream is over and you end up back in the pond.

"Sounds cool," Scott said eagerly. "But just one question. How do you take a breath underwater without drowning?"

"It's not really water," Azinine explained. "But that's the only way to describe it. It just looks and feels like water. When you are done and you step out, you're not wet or anything."

Scott could barely contain his excitement. "Let's go!"

Chapter 6

The Dreaming Pond

When they arrived at the dreaming pond they were a little disappointed to see how long the line was. But undeterred, they decided to go ahead and get in line. They waited almost two hours before it was finally their turn. As they were passing the time, Scott watched how groups of people jumped in, sank, and then eventually came up six or seven minutes later.

"They aren't down there for very long," Scott commented.

"No, but while you're in the dream, it can seem like hours," Azinine replied.

When it was finally their turn, they stepped up to several platforms that ran out to the middle of the pond. Scott looked down into the dark, murky liquid and began to feel the smallest of butterflies in his stomach. A little nervous, he had to remind himself that he had seen person after person jump into the pond and eventually come back up. What truly amazed him, however, was to see each person exit the pond as dry as when they entered it.

"Okay, Scott, remember. Let yourself sink and then inhale the fluid. It will be scary at first, but you'll just have to trust me," Azinine said, trying to reassure him.

The three of them jumped in and Scott felt himself sink. He tried to make himself breathe in the liquid, but he just couldn't do it. He began to panic and tried to swim back up to the surface, but Azinine grabbed hold of his hand and wouldn't let go. He jerked free from her grasp and stroked madly for the surface. This time, Ned grabbed him around the waist while Azinine reached for his shoulders. In full panic mode now, Scott kicked wildly, dragging all of them towards the surface. Knowing Scott only had a few more seconds of air in him before he'd have to take a breath, Azinine tickled him. Scott reacted instinctively by throwing an elbow, which connected with her head. She fell off immediately and floated motionlessly.

Azinine! his mind screamed, suddenly realizing what he had done. He reached out to grab her, but she had floated too far toward the bottom and he wasn't able to reach her. He could feel himself starting to black out. Remembering what she had said about breathing, he opened his mouth and felt the fluid enter his lungs. It was a weird feeling, but not near as weird as what happened next. Suddenly, he felt himself falling while at the same time, the sensation of his body mutating overcame him. When he landed, he discovered himself in the form of a tiger, surrounded by bars. Realizing he was in a cage, he looked wildly around and noticed both Azinine and Ned close by, also in cages and waving to him. Although they had taken on other forms, he somehow knew it was them. Azinine was in the shape of a unicorn and Ned was in the form of an animal Scott had never seen before. It stood upright like a large ape, and it had large, long claws, thin fur, and a head similar to a lion.

As Scott took in his surroundings, he noticed they were on the outer rim of an island that was covered by a thick jungle. Somehow, Scott knew there was a golden egg in the middle of the jungle and the object of the game was to be the first to get the egg and return with it to the cage. Shaking his head in amazement, he wondered how he knew all this.

"Sorry for the elbow," he called over to Azinine.

"It's okay. I should have seen it coming."

"A tiger, Scott?" Ned teased. "That's the best you could do?"

"What is this place?" Scott asked, ignoring Ned's comment.

"Didn't you listen to anything I said?" Azinine asked in exasperation. "This is a conscious dream world."

"So this isn't really real?"

"No. Right now your real body is still in the pond."

"Whoa! This is so cool. I..."

He was cut off by the sound of a voice counting down. "Five, four, three, two, one, go!" the voice yelled. The cages flew open and Ned and Azinine shot from theirs like a bullet. Scott hesitated for just a second and then jumped from his cage following his friends. He hit the ground on all four legs. The sensation was like nothing he'd ever felt before. It was extraordinarily exciting. He could feel the power of his legs underneath him as he picked up speed. He looked ahead and could see Ned, but there was no sign of Azinine. He quickly caught up to Ned and began to pass him when Ned turned and struck out with one of his powerful arms and sharp claws. Scott screamed out in pain, more than a little surprised as he heard the roar of a tiger, not the yell of a human. Ned had hit Scott with such power that it sent him flying end over end into the undergrowth. As he lay there for a moment catching his breath, he heard Ned, or at least the beast Ned was formed as, howl out in glee.

"So, you want to play dirty, do you?" Scott said to himself. He went to get up, but an excruciating bolt of pain shot through his right side. He looked down to see a huge gash in his shoulder. He struggled to his feet, but could barely manage to limp along.

"This sure doesn't *feel* like a dream," he muttered. "Wait a second! This is a *dream*," he told himself, remembering what Azinine had said. "I can take on any shape I want to." He immediately shed the shape of the tiger, turned into a house fly and sped off. He figured he could sneak up on Ned and he'd never see him coming.

Scott zipped in and out of trees making good time. This was more fun than being a tiger. Being this small, it was easy to avoid the jungle brush. No more than two minutes went by and he saw Ned ahead of him. He easily caught up and landed on his shoulder. He decided to rest for a bit and let Ned do all the work. Then, when he was ready, he'd change into something big and squash him. But no sooner had he decided this, when Ned came to a screeching halt, diving to the left to avoid being skewered by Azinine's horn. She had apparently seen Ned coming and had been waiting for him behind a tree.

These guys mean business, Scott thought as he quickly flew off Ned's shoulder and landed on a leaf, fascinated to see what would happen next. Azinine had turned and was once again charging toward Ned. Meanwhile, Ned leaped into the air, grabbed a branch and hoisted himself into a tree. Azinine snorted in triumph and ran around the tree several times hoping to get at Ned. Here and there, Ned would swing down and try to get a claw into Azinine.

"Enough of this," Scott said to himself. "Those two can play all they want. I'm getting that egg." He sped off again and was making good time when something grabbed him, pulling him back.

"Ahhh!" he yelled. He struggled to free himself and found he was getting more tangled up than ever. Realizing this, he calmed down and discovered he was stuck in a spider's web and the spider, three times his size, was wasting no time in hurrying to its meal. The thing was huge!

"Time to change," he said. But he couldn't think of what to turn into and the spider was getting closer. Out of desperation, he changed into an elephant. Immediately he was free from the web, as he dropped to the ground. However, he quickly discovered that an elephant couldn't exactly move through the thick jungle so easily. He tried changing back into a fly, but found he couldn't do it. Guessing that a person could only change into a form once, he decided to remain an elephant and just smash his way through the jungle. Although he was making progress, he was also giving away his location and he soon found a terror hound bounding up behind him. Scott whirled around, and noticing that it was Azinine, stood up on his hind legs and blew his trunk at her.

Not to be deterred, she leaped into the air with jaws wide open, ready to sink them into whatever she could find. Scott came down on all fours, expecting to flatten her. Azinine, however, was too quick and had turned into a Nonbee, a type of bird Scott had encountered on Lumen during his last visit. She was about to charge, when Scott yelled at her. "Azinine! What has gotten into you and Ned? Why do you guys keep attacking each other?"

"That's part of the game. You have to outdo each other. Part of that is destroying your opponents' form. If you injure another form, you get stronger. If you destroy their form before they are able to change, they are out of the game and you become really strong."

"Now you tell me!" Scott snorted. "It would have been nice to know that from the start." Looking up, he saw a horrible looking alligator-like creature, descending from the trees. "Watch out!" he yelled. The alligator, with its jaws open wide, was heading right for Azinine. She zipped out of the way just in time as it slammed into the ground. Scott instinctively started stamping on the creature. As he did, he felt a burst of energy coursing through his body and understood what Azinine had been talking about. The alligator-like creature quickly turned into a butterfly and fluttered off.

"Thanks," Azinine said. "I would have been out for sure."

"What was that thing?" Scott asked.

"They're called water dragons. They don't have wings and they don't breath fire, but they float like dragons just the same. They're able to move quietly and quickly through the forest and water searching for prey."

"They really exist?"

"Yes, and you don't ever want to meet one in real life."

Scott shuddered. "That wasn't Ned. Who was it?"

"No, it was another player."

"We should stick together then, and play as a team."

"Good idea," Azinine agreed.

The two of them headed further into the jungle. They knew they had to be close, but they still hadn't located the egg. They continued searching until finally they came to a clearing where they could see the egg on a dirt mound that was covered with sharp, thick thorns. They noticed a few other creatures already there too, standing on the perimeter. So far, no one had made a move for the egg and Scott shot towards it.

"Scott, stop!" Azinine yelled.

Scott skidded to a stop and turned around. "What's wrong? There's the egg."

"It's not that easy," she explained. "There's a reason no one has made a move yet. The egg itself will try to avoid being caught, and there have been many players eliminated in the act of trying to grab it. Those thorns might shoot out at you or the mound might explode. No one knows what it will do. Look at the others. They are all hoping that another player will try to do just what you were about to do. As soon as the egg tries to escape, it will be vulnerable, but the person who usually grabs it first is the one who fares the worst."

"Okay," Scott said, once more amazed at the details of this game. "I've got an idea. I'll change into a bee and fly over to the egg. Once I'm directly over the egg, I'll change into a turtle and drop on it. My shell should protect me. This will give you a chance to grab the egg."

"Okay," she agreed. "But I can't guarantee that will work. You might lose."

"It's just a game."

Scott turned into a bee and flew directly over the egg. The platform the egg rested on began to tremble. Watching the others back away, Scott took in a big breath. He turned into a turtle, quickly pulled in his head, arms and legs, and fell like a rock. He heard or rather felt an immense explosion and felt himself hurtling towards the sky. He knew he had to change form soon because the fall back down to the ground would certainly kill him. He was about to change, when he landed softly on the ground and found himself rolling end over end down a hill until finally he came to a stop with a thud.

He cautiously poked his head out and what he saw surprised him. He was on a ledge about halfway down a very high mountain. Looking up, he saw that the tip of the mountain came to a sharp point and at the very top of the point sat the egg. The mound had grown into a mountain! Below, he could see various forms of birds circling and attacking each other. It looked like a dogfight. Two of the bird forms weren't birds at all, but dragons, with Ned being one of them. Azinine was still in the form of a Nonbee and was ferociously jabbing anything she could sink her horn into.

The dragons kept trying to fry her with their flames, but she was too quick. One of the dragons actually succeeded in destroying a sparrow-sized bird. Scott watched as it fell like a rock. That person was obviously out of the game, because the dragon immediately grew in size and increased in speed.

Scott was so fascinated by the display before him that he forgot about the egg for a while. But as the group approached, he realized he was losing a competitive advantage. The others hadn't seen him yet. He turned his attention to the egg and looked up at the tip of the mountain. There was no way he could get to the egg as a turtle, he would have to change into something else. He decided on a red-tailed hawk. A hawk may be able to approach the egg fast enough before it had a chance to react. He quickly changed and launched himself from the ledge he had been sitting on.

It was the most incredible feeling to fly and soar like a hawk. He began to circle, pushing himself higher and higher. He'd have to get considerably higher than the egg if he was going to pick up enough speed. As he did so, he noticed the spectacular view. Below him he could see the whole island surrounded by water as far as the eye could see.

By the time he had reached a height sufficient for his strategy, the others had reached the egg and had once again surrounded it. But as before, no one dared take it. Scott pulled his wings in and sent himself into a dive, picking up incredible speed. It was exhilarating and terrifying at the same time.

"This is just a dream. I can do anything I wish," he repeated to himself over and over. He unfolded his wings slightly and targeted the egg, at what he estimated must have been close to 100 miles per hour. He whizzed by two of the players, opened his talons and reached for the egg. Success! He had the egg in his talons. But no sooner had he grabbed it, than the egg began to vibrate violently. He tried to hold on, but the vibration became so intense that it wiggled free and fell. The others shot after it. Ned, who was still a dragon, let out a stream of fire, slightly burning a big bird in front of him, sending the bird careening out of control. The bird eventually changed into a big fish, which Scott thought was strange, until he realized that below them, a great body of azure blue water had appeared in the middle of the island. The egg had obviously decided to hide itself there.

Soon everyone in the group, except Scott, had changed into some sort of water creature. Scott hadn't changed because he still hadn't decided what form to use. There had to be some form he could take that would give him an advantage. He desperately wanted to make himself invisible. Then a thought occurred to him. *If I can't make myself invisible, perhaps I could turn into something so small, no one will see me.* He remembered discussing zooplankton in his science class. These creatures were some of the smallest living creatures in water. He flew towards the water and when he got close enough he changed into a zooplankton. He floated along with the current keeping an eye out for the egg. It wasn't hard to spot. The other players had already found it, and just as before, they were watching from a distance. Scoping out the situation, Scott noticed that this time the egg was guarded by a large sea monster. Scott slowly half swam, half floated next to the egg, which gave no sign of it even being aware he was so close. No one else seemed to know he was there either.

So far so good, he thought. He floated over to the egg and hovered above it. The egg didn't react and Scott was just seconds from victory. However, he quickly realized that he was so small there was no way possible to lift the egg. Realizing his mistake, Scott knew he would have to change into something of substance to grab it. The problem was, however, that as soon as he changed, the egg would react just as it had before, and the sea monster would eat him or something along those lines would happen. He needed a form with speed and agility, so he decided on a barracuda.

He counted to three and changed. As soon as he did, the sea monster turned on him. Scott grabbed the egg in his mouth and shot away. The monster was no match for his speed and he easily slipped away. He sped through the water with lightning speed and even though he couldn't see them, he knew the others were pursuing him. Wasting no time, he swam up to the shore, shot into the air, changed into a wolf, and hit the ground running. He heard the others shoot from the water and land behind him and knew he had to move quickly. He shot forward in the direction of the cages. That of course was the logical direction they would expect him to go. However, once in the thick jungle and out of sight, he darted left and hid in the brush until everyone passed by him. Everyone except Azinine.

Wondering if she was out of the game Scott waited for a moment longer to see if she too would eventually pass. When she didn't, Scott jumped up, shot around the corner, and just about slammed into a player morphing into a large pelican-type bird. It was Azinine. Fearing the egg might slip away somehow if he spoke, he morphed into a large gorilla and held the egg tight in his fist.

Approaching her he asked, "What happened?"

"The big one trampled me and almost put me out of the game." Then noticing the egg in his hand, she exclaimed, "You still have the egg?"

"Yep. If I've got this right, I have to get back to my cage, right?"

"Yes, but it won't be so easy. You can bet someone, if not all of them, will be guarding the cage."

Scott shrugged his shoulders. "We'll just have to give it our best try, but I have an idea," he said with a twinkle in his eye. He moved closer to Azinine and whispered his plan in her ear.

Scott needed something fast, so he stuck the egg in his mouth and morphed into a cheetah. As he made his way through the jungle, he expected all of the players to be guarding his cage, so he was surprised when a water dragon came out of nowhere and just about snagged him. His quick reflexes allowed him to dodge those horribly sharp jaws. The water dragon, however, was not about to give up and continued to chase him. Scott was amazed at how fast and agile this terrible beast was in the woods. It floated, using the branches of the trees and the bushes to propel itself through the brush very effectively. Because of the thick undergrowth, Scott was never able to pick up much speed and it was only because of his quick reflexes that he barely escaped several close calls. He desperately tried to think of another form that could out maneuver the water dragon, but couldn't think of anything but a bird. He knew he couldn't take on the form of a bird, because a small one wouldn't be capable of carrying the egg and a big bird would take too long to take flight. He'd be caught for sure.

He had just barely escaped another chomp when a male unicorn charged from behind a tree with its horn aimed directly at him. Scott hit the ground, flattening himself as close to the ground as he possibly could. The unicorn missed him by a hair and ending up spearing the water dragon instead. This gave Scott a little breathing room, but not much. Then things only got worse. The others apparently heard the racket and came looking. With his path to the cages cut off, Scott turned around and led the others back through the forest. They ended up back at the lake again, where Scott quickly changed into an eagle. As he lifted into the sky, one of the other players leaped into the air, caught his leg and pulled him down to the ground. He knew he was finished and he braced for the impact.

Before he felt anything though, the island disappeared, and each of the players, back to their normal selves, found themselves bobbing up and down in the pond.

"How can the game be over? He hasn't reached the cage yet!" one of the other players yelled.

"Congratulations!" a man on the shore was saying. "You retrieved the egg. Please exit the pond and pick up your certificate."

"Who won?" Ned asked in surprise.

"The young lady," the man replied pointing to Azinine.

"I thought you had the egg," Ned said looking at Scott.

"Nope. I had a rock in my mouth. While you guys were chasing me, Azinine made her way to the cages."

"That's cheating! We're all supposed to play against each other."

"We were playing against each other. She was ruthless the way she batted those brown eyes at me. I couldn't help but hand over the egg," Scott said teasingly.

"Oh brother! I cannot believe you let her win," Ned shook his head in disgust.

Chapter 7

Bad News

The three of them picked up Azinine's certificate for winning and headed towards their MOC. They had just exited the fair when Ned stopped in his tracks.

"What's wrong?" Scott asked.

"Pretty sure I just saw Magus Mitle enter that building over there," Ned answered, pointing across the way.

"So, what's wrong with that?" Scott asked in bewilderment.

"He's suspected to be one of Cohar's followers," Ned explained. "Our father and others on the council have reason to believe that Cohar and his Kingmongers used to meet down here somewhere to make their secret plans. That building over there is an old potions factory that hasn't been in business for years. So, I'm curious why Magus Mitle would be interested in a place like that."

"But Magus Cohar has been captured. The head of the snake has been cut off. Why do we care anymore what Magus Mitle does?" Scott asked.

"Scott, we assumed Cohar was the leader, but what if he's not?"

Scott nodded slowly. With a chill running down his spine, he remembered the conversation he had with Cohar a couple of weeks ago just before Headmaster McDougal and Buzz showed up to rescue him. Cohar had told him that he wasn't the leader, but just a pawn. He had to know if Cohar was telling the truth.

"Maybe we should go find out," Scott suggested.

"NO!" Ned blurted out. "Only an idiot would do that. It's far too dangerous. If he discovers us, especially you, who knows how he'll react?"

Azinine took in a deep breath. "I don't like the idea either but if there are still magi planning a rebellion, knowing their secret hideout could really help the magi council put down the rebellion. Scott's right. We have to find out," she argued.

"It's too dangerous for Scott. I would never forgive myself if something happened to him."

"So, would I. I feel just as responsible for him as you do," she assured her brother, "but we've got to take this chance while we have it. I tell you what, I'll go inside myself. If…"

"No way! You're not going in there all by yourself," Scott protested cutting Azinine off. "I'm not some little kid you guys need to babysit. I know the risks."

"Let's go get Father and let him investigate," Ned suggested.

"No, it might be a false alarm. We don't want to disturb him unless we know for sure something is wrong," Azinine argued.

"Ned," Scott began, "we have to find out. If we take the time to get your father, Mitle might be gone by the time we get back. We can't let this opportunity get away. If it's nothing, then we shouldn't be in any danger. We may not have another chance. Let's just go in and have a look around like we're a bunch of dumb kids exploring an old building."

Ned blew out a long breath. "Okay, but one of us should stay behind in case something does happen to the others. That way they can go get help."

"That makes sense," Scott said.

"Azinine, I think you should be the one to stay behind," Ned suggested.

"Why me? You're the one who's scared to go in there. I think you should stay behind?"

"I'm not scared to go in there. I just don't think it's a good idea. But if we're going in, you're the best person to go get help if something happens," Ned argued. It was a weak argument, but Ned could never face his parents if something happened to her.

"What do you mean by that?" she asked with her hands on her hips, demonstrating her annoyance.

"I'm just saying that we don't know what's going to happen. If you need to run for help, they're less likely to chase you than me. Plus, you know magic a lot better than I do."

"That argument makes no sense. You just don't want me to come because I'm your sister."

"Azinine," Scott said butting in, "if they catch us and start to torture us or something like that, I don't think I could bear seeing that happen to you. I don't care what happens to Ned," he said, poking an elbow in Ned's ribs and laughing slightly. Then more seriously he continued, "Please, for my sake, stay here and watch. If we don't return in one hour, go get your father. All right?"

"Oh, fine," she replied, unhappily crossing her arms across her chest. "But please be careful."

They walked over to the building and stood in front of the closed entrance.

"It's most likely protected," Ned said. "Any ideas how to open it Azinine?"

Azinine furrowed her eyebrows and thought for a moment. "Let's see," she said. "How about 'ewftenin af.' "They waited a moment but nothing happened. "Okay, let's try 'gagin kosig af'. Still nothing happened. Shrugging her shoulders, she turned to her brother. "I don't know, Ned. It could be anything."

"Af," Scott said. The door instantly opened. Ned looked at Scott in wonder while Azinine burst out in laughter.

"I can't believe it," she said. "Why would they leave the door unprotected?"

"They probably don't think anyone would suspect this old place," Scott reasoned. He nodded his head at Azinine and walked through the door.

"Remember, Azinine," Ned reminded her as he turned to follow Scott. "One hour. If we don't return, go get Father."

The two boys crept into the factory and quietly made their way down a hall. There was no sign that anyone was in the building. But the boys knew Magus Mitle had to be there somewhere. They had watched him enter. They continued along the hall until they came to a large room filled with cauldrons of different sizes. As they gazed around, they noticed several bottles sitting on the shelves lining the walls. Scott wrinkled his nose when he took a closer look at one and saw it was filled with the feet from some sort of small rodent. There were other bottles that contained eyeballs, hair, claws, liquids of all different colors and all sorts of other ingredients. Scott picked the bottles up one by one, wondering what in the world the contents would be used for. For a moment he forgot their original purpose for coming into the factory and jumped when Ned tapped him on the shoulder.

"It's just common stuff for common potions," Ned said. "No big deal. Come on, let's keep going."

Sheepishly, Scott placed the jar he had been inspecting back on the shelf. It was then that he noticed a small potion labeled 'Terror Hound.'

Terror Hound? Sweet! he thought. Scott quickly placed it in his pocket and followed his friend to the other end of the room. They discovered a door that had been left ajar. They walked inside and found themselves in a hall where several doorways opened into several other rooms. Slowly they walked up to each room and quietly looked inside, only to discover each one empty. At the end of the hall, they discovered a set of stairs that led to an upper floor. The two quietly made their way up, trying to keep the stairs from squeaking, but failing numerous times. Each time a stair would squeak in protest of their weight, they would stop and listen for any sound that might indicate someone had heard them. Fortunately, no one had.

When they reached the top, they found a room that had potion recipes hanging on the walls. Scott couldn't resist. He walked in and examined several of them. The first one he came to read 'Beauty Potion.' He read the ingredients:

Three strands of princess hair

Three petals Lorilauldi flower

One kettle Shooner water

Three sprinkles fairy dust

Three shots of dragon's breath

Boil and stir under a full moon for twenty minutes while repeating the words "eyes of starlight, hair of gold, give the drinker a face to behold."

"Scott," Ned urged, after he realized Scott wasn't following him. "What are you doing?"

"Sorry! I couldn't help myself. This stuff is so interesting."

"We only have an hour, remember?"

"Okay, okay. I'm coming."

Scott followed Ned out into the hall. They explored several more rooms, but found no sign of Magus Mitle.

"He's got to be here somewhere," Scott said.

"You're right. We haven't checked the basement yet. Let's try there. They walked to the end of the hall where Ned opened a door with a sign that read, 'float pad.' To Scott, the inside looked like nothing but a large hole. But as soon as they approached the edge a floating pad appeared quickly from below. Ned explained it was similar to an elevator, except there were no walls connected to the pad. When the pad moved it held you tight to the floor like a MOC.

"Cool," Scott said, as they both stepped onto it.

"Basement," Ned spoke and the float pad began to descend.

"Get ready," Ned warned. "If they see us before we come to a stop, we'll be sitting ducks." The float pad continued past a lower-level floor that was completely dark. However, as it continued its descent, Scott could see a light coming from the basement.

"Look," he said pointing to the light.

"I know. I see it too. We probably should have taken the stairs down," Ned replied with a grimace. "Halt," he commanded, but the float pad didn't stop. "Halt now," he tried, but to no avail.

"Why won't it stop?" Scott asked.

"I think I know why the front door wasn't protected," Ned replied.

"You think it's a trap?"

"Pretty sure, and we're about to find out."

The float pad landed. The boys could see down the lighted hallway, but to their relief, no one was there.

"Main floor," Ned spoke. The float pad didn't budge. He turned to Scott, shrugged, and said, "I guess our only option is to get off."

They cautiously stepped off, wary of a trap. They noticed a hallway leading to the left, but it was sealed off. The only way to go was straight ahead.

"I'm going to guess that he knows we're here," Ned commented.

"If he does, do you have any good magic tricks to get us out of here?" Scott asked.

"Not really. I haven't studied magic that seriously. The magic I know is simple compared to his magic."

"Do you have any suggestions?" Scott asked.

"There's always the small possibility he doesn't know we're here. Let's see if we can find him and figure out what he's up to," Ned suggested.

"Sounds good to me. If they catch us, we'll pretend we're just exploring an old factory."

"Fat chance they'll believe that."

Whomp! Whomp! Suddenly two glass cages formed around each boy and moved them involuntarily down the hall.

"Oh, great! These again," Scott muttered. "What is up with these glass cages? Don't they know any other spells they can use to trap people?"

"You have to admit, they are effective," Ned replied.

"I guess."

"I hate to say I told you so, but I told you so. I knew this wasn't a good idea," Ned said regretfully. He paused and then added, "I should have been more careful. I'm sorry, Scott."

"Don't be sorry, we both knew it was risky," Scott replied. "Besides, it may still be worth it. Let's just keep cool heads and see what he wants. We'll find some way out of this."

The two boys ended up in a very nicely decorated room that was decked out with plush chairs, couches and carpet. At first, it looked as though no one was there. But after a moment Scott spotted someone sitting in the corner of the room. The figure stood up and removed his hood. It was Magus Mitle, just as they had suspected.

"Welcome, Scott," Magus Mitle said, ignoring Ned. "It's nice of you to visit us in our world. We have been waiting for you."

"How did you know I was here?" asked Scott.

"We knew you'd return," the magus laughed. "And it takes more than blue hair to keep us from finding you."

Scott felt his hair again and looked at Ned. Ned nodded and gave a slight smile.

Scott's mind raced, trying to come up with some way to stall. "Actually, the blue hair was Ned's idea of a joke. There's no reason for me to hide now that Magus Cohar has been caught, right?" Scott said as though Magus Mitle was one of the good guys.

"Right," Magus Mitle dryly agreed. Then he added, "As long as you cooperate."

"Cooperate?" Scott said, faking bewilderment. "I've always cooperated with the magi council. In fact, I'm not sure why an upstanding member of the council like you, would treat us like this," he continued, trying to get some sort of confession out of the magus.

Magus Mitle smiled. "I do what I think is right. It's hard to know people's intentions, so I have to be careful." He mumbled a word and the glass prisons disappeared. "Now, you will tell me what I need to know," he commanded.

"Sure. What is it?" Scott asked, keeping up the charade.

"I want the Eigenholle. Where is it?"

"What is up with this Eigenholle thing?" Scott questioned. "Cohar asked me the same question, but I don't have a clue what it is."

Magus Mitle seemed to consider this. "Well, then," he said in an offhand way, "you'll just have to stay here until your mother tells us."

"My mother?" Scott repeated, taken aback. "How do you know about my mother?"

Again, Magus Mitle laughed. "We know she's alive and we know where she's living. She'll know where the Eigenholle is. And with you right here beside us, I'm sure she'll be very happy to tell us its location."

"We? Who's we?" Ned interrupted.

"Never mind," Magus Mitle replied. "You had both better take a seat. You might be here a while. Unless, of course, you change your mind and decide to tell me what I want to know," he paused, giving them one more chance.

"I swear, I don't know where or even what this Eigenholle thing is," Scott insisted.

"Very well. If your mother is anything like her father, it might take a while to make her talk, even after we've tortured her several times."

"Yeah, she's a tough one," Scott said casually. Then he rushed at Magus Mitle as fast as he could. A bit startled at first, the older man quickly regained his composure and brought up his staff. Before Scott could reach him, he felt the all too familiar choking sensation of the death grip. He clutched his chest, but still tried to force his way toward Mitle.

Meanwhile, Ned jumped from the chair he had been sitting in and with amazing speed, levitated a book and hurled it towards Mitle, causing the magus to temporarily drop the death grip and handle the book. Magus Mitle turned to Ned and once again imprisoned him in glass. Scott took in a deep breath and tried to rush Mitle again. Once more, Mitle was too quick and he raised his staff and caught Scott in the death grip. Scott leaped forward in one last attempt to grab hold of Mitle, but he fell short.

"A valiant try," Magus Mitle said with an evil smile. "But you won't get away this time."

Magus Mitle increased the death grip causing Scott to fall to the ground writhing in agony. He desperately needed air. He thought for sure this was the end and he was going to die. However, a second later the pressure left him and Magus Mitle fell to the floor. Surprised, Scott looked up and saw Magus Noka standing above him with a club in his hand.

"Magus Noka," he gasped. "Thank...you."

"You're welcome," Magus Noka replied, helping Scott to his feet. "What are you two doing down here?" he asked scolding them. "This is a dangerous place."

Still a little out of breath, Scott answered, "Yeah, we noticed. We saw Magus Mitle enter the building and we were curious. We wanted to see what he was doing."

"I believe your world has a saying...hmm...oh, yes. Curiosity killed the cat. You need to be more careful about who you start chasing," Magus Noka scolded again. "Ned, at least, should have known better."

"Speaking of Ned, can you release him?"

"Of course." The magus raised his staff, mumbled a few words and the glass prison disappeared. "Are you okay, Ned?"

"I'm fine. But what are you doing here?" Ned asked suspiciously.

"I came to help you."

"You came from the other direction. Not from the entrance," Ned pointed out. "That means you've been here the whole time."

"Ned!" Scott said in surprise at his friend's attitude. "The guy," Scott took in another painful breath of air, "just saved our lives. How can you accuse him of being a part of this?"

"Because I am," Magus Noka answered for Ned.

"But you just..." Scott began.

"Let me explain," Magus Noka interrupted, holding up his hand to stop any further questions. "Magus Polimar, your father," he nodded at Ned, "asked me to infiltrate the group in order to spy on them. I was supposed to figure out what they're up to. As far as they know, I am one of them."

"So Magus Cohar's capture didn't stop the rebellion?" Scott asked.

"Magus Cohar? No, no, he was only a small part of this whole plan."

"But I thought he was the leader of this rebellion. He told Azinine he was and that he was the one that killed the high king."

Magus Noka thought for a moment before answering, "Well, I don't know about killing the high king, but if he was the leader, he isn't any longer. Magus Mordi is the leader now."

"How come my father never mentioned anything about this?" Ned asked, still suspicious.

"No one on the council knows of this but your father. We just don't know who we can trust. If these Kingmongers found out I was a spy they would kill me for sure."

"Don't you think that's going to be obvious, now that you've just clubbed Magus Mitle over the head?" Scott pointed out.

"Possibly," he conceded. "I have taken a huge risk. But I couldn't stand by and let him kill you. However, last time Magus Mordi held you in the death grip, something hit him over the head and knocked him out. Who's to say you didn't do it again? Magus Mitle still believes you have uncanny powers so I'm hoping he'll simply believe you did it again. As soon as you leave, and you better leave soon, I'll revive him. Hopefully that will remove any suspicion."

"I'm sorry," Ned apologized, bowing to Magus Noka. "I didn't know. Thank you for your help."

"How do you know it was Magus Mordi who used the death grip on me in the street that night?" Scott asked.

"I am one of them, remember?"

"Oh, yeah. Well, thanks again for coming to our rescue."

Magus Noka gave them a gentle smile. "You're welcome. Now you'd better leave. And remember, not a word of this to anyone. I have placed my life in your hands by telling you this. I trust you can keep it a secret."

The two boys promised they would keep everything to themselves and then left the room. Apparently, the float pad had only been spell-rigged for a short period of time, or Magus Noka had removed the spell, because it worked fine as they hopped on and commanded it to take them to the main level. It had been just under an hour since they had entered the building and they hurried outside in an effort to catch Azinine. However, as they stepped out into the sunlight, she was nowhere to be seen.

"She must have already left," said Ned. "We better go and find her."

"Ned," Scott said with concern in his voice. "I have to get home. You heard what Magus Mitle said. They're after my mother."

"Okay," Ned agreed. "I'll take you to Cylindhall. You should be able to make your own way to CastleOne from there. After that, I've got to try and intercept Azinine before she has the whole magi council out looking for us."

Chapter 8

Robbed?

Scott made it back to CastleOne and immediately went to look for Headmaster McDougal. He found him in his office and gave him a modified version of what had happened, being careful to leave out the part about Magus Noka.

Headmaster McDougal looked at Scott in disbelief. "I thought I told you to stay away from Lumen," he said angrily.

"I know and I'm sorry. We originally planned to be there only for a short time. Just long enough for Azinine and Ned to teach me some magic."

Headmaster McDougal stood there with his mouth gaping open. "They taught you magic?" he cried out in anger. "That is forbidden. They know better. Those two should not be teaching you any magic without permission."

"But my mother gave me a Shalle. We figured she wanted me to learn magic," Scott replied in defense of his friends.

"Learning magic is fine, Scott. But only under the right circumstances." The headmaster threw his hands up in exasperation. "What were they thinking?"

"Okay, I get your frustration. But can we please get back to my mother?"

Headmaster McDougal's expression seemed to soften. "So you think your mother may be in danger?" he asked.

"Yes. Can you take me to her?" Scott pleaded.

"Yes. We'll go right away," answered Headmaster McDougal in a slightly calmer voice.

Relief flooded over Scott as they arrived at his home to find his family, including his mother, safe. However, there was still cause for concern because the house had been torn apart. Someone had broken in and was obviously looking for something.

"Scott! Magus McDougal! What are you doing here?" Scott's mother asked in astonishment.

"We came to see if you were okay," Scott said hugging her.

Mrs. Frontier was more than a little surprised at the visit. "It looks like someone tried to rob us, but I can't see that anything has been taken. How did you know? We just barely got home ourselves."

Headmaster McDougal gravely shook his head and said, "I don't think they were the kind of robbers you're thinking of. Scott, do you want to explain what happened?"

"Sure, I guess," Scott recounted the same story he had told the headmaster just hours earlier. His mother's eyes widened as he mentioned the Eigenholle.

"Did they get it?" Headmaster McDougal asked Mrs. Frontier when Scott had finished.

"No," she replied, still in disbelief at what her son had just been through.

"Good. Keep it safe. It cannot fall into their hands," the headmaster warned. "I need to get back to the school and monitor the portal. Please be on your guard. I'll increase the security at the portal, but they may still be here. Scott will be safe at the castle. If you feel it necessary, please feel free to bring Eric and Josh to the castle. They can live there for a while."

"Really?" Josh exclaimed, excited by the prospect.

"Headmaster McDougal," Eric piped in with a smirk on his face, "you may want to reconsider your offer. You have no idea what kind of damage Josh might do to the old place."

The others laughed and then Mrs. Frontier turned to Scott, saying, "I thought you were told not to enter Lumen until it's safe."

"Well, with Cohar gone we thought it would be safe," Scott replied.

Valar looked at Headmaster McDougal. The headmaster held up his hands. "I didn't tell them that. I specifically told them we didn't know for sure and that they should stay on earth."

Valar looked back at Scott, waiting for a better explanation from her son. Knowing she would not accept any further excuses, he simply muttered, "Okay, okay, I'm sorry."

"No more going to Lumen. Do you hear me?" his mother said sternly.

"I hear you," Scott replied glumly.

They said their goodbyes to Scott and the headmaster. On the way back to the castle, Scott was burning with curiosity about the Eigenholle. He wanted to know what it was and why the Kingmongers wanted it so badly. As they rode back to the castle, he asked the headmaster about it.

Magus McDougal looked over at Scott, knowing this question was inevitable. "The Eigenholle is a magical device created long ago," he explained. "It allows a person to see things as they really are. I believe the Kingmongers want the Eigenholle in order to get their hands on the Ancient Book of Magic which is hidden in the Pyramids of Death. No one has ever entered the pyramids without the Eigenholle and returned. Several people have tried, sure enough, but no one has succeeded."

"What do the Kingmongers want with the book?" asked Scott.

"The majority of the council still believes the amulet should select a king. The Kingmongers want to select their own king. My guess is they are running out of patience and are looking at another option."

"What other option?"

"War," the headmaster said solemnly.

"War?" asked Scott.

"Yes. If they force themselves into power, they don't need the voice of the magi council or the people, for that matter."

"With men like that in power, Lumen would probably be a miserable place to live," Scott admitted. "But I still don't see what this has to do with this book of magic."

"The Ancient Book of Magic," Headmaster McDougal corrected. "As you said, Lumen would be a miserable place to live if the Kingmongers came into power. You can see why we are so anxious to find a king. If the amulet chooses a king, we'll have all of Lumen, Diggermen, and maybe even the Greymen on our side. As it stands, there are many that currently side with the Kingmongers. It has simply been too long. They're convinced that the amulet no longer works and it's time to move on. But if a king were chosen by the amulet, most of them would come back to our side in a heartbeat. The Kingmongers would lose most of their support and would have a hard time building an army. Unless," he paused, "they were able to create an army or recruit other magical beings to fight for them. I'm sure that's one reason they want the book. But it also contains many powerful spells that could aid them in other ways."

"This one book can do all that?" Scott asked incredulously.

"The book contains spells that are written in the ancient tongue. The ancient tongue is very powerful. It can be used to control the elements of nature, meaning, wind, fire, water and earth. We believe that by its power this world was created. Not only was it used to create this world, but also the magical creatures that live on it, such as trolls and nymphs."

"Trolls were created by the high kings?" Scott asked.

"No," Headmaster McDougal answered. "They were created by evil warlocks who got their hands on the book. That's why it's now secured in the Pyramids of Death."

"What's a nymph?" Scott asked.

"They are unnatural beings who are able to melt into the trees, the water, and many other elements. Sometimes, if you look hard enough at a tree, you might see a face looking back at you. But they are camouflaged so well that it isn't easy to spot them. They were created to act as spies. Most of them live in the water and in trees and are harmless. But if they want to, they can leave the element they are taking refuge in and take on an actual, physical form with arms and legs. Water nymphs usually take the form of a lady. When they do this, you have to be careful not to let them lure you into the water. Many people drinking at a stream have been caught and dragged in by these horrible creatures."

Continuing with his questions, Scott asked, "And who are the Greymen and the Diggermen?"

"Greymen are very elusive beings. They stick much to themselves for the most part and have little to do with Lumens, unless of course, our actions impact their way of life. Then they can be quite ill-mannered."

"Where do they live?"

"There is a land within the Grey Forest Hills that they inhabit. But I wouldn't advise looking for them or even going near their borders," the headmaster warned. "They're very good at camouflaging themselves and they have a nasty habit of shooting first and asking questions later."

"I'll make a note of that," Scott commented.

"The Diggermen, on the other hand, are usually quite friendly when you meet them. They spend most of their time underground either mining stones or quarreling with goblins about whose mine belongs to whom. Chances are you'll probably never meet one."

Chapter 9

More Bad News

When they arrived back at CastleOne, Scott made his way to his room and opened his books. He had a lot of studying to catch up on and he had been working hard at it when three hours later Ned opened the door. One look at his grave face and Scott knew instantly something was wrong.

"Ned, what's up?" he asked cautiously.

A panicked look crossed Ned's face as he answered Scott's question. "I can't find Azinine or my parents. I've looked everywhere for them. I just spoke with Magus McDougal and he asked me to stay here at CastleOne for a while until he can find them."

"I'm sure they're fine, Ned," Scott said with more reassurance than he actually felt. Then trying to take his friend's mind off his worries, he suggested, "There's a movie tonight. Do you want to go?"

"I don't know. I'm not really in the mood."

"Come on! It will keep your mind occupied so you don't fret and stew over this. Headmaster McDougal will probably have found your parents by the time it's over."

They talked for several more minutes, with Ned recounting to Scott about his search and coming up empty handed. Scott then told Ned about the break-in at his parent's house. Scott had just begun to tell Ned about the Eigenholle when a knock came at the door.

"That's probably your parents right now," Scott whispered, smiling at Ned. He walked to the door and opened it. Headmaster McDougal walked in with a look on his face that alarmed both boys. They knew this couldn't be good news.

"I'm sorry to disturb you two, but I must talk to you immediately," the headmaster said. "There isn't any easy way to say this, so I'll just get right to the point. Scott, your father just called. Your mother seems to have disappeared." Scott fell back a few steps and tripped over his bed. The headmaster didn't wait for him to sit up. "She left just after we did to get some groceries from the local market and didn't ever come home. They found her car on the side of the road, but she wasn't in it. Your father is bringing Josh and Eric here until the local police can work things out. However," he continued with a heavy sigh, "I have to tell you that I don't think they'll find her. Just before your father called, someone used the main portal back to Lumen. There is no way for me to know for sure, but I have a hunch she was with whoever it was. I'm probably too late, but I can't take the risk of anything else like this happening again. I'm going to place a protection spell on the main portal so no one can use it. The only way back and forth between our two worlds will be through the council room." Then as an afterthought, he added, "And I'm going to protect it also so only I can use it right now."

Startled by this last comment, Ned jumped to his feet with a concerned look on his face. "But I won't be able to get back home if you do that," he exclaimed.

"Exactly," replied Headmaster McDougal. He laid his hands on Ned's shoulders and tried to make him understand. "Home is not the safest place right now, Ned. We still haven't come up with any clues as to where your family is. It's possible that whoever has Scott's mother may also have your family. Right now, the safest place for you is right here at CastleOne. Please try to understand. I have to go back to Lumen and meet with members of the council. In the meantime, Buzz is here if you need anything. I'll be leaving as soon as Scott's father arrives."

"Are you sure there isn't anything we can do to help?" Scott asked.

"There might be, but I won't know until after I meet with the council. In the meantime, I don't want you to panic. What I do want is for the both of you to stay together as a safety precaution." The headmaster gave them a smile to reassure them. "I don't think there's any danger here but there is a slight possibility that one or more of them could have stayed behind."

The two boys nodded and Headmaster McDougal left the room. They were silent for a while, each thinking about the turn of events.

"Still want to see that movie?" Ned asked.

"Not really, but it's better than sitting here doing nothing," Scott replied in a whisper.

The movie was just about over when Scott's father came in and pulled the two boys out of the room. Scott's heart went out to his father when he stepped into the lighted hallway and glanced at his father's face. He looked very old and tired. Seeing how worried his father was, he desperately wanted to say something to make him feel better but he didn't know what. Knowing there really wasn't anything he could say, he put his arms around him and gave him a hug.

"Are you okay, Dad?" he finally asked, pulling back so he could look at his father's face.

His dad gave him a slight smile and rumpled his hair like he used to when Scott was younger. "I'm doing as good as can be expected," he replied. "I'm worried about your mother and about the safety of your brothers, especially Josh," he added. "I hope you won't mind him staying here for a while."

"No problem. What are you going to do?"

"I'm going to take a few days off and work with the police."

"Headmaster McDougal says he thinks she's been taken to Lumen," Scott replied.

"I know, but we can't be sure. If she's still here, I need to try and find her."

"Okay," Scott said.

Mr. Frontier left the four boys in Scott's room, each of them deep in their own thoughts. The magnitude of what was happening was beginning to sink in. Even Josh was mellow, which for him was rare.

Finally, Eric broke the silence. "I know Headmaster McDougal told us to stay here, but I can't just stand by and wait. Ned, isn't there any other way back to Lumen?"

Ned shook his head. "There are only two portals, and they have both been protected by Headmaster McDougal."

"Could you try and break the spell that protects it?"

"I could try, but it's a long shot."

"Whoa, wait a second," Josh said grabbing Ned's shoulder, "Did you say 'spell'?"

"Yes, I did," replied Ned forgetting that Josh hadn't been informed about the magic yet.

"As in magic spells?" Josh asked slowly.

Ned suddenly realized what was going on and looked at Scott and Eric for help. The three of said nothing for several seconds, each contemplating what to say. Finally, Scott spoke up.

"Josh, you might as well know. Lumen is a little different from earth. Magic here on earth is mostly just illusions and sleight of hand tricks. However, on Lumen magic is real. Do you remember that trick I showed you last year just before Christmas?"

Josh's eyes were as round as poker chips and he had a huge grin forming on his face. "You mean the one where you made the card fly from my hand into yours?"

"Yeah, well that was done with real magic. It works here at the castle because it's so closely tied in with Lumen."

"Sweeeet!" Josh said slowly, but with excitement. "Can you show me how to do that trick and maybe some other ones too?" he asked hopefully.

"Some other time, Josh," Eric said butting in. "We need to spend our time trying to find a way back to Lumen." Eric then turned to Ned. "I know we're reaching for straws but as long as there's a shot, let's try."

"Eric," Ned said, "you've only been to Lumen once. Are you sure you want to do this? It's not a very safe place to be right now."

"I know," Eric answered, "but I would have a really good guide." Then with a grin he added, "In fact, I would have two really good guides. You're not planning to just sit around here are you?"

"That's three very good guides," Josh piped in.

Ignoring his younger brother, Scott now jumped in. "Last couple of times I was on Lumen, I just about lost my life. Maybe we should wait for a few days and see if the magi council finds them.

Eric was dumbstruck. "You can't be serious. Of all of us, you're the one I would think would be the most adamant about going."

"Hey, I'm all for going too. I just think we should wait a little and see what Headmaster McDougal comes up with. Also, Dad will kill us if he finds out. Especially if something happens to the squirt here," Scott said, pointing to Josh.

"Hey, I can take care of myself," Josh protested.

Again, ignoring the youngest of the Frontier brothers, Eric continued arguing. "Scott, I won't be able to live with myself if Mom ends up dead and I just sat here doing nothing. I'm going with or without you guys."

"That assumes we can find a way to break the spell," Ned reminded him.

"Okay, fine," Scott replied. "If we can break the spell, then we'll go. But we just need to be really cautious."

"What about you, Ned?" Eric asked.

"Of course!" Ned assured them. "It's my family too. I'm all for it if we can find a way in. But I have to tell you, I don't think it's going to happen."

"We have to at least try," Eric pleaded.

For several hours they tried to break the spell, but nothing worked. Ned tried everything he could think of, but to no avail. Finally, exhausted, but not at all surprised, Ned suggested they sleep and have another go in the morning.

"Maybe if you taught me some magic, it would jog your memory or give you some inspiration on how to crack it," Josh suggested hopefully.

"I'm sorry, Josh. I'm really just too exhausted right now. Can we please just sleep now," Ned pleaded.

They reluctantly agreed and all four slept. Over the next couple of days, Eric and Scott urged Ned to think of anything he hadn't already come up with, but there just wasn't anything he could do with his limited experience. After all, Headmaster MacDougal could have used any number of protection spells and phrases. They even tried re-opening the main portal located in the forest, but with no luck there either.

Tired of watching Ned fail, Josh decided to explore the castle. He checked in with them every once in a while, to see how they were progressing, or in this case, not progressing. But for the most part, he was fascinated with the castle and spent most of his time exploring the many corridors and rooms.

On the fourth day, after 'accidentally' breaking a very worn-out lock on one of the doors, Josh found his way to the wall walk of the castle. The wall walk was built toward the top of the castle. Long ago, it allowed soldiers to move quickly between towers and keep a look out for enemies. Today, however, the wall walk was off limits and students weren't allowed up there. Of course, Josh didn't know this and the chain that kept the door secure, and which he broke with a great deal of effort, didn't seem to clue him in either.

When he arrived on the wall walk, he discovered it led around the entire perimeter, leading to each wing. Looking over the high walls, Josh was amazed at the scenery below him. He could see over the entire castle grounds and then beyond some too. It was such a magnificent site that even Josh, at his young age, took a moment to enjoy the view. Bending over, he picked up a rock and hurled it as far as he could. Most of the time he easily made it over the moat, for it was only about fifteen to twenty feet wide, but once in a while the rock hit the water with a plop. When he ran out of rocks, he went down into the cellar and grabbed a bucket which he filled with more rocks from the castle grounds and hauled them back up to the top.

After catching his breath and resting for a bit, he wiped the sweat off his brow and continued his barrage. Flinging them as far as he could. He tried over and over to outdo his best shot. Eventually that game got boring and he turned his attention to the murky water of the moat below. He noticed fish of some sort swimming below and an idea hit him for another game. Having all the time in the world, he went back outside the castle walls and collected several softball sized rocks. He then hauled them up to the top of the castle and proceeded to drop them on the fish or at least he tried to. He kept at it for quite a while but none of the rocks ever seemed to actually hit the fish. However, he was having fun just tossing the rocks over and watching them splash into the water.

It was while he was playing this game that a very strange thing happened. A little way out, Josh noticed a large fish swimming near the bank of the moat, near the castle. Excited about a bigger target, he scampered down the walkway until he was directly above it. To hit the fish, he knew he would have to throw the rock out about five feet, not just straight down. He picked up a fairly large rock and heaved it over the wall. The rock left his hands, but about three feet out, it disappeared. Wondering if his eyes had deceived him, he threw another rock. Again it disappeared. He could hardly believe his eyes. Here was a riddle he had to solve. He took several steps to his right and threw another rock. This time the rock fell and hit the water with a great splash. Taking the same number of steps back to his left, he threw one more rock. Sure enough, it disappeared just like the others had.

Then he had another idea. He hurried back inside the castle and found a broom. By this time, Josh had explored the entire castle and knew where everything was. With the broom in hand, he hurried back up to the wall walk. He approached the spot where he thought the rocks disappeared. He picked up a rock and tossed it. It didn't disappear, but plunged into the moat. He took a step to his right and threw another rock. It too plunged into the moat. He repeated this several times before one of the rocks finally disappeared.

"Jackpot," he whispered to himself.

He held on to the brush end of the broom and reached the stick part out over the castle wall. To his amazement, about three feet out, the end of the broom handle disappeared. Slowly he lowered the brook stick, watching to see if the end of the broom would reappear. He had only let it fall about two feet, when it hit something hard and came silently to a stop. His eyes widened and he could hardly believe what he was seeing or not seeing in this case. The broom handle was actually resting on some type of invisible ledge or floor about three feet out from the castle wall.

"Whoa!" Josh breathed out. This riddle was getting better and better and he was determined to solve it. But how was the question. He didn't dare jump, just in case there really wasn't something there. Then he had an idea. In the utility closet where he had grabbed the broom, was a ladder. He ran back inside, put the broomstick away and grabbed the ladder. He hauled it up to the top, but couldn't remember where the correct spot was. He cursed himself for not marking it. He placed the ladder on the wall, estimating the correct location the best he could, and slowly pushed it out over the wall where he thought the invisible ledge was. The end of the ladder didn't disappear like the broom had, so he continued to push it further and further out over the wall. Finally, the part of the ladder hanging out over the wall became too heavy for him to hold, and it fell. He clung desperately to the ladder rung, as it slammed against the outside of the castle wall. He almost lost his grip on it. With a grunt, he pulled the ladder back up until it was resting on top of the wall.

After taking a short break to rest his muscles and calm his heart, he picked up a few more rocks and started tossing them again until he finally found the spot. He then leaned over and picked up a sharp rock and scratched the wall to mark the exact spot so he would know where it was. Then he picked up the ladder and placed it on the wall. He slowly slid it outward until he saw the end disappear and come to rest upon...what? He let go of the ladder and sure enough it held. It sat there as though the end were resting on something.

Carefully, he climbed upon the wall and put as much pressure on the ladder as he possibly could, while still hanging onto the wall, just in case the ladder gave way. It felt solid enough, but he still didn't trust it enough to put his whole weight on it. Josh was pretty much a daredevil, but even he drew the line when his life was at stake. In the end, he found a rope and tied one end around his waist and the other around an iron ring fastened to the castle wall on the opposite side of the walkway. This way, he reasoned, if the end of the ladder hanging out over the wall gave way, the rope would at least save him from falling, and he could climb back to safety.

Slowly he crept out onto the ladder, crawling backwards as if he were climbing down the ladder. His heart was racing and his entire body broke out in a sweat. Not one to back down from an adventure though, he continued along until his feet disappeared and eventually landed on what felt like a brick floor. He brought the rest of his body up and suddenly found himself in a small hallway leading to a rectangular room. He couldn't believe it. Looking back to see the castle and the ladder still there, he turned around, walked down the small hallway and found himself inside some sort of secret room. It was impossible, but yet here he was. The walls were covered with a few tapestries and a couple of portraits. There were two large bookshelves along one wall that were filled with all kinds of books. Several small poles made of what looked like gold were set throughout the room. A very large, ornate chair was placed in one corner among various other things. As he took in his surroundings, he noticed the room also had five doors, one behind him and two others on each side of him.

He tested the handle on one of the doors to his left, but it was locked. He tried the second door to his left, and it swung open to another small empty hallway. He took a few steps inside and stopped. At the end of the hallway, he could see a very realistic picture of a forest. So realistic, in fact, that he wondered for a moment if he weren't looking out a window. He stared at it for several seconds, thinking how odd it was to put a picture at the end of an empty hall. He turned around to leave and saw that the door was no longer there. He was now standing in a hall that led directly back into the rectangular room from where he had come. He closed his eyes and rubbed them just to make sure he wasn't seeing things.

As he entered the room, he noticed it was exactly as he had left it. There were five doors and no sign of any hall that led back to the castle. Panic surged within him and he hurried across the room and checked one of the other doors. The door opened, but it was another empty hallway. At the end, was another picture, but it was all black. Nothing to see there. He tried another door, but it was locked. He started to hyperventilate. *Was he trapped in this room forever?* he wondered. He tried the last door. It opened and astonishment quickly replaced the panic he was feeling. He stood at the head of another long hall and saw what looked like another picture at the end of it. However, this was a picture of the castle wall with a piece of ladder protruding out of it. As he approached the picture, it grew larger and larger until it was full size. It dawned on him that what he was looking at wasn't a picture at all, but the real thing.

"It's an illusion," he whispered to himself. He started to walk backwards. As he did, the doorway back to the castle began to shrink in size until once again it looked like a picture at the end of the hallway. Then the thought struck him that the picture of the forest in the other hallway, might not be a picture at all, but a real forest. He walked back to the door where he had seen the forest, and opened it. He walked inside and continued towards the picture. As he got closer, the picture grew larger and larger until he was no more looking out a window, but a doorway of sorts. Below him was a lake surrounded by forest. He could see the branches of the trees gently swaying back and forth. A bird flew by below him and he watched it as it landed on the lake.

This is unbelievable, he thought. *How can this be real? What is this place? This is like the sickest hideout ever!*

He turned around and noticed that the door was missing just like last time. The hall led directly back to the room. As he entered the room, he quickly turned around and found that the door was once again there.

I'm going crazy. This doesn't make any sense," he mumbled to himself. He opened another door. It was the hallway he had looked at earlier with pitch black at the end. No, not pitch black. As he looked closer, there were tiny lights flickering. Josh walked through the door and approached the end of the hall. As he did so, the picture, just like the others, grew until he was standing, looking out of the doorway into nothingness, or at least that's what he thought at first. Then he noticed, far in the distance, lights.

"Oh my freak!" Josh exclaimed with a chill. "That's space out there. Those are stars!" A chill ran down his back as he thought about what would happen if he actually stepped out into it. Against his better judgment, he walked closer until he was right up against the doorway. He stuck his hand through it. It was freezing cold and he quickly pulled it back in. Then he very cautiously stuck his head through. Again, it was very cold, and he also couldn't breathe, as there was no oxygen. He pulled his head in and quickly took a few steps backwards. This was one door he didn't want to ever get close to again.

He walked back and found the door leading to the castle. Sure enough, the ladder was still there. He climbed back on and quickly returned to the castle. For just a moment, Josh considered not telling the others about the place. It would make a great hideout. But then again, this was too great a discovery and he knew himself too well to think he'd ever be able to keep it a secret for long. However, he did decide not to tell the others right away. The wheels in his brain began to turn and he wondered how he could use this place to have a little fun.

Still contemplating this, his stomach growled and he decided to get something to eat. He returned the ladder and made his way to the dining hall. As he did, he contemplated the picture of the forest he had seen down the first hall. He knew without a shadow of a doubt that the forest was real. But what forest was it?

Chapter 10

Kirtsvag Roum

The three older boys discussed their options, while Josh sat in silence listening to them banter back and forth. It had been five days since they had learned of the disappearance of their family members and still they had had no luck in finding a way back to Lumen. What worried them more was that Headmaster McDougal was long overdue.

"Ned, isn't there a way for you to contact *someone* who could help us?" Eric asked.

"Not that I can think of. Besides, who would I contact? I can't find my family and the rest of the magi council are probably on Headmaster McDougal's side." He lowered his voice to that of a man's and mimicked the magi, "Those boys will be safer at CastleOne. Let's just lock them up so we won't have to worry about them too."

"I could try Azinine's bracelet," Scott suggested.

"Perhaps..." Josh started to say, but was cut off.

"That's not a bad idea," Eric replied.

"I think..." Josh tried again, but was cut off once more.

"Azinine is missing also. She's probably with my parents. Even if she got the signal, and that's a big if, Headmaster McDougal has closed everything. There's no way she could help us. At this point, only Headmaster McDougal can open the portal."

"Maybe I could…" Josh tried but was interrupted again.

"Ned, what if he gets captured or even killed. You'll be stuck here forever," Eric pointed out.

"I have…" Josh began again, getting a little perturbed that they weren't listening to him.

"The spell may not be permanent," Ned continued, ignoring Josh. "Hopefully he put some sort of time limit on it."

"Yeah," Scott gave a little laugh. "But by the time it releases the lock, you'll be old and gray."

"Would you guys shut up and listen to me!" Josh yelled.

Surprised at his outburst, all three boys stopped and stared at him. "What's up with you, squirt?" Scott asked.

"I have something to say and you're all treating me like some insignificant little bug!" Josh retorted.

"Okay, little brother," Eric said, trying to calm him down. "What's on your mind?"

"I may have a possible solution to our problem."

"Don't tell me. You want to build a space ship and fly there," Scott joked.

"Funny, funny. You're a comedian," Josh said, sticking his tongue out at him. "You just watch. I'll have the last laugh."

"Josh, there's no way to open up those portals. We've tried everything," Ned replied trying not to get Josh's or anyone else's hopes up.

Eric turned to his youngest brother. "Josh, if you have an idea that you really think will work, then we'll listen. But I'm warning you, this is not a time for jokes."

"I'm not promising anything, but I think there might be a way. Follow me."

Scott and Ned looked at each other. Unlike Eric, they both seriously doubted Josh, but they were curious enough to follow him and see what he had in mind. Josh led them up the stairs and out onto the wall walk.

"Where is he taking us?" Ned whispered skeptically to Scott.

"Who knows? It's Josh," Scott replied, as if that explained everything.

Josh told them to stand by the doorway and not move. He then walked along the wall searching for the spot he had marked. He was at least going to have some fun before he showed them his discovery. He had to make sure he was right on target or this little stunt of his could prove fatal. He found the mark he had made and then picked up a small pebble. He threw it to make sure it disappeared, which it did. The pebble was small enough that the older boys paid no attention to it.

"Okay," he began. "What Zandor the Magnificent is about to show you will both fascinate and amaze you, something beyond your comprehension. But remember, this is for professionals only. So kids, please do not try this at home."

Growing a little angry at what he figured was Josh's way of getting attention, Eric warned, "Josh, I said no jokes!"

"I assure you this is no joke," Josh said as he climbed up on the wall. "Now I, Zandor the Magnificent, will amaze and astound you."

"Josh! Get down from there! This is not funny!" Eric yelled.

"It's not meant to be funny. It's meant to amaze you and it will," Josh replied calmly even though his heart was racing. He flashed his boyish grin at them. He turned and faced the castle grounds with his heart still racing. "This better work," he muttered to himself.

Ned leaned over to Scott. "Is your brother psycho?"

"Most of the time. Why?" he replied joking.

"Because it looks like he's about to jump?"

"He's not really going to jump…I don't think. I mean, he's always been short of few marbles, but he's not that crazy."

"No, Scott. He's going to jump," Ned said very seriously.

"Josh, what are you doing?" Scott yelled, all joking quite gone now.

"We've got to stop him!" Eric yelled and sprinted toward Josh. But just before he reached him, Josh jumped.

"Josh!" all three cried out simultaneously.

"Huh? Where did he go?" Scott asked in bewilderment. They looked over the wall expecting to see him splattered on the ground or swimming in the moat, but he wasn't down there.

"I...don't know," Eric replied just as confused. "He just...disappeared."

Not saying a word, Ned studied the place where they had last seen Josh with a very curious look on his face.

Noticing his friend's reaction, Eric asked, "Ned, do you know what just happened?"

Slowly Ned shook his head as he answered Eric's question. "I don't know. I've never actually seen anything like it before, but I've heard stories. Myths really. I just never believed it could really exist."

They couldn't see Josh, but Josh could see and hear them, and he was enjoying himself immensely as he watched their reaction. Finally, he decided it was time to show them. He took a couple of steps back to give him some running room. He then ran and jumped back onto the castle wall. To the older boys it looked like Josh had reappeared out of nowhere and landed on the castle wall.

"Josh!" Eric and Scott exclaimed, with both relief and anger registering on their faces.

"What just happened?" demanded Eric.

"How in the world did you do that?" asked Scott, at the same time.

Josh just winked at them. "A magician never reveals his secrets," he said smugly. Then noticing the looks on his brother's faces he figured he better spill the beans before they killed him. "But in this case, I'll make an exception," he hastily added. Pointing to the wall, he instructed them, "Stand right here. It has to be on this spot or you'll fall like a rock to the ground below. Believe me, I know, I've tested it. Then you just leap out about three feet and you'll land in an invisible room."

"So it does exist," Ned said in wonder.

Scott stared at him, his jaw hanging open. "You expect me to stand on the edge of this wall and jump? Are you mad!" he exclaimed.

Eric climbed up on the wall and looked at Josh soberly. "If you say this really works, I'll trust you. But if this is a joke, you better tell me now before I jump."

"I'm telling you, it's really there. I'm not making this up," Josh replied.

"Okay, here goes." Eric took in a deep breath and got ready to jump. He looked down at the water below and then once again out in front of him. There was no evidence that this room actually existed. He believed Josh, because he saw what Josh had done, but he was jumping out to something he couldn't see. He could feel his heart hammering in his chest. The others stood there silently, waiting to see if he would really do it. He tried hard to bring himself to jump, but his legs wouldn't move.

Josh tapped him on the back. "Let me go first. Maybe if you see me do it again, it will give you more courage, big brother."

Eric nodded, relieved he didn't have to jump. Josh climbed back on the wall and jumped as though he'd done it a million times. About three feet out, just as he had said, he disappeared into thin air. Seconds later he poked his head out, taking the others by surprise. It looked as though his head were floating in midair.

"Piece of cake," he grinned at them. "As long as you jump from that particular spot, you have nothing to worry about."

Eric climbed back onto the wall. "Okay, here goes nothing," he muttered. He made sure his footing was sure and jumped. Seconds later he landed in the hallway, on a brick floor as solid as any he had ever felt.

"Wow…" he said looking around. "This is amazing." He was about to ask Josh a question, when he was almost knocked over by Scott who had just jumped. Scott stood up and looked around, trying to take it all in.

"What is this place?" Scott finally asked.

"Not really sure," Josh replied.

The others looked back. Ned had just climbed upon the wall, but he wasn't jumping. They could tell he wanted to, but his brain just wouldn't let him. Scott and Josh both snickered at the look of sheer terror on Ned's face.

"I know how he feels," Eric said. He walked over and poked his head out. "Ned, you just have to trust. The room really is here. You just have to jump."

Ned nodded. He took in a deep breath and jumped. He let out a little scream, but quickly stifled it when he actually landed in the room on solid footing. He had leapt about five feet in an effort to make sure he made the jump, and slammed into Josh as he entered.

They walked down the hall and into the room. Amazed, nobody said a word for several minutes. They simply stood there taking it all in. Josh had grabbed one of the golden rods and was now sitting in the chair like a king upon his throne.

Eric was the first to speak. "Ned, what is this place?"

"I think it's a Kirtsvag Roum, but I've never actually seen one before so I can't be sure."

"What's a…Kirtsvag Roum?"

"Kirtsvag Roum. It means 'shortcut room.' But the stories around these rooms describe it as an escape portal."

"An escape portal?" Scott questioned.

"A long time ago, there was a High King named Blutenbar. Blutenbar was under attack by a neighboring king named Tritanar. One night, Blutenbar had a dream that Tritanar had surrounded his castle with a huge army, trapping Blutenbar inside. Blutenbar's men betrayed him and let Tritanar and his army inside the walls. Even though it was just a dream, it scared Blutenbar enough that he commissioned a magus named Luten to figure out some sort of escape route, in the event his dream came true. The story goes on to say that Luten created a room that existed in two places at one time. The idea is pretty absurd and virtually every magus will tell you it's only a myth. But I really think this must be a Kirstvag Roum."

"But this castle isn't Blutenbar's castle," Eric pointed out.

"No, you're right about that," Ned conceded. "But later on, Luten was one of the first magi to live in this castle. He helped move a group of Lumen here from England, because of a war between the Lumen and the Druids. For years, these two groups lived in peace in what is now called England. Then one day a magus named Taranis disappeared and that's when the trouble started. You see, Taranis used a combination of simple magic and farming techniques that he learned on Lumen, to teach the Druids how to farm, and breed animals, so the earth would continue to provide for them. He was highly respected among the Druids. When he disappeared, the Druids blamed the Lumen and attacked them. Instead of fighting, the Lumen decided to relocate themselves."

"So they moved to Germany?" Scott noted.

"It wasn't Germany at the time. It was part of the Western Roman Empire. But it was inhabited by several different tribes. Eventually, those tribes defeated the Romans and then started warring against each other. Luten and the others disguised themselves as peaceful monks, but that still didn't mean they were out of danger. I don't really know, but maybe Luten created this room as a way to escape any marauding tribes."

Fascinated by this story, Scott asked, "The portal in the forest, next to the castle, looks a lot like Stonehenge in England. Is there some relation there?"

"I suppose Stonehenge could have been a portal at one time. They needed portals that were large enough to transport large groups of people. For years they used to move people back and forth between the two worlds. There were several portals created. Some are here in Germany, some in England, China and many other countries. The ancient Chinese traded with Lumen a lot. In fact, the Chinese learned how to make their fireworks from Lumens. They were also notorious for trapping baby dragons on Lumen and taking them back to China. They..." he continued, but was cut off by Eric.

"Enough history for one day. Do you think this room can get us back to Lumen?"

"I honestly have no idea. Up to this point, I've always thought it was just a myth. That's assuming this really is a Kirstvag Roum."

At this point, Josh jumped off the chair and opened one of the doors. "Right this way, gentlemen," he said, bowing low as though he were a butler.

Curious, the three of them walked over and looked inside. The hallway was empty except for a painting at the end.

"And your point is?" Ned asked.

"You surprise me, Ned," Josh said in mock astonishment. "Of all of us, I would think you'd understand the best."

"What are you talking about?"

"That picture is only an illusion. Get up closer to it and you'll see what I mean." The four of them walked down the hall approaching the picture. As they did, it began to grow until it encompassed the entire wall. They could see the branches of the trees slightly swaying and ripples of water on the small lake directly beneath them. The room they were in stood about forty feet above the middle of the lake. The four of them stared silently in wonder for several minutes until Ned turned to Josh.

"So you think this is Lumen?"

"Well, I think there's a good chance it's Lumen since this castle seems to have been inhabited by Lumens for centuries. Doesn't it make sense to you?"

Ned nodded slowly. "I guess there's some logic in that. But on the other hand, this may not be Lumen. It may just be another part of earth, or some other planet for all we know."

Chapter 11

Lardior

They sat in silence contemplating what they should do or how they could determine if the land beneath them was indeed Lumen. Finally, Scott spoke up.

"Well, there's only one way to find out if it's Lumen," Scott said. He moved to jump into the lake, but Ned grabbed his shoulder.

"Wait a minute, Scott," Ned said. "If it's not Lumen, there's no way to get back up here. Not to mention that we may never even be able to locate this door again since it's invisible once we leave it.

Without a moment's hesitation, Scott answered, "Josh will stay behind. He can let a rope down and we can pull ourselves back up."

"No way!" Josh objected. "I'm coming with you guys! I was the one who found this place. Without me, you would still be back in the castle muttering magic mumbo jumbo spells and stuff."

"Josh," Eric tried to reason with him, "we need someone to stay here so we can get back up. Even if this is Lumen, this may be the only way back. It's not that we don't want you to come with us, but we need someone here to let us back in."

"But I found the portal. Why can't someone else stay behind?"

"Because Ned and Scott are the most familiar with Lumen and they both speak the language."

"I speak it too!" Josh replied quickly.

Josh had a point. Logically, Eric was the one who should stay behind, but he wasn't about to do that. He had to find a way to convince his younger brother that he should be the one to stay behind. He came up with an idea, and putting his arm around Josh's shoulder, he said, "Which is exactly why you need to stay behind. If something does happen to us, we'll need someone who can rescue us. And that person will need to speak Lumen. You're perfect for the job."

"Hmm, that's true, I guess," Josh said, nodding his agreement. "And knowing you boneheads, you probably will get in trouble."

"Good," Eric said, giving him a pat on the back. "Now go find a rope and secure it so we can pull ourselves up."

Knowing he'd been tricked, but also realizing there really was some logic to what Eric had said, Josh resigned himself to being left behind. He turned and left the room to go find a rope.

"Very sly, big brother," Scott said.

Eric smiled slightly and looked back out the portal. He was getting worried. It looked as though it would be dark in a few hours and he didn't want to wait until morning. They had to go now. "Are you guys ready?" Eric asked.

"Don't you think we should prepare for this? You know, bring stuff with us?" Ned asked.

"We're just going to see if this is Lumen. Once we know whether it is or not, we'll come back and get what we need. There's no reason to lug our stuff with us if this isn't the right place."

"We don't even know what's down there. We don't know how far we'll have to go and what we'll encounter. We should at least bring a jacket and some food," Ned said trying to reason with Eric.

"I don't like it either, but we can't wait a whole night. It's going to be dark soon. I just think we need to check it out first. We won't go far and we'll make sure we're back here before dark. If, after that, we still haven't been able to determine if it's Lumen, then we'll wait until morning and go better prepared. Okay? Deal?"

Ned let out a long breath. "Oh, alright," he agreed.

Scott," Eric said turning to his brother, "since you're the best swimmer, I vote you go first. Ned, you go second and I'll go last."

"Well, there's no time like the present. Geronimo!" Scott yelled and jumped. He hit the water and went in over his head. Seconds later he emerged and looked up at the others.

"Come on in, the water's warm!" he hollered.

Ned was just getting ready to jump when Scott let out a yelp and was pulled under the water. He managed to make his way to the surface long enough to scream for help and was once again pulled under.

"Scott!" Eric and Ned yelled simultaneously. The two of them jumped at the same time, the water engulfing them as they landed. Both came to the surface, frantically looking around for any sign of Scott.

"Scott!" Eric yelled. "Scott!" But there was no sign of him. They dived down again straining to get a glimpse of him, but with no luck. "Ned, anything?" Eric asked.

"Not here. You neither?" Ned asked concerned. Eric looked around frantically. Just then Eric noticed Josh's head poking out of the portal.

"Josh, can you see any sign of Scott?" Eric yelled up to Josh.

"Yeah," he answered with a huge grin. "He's sitting on the shore laughing at you two morons."

Eric and Ned both turned to look towards the shore where they saw Scott sitting on the bank waving at them.

"Oh, he's dead meat!" Eric growled turning to Ned. "Let's get him!" They swam over to the shore and dog piled onto Scott.

After a few minutes, Eric stood up. "Scott, you scared the bejeebee's out of me."

"Sorry, just having a little fun," Scott replied.

"Okay," Eric said, "we have about two hours to discover what this place is and then get back. Any suggestions?"

"Uh…if I'm not mistaken, I'm pretty sure we're on Lumen," Ned replied gravely.

"How do you know?" Eric asked.

"Look over there," he replied, pointing to the far side of the lake.

They turned and saw six men on flying discs coming towards them at full speed. They were getting close enough to see that the men wore black robes with a red collar.

"Who are they?" Eric asked.

"Men of Lardior," Ned answered. "I guess the best way to describe them would be the equivalent of the mafia on earth. They're bad news."

"We can't outrun them," reasoned Eric. "So, we'll just have to act like three kids taking a swim. We don't have anything valuable on us, so there's no reason they should be concerned about us."

"It's worth a try," Ned replied. "But if they weren't concerned about us, they wouldn't be flying at full speed towards us."

While they stood there waiting for the men to approach, it dawned on Eric that Scott wasn't standing with them. Looking around, Eric found him walking in a circle, touching some rocks and picking others up. "What is he doing?" Eric said, more to himself than as an actual question.

Ned glanced over at Scott, just as perplexed. "I don't know. Collecting rocks?"

At that moment the men flew up to them, coming to a stop right in front of Eric and Ned. Scott, who was at the moment standing behind them about fifteen feet away, stopped to watch.

"Hello," Ned hailed them. "Are we okay swimming here?"

One of the men jumped off his disc and walked over to Ned while two of the men flew over to hover by Scott. The remaining three men stayed on their discs and stood guard around Ned and Eric.

"You are Magus Polimar's son, are you not?" the man addressed Ned. His voice was not angry, but rather friendly, which was a relief to the boys.

"Uh..yes, I am," Ned stammered, surprised this man knew who he was. "How do you know that? Do you know my father?"

"Yes, I guess you could say that. What are you boys doing all the way out here?"

"We just came for a swim?" It came out more as a question than an answer.

"You came all the way out here just to swim. How did you get here? We didn't see you come."

Ned was at a loss for words and Eric had no clue what was being said.

Scott, who was still standing apart from them, joined in the conversation. "Don't tell him, Ned. You promised your dad."

The man whirled around to face Scott. "Bring him here!" he ordered the two who were guarding him. They both jumped off their discs and each grabbed one of Scott's arms.

"Let me go!" Scott yelled as he tried to jerk himself free, but the men held him tight. Scott jumped up, swung a leg around the inside of each man's leg and threw himself backwards. The unexpected force surprised the men and both fell backwards, taking Scott with them. The three of them landed on their backs with a humpf, almost knocking the wind out of them. One of the men smacked his head on a large rock and began writhing in pain. The other scrambled to his feet just a second after Scott, who put up a fist as though he were going to punch the man. "I'm not going to run, so keep your paws off me," Scott said, daring the man to come any closer.

The man who appeared to be the leader clapped his hands, giving Scott an appraising look. "Well done, Scott Frontier. I like your spunk. Perhaps I'll be able to convince you to join my little band. You'd be a great asset to us."

"Are you Lardior, their leader?"

Ned looked at Scott like he'd just given away some sort of precious secret.

"Why, yes, I am. That's very perceptive of you. What do you know of the Lardior band?"

Scott, sensing he'd just made some sort of blunder, tried to recover, "Not much. It was really just a guess. After all, who but the Lardior band would be camping out here."

Lardior smiled, obviously not convinced in the least by Scott's reply. "I see you went swimming with your clothes on. It will be dark soon and you'll need a place to shelter. Tonight, you will be my guests." It was given as an invitation but the boys sensed it was more of a command.

"Oh…we wouldn't want to impose on you. Besides, our parents will be expecting us back home very soon," Ned explained hoping to get out of this very precarious situation.

"On the contrary, young Polimar. Your parents won't be expecting you at all," Lardior replied with an evil grin. All of the former warmth and friendliness had disappeared from his voice, sending a chill down Ned's back.

"What do you mean by that?" Ned asked nervously

"I mean just that," he replied cheerfully. "Your parents are in no condition to be expecting anyone."

"What's happened to my parents?" Ned demanded.

"You'll find out soon enough, I'm sure." Before Ned could question him any further, he nodded to his men. "Take them."

The men escorted the young boys to their camp, where upon arrival, they were immediately taken to a tent-like structure. Lardior had large robes brought for them so they could change out of their wet clothes. As they studied their surroundings, they noticed the enclosure was actually very solid and there was no way out except for the door, which they ruefully noted was guarded.

"Scott," Ned muttered, "do you want to know the secret to keeping out of trouble?"

"What's that?"

"Breath through your nose. That way your mouth stays shut."

"What did I do?"

"What did you do!" Ned exploded. "What do you think happens when you walk into a mob leader's home, a person who is wanted by the law, and you identify him? Do you think, for one moment, he's going to let you go? I'm telling you, we're toast."

"I was trying to pique his curiosity so he wouldn't kill us," Scott said defending himself. "If he thinks we have something of value, he'll keep us alive."

"Oh, great idea! And then maybe he'll torture us to get this so-called secret out of us that doesn't really exist."

"Okay, maybe it wasn't such a great idea, but you weren't doing any better," Scott pointed out.

"At least I..." Ned started to say, but was cut off by Eric.

"Listen, guys. What's done is done. We're here and what we need to do now is come up with a plan to get us out of this situation."

"Maybe Josh will rescue us," Scott said sarcastically.

"Oh man! I forgot all about Josh," Eric groaned. "He probably watched the whole thing, and knowing 'Zandor the Magnificent,' he's probably on his way right now with some hair brained idea. Ned," he turned desperately to his friend, "any possibility you have some sort of magic to get us out here?"

Ned shrugged his shoulders. "Maybe, but so does Lardior. He's an incredible warlock from what I hear. He used to sit on the magi council before he was ostracized. He won't be easy to escape from."

"I have a plan," Scott broke in. "But we need to wait until they're all in bed."

He had just started to explain what he had in mind, when Lardior entered the tent and invited them to dinner. His voice was back to its friendly nature, which the boys took as a good sign. The dinner itself wasn't great, but they enjoyed the entertainment. Lardior's men took turns jousting with each other on flying disks. It was similar to the jousting they had watched at the fair, but since most of the men were drunk, they usually fell off without even being hit. The boys were careful not to drink the liquid, as they needed to have their wits about them if they were going to escape.

All through dinner, the man Scott had injured earlier kept glaring at him. Finally, he arose and challenged Scott to a disking duel. Scott turned him down, not wanting to bring attention to himself. However, the man kept insisting until eventually the rest of the band picked up on the challenge and began chanting, "Scott! Scott! Scott!" Two of the men approached Scott and picked him up off his chair, sat him on a disk and shoved a pole in his hands.

Not wanting to anger the man further, Scott stood there for a moment studying the pole in his hands. It was unusually light and he noticed the tips were blunt on both ends just like the ones he had seen at the fair. The man who had challenged him jumped on a disc and rose up about three feet, floating in midair. He stood there, apparently waiting for Scott to rise. Meanwhile, the crowd now started chanting, "Berto! Berto! Berto!" which Scott assumed was the man's name.

"Scott!" Ned hollered. "They work kind of like the flying shoes. They're just not attached to you."

Scott nodded at his friend and rose into the air. He was surprised at how much like the shoes they really were and it didn't take him long to get the hang of it. The two squared off, eyeing each other as a wolf eyes its prey. Berto charged with his pole in his right arm and pointed directly at Scott. Scott faked to the left and turned sharply to Berto's right. This allowed Scott to get inside of Berto's striking range and with the blunt end of his own pole, he swung for Berto's head. Scott had fully expected to connect, but Berto ducked with lightning speed and Scott's momentum almost sent him sailing off his disk. Below, the crowd of men went wild. Scott barely had time to recover when out of the corner of his eye he noticed Berto had turned and was rapidly heading in his direction.

Scott shot straight up to get out of the way. He succeeded in avoiding Berto's pole, but when he came to a sudden stop, his own upward momentum sent him flying upward off the disk. He was close to thirty feet off the ground, and his heart jumped into this throat. To make matters worse, he hadn't shot up exactly straight and as he began to drop, he realized he wasn't going to land on the disk. He let go of his pole and reached for his disc with both hands. He grabbed the edge, and barely managed to hold on. Hanging there like a sitting duck he could hear Ned yelling at him.

"Watch out, Scott! Here he comes! Use the disk!"

Scott looked down in time to see Berto heading up towards him. He tried to move the disk forward to avoid Berto's attack, but he was too late. Before he could get out of the way, Berto swung his pole and slammed it into Scott shins.

"Ouch!" he screamed out.

"Use the disk! Use the disk!" he could hear Ned screaming.

"I'm trying to use the disk!" he muttered under his breath.

At this point, he did the only sensible thing he could think of. He lowered the disk back down to the ground so he could pick up his pole and get back on. He made it down okay, but before he could pick up his pole, Berto swooped down, and despite Ned's continued warnings to Scott, rammed his pole into Scott's back, knocking him to the ground.

"Auugh!" Scott screamed out. Frightened at this point, Eric jumped out of his seat to help Scott, but two men grabbed him and pulled him back down. Meanwhile, despite the incredible pain he was feeling, Scott picked up his pole just in time to ward off another blow by Berto. He jumped back onto his disk, and waited for Berto to make the next move. Berto slowly made his way to Scott, stopping as he came within striking distance. The two stared at each other for several seconds and then without warning Berto circled around to Scott's back and struck hard. Scott saw this coming, and reacted quickly. He countered Berto's blow and swung hard at his legs. Berto avoided the blow by jumping over it. He then flew some distance away from Scott and stopped.

Scott was impressed with his opponent's ability to maneuver and he knew he'd have to come up with something better if he were to beat this guy. *What's he up to now?* he wondered. He didn't have to wait long. After only a few seconds, Berto shot towards Scott at tremendous speed. Scott held up his pole trying to anticipate Berto's move. Berto wasn't quite within striking range when he threw his pole at Scott like a spear. Scott swung his pole to block it, but missed and Berto's pole struck him square in the chest, knocking him off the disk again. As he lay on the ground gasping for air, Berto flew over to him and jumped off his disk.

"Now you'll pay for what you did," Berto bellowed angrily. He picked up his pole and raised it high above his head. Berto was poised for a deadly strike. Scott brought his legs into a fetal position, and placed his arms over his head to protect his vital areas from the blow. Berto had just begun to swing the pole down when he was suddenly jerked off his feet.

"I need the boy alive," Lardior said to Berto in a cold voice. He lifted Scott off the ground and helped him to his feet. "You're an interesting mystery, Scott Frontier. Once you defeated Magus Mordi and once you defeated Magus Mitle. Twice you defeated Magus Cohar. And twice you defeat the goblins, in their own lair I might add. Yet we are able to take you captive and you can't even beat Berto, a common thief, in a disking dual."

Scott shook his head, struggling to regain his composure. "How do you know I didn't *let* you capture me? And maybe I *let* Berto beat me," he finally blurted out.

Lardior eyed him for a second, and then his face broke into a sly smile. "Maybe," he conceded. "Although I can't think of one good reason why you would do such a foolish thing."

"Lardior!" At that moment, from out of the darkness, a guard came running up to them, gasping for breath. "Lardior! There's something you must come and see."

Lardior's eyes narrowed as he listened to the man. "Take the boys back to their room," he instructed members of his band who were standing close by. "I'll call for them later."

Five men escorted the boys back to their tent. When they walked in, they were a little surprised to see what was waiting for them. Apparently, while they had been to dinner someone had brought them some blankets and cots to sleep on. Their clothes, now dry, lay on their cots.

"Well, this is a good sign," Eric said. "At least they don't plan on killing us until morning."

"We're not going to wait until morning to find out," Scott replied.

"Does the powerful Scott Frontier have something in mind?" Ned asked sarcastically.

"Possibly," he answered with a shrug. "But we'll have to wait until the time is right."

"Could you let us in on your plan in advance?" Ned asked. "Because if it involves me, I'd like to decide in advance whether or not to participate."

"No problem," Scott answered. But just as he was about to unfold his plan, he was interrupted, once again by Lardior, who had just entered the room.

"You!" he said pointing to Eric. "Come with me."

Eric knew Lardior was speaking to him, but because he couldn't under-stand Lumen, he had no clue what the man had said or what he wanted him to do. Eric glanced at Scott and then over at Ned. Just then, Scott began to laugh hysterically causing everyone, including Lardior, to glare at him.

"What is so funny?" Lardior demanded.

"If you plan on torturing him first," Scott pointed at Eric, "it won't do you any good. He can't talk. He can make sounds and all, but nothing understandable."

Annoyed, Lardior then pointed to Ned. "Okay, then you come. I don't really care who I torture first." He turned to the guards. "Shackle them all and then bring the short one to my room."

Ned looked at Scott. "Thanks a lot! Didn't we just talk about keeping your mouth shut?"

"He was going to take Eric!" Scott replied.

"Yeah, and now he's going to take me." Before the boys could say any-more, the guards grabbed Ned, and escorted Ned out the door.

Scott softly whispered, "Good luck."

Chapter 12

Escape

The guards returned Ned about a half hour later, and thankfully in good shape. As it turned out, Lardior wasn't serious about the torture bit. He just had a few questions he wanted answered.

"So, what did he want to know?" Scott asked.

"Apparently one of the guards found four other guards completely unconscious in the same area where they found us. He wanted to know if there was anybody else in our group that we hadn't told him about. Of course, I told him there wasn't. And even if there was, one of us certainly couldn't take out four of his highly trained men. Then he wanted to know more about how we got past his guards in the first place."

"What did you tell him?" Eric asked.

"I told him his guards were probably sleeping on the job just like the ones he found tonight. Because we simply walked right up to this place without even hearing a boo from them."

"Good thinking," Eric said complimenting him.

"You don't think Josh is out there do you?" Scott asked, turning to Eric.

Eric thought about that for a moment. "I don't think so. Josh may be stupid enough to try and rescue us, but there's no way he could take down four guards."

Later that night, when everyone was in bed and the camp was quiet, Scott woke Eric and Ned. "It's time to get out of this place," he whispered. "Ned, is there a certain distance the command 'abtu' won't work?" Abtu was the command used to retrieve an object that has been magically bound to a person by the use of another command, 'hortu.'

"I'm sure there must be some limit, but I don't know for sure what it is," Ned answered. "I think it works from pretty far away, as long as no other objects get in the way and you're able to adequately concentrate on the object. Why?" Ned asked dubiously.

"Because it's time to put my plan into action," Scott replied.

"Oh, great! Here we go," Ned rolled his eyes. "Another one of Scott's plans. Does this involve death? Because I'm not sure I want to participate if it does."

Scott ignored him and proceeded to give out instructions. "Eric, there are two guards stationed outside our room. We'll tell them you have to use the bathroom. They'll have to unlock the door and one of them will have to escort you, leaving only one guard on duty. You'll have to watch for the right moment, but your job is to take him out. You'll have to do it quickly though, before he can use the shackle against you, otherwise it won't be pretty. But," he cautioned, "don't do anything until you know for sure that we've already taken out the other guard. Then meet us outside camp by the large black tree we passed on the way in here."

"I'm sure I can find a way to take out the guard accompanying me, but how do you plan on taking the guard here out?" Eric asked.

"Magic," Scott replied.

"Magic? You?" Eric asked in disbelief. "Ned already told us he didn't have any magic powerful enough to use. What makes you think you do?"

"I'm not exactly sure I do, but we have to try something. However, I think it will work. But, just in case it doesn't work, I'm asking you to wait to take care of your guard until after I've done my part."

"Okay, I suppose it's better than doing nothing. But I hope you know what you're doing," Eric replied. "This could go bad pretty quick," he said pointing to his shackle.

Eric walked over to the door and Ned hollered to the guard that he had to use the bathroom. The guard growled, but opened the door and motioned for Eric to come out. But immediately after Eric emerged, the guard quickly locked the door behind him. Scott and Ned looked at each other.

"What do we do now, Magus Frontier?" Ned asked sarcastically.

"We'll take care of this guard and hope Eric can handle the other one without waking the entire camp."

"Eric is strong and well trained in combat. I don't worry about him. It's you I'm worried about."

"O ye of little faith," Scott replied to Ned's pessimistic words.

With what little moonlight there was, Scott could just make out the silhouette of the second guard through the canvas-like material of the tent. He placed his hand directly behind the guard's head.

Then concentrating as much as he possibly could he whispered, "abtu." Although he couldn't see the baseball size rock he had touched earlier that day, and magically bound to himself before they were captured, he somehow knew it was making its way toward him. It wasn't flying through the air as he had anticipated, but rather just rolled along the shore until it hit a larger rock and stopped.

"Ned, what am I doing wrong?" he asked. "I used 'hortu' on a rock earlier and it's barely moving. How come it doesn't fly through the air?"

Remembering earlier that day when he and Eric had joked about Scott collecting rocks, understanding began to dawn on Ned. He quickly answered, "The further away the object is, the more you have to will it towards you. You just need to concentrate harder."

Scott closed his eyes and pictured in his mind the rock flying through the air. He lifted his hand one more time and whispered "abtu." This time he somehow felt the rock lift off the ground and fly towards him, but it only made it about half way before it dropped again.

"Dang it," Scott muttered under his breath.

"What happened?" Ned asked.

"I think it hit something, a tree maybe."

"Well, just keep trying until it makes it here."

Scott took a deep breath. "Okay, here goes again."

He lifted his hand, concentrated and spoke the command. Just like before, he felt or sensed the rock lift off the ground, but as before, it hit another tree and clattered to the ground. Only this time, just yards away from the guard.

"Halt! Who goes there?" the guard yelled out. When no one answered he left his post to investigate.

Scott gave Ned an 'oops' look.

"At this distance," Ned cautioned Scott, "the rock won't pick up enough momentum to knock him out unless you really concentrate on speed. Think of the rock as a bullet leaving a gun."

"That's assuming he comes back," Scott said dryly. "I…" He went silent at the sound of footsteps. It was Eric and the other guard returning.

"Crap!" Ned whispered. "With the other guard away, there's no way we'll get out of here."

"What is the range for the shackles to work?" Scott asked.

"Long enough," Ned answered. "There's no way for us to escape unless we take out both guards. Otherwise that second guard will fry all of us as soon as he discovers we're gone."

"Hopefully he'll come back when he hears Eric and the other guard. Either way we have to try. Nothing ventured, nothing gained."

"Oh yeah? What we'll gain is a lot of pain."

"If we stay, we're guaranteed a lot of pain," argued Scott.

"I guess you have a point there."

Eric and the guard were now at the door. As the guard opened the door to let Eric in, Scott placed his hand directly in front of the guard's head, concentrated on the rock as though it were a bullet and spoke the command. The rock shot through the air, between two very large trees and smacked the guard hard on the head. He made a grunting sound and crumpled to the ground.

"Wow! That was pretty impressive," Eric whispered. "Where's the other guard?" he asked holding the door open.

"We don't know," Scott and Ned both replied as they slipped out the door.

"What do you mean you don't know?" Eric asked with concern.

"This is hardly the time to discuss it," Scott pointed out as they headed toward the portal. "We have to get out of here now."

They ran as fast as they could through the dark, trying to make it to the edge of the lake. They ran for several minutes when suddenly they felt their shackles activate, followed by the most horrifying pain shooting through their bodies. All three hit the ground writhing in pain. Seconds later, three men appeared before them. One was the guard who had left his post. The second was a new guard, and the third they recognized as Lardior. He was carrying his staff, and the crystal was lit up like a light bulb. Despite the pain racking his body, Scott glanced at Lardior and cringed at the anger twisting at his face.

"Get up!" Lardior demanded in an icy cold voice. The shackles stopped and as the pain subsided, the three boys stood up, not knowing what to expect. Lardior began to speak again, but this time with more control in his voice. "What kind of guests are you? I take you into my home. I feed you. I give you a place to warm yourself and a bed to sleep in. And this is how you repay me? If you are not my friends, then you are my enemies and you will soon find out what happens to my enemies."

He gave the guard a nod and the pain shot through their bodies again. The three boys fell to their knees and then onto their backs writhing in pain, until the signal once again stopped.

"I expected more resistance than this," Lardior mocked. "Especially from the son of Magus Polimar, and certainly from the great Scott Frontier. I should..."

He was cut off as something suddenly hit him, and he dropped to the ground as though he were dead. The two guards spun around just before a very tall shadowy figure grabbed them both and smashed their heads together as though they were rag dolls. The guards crumpled to the ground beside him. The three men lay on the ground motionless. The figure stood there looking down at the three boys. From what they could tell, it, whatever it was, stood about ten feet tall and it had a long black robe draped around it. It didn't have any legs that they could see, but it stood facing them, floating like some silent wraith.

They lay on their backs, not knowing whether to run or to stay put. Finally, Ned spoke up. "Uh…thank you for saving us." When the figure remained silent and motionless, Ned continued. "Are you a friend?" he squeaked out.

Still, it said nothing.

"Who are you?" Scott asked, gathering his bearings.

Finally, the figure spoke, "I am he who goblins fear and king's revere. Whose name is great and who controls your fate. Do as I say and your life you buy, but double cross me and surely, you'll die."

Whoa! This thing speaks in rhymes just like the dragons do, except it's audible," Scott thought, remembering his experience with dragons a while back.

"What do you want from us?" Eric asked.

"First, you will kneel before me and show me the respect I deserve," the figure hissed.

Ned and Scott slowly got to their knees, but Eric stood up. "I'll tell you what," Eric began, "you get your scrawny little butt over here and we'll let you live."

Ned swung an arm into Eric's leg. "Are you crazy? You're going to get us killed!"

"No, Eric's right," Scott said as he stood up. "Don't get us wrong. We do appreciate your help, but we're wasting time with this little charade of yours."

"How did you know it was me?" Josh asked in his normal voice.

"Because you spoke to us in English," Eric replied. "You're the first person in this world I've understood. But what I don't understand is how you made yourself so tall and how you were able to handle those men like you did."

"Can we talk about this later?" Scott interrupted. "I'd like to get out of here before those goons wake up."

"Good idea," Ned agreed. He pointed at the men lying motionless on the ground. "Josh, each of those guards are wearing senders. We can't release ourselves because we are all wearing receiver shackles and it would just end up shocking us."

"Why?" Josh asked.

"It's just the way they work. Since you're not wearing a receiver, all you have to do is reach down and press the green stone for two seconds, and it will set us free."

As Josh moved down towards the guards, they could see he was floating rather than walking. He did as he was instructed and soon all three shackles fell open and were quickly discarded.

"That explains the height," Ned said pointing to the disk. "We'll make better time if we fly back to the portal. Josh, we'll each hold on to the edge. Just don't fly too fast in case one of us loses our grip and falls. Okay?"

"Roger, Dodger," Josh replied. "But I have to warn you, I'm still trying to get the hang of this thing."

"How did you get it anyway?"

"Two guards down by the lake were nice enough to give theirs up, if you know what I mean."

"So you're the one who knocked out Lardior's guards?"

"Yep."

"How?" Eric asked with admiration as he grabbed hold of the disk.

Josh flexed his scrawny muscles. "Brute strength, brother. Brute strength."

"Can we please get out of here?" Ned said with some urgency, while at the same time, rolling his eyes.

Once all three boys had grabbed a hold of the disk, Josh lifted them up in the air and moved towards the lake. Instead of flying around the lake, he chose to fly over the lake. That way they wouldn't run into any of Lardior's men on guard duty. And if they fell off they would hit water instead of the ground. They were just about halfway across the lake when a warning siren went off.

"Josh, we've got to hurry! It won't be long before this place is crawling with Lardior's men!" Ned yelled.

"I'm trying," Josh replied. Despite his inexperience with the flying disk, he was handling it pretty good and was able to bring the boys to the approximate spot where the portal was. But instead of stopping, he kept moving towards the shore.

"Josh," Scott yelled, "what are you doing? The portal is back there!"

"It's too hard to find the portal without the rods," he yelled back.

"What rods?"

"Just hold on and I'll show you."

Josh landed about twenty feet from the shore inside a grove of trees. Once the older boys let go of the disk, he rose back up in the air. Approaching one of the trees, he grabbed four golden rods that were similar to the ones they had seen earlier in the invisible room. He flew back down to the ground and hopped off.

"Without these," Josh said, handing each one a rod, "it's really hard to find the door. These rods however, will take you directly there. They're pretty cool. You can make them shrink down to about a foot and then make them grow to about six feet. If you push this black stone, two blades on both ends pop out. How's that for a switchblade? Push it again and the blades retract back inside."

"How did you figure all this out?" Scott asked, impressed.

"I was bored. I..." he started to say, but was cut off by Eric.

"Never mind that now," Eric interrupted. "How do we get back before this place is crawling with goons?"

"Walk over to the edge of the water and push the blue stone. But I have to warn you, when you push it, hold on tight. These babies drag you through the air like they are connected to some sort of cable. It's actually kind of fun. But you really have to hold on. If..."

"Okay, okay," Eric held up his hand, signaling Josh to stop. "We get the point. We can talk more once we're safe."

"Too late for that. Look!" Scott interjected. Through the trees the boys could now just make out several men combing the beaches. Some were on disks and others on foot. "We'll have to create a diversion."

"Do you have something in mind?" Eric asked.

"Nothing very appealing, but I do have an idea. One of us will take the disk and fly to the tops of these trees where they won't be looking."

Eric gave Scott a concerned look. "Scott, flying a few feet above the ground is one thing, but flying above the treetops could be fatal. You could fall off and kill yourself."

"Who said anything about me? I was thinking more like Ned."

"Me?" Ned yelped.

"Sure! You've had more practice on these than any of us, haven't you?"

"I guess I could sit down and hold on," Ned said.

"Boys, boys," Josh interrupted. "This is a man's job. I'll do it."

Scott shook his head. "You'd kill yourself for sure. Plus, with those *strong* hands of yours, we need you here just in case we run into trouble before we have a chance to use those rods."

Josh lifted his hands and looked at them. "I hope you don't mind me borrowing these.

"How did you even know about them?" Scott asked. "I've never said anything to you."

"No, but I overheard you and Ned talking about them the other night and I couldn't wait to get my hands on them...or under them. Ha ha. Get it? Under them?"

"Yes, we get it," Scott said rolling his eyes.

"Anyways, when I saw you guys get captured, I knew I was going to need some help, and you weren't around to ask, so I had to take things into my own hands. Ha! Get it? My own hands. Man, I'm getting good at these puns, aren't I?"

Though he couldn't see them, Scott looked at Josh's hands and knew his younger brother was wearing his gloves. They were the same gloves he had acquired several months ago, while searching for the golden sword. Without the gloves, which gave anyone wearing them incredible strength, the sword could not be wielded. He had retrieved the sword, but then had lost it while escaping from Goblin Mountain. He did, however, manage to keep the gloves.

Scott lightly punched Josh on the shoulder. "Normally I'd pummel you for taking them. But under the circumstances, I'll let it go."

Josh smiled. "You'll be glad to know I left your leotard in your drawer. I'm not into that kind of thing."

"Your leotard?" Eric asked, raising his eyebrows.

"It's not a leotard," Scott retorted.

"Then what is it?"

"Don't we have more important matters to take care of right now?" Scott asked, changing the subject.

"You're right. But I want to see this leotard when we get back."

Ignoring his older brother, Scott continued, "Listen, these discs aren't that much different than a skateboard. Since I'm the best boarder here, I'll create the diversion."

"Excuse me?" Josh said cutting in. "Who's the best boarder here?"

Eric looked at both of them skeptically, but didn't argue. Scott ignored Josh and hopped on the disk. He slowly rose higher and higher until he was above the trees. This actually wasn't much different than when he had played tag with Azinine in the clouds, except the disk wasn't connected to his feet and he truly could fall. He decided to sit down on the disk as Ned had mentioned to ensure a better grip. Once he got above the trees, he quickly moved a little way off from where the others were hiding. Then he lowered himself back down among the trees. He jumped off the disk and walked out in the open towards the shore. He left the disk in the trees so he could escape without his pursuers catching him. Once he got out in the open, he acted as though he had lost his friends and that he didn't know the men were there.

"Eric! Ned! Where are you?" Scott yelled. Lardior's men immediately spotted him and headed in his direction. Running back into the forest, Scott jumped onto his disk and shot straight upwards. Once above the trees, he looked out over the lake.

"Now," he whispered to himself. "Go!" He didn't have to wait long. In the moonlight, he watched as a shadow emerged from the trees where the boys had been hiding. Scott couldn't tell who it was, but he guessed it was Josh. Eric would have sent him first. Not only because he was the youngest, but because he would want to see how it was done.

The shadow ran to the edge of the lake, shot like an arrow silently through the air and then disappeared. If Scott hadn't known the portal was there, it would have been a very strange sight to see. Once Josh had gone, another figure emerged and then a third. They were all safe now except Scott.

Scott looked around to get his bearings and to see if there were any guards that hadn't fallen for his diversion. The coast looked clear so he darted towards the portal. He was halfway there when two guards spotted him. One was flying directly towards him and the other from his left side. Scott dropped as close to the ground as possible. If he was going to get knocked off, he wanted to make sure he would at least survive the fall. He pulled out the golden rod Josh had given him, extended it to its full length and flipped out the blades.

The man who was coming in from the front brought up his own pole, getting ready to use it. Meanwhile, the man coming in from his left had now fallen in behind Scott and was closing in. Scott decided to try to dodge the front guard's pole just as the guard behind him was about to strike. He hoped the two might actually hit each other. They didn't though, and soon they were both behind him, closing in. It was difficult to effectively use the golden rod while sitting down, so Scott slowly rose to his feet, hoping that his boarding instincts wouldn't fail him.

Scott did so just as the guard closest to him held his pole like a baseball bat and swung. The pole struck his ankle, not hard enough to knock him off, but hard enough to really sting and spur Scott forward. He flew out over the water with the two guards close on his heels. Once over the water, where he felt he could take greater risks, he came to a sudden stop and whirled around, the golden rod stretched out. Before the first guard could react, Scott struck out with the rod, slicing him across the chest and knocking him clean off his disk and into the water below. The second guard thrust his pole forward trying to ram Scott with his pole, which Scott narrowly dodged. He swung out with his own pole. The blade caught the other guard's pole and sliced a piece of it off.

"Whoa, those are sharp!" he said to himself.

The guard circled Scott, catching him off guard. He reacted instinctively by shooting straight upwards. This time, however, he came to a stop slowly, to avoid leaving the disk as he had done in his duel against Berto. He looked down to see where his assailant was, but couldn't find him. Unbeknownst to Scott, the guard had followed him up and was now right behind him.

"Say goodbye," a voice from behind him hissed. Scott whirled around just in time to feel a pole ram him in the chest forcing him off the disk. He tried commanding the disk to follow him down, but it was no use. He was just about to hit the water, when he remembered the golden rod. Holding on tight, he quickly pushed the blue stone, but not before he plunged into the water. The rod ripped him from the water and dragged him in a straight course toward the portal. He landed inside with a thump where he released his grip on the rod.

"Scott! Are you okay?" Ned asked as he picked him up from the floor.

"Uh…yea, I think so. This rod saved me. But my chest is going to have an ugly bruise on it," Scott groaned.

"Did the guard see what happened?" Ned anxiously asked.

"I don't know," Scott said, shrugging his shoulders. "It all happened so fast. I didn't look to see where he was. But it was dark. Besides, even if he did see, I'm not sure he'll be able to make much sense of it."

"No, maybe not. However, if Lardior gets wind of it, he might. This portal will no longer be safe to use."

"It was the only choice I had," Scott said defensively.

"I know," Ned said. "I'm not blaming you. It's just that this is the only way into Lumen until Magus McDougal gets back."

Scott shook his head. "If he is back, you know he'll never let us leave again. We'll just have to chance using this one more time. But maybe it would be better to wait a couple of days when things calm down."

Eric shot Scott an incredulous look. "I don't know about you, but I'm not waiting another day. The longer we wait, the greater chance our parents…." He paused for a moment. "Well, you know what I mean. I, for one, am going to grab some essentials and head back."

"I'm cool with that. We just need to be careful, that's all," Scott replied.

Ned heaved a big sigh. "Okay, but it won't be easy. We'll need food and water and any type of weapons we can find."

"We have plenty of paint ball guns," Scott suggested.

"They may help with some of these guards, but they'll be useless against a magus."

"They're better than nothing," Eric chimed in. "Let's get back to the castle. Scott and Ned, you track down some paint ball guns. Josh and I will grab some grub and we'll meet back here in an hour. The faster we move, the less opportunity Lardior has to organize his men."

Chapter 13

Meking Their Way Home

There was no sign of Magus McDougal. It was obvious he had not returned to the school, but their father had. Not able to find his sons and figuring they were simply out on the grounds goofing around, he left a message for them that he would be back soon. Feeling a little guilty, Eric and Josh decided they should at least leave a return note for their father. They let him know what they were planning on doing, just not how they were actually going to do it.

In their dorm, Scott and Ned decided to change clothes before they took off again. When Ned left to use the restroom, Scott quickly undressed, and pulled out the bodysuit the old lady had given him months ago. This suit appeared to make him invulnerable to magic, which he thought just might come in handy while on Lumen.

"This is not a leotard," he muttered to himself.

After grabbing four paint ball guns and some ammo from the weapons shed, Scott and Ned made their way back to the top of the castle where they found Eric and Josh waiting for them inside the Kirtsvag Roum. Eric had been watching Lardior's men from the portal entrance. He had seen several of them scouring the shores and the water, most likely still looking for signs of Scott. They decided this was a good sign the guard hadn't seen Scott enter the portal. However, now they had the seemingly impossible task of entering Lumen again without being seen. And even if they accomplished that, they still had to get past the other guards posted all over the area.

"Josh, will you keep watch while we try and figure out a plan?" Eric asked. "Look for any signs of Lardior's men taking up posts around the lake or even looking for this place."

"Sure," Josh replied, feeling dejected and left out again. Regardless of his feelings though, Josh took up a post at the portal entrance while the other boys discussed different options. They needed to know what to do once they landed on the lake's shore. They talked about making their way through the woods separately to give them a better chance of escaping, but decided that would be too dangerous. They would have more strength together.

As the boys continued discussing strategy, Josh kept watch on Lardior's men. As he watched, he could see two guards flying directly towards him, and was sure they were going to hit the entrance. He quickly raised his pole ready to fend them off. As it turns out, they missed the entrance, but only by inches. Josh, who reacted more out of instinct than on purpose, stuck the pole out the entrance and 'clotheslined' the two men. Since they weren't expecting anything like that, they easily lost their balance and fell from their disks, plunging into the water below. Much to his surprise and complete satisfaction, Josh noticed that the disks had stopped the second the men fell and now hovered in mid-air, not two feet from the entrance. He quickly leaned out as far as he could and grabbed them, pulling them inside. Just then the others returned to inform Josh of their plans.

"Hey, how did you get those?" Eric asked.

"Let's just say I've been fishing," Josh answered smugly.

"Fishing?" Eric questioned.

"Look," he said pointing down. The three older boys looked down and noticed two of Lardior's men swimming to the shore.

"You didn't!" Ned exclaimed.

"Hey, don't look a gift horse in the mouth," Josh replied.

"That's one I haven't heard. What's a gift horse?" Ned asked.

"Never mind that now," Eric replied. "I'm sure these disks will come in very handy, but we do have ourselves a slight problem. If Lardior wasn't suspicious before, he's bound to be now."

Scott nodded. "If we plan on entering Lumen through this portal, we've got to do it soon. It won't be long before Lardior has this place crawling with men looking for the portal. If you'll notice," he continued, pointing downwards, "there are three other men on disks down there. If we attack them right now, while we're not outnumbered, we might be able to snag two more disks and get away through the woods."

"Scott," Ned objected, "those disks aren't meant for travel, especially high-speed travel. Besides, Eric and Josh don't have much experience with them. If one of us fell, we could seriously get hurt, if not killed."

"I think we'll be okay," argued Scott, "Earlier, when I created the distraction, I sat down and held on. I used to do that as a kid when I was learning to ride a skateboard and it worked pretty well. I don't want to walk and I don't think you do either. These discs are better than nothing. If we fly above the tree line, we won't be in any danger of running into things. Once we're far enough away, we can slow down."

"I like it," Eric stated. "Scott, you and Ned take the two disks we have and distract those men. When they're not looking, Josh and I will use the golden rods to reach the shore. You lead the men past us and we'll knock 'em off."

"It's worth a try," Scott replied.

"Worth a try?" Ned sputtered with his eyes bulging out. "This isn't a game, you guys! We could get captured again or even killed!"

"How come you're always so worried about getting killed?" Scott joked, trying to ease the tension.

"How come…" Ned started to reply, but Scott cut him off.

"Ned, I'm kidding. But we're not going to just sit around and do nothing while our parents need help. They could just as easily end up dead if we're too late." He paused, letting that sink in. Then he continued, "I'll tell you what. I'll go first and act as a first distraction. When they start chasing me, you fly up from behind and knock 'em off if you can. Between you and Eric, we might just pull this thing off."

"Excuse me," Josh interrupted waving his hand. "I'll be there kicking butt also."

"Of course you will," Scott replied. "Just don't get in Eric's way and don't scream if one of them catch's Ned and rips his eyes out."

Ned rolled his eyes. "Funny. Scott, you go through life like you're invincible, but you're not. One of these days, life is going to catch up to you."

"Well, I guess I better enjoy it then until it does," Scott said with a wink. "Now let's get going."

He grabbed a golden rod, jumped on a disk and flew out the door without another word. Lardior's men had just managed to drag their friends out of the water and onto the shore when Scott caught up to them. One of the men spotted Scott and motioned to the others before he was able to catch any of them by surprise. He quickly banked to the right, out over the water. From the corner of his eye, he saw Ned leave the portal on the other disk with someone hanging from the bottom. Even though he couldn't see who it was, he knew it must be Josh since the figure was too small to be Eric. He wondered what they were up to, but didn't have much time to think about it. He needed to concentrate on his own situation. Chancing a backward glance, he could see two men hot on his tail. He darted to the right and then to the left, but couldn't shake them.

Meanwhile, Josh, who was still hanging from Ned's disk, was spotted by the third man on a disk. He was now shooting towards them. Clearly, he considered Josh a sitting duck and was going to run him through with his pole. The two discs were now on a collision course headed straight for each other, with the guard stretching out his pole like a skewer.

"Now!" Josh yelled.

Ned launched his disk a little higher into the air as though he were going to fly over the man. Josh let go of the disk, shoved the guard's pole aside and slammed into him with his hands outstretched. He was counting on Newton's third law of motion to carry out his plan. He hoped the man's forward motion would stop his own momentum, landing him on the disk while knocking the guard off the disk at the same time. He was only half right. His momentum did knock his attacker off, but he didn't land on the disk. Instead, he fell over the edge of the disk also. He barely caught hold of the edge and almost plunged into the water with his attacker. Normally, this would have been impossible for him to do, but the gloves he was still wearing gave him the strength to hold on. Now he hung from the disk by one arm suspended in midair.

The two guards on shore spotted Eric as he landed on the shore and started running towards him. Growing concerned that he might get caught, Eric looked around frantically for Scott. Relief flooded over him as he saw his younger brother racing towards him. Judging by Scott's speed, Eric knew Scott would reach him in plenty of time before the two guards running towards him on foot arrived. The real question was whether he'd be able to obtain a disk and take off in time.

Scott had just about reached Eric when the guard flying closest to him pulled out a whip and whirled it towards Scott. The whip followed Scott, like a heat seeking missile and wrapped itself around Scott's neck. Pulling back hard, the man jerked Scott off his disk. Instinctively, Scott grabbed the whip around his neck and held tight to keep from being seriously injured, but it still gave him quite a sting. He plunged into about five feet of water, his feet hitting the sandy bottom.

The whip unwrapped itself from around Scott, but Scott held on. The man yanked it back, trying to free it from Scott's grasp, but Scott wouldn't let go. By this time, the second guard had reached them and brought himself up behind Scott. Leaping from his disk he landed on Scott's back, causing Scott to release his grip on the whip, and sending them both under water.

"Scott!" Eric yelled, running into the water to help. At the same time, the man with the whip had recoiled it and now poised to attack Eric when he came within reach. To make things worse, the two guards on the beach were getting closer. That made four against two and even though Eric was extremely strong for his age, he didn't like those odds. He would have to reach Scott quickly and free him. Their only chance was to make a run for it.

As he approached, the man with the whip started whirling it in the air. Eric darted left and then quickly to the right. The whip lashed out and followed Eric's every move. It wrapped around his arm and held him tight. Eric jerked hard, but the whip held tight, while still giving just enough slack to keep the guard from being pulled off his disk. Out of the corner of his eye, Eric could see a figure rapidly approaching. It was moving too fast to be one of the men on foot, which surprisingly hadn't shown up yet.

Josh blew past Eric. He circled the guard with the whip who was still struggling with Eric. With the help of his gloves, he slowly approached the guard from behind and plucked the man from his disk. It surprised the guard so much that he let go of the whip, and tried desperately to release himself from Josh's grip. Josh knew he probably only had seconds before the man was able to twist himself around and grab the disc, so he accelerated further out over the lake and dropped him.

Eric grabbed the whip and then lunged towards the man who was struggling with Scott. He wrapped the whip around the man's neck and pulled him off. Josh came flying over to help. He grabbed the second guard and hauled him out over the water and dropped him. By the time Josh returned to his brothers, Ned had joined them. Eric and Scott grabbed the two empty disks and hauled themselves up onto them.

"Our stuff is still on the beach. Let's grab it and get out of here!" Eric yelled.

Scott, Josh and Ned all took off, but Eric was still sitting motionless. Noticing, Scott swung around to see what the problem was. "What's wrong?"

"I don't know. It won't move."

"You're trying to force it to move," Scott quickly explained. "Think of it as part of your body, like your arm or something. You don't think about how you're going to move your arm. You just do it. The disc works the same way."

"Okay..." replied Eric, not very sure of himself. He leaned forward, lost his balance and fell into the water.

Scott tried hard to stifle his laughter. "Get back on. We don't have time for this." Scott looked to see where the other guards were. Two were still swimming back to shore, two others were laid out on the beach and he couldn't tell where the fifth one was.

"Don't you think I know that?" Eric yelled back, both frustrated and embarrassed that he couldn't get the hang of it. He climbed back up on the disk and this time sat down. He thought about how he moved his arm and then aimed for the beach as though it was the most natural thing in the world. The disc moved and they both made their way over to where Josh and Ned were waiting for them. They all strapped a paint gun around their waist, pulled their backpacks on and climbed on their disks.

"Guys, we've got company," Ned warned. They looked behind them and could see about fifteen to twenty figures on disks heading in their direction.

"Fly into the woods and then straight up until you're above the tree line," Scott ordered. "Hopefully that will confuse them long enough for us to get away." Not wanting to take the time to argue with him, the others immediately followed him. They flew into the woods about ninety degrees from the direction they intended to get away. Approximately fifty yards in, Scott shot straight upwards and the others followed. Once they had reached the top of the tree line they stopped and waited for Lardior's men to enter. They waited only long enough to be sure they wouldn't be seen flying out again. The sun was just starting to rise, so they needed to put as much distance between themselves and Lardior as possible. Even so, they were well aware that Lardior had spies everywhere and once word got out, it wouldn't be easy to hide from him.

They zoomed along the tops of the trees for about a half an hour when Eric turned to Ned and asked, "Do you have any idea where we are?"

Ned ruefully shook his head. "I don't recognize this place. It just looks like another forest to me."

"Well, just keep looking for anything that might look familiar," Eric suggested.

A few minutes later, a flock of birds merged into their path, flying just to the right of them. They flew in a 'V' formation like geese, but they were slightly larger, and their wings were copper with white streaks running through them. Because of the bright coloring, they glistened in the light of the rising sun and Scott couldn't help thinking how beautiful they looked. They soon began to squawk back and forth to each other. At least, to Eric and Ned it sounded like squawking, but to Scott and Josh it was a different matter. The lead bird would sing a phrase and the others would repeat it. Both boys got a kick out of it, and it reminded them of an army show where the soldiers sang as they marched.

"We are Meking of the West, flying east to be the best.

We fly high and we fly low, we'll give the Weking quite a show.

We'll strut our feathers till they swell, we've always done it really well.

We are Meking of the West, they'll pick us to make their nests."

Josh looked over at Scott with a quizzical look. "Don't even ask," Scott said before Josh could say anything. They both broke out in laughter.

"What are you guys laughing at?" Ned asked.

"I think those Meking birds are on their way to makin' baby birds," Josh hollered back.

"How do you know they're Meking birds?"

"They said so."

"Man, that is so cool you guys can understand them," Ned said wistfully. "The Meking fly from all over the country this time of year to a special breeding ground. They do all kinds of spectacular stunts to impress the females or the Weking."

"So we heard," replied Scott with a chuckle.

"It's really quite a sight. If we had more time, I'd take you there to watch."

Eric glanced over at Ned. "What did you just say?"

"I said I'd take you there if we had more time."

Eric looked incredulous. "You mean you know the way to the Meking breeding grounds, but you don't know the way home?"

Ned's eyes grew wide. "Oh my word! I know where we are! Or at least I know how to get home. We simply need to follow these birds and they'll lead us to their breeding grounds. They are only about thirty minutes outside of Lux."

"We probably shouldn't just fly into Lux like this," Scott cautioned. "We'll attract too much attention. We need to drop down a few miles before we get there and walk the rest of the way."

The others nodded in agreement and they continued to follow the birds, who continued to sing.

"We are Meking of the West, we'll put the others to the test.
Like Leland's diving from the sky, we'll make the others turn and fly.
We are charming without guile, those Weking really dig our style.
We are Meking of the West, they'll choose us since we're the best."

"Are we there yet?" Josh yelled over to the others. "I think I'm gonna be sick." Scott laughed at Ned and Eric's puzzled expressions.

Chapter 14

More Bad News

A couple of times the birds landed by nearby ponds to rest and eat, so the boys took this opportunity to rest also. The disks weren't meant for long distance travel, and so they were grateful to have a break now and again. They traveled for most of the day and arrived just outside of Lux in the late afternoon. Hiding the disks, they walked the short distance into town. In an effort to keep from being spotted by any of Lardior's men, they split up into pairs. Ned and Josh went in together one way and Scott and Eric another, planning to meet up at Ned's place.

The last time Ned was on Lumen he hadn't been able to find his parents or Azinine, and Lardior's comments about his parents not expecting him really had him concerned. They figured the best place to start looking was back at home, hoping to find any clue that would tell them about his parents' whereabouts.

Ned and Josh entered Lux on the north side of town. As they came deeper into the city, they found a large group of people gathering to listen to a man on a makeshift stage.

"People of Lux," they heard him say. "It has now been twenty-six years since the high king was murdered and the amulet still hasn't chosen a king. Is that because the amulet simply hasn't chosen one yet? No! It's because certain magi on the magi council have hidden it so it can't choose a king. As long as there is no king, they remain in power. The time has come to take things into our own hands. Since the amulet isn't available to choose a king, we have no choice but to force them out of power and place our own king upon the throne.

"There are others on the magi council who believe this also. With their help, we can do this. We hope it can be done without any bloodshed. However, it might just come down to war and you will need to decide whose side you're on. Do you want a king to rule us or do you want to continue to be ruled by that upstart Polimar and his cronies?"

A group in the crowd starting chanting, "Down with Polimar! Down with Polimar!" Ned noticed others joining in, but he also noticed there were some who didn't chant. He hoped that meant they were still with his father.

"Come on, Josh. Let's keep going," Ned said rather sullenly.

Scott and Eric entered Lux on the east end of town. This must have been where many of the rich and famous of Lux lived because the homes were huge and sat on large lots. Neither Scott nor Eric really knew their way around, but they could see Polimar's castle on the hill and so they made their way through the streets the best they could in that direction. As they walked, they came to a market place where they ran into a group of kids around their age drinking mystery potions. Scott was still fascinated by this and it was completely new to Eric, so they stopped for a moment to watch.

A girl had just drunk a potion. She sat there with her eyes closed for several seconds with everyone watching closely. Eric and Scott walked closer to get a better look. Suddenly she opened her eyes and looked directly at Scott. Then, she started to change. Her hair turned blond and became short. Her eyes turned brown and she grew about a foot. The kids watched with intense curiosity. Eric couldn't take his eyes off her. This was the most fascinating thing he had ever witnessed. Scott couldn't either, but he soon began to feel very uncomfortable. As more seconds passed, the girl was beginning to look more and more like him. In fact, exactly like him.

"Hey, that's the kid the magi have all been looking for," one of the kids yelled. The kids in the group gasped and quickly whirled around to see who the girl had last looked at.

She had taken a mirror potion, which causes the person taking it to look just like the first person they see after taking the potion. When the girl opened her eyes, she saw Scott and thus the potion had morphed her into a figure that looked just like him. Though none of these kids were alive when the high king reigned, they had all seen pictures of him, and many of their parents had commented that the kid in the wanted pictures looked just like the late high king. As a result, they were very surprised when the girl appeared like Scott before them. They saw Scott and Eric standing there. Eric kept looking back and forth from Scott to the girl with amazement.

"She looks just like you!" he finally said. Scott was speechless and wanted to get out of there. He started to walk away, but one of the kids caught him by the sleeve.

"Hey! You're the kid everyone's been looking for, aren't you?"

"No, I don't think so," Scott said shaking his head.

"Hey, guys! This is the kid everyone's been searching for," he said to his friends.

"You're right! That's the guy," another one said.

The kid holding him, now grabbed him tighter. "Let's take him in and get the reward!" he yelled to his friends. Scott quickly jerked his arm free and gave Eric one of those, 'let's get out of here' looks. The kid grabbed Scott's arm again. Two other kids jumped up now and also grabbed him. Eric was confused. Because of his language barrier, he wasn't sure what was going on, but he could see the look of alarm on Scott's face and knew it wasn't good. The kids seemed to ignore Eric and were focused on dragging Scott to some unknown destination. Eric didn't know how to say, 'Let him go or else,' so he simply grabbed the paint gun he was carrying and started shooting. The pellets weren't deadly, but they stung something fierce and soon the kids turned their attention to Eric, who kept shooting until the last kid let go of Scott.

Once Scott had his arms free, he too, took up his own gun and pointed it at the crowd. The boy who had originally grabbed Scott turned to one of his friends and told him to go get Magus Mordi. The name sent chills down Scott's spine.

"We have to get out of here, now!" Scott said to Eric. The two of them started backing away from the crowd. But the crowd started moving towards them, but at a distance.

"Leave us alone!" Scott said in as stern a voice as he could muster. Ignoring his threat, the kids kept following.

Scott turned to Eric. "We're going to have to ditch them." Then Scott pointed his gun at them and started spraying pellets. The crowd quickly dove for the ground or tried to find something to hide behind. Scott turned and he and Eric took off running as fast as they could. As they ran, they could hear the group of kids getting up and running after them.

"Keep them in sight," he heard one of them yell.

Eric stopped, turned around and started shooting again. Once more, the kids scattered for cover. Then he and Scott continued to run as fast as they could, trying to shake the pack of kids following them. Although not as many now, there were still several boys who were pretty good runners and the two brothers were having a hard time losing them. They came to a hill and started up it, but they were quickly losing steam. At the top of the hill, three men were talking like neighbors might chat over the fence on a nice summer day.

One of the kids chasing Eric and Scott, yelled to the men, "Anweer, stop those boys!"

The men looked up and saw Eric and Scott coming their way. Scott and Eric stopped running. The men at the top of the hill started moving toward them and the boys at the bottom were coming at them from the other direction. They were trapped. Scott and Eric frantically looked around, hoping to find a yard or an alley they might escape through, but it was mostly houses and fences.

"I guess we're going to have to fight our way out of here," Eric said. "And I like our chances better with the boys."

"Yeah, I guess you're right," Scott replied. As he brought up his gun, his hand brushed up against his pocket and he felt the potion he had taken from the factory. He had kept it with him, hoping to find some time to try it out, but up until now, never had a good moment. He put his hand in his pocket and pulled out the potion. He looked at the label again. It read, 'Terror Hound.' He was just about to drink it when he remembered he was wearing the body suit the old lady had given him. Knowing that it deflected all magic, he was sure it wouldn't work.

"Eric, quickly! Drink this," Scott said, handing it to Eric.

"What is it?" Eric asked.

"It's a potion," Scott replied.

The men and the boys were getting closer. Eric pointed his gun at the boys coming up the hill and Scott pointed his at the men coming down the hill and both pulled their triggers. Both groups hit the ground or hid behind whatever cover they could find.

"Why don't you take it?" Eric asked.

"Because it won't work on me."

"Why not?" Eric asked.

"It's too hard to explain right now. If you take this, I think it will get us out of this mess," Scott said, but not very convincingly.

"What's it going to do to me?" Eric asked.

"Turn you into a very large dog," Scott replied. And then added quietly to himself, "I hope."

Just at that moment, Scott ran out of ammunition. "I'm out," he said to Eric. He once again held out the potion for Eric to take. The men were getting up. Eric turned around and fired a few more shots in their direction, forcing them back to the ground.

"Are you sure this is safe?" Eric asked.

"Of course it's safe. You saw those kids taking potions, didn't you? They take them all the time here on Lumen."

"It's not permanent, is it?"

"No. Ned said they're only temporary," Scott replied. And then again to himself, "At least, that's what I think Ned said about potions."

"Okay. This had better work, and it better not be permanent," Eric yelled back, not happy at all about the prospect of being turned into dog. Due to the circumstances though, he opened the bottle and drank it down. "Yuck!" he spluttered. "That stuff tastes awful."

The men and the boys were now both on their feet running towards them. Eric dropped his gun and pulled off his backpack as he started to jerk and then convulse. Dark hairs started poking out everywhere and then his arms and legs started to grow. Scott picked up the gun. He shot a few more bullets at each side to try and buy them a bit more time. But as Eric started to morph, both the boys and the men slowed their pace, until finally both sides came to a complete stop as they watched what was happening. In a matter of seconds, Eric had turned from a boy to a large dog the size of a moose.

Scott grabbed Eric's backpack and jumped on his back. "Let's get out of here!" he yelled. Eric turned towards the men and let out a deep growl. The men turned and quickly ran back up the hill while Eric bounded up after them. It didn't take Eric long to catch the men and bowl right through them, sending them, sprawling to the ground. Not stopping to see if they were still chasing him, he put himself into a full run. Scott, however, did look back and neither the kids nor the men could be seen.

"Just keep heading for the castle," Scott yelled. Eric ran down one street and up another, trying to find a path that led up to the castle. It took several tries, but they finally found a path that led to their destination. They had just made it to the foot of the castle, when Eric began changing back to his normal self. The transformation into the terror hound had completely destroyed Eric's clothes, and Scott could tell that in about thirty seconds his brother was going to be standing next to him completely naked. Knowing he wouldn't be thrilled about that, Scott delved into Eric's backpack and pulled out a sweatshirt Eric had packed.

When Eric finished transforming, he looked at himself and then at Scott in disbelief. "Where are my clothes?" he yelled.

"Here, take your sweatshirt. Put your legs through the sleeves and pull it up around your waist," Scott instructed. Scott then took off his belt and handed it to Eric. "Use this to keep the shirt from falling down."

Eric took the shirt and did as Scott said. "I look like a complete idiot!" he said looking down at himself.

Scott started to laugh. "Yeah, you do look pretty stupid. But it's better than nothing."

"Scott, I can't go running around Lumen looking like this," Eric shot back.

"Let's get inside the castle. I'm sure they'll have some clothes up there you can wear."

The two boys made their way up to the castle without any resistance. In fact, it looked like the castle was deserted. There weren't even any guards posted. The door was wide open, which left Scott thinking that Lardior was correct about Ned's parents. But now, he was also worried about Azinine. If Azinine were safe she should be home. But he knew she would have locked the doors. There were also no signs of any of their servants scurrying about their duties.

Scott and Eric cautiously entered. Even though it looked deserted, after what they had just been through, they weren't taking any chances. They checked the majority of the rooms on the main floor, but just as they feared, no one was there. They wandered into both the kitchen and the veranda, but they too, were deserted.

"This is kind of eerie, seeing this castle so deserted," Scott said.

"Well, it's a good thing it is. Can we find me some clothes please?" Eric asked impatiently.

"None of Ned's clothes are going to fit you. We'll have to find his father's room. Something of his should fit. He's not quite as broad as you, but you are about the same height. I would feel better though if we waited for Ned.

Somehow, I feel like we're invading their privacy, even though they aren't here."

"Fine," Eric growled.

They were just about to head back outside to wait for Ned and Josh when they heard a sound coming from upstairs.

"Who do you think that is?" Scott asked.

"Maybe Ned and Josh beat us?"

"I doubt it. Besides, one of them would have waited for us."

"My better sense tells me we should leave now," reasoned Eric. "But whatever made that sound may lead us to Mom. We have to check it out."

"Definitely," Scott agreed. "I'll lead out since I know the layout. If I get in trouble, you're there to back me up, right?" Scott asked, once again looking at Eric who was still wearing his shirt upside down. Scott started to smirk again, but the look on Eric's face told him this wasn't a time for humor.

"It's your life, little brother," Eric replied.

They crept up the stairs and into a hallway. Stopping for a moment, they listened for anything that would give away the intruder's whereabouts, but the place was silent. Let's check Azinine's room first," Scott whispered. Eric nodded and followed his brother toward a wall. He looked questioningly at Scott, who just smiled and said, "Af." No sooner had he spoken the word, when a doorway appeared. The two silently crept inside, watching for any sign of life. After a quick look through the room, they found it empty and decided to try another room. They were headed for Ned's room when they heard another sound. It was coming from the guestroom Scott had stayed in several months ago. They made their way silently up to the guestroom and Scott pressed his ear against the wall, listening. Someone was in there alright.

"As soon as we enter, whoever's in there will know we're here. Not to mention we might be sitting ducks. Any suggestions?" Scott whispered.

Eric thought for a moment and then answered, "We've got a gun that still has bullets. Not many, but hopefully enough to distract them. We need to charge in quickly, catch him by surprise and let 'em have it. That should distract him long enough for us to look things over and take them if necessary.

"Okay then, on three," said Scott. "One…two…three." The two of them charged, Eric in the lead. He only made it two steps when a flash of light pierced the doorway stopping him in his tracks. Scott halted in his tracks, stunned at what had just happened. Eric stood just beyond the doorway as still as stone. In fact, he *was* stone. He had been hit with a stone spell. Hearing footsteps moving towards the doorway, Scott shook his head to clear his mind. He knew he had to come up with something quick. He couldn't just leave Eric standing there. Counting to three, he stepped into the doorway and began firing. A cloaked figure, who was only ten or so feet from him, began to scream as several bullets hit him. Then he immediately began to retaliate by casting several spells at Scott. The spells, however, had no impact on him as he was wearing the body suit.

"Scott, stop!" the person yelled.

The voice was familiar and Scott stopped shooting. "Who are you?" he demanded.

The figure removed the hood revealing beautiful blonde hair.

"Azinine!" Scott cried out, running to her side. "Are you okay? I didn't know it was you. I thought you were someone else."

"It doesn't matter. I'm so glad to see you," she cried. She threw her arms around him and started to sob. Scott held her tight until she was ready to talk. She finally got control of her emotions and began to explain what she had been doing. "I tried desperately to get to CastleOne, but it was locked and I couldn't break the protection. I knew you and Ned were there and I needed your help. Oh, Scott," she moaned. "It's awful! They've taken my parents and Magus McDougal. I think they even have your mother."

"Oh, no," Scott replied, realizing the worst had happened.

"We…" but just then Ned and Josh entered the room.

"Ned!" Azinine squealed out loud. "You're safe!" She ran over and gave him a hug. "I was so worried about you."

"What about me?" Josh asked with his arms held open.

Azinine laughed. "Yes, of course. Especially about you," she replied giving him a big hug too. She turned to Eric. "What about you? Do you need a hug?" The stone-like figure said nothing. All four of them turned and looked at Eric as if he were some sort of strange alien. It was Josh that broke the silence first.

"What the crap?" he said and then broke out laughing so hard that tears began streaming down his cheeks.

"What is he wearing?" Ned asked in disbelief, turning to Scott. Scott had his hand over his mouth trying very hard to stifle his laughter. He wasn't sure if Eric could hear them or not. Once Scott got himself under control, he said, "I'll explain later." He then turned to Azinine. "That's one of those stone spells, right?" he asked.

"Yes, I forgot I hit him with that spell." She put her hand on his head and spoke, "yederharstal." Eric's body become limp and he would have fallen to the floor had Scott not grabbed him and helped him to his feet.

"What happened?" Eric asked.

Azinine's English wasn't very good, but she understood his question. "Sorry. You okay?" she asked in her best English.

He nodded. "Yeah, I'm okay. But don't ever do that again. It hurts."

Josh was still on the floor laughing his head off and Eric looked down at himself with embarrassment. Next, he looked up at Scott with a look that said, *I'm going to kill you!*

"Uh, Ned? Do you have any clothes that might fit Eric?" Scott asked trying to remedy the situation as quickly as possible.

"I don't have anything that would fit him, but my dad might." Ned led Eric to his father's room and found some clothes for him. Eric put them on and felt a little better about the way he looked.

"Well, on the positive side," Ned said, "you look authentic now. No one will wonder why your clothes look odd."

"I guess," Eric replied, still a little uncomfortable wearing someone else's clothes.

"Where is everyone?" Ned asked Azinine.

"I told you, the Kingmongers took them."

"I mean the guards and the servants?" he asked

"I don't know. The castle was locked when I got here. I entered through my bedroom balcony. They couldn't lock that since I'm the only who knows the spell to open that door. Once inside, I looked around, but it was empty. I searched the grounds, but they were empty also."

Eric then turned to Azinine. "Do you know where they have taken our parents?"

She didn't understand everything Eric had asked, so Ned stepped in and translated.

"No," she answered after hearing the question. "Several on the magi council are looking for them, but no news so far. I was hoping to locate them through the crystal ball. But I can't find them."

Chapter 15

Noka

The group sat in silence for a moment, contemplating the seriousness of the situation.

"Have you tried Magus Noka?" Scott finally asked.

"I haven't been able to locate him either," Azinine replied.

"We might find him at the potions factory. At least, that's where we saw him last."

"The potions factory?" Azinine looked confused. "Isn't that where we saw Magus Mitle go?"

"Yes."

Forgetting that Azinine still didn't know about their adventure at the factory and their meeting with Magus Noka, he explained, "He was spying on the Kingmongers. He might still be there if he hasn't been discovered yet. Maybe he knows where they are holding our parents."

"Magus Noka is working as a spy?" Azinine asked doubtfully. "That doesn't sound right. Do you think we can trust him?"

"He saved our lives," Scott replied.

"Yeah, he whacked Magus Mitle over the head to do it," Ned added. "He said it was an assignment given to him by father and that he and father were the only ones who knew about it."

Still not convinced, Azinine asked, "Why would father keep it secret? Normally all decisions are made by the council."

"That's true," Ned patiently agreed. "But since we're not sure if there are any Kingmongers on the magi council, it would be too risky to tell anyone else."

"I guess that makes sense," she replied.

"Besides," Scott pointed out, "he's our only lead right now. We have to chance it."

"Okay," Azinine said, giving in. "Let's take my MOC. It'll be faster."

"No!" Ned cried. "We're being hunted by Lardior's men. It'll be safer if we walk and take the back roads."

"Actually," Scott said, "Azinine should take her MOC with one or two of us. The others can walk. If we split up we're less likely to attract attention."

"All right," Ned agreed.

Without waiting for any assignments to be made, Josh sidled up to Azinine. "Looks like it's just you and me, sweetheart."

Ned rolled his eyes. "I'm afraid Scott has to go also."

"Ugh!" Josh let out. "Why does he always have to tag along?"

Scott looked at Josh incredulously. "Tag along?"

"Oh, okay. I guess you can, if you must, and don't mind being a third wheel," Josh finally said in response to Scott's reaction.

"A third wheel?" Azinine asked.

"Never mind," Scott replied. "He's just being a dork."

"A dork? What is a dork?" she asked.

"I'll explain later. We need to get going," Scott said.

Ned and Eric made their way down the stairs and outside the castle. The other three walked out onto Azinine's balcony where she kept her MOC.

"So, where's this MOC thing?" Josh asked.

"You're standing on it," Azinine replied with a smirk.

"Huh? I'm standing on a rug," Josh replied as though they were all idiots.

"It's a flying carpet," Scott said dryly.

"Really?" Josh's eyes lit up. "Oh, this is going to be sooo cool! Can I drive?"

Azinine turned to Scott. "He scares me."

"Yeah, he scares most people. But don't hold it against him."

"Does he have any fear in him at all?"

Scott chuckled. "Yeah, he does. He just hides it well."

They all sat down and Azinine directed the carpet off the ground. They rounded a corner and were headed towards the potion factory when she suddenly dropped to the ground.

"Where are we going?" Scott asked.

"I haven't seen Yorim for days and I'm concerned about the unicorns," she explained. "Don't worry. We have plenty of time before Eric and Ned arrive."

"That's not what concerns me," Scott replied. "It's those deadly horns. What exactly do you plan on doing?"

"I'm going to drop down low enough for you to talk to them." She laughed at the worried look on his face. "But high enough that they can't hurt us," she reassured him.

"You want me to talk to them?"

"Well, I certainly can't do it."

"Okay, what do you want me to ask them?"

"Just find out if they need anything."

She lowered the MOC down inside the pen, but was careful to keep them high enough where they were out of reach of the deadly horns. The unicorns began to stamp their feet restlessly and one charged with a feeble attempt to skewer them.

"Are these what I think they are?" Josh asked in wonderment.

"Yes," answered Azinine. Then giving him a sharp look, she added, "Don't even think about trying to pet one, they are very dangerous."

Scott looked down at the unicorns. "We're not here to hurt you," he said. "We just want to know if someone is still caring for you."

The unicorns stopped their stamping and looked up at Scott for several moments. Not knowing whether they had understood, he was about to speak again when the largest of the group stepped forward. "It's you again," the unicorn stated. "What do you want?"

Scott took a deep breath. "My name is Scott. I am the son of Valar, the daughter of…"

"I know who Valar is," the unicorn interrupted. "But I don't believe you. If Valar still lived, we wouldn't still be penned up in this lousy excuse for a home. She would have let us go." Scott was surprised to hear them speak. Their language was a lot like the dragons. Instead of noise, they sent thoughts.

"If she were able, I'm sure she would. But when the high king died, she escaped with just her life to a place very far from here. Those same evil magi have now captured her and we are trying to rescue her."

"That is very admirable. But what has that got to do with us?"

"Nothing really. We just wanted to know if you were okay and if you needed anything."

"If you really want to help us," the large unicorn said scornfully, "then let us go. The High King is dead and no longer requires our services. There is no reason for us to be here anymore."

Scott turned to Azinine. "They want to be let go," he said. "They say there's no reason for them to be here anymore."

Azinine nodded her head. "I agree, but wouldn't it be dangerous to let them go? They might hurt someone."

Scott turned back to the unicorn. "We agree you should be set free. Will you promise not to hurt anyone if we let you go?"

The unicorn looked offended, as only a unicorn can. "We are not malevolent creatures. We don't senselessly attack things. We only fight if we are in danger or there is some other compelling reason."

"Hmm, you could have fooled me. A year ago, you and your friends just about killed me," Scott replied.

"But we didn't kill you. Even though you were encroaching on our territory."

"True," Scott replied. "All right, do you promise not to hurt anyone?"

"Of course! Didn't I already tell you that?" the large unicorn responded.

"Fine," Scott said, a little surprised at the scolding he had just received. "Hold on and we'll try to figure a way to get you out of there." He turned back to Azinine. "They're not going to hurt anyone. How do we let them go?"

"The gate is locked and I don't know how to unlock it," she answered.

"What just happened?" Josh asked, full of wonder.

"What do you mean?" Scott asked.

"I heard every word you just said to that unicorn, but I heard it in my mind, I think. Am I going crazy?"

"No, you're not going crazy. Unicorns, and dragons for that matter, communicate by sending thought waves," Scott answered.

"That's awful, everybody can hear everybody else. There's no privacy."

"Not really. If I send the thought waves out to all the unicorns, like I just did a moment ago, then all will hear. But if I concentrate on just one unicorn, then only that one unicorn will hear it."

"Oh, That is so cool!" Josh replied. "And it works the same way with dragons?"

"Yep."

Josh concentrated on Scott and then sent out a thought wave. "Can you hear me, Scott?"

Scott grinned and replied, "Whoa! Do you realize how cool this is? We can talk to each other and nobody will hear us."

"I know," Josh replied with a mischievous grin.

"Are you going to help us or not?" a voice interrupted.

"Oh, sorry," Scott said to the unicorn. "We just need to figure out how to release you."

"Just leave it to me," Josh said, lacing his fingers and cracking his knuckles. He turned to Azinine and instructed, "Set us down over there. Just outside the gate."

Azinine did as he asked, and Josh jumped off. He found a large log, and with the strength of many men, due to the gloves he was wearing, he slammed it down hard against the fence. He damaged the fence, but that was all. He repeatedly hit the poles with the log until he finally had a small hole started. Dropping the log, he pulled at the fencing until the opening was large enough for the unicorns to get through. He walked inside cautiously, ready to take care of the inner fence, but it was bulging from the throng of unicorns now pushing against it.

"Excuse me," he politely called out. However, they paid no attention to him. "Excuse me," he tried once more, but still no heed was given. "EXCUSE ME!" he yelled. The unicorns all stopped and looked at him in surprise. "That's better!" Josh exclaimed, brushing his hands off. "Now if you want out, I need you all to BACK OFF so I can open the gate!"

The unicorns, being very proud animals, normally would never have let Josh speak to them in that manner. However, they wanted to be free much more than they cared about his manners. They backed away and Josh approached the gate of the inner fence. It was also locked, but not quite so heavily as the outer gate. He pulled on the bar with all his might. At first it didn't budge, but then, slowly but surely, it moved and eventually gave way. Josh barely had time to get out of the way before the unicorns stampeded out. The last unicorn out, the one Scott had spoken to, stopped where Josh stood.

"I apologize for the actions of my friends. They have been here for so long and now they are finally free. Thank you. We will never forget your kindness. If you are ever in need of our services, you may call on us. Ask for me. My name is Nimone." With that, he trotted over to Scott and Azinine, thanked them and ran to catch up with his friends.

"Wow! They are so cool," Josh said as he walked back to Scott and Azinine.

"Yeah. Just make sure you're always on their good side," Scott warned.

"So, can we talk to all the animals?" Josh asked.

"So far as I know," Scott replied.

"Awesome!"

They climbed aboard the MOC and headed toward the factory. They passed just to the left of a huge park enclosed by a semi-see-through bubble that had a bluish tint to it. Inside, Scott thought he could see what looked like various animals.

"That's the Animal Showplace," Azinine commented, noticing Scott's curiosity.

"What's with the blue bubble?"

"It's a security perimeter. They say it's to keep the animals from escaping, but I think it's to keep other animals from getting in."

"Why would animals want to get in?"

"Most wouldn't," she shrugged. "But some, like dragons, would tear the place apart if they knew one of their own kind was kept there."

"Are you saying they have a dragon in there?" Josh asked incredulously.

"Yes," Azinine replied. "And I've been told that dragons communicate through their thoughts instead of sound waves, and are able to contact their own kind miles away. Of course, Scott, you'd know better than I would on that point, but I think the bubble blocks the dragon's ability to call for help."

"Don't you think that's wrong?" Scott asked. "Dragons have families just like you and I do."

"I suppose so," she agreed. "I never really thought of it in that way before. But I don't really have much of a say in the matter."

"Maybe we don't have to say anything," Scott said with a glint in his eye.

"What do you mean?" she asked.

"I mean, maybe we could spring her," Scott said.

"Spring her? What does that even mean?"

"It means that we could find a way to help her escape," Scott answered.

"Oh, we'd get in a lot of trouble for doing that."

"I'm not saying we do it now. But, you know, after all this is over," he said.

"Hmm, okay," Azinine said thoughtfully. "I agree in principle, but I'm not sure how we'd do it."

"I don't either, but we can discuss it later. Now, I think that's the factory over there and I think that's Eric and Ned back there," Scott said pointing in a direction about a quarter mile from the factory.

Azinine lowered the MOC down just outside the factory where they waited for Eric and Ned to arrive. Once there, the group entered the factory, and just as they had expected, it was open. They wondered for a moment if their presence was already known. They walked down the hall and found the large room with all the cauldrons that Ned and Scott had seen before. Entering the room cautiously, they looked to see if anyone was there. The coast was clear so they made their way across the room. They were about halfway when Azinine noticed that one of the cauldrons was simmering. Curious that they hadn't smelled any sort of odor, she wandered over to see what was inside. She peered in and found what looked like boiling water.

"This cauldron hasn't been burning for long," she whispered. "Someone was here not too long ago. It's strange that it's burning at all. Magi don't normally make potions. Those are usually brewed by witches and hags."

"Hags?" Josh asked raising his eyebrows.

"A hag is an evil witch. Just like a warlock is an evil magician," Ned explained.

"Oh," Josh replied. His mother had explained a lot about Lumen to him, but he was discovering that there was a lot she hadn't explained. He was amazed at everything he saw and was soaking it all in like a sponge. There was still so much he didn't understand.

"Hello! Could someone please tell me what's going on?" Eric asked, frustrated that he couldn't understand Lumen. So Ned patiently explained their concern about the cauldron.

Meanwhile, Azinine had been trying to determine the purpose of the potion that was brewing, when a blaze of light pierced the room. They all whipped around to see Josh, who had wandered over to a door, standing still as a statue. Recognizing a stone spell, Azinine pulled out her wand ready to protect herself from whoever was on the other side of the door. Ned and Eric ran behind a giant cauldron while Scott crept over to Josh to offer his help.

"Scott!" Azinine whispered. "Get back here."

Paying her no heed, Scott continued on. He spied a large wooden paddle, most likely used to stir the cauldrons, and picked it up. As he reached the doorway, a man appeared and Scott reacted by bringing the paddle down hard on top of his head. The man blocked the blow with his staff, and was just about to zap Scott when the two of them recognized each other.

"Magus Noka!" Scott exclaimed.

"Scott?" the magus asked completely caught off guard. "What are you doing here? There are people looking for you everywhere."

"Really? Why?"

"Apparently our once good friend, Magus Lardior has a very bruised ego."

"Oh, him."

"What are you doing here?" he asked again.

"We think our parents have been kidnapped by the Kingmongers. We were hoping you'd know where they are keeping them."

Looking around quickly, Magus Noka said, "You are taking a huge risk being here and I am taking just as big of a risk talking to you. They already suspect me. If they catch me talking to you, everything I've done up to this point will be ruined. Quickly! Follow me. I know a place where we can talk safely."

"What about my brother?" Scott asked, pointing at Josh.

"Oh, yes. Sorry about that. I didn't know who he was. You really need to teach him not to startle an old paranoid magus."

"I'll be sure and bring him up to speed."

Magus Noka reversed the spell and Josh became limber once again.

"That was not cool!" Josh said once he could move again. "What just happened?"

"I am so sorry, young man. But I didn't know who you were. I was just trying to protect myself," Magus Noka explained to Josh.

"Ah, it's cool," Josh replied. "Can you teach me how to do that?"

Magus Noka gave him a curious look and then asked, "Did I hear correctly? Are you Scott's brother?"

Josh eyed him for a second. "Well…" he drawled, "that depends on whether being Scott's brother is going to help me learn that trick or not."

Magus Noka smiled. "I see. Well, first of all, it is not a 'trick', it's a spell. Second, being Scott's brother won't help you one way or the other. You see, we have rules on Lumen regarding the use of magic. If you want to learn that spell, you will need to be trained by someone who is authorized to teach you. Now, we really need to get somewhere more private. Please follow me."

He led them up a staircase, down a long narrow hallway and into a corner room of the building. As the children looked around, they could tell this was obviously his sleeping quarters while he was in town. It was quite a downgrade from his palace in Tonwah.

When they were all inside, Magus Noka protected the door with a spell and then produced another spell, which Scott figured was probably to keep eavesdroppers from hearing their conversation.

Magus Noka turned to face the children. "Okay," he said. "We can talk, but we must hurry. What is it you want?"

"Our parents," Ned demanded. "We want to know where they are."

Magus Noka sadly nodded his head. "I know where your parents are, along with many others on the magi council. Those treacherous scum have taken many of them."

"What are they doing with them?" Scott asked.

"I'm not exactly sure why they've taken so many, but I do know why they've taken your mother."

"Why?"

"They want the Eigenholle. When your grandfather died, they searched the castle for it, but didn't ever find it. When they discovered your mother was still alive, they were sure she had it."

"Is she okay?" Scott asked.

"I haven't seen her for several days. When I last saw her, she looked tired, but other than that she appeared fine."

"Where is she? How can we find her?"

"They are holding her and the others in Cohar's Gorge."

Ned gave out an audible gasp.

"I don't want to sound discouraging," Noka continued, "but it'll be next to impossible to rescue them."

"Why...not?" Scott asked hesitantly, noticing the look on Ned's face.

"Cohar's Gorge is a very deep triangular hole in the ground and consists entirely of Amblar rock. The face of each triangular side drops straight down, which means the only way down is by flight. But where it gets tricky is that about a hundred yards down is a platform suspended on three sides by polar light beams and encased by a polar sheer, a kind of shelter or room. Each polar light beam is protected by a spell from a different magus.

"In order to remove a prisoner from the platform, each magus must simultaneously remove the protection, raise the platform and remove the sheer. Only then can they be rescued."

"Why couldn't we fly down inside the hole with a MOC, destroy the sheer, and remove the prisoners?" Scott asked, forever overconfident in his abilities.

"The sheer and polar light beams are connected. If you destroy the sheer, you'll also destroy the polar light beams.

"Maybe we could destroy just one of the polar light beams and a section of the sheer. Would that work?"

What happens when you remove one leg on a three-legged stool?"

"It falls over," Scott whispered, the light going on in his head.

"Yes," Magus Noka affirmed. "And the contents fall off. Everyone would be killed."

"Unless, we had some sort of net that would catch them," Scott replied hopefully.

"In theory that might work, but would you be willing to take that risk? In any case, it would be highly unlikely that you would even get close enough to try. Cohar's Gorge is guarded very heavily by men during the day and goblins and trolls by night. If you did somehow succeed to get past the guards, you'd have to find a way to set up a net or whatever you have in mind to catch them. And last of all, you'd have to find a way to remove one of the polar light beams, all at the risk of your lives and the lives of your parents."

Not to be discouraged by Magus Noka's words, Scott asked, "So you're saying we should just give up and let our parents be tortured?"

"Do you know where the Eigenholle is?" Magus Noka asked, not bothering to answer Scott's question.

"You...want us to give them the Eigenholle?" Scott asked warily.

"No. But you could use it for the same purpose they would."

"And what's that?"

"They want the Eigenholle to retrieve the Ancient Book of Magic."

"So I've heard," Scott said dryly. "But even if we got the book, how would it help us rescue our parents?"

"I keep forgetting you are not from Lumen. The book contains very powerful spells written in the ancient language. I've never read it, but I think it would certainly have spells strong enough to get you past the guards."

"What about the polar light beams and the sheer?"

"Because the spells in the book are in the ancient language, I'm certain it contains something that would override those currently binding the platform. As I mentioned, the magic contained in this book is very powerful. Which is why it is locked up in the Pyramids of Death."

"You think it will get us past the guards?" Ned asked skeptically.

"If you can get the book," Magus Noka affirmed, "I'll find a way to get past the guards."

"Ned, can you get us to the Pyramids?" Scott asked.

"I'm not sure," Ned answered. "but I think Azinine knows the way." He turned to Azinine and asked, "Didn't you and Father fly over them when you accompanied him on business?"

"Yes, I think I could get us there," she replied.

"You're forgetting one thing," Magus Noka pointed out. "No one has ever entered the pyramids and returned without also having the Eigenholle. Do you know where it is?"

"No," Scott admitted. "But I might have an idea of how we can get the book."

"Why does that worry me?" Ned muttered under his breath.

"Scott, don't do anything foolish," Noka warned. "Many men have tried and failed. These were not ignorant men either. They were powerfully skilled in magic and none of them ever returned."

"Foolish or not, we have to try," Scott argued.

"Can't you come with us and help?" Azinine asked.

Magus Noka smiled and let out a sigh. He walked over to Azinine and put his arm on her shoulder. "Have you forgotten? You are wanted. If I were seen with you, especially helping you, the Kingmongers would brand me as a traitor and kill me for sure. Your chances of getting the book are very slim. Even if I came with you, I'm not sure how I'd help you without the Eigenholle. I can do better as a spy."

"If we were able to get the book, you're sure we could use it to rescue our parents?" Scott asked.

"Yes," he replied.

"And you would help us?" Scott questioned.

"Yes," the magus assured him. "If, by some luck, you get the book, it won't matter if they know I'm a spy. We'll be able to confront them directly."

"We understand," Scott replied. Then he turned to the others. "Let's go discuss this over some dinner. I'm starving."

Magus Noka unlocked the spells he had placed on the room and as they all exited, he reminded them, "Be careful as you leave. I don't believe there are any Kingmongers here right now, but they have several hags brewing who knows what for them. Do not let them see you. If you go down the stairs we came up, you'll see a back door. Exit that way and you'll avoid the brewing room. Remember, you must find the Eigenholle first. Without it, you will not succeed. If you're able to retrieve the book, come directly to me. Do not let it fall into anyone else's hands. If it falls into the wrong hands it would be a disaster."

Chapter 16

Water Dragon

By the time they arrived back at the Polimar's castle, it was dark. They were all starving so they made some dinner and sat down to make plans.

"Okay," Eric began. "I think Josh has done a pretty good job of translating for me, but let me just repeat what I've heard to make sure I understand. Our parents are being held in some invincible fortress. The only chance we have of rescuing them is to find this ancient magical book. This book is locked in a pyramid that's impossible to get out of unless you have some sort of eye hole with you.

"Basically, that's correct," Ned replied. "Except it's not quite so simple. The book is like a bomb. It works for whoever has it, and can read it. If it were to get in the wrong hands, it could be used against us. So you see, once we pull it from the pyramid, assuming that's even possible, we put our whole world at risk. If the book falls into the wrong hands, who knows what they'll do with it?"

"Where do we find this eye hole thing?" Eric asked.

"Eigenholle," Ned corrected him. "They seem to think your mother has it. We think that's what they were looking for when they broke into your parent's house."

"Well, I don't know where it is," Eric exclaimed. "I've never even heard of the thing before."

"Me neither," Scott shrugged.

"There must be another way in," Eric continued. "When computer programmers create a program, they always leave a back door in case the main password is forgotten. Certainly, whoever created the pyramid would have realized the Eigenholle might get lost or broken. They must have created a back door."

"Maybe," Ned said doubtfully. "But we don't know where it is and it could take years to figure it out."

"True, but we have to try. We can't just sit here and do nothing."

"Why not take a ball of string with us?" Josh suggested. "That way if we get lost, we can always follow it out."

"That might work," Scott replied.

"It's too simple," Ned interjected. "Remember what Magus Noka said? Many have already tried numerous ways. Certainly, someone would have thought about leaving a trail to get back out."

"Hmm…you're probably right," Eric replied. "We need to know more about the architecture. Do you guys have any books describing the pyramids? Is there any chance someone has documented how it was built? How it works? Anything?"

Ned shook his head. "Not really. There are tales or rumors that have been handed down from generation to generation about the pyramids. But who knows how true they are or how twisted they might have become over the years?"

"Well, at least it's a start," Eric said. "Tell us what you've heard."

"Okay, what we know is that there are four pyramids all right next to each other. The pyramids themselves are sand colored, except for the tops of them. One has a white colored tip. The next one has a yellow tip, then a grey tip and the last one has a black tip. There are no entrances into any of the pyramids except from the white tipped one. From past kings, we know that all the pyramids are connected. Once inside, you have to pass through the white tipped pyramid in order to get into the yellow tipped pyramid. A person would then move from the yellow tipped pyramid into the grey tipped pyramid. And from the grey to the black one, where supposedly the Ancient Book of Magic rests.

"But it's not just a matter of simply walking through each pyramid. In order to pass from one pyramid to the next, you have to pass a test. What those tests are, we don't know. I've heard rumors, nothing factual, that the test in each pyramid is different for everyone. No one experiences it the same."

"Maybe it's just an illusion and the illusion changes for each person," Scott suggested.

"Illusions aren't real. These pyramids are definitely real," Ned declared.

"Maybe the outer walls are real, but the inside is an illusion."

"Nice try! There are spells to detect illusions, even dissolve them."

"I tell you what," Eric started. "Let's get a few hours of sleep so we're at least somewhat rested. In the morning, we'll gather our things, we'll bring a ball of string, the paint guns and whatever else we think might be useful and head to the pyramid. On the way, hopefully we'll think of something. If not, maybe once we're there, we'll find some clues."

"Sounds good," the others all agreed. All but Azinine, who only understood a little of what they said.

"What are we doing?" she asked. Ned explained what they had talked about and repeated Eric's suggestion. Azinine didn't have any objections, so they all headed off to bed. There were plenty of bedrooms, but they all chose to sleep in the same room, just to be safe. However, morning came without incident and they hurriedly ate some breakfast and grabbed their stuff. They took whatever they thought would be worthwhile. They still had most of the food they had gathered from CastleOne and Josh had snatched about every trinket he had brought with him to CastleOne. Ned and Azinine gathered their gear and more food. Once everyone was ready, they all boarded the MOC and took off.

It was a sunny day with few clouds, which was unfortunate because it gave them little cover. Nonetheless, they were determined to make it to the pyramids with as much speed as possible, so Azinine took them on the most direct route.

Eric turned to Ned. "If I didn't know better, I'd say we're heading back the way we came from Lardior's stronghold."

"I don't think so," Ned said. "The pyramids are north and east of the Grey Forest Hills. Lardior's camp, I believe, is north and west of the Grey Forest Hills." Eric figured Ned knew better than he did, so he didn't say anything else.

About mid-afternoon they decided to set down to stretch their legs and get a bite to eat.

"So, anyone thought of any great ideas about how to get in and out of the pyramids?" Eric asked.

"Not really," Scott admitted.

"Not me," Ned added.

They all looked at Azinine who must have at least understood enough because she shook her head.

"It's not a great idea," Josh said slowly, "but it might help. I brought my video camera and remote monitor. One of us will enter the pyramid and video everything inside. The whole thing will be taped on my remote monitor. If, for some reason, the string doesn't work, we'll at least have a good idea of how the pyramid works. From that, we might be able to figure out how to get the person out. I also brought my two-way radios so we can keep in contact."

"Josh, you're brilliant!" Eric exclaimed.

"Finally! You admit the obvious," Josh replied with a grin on his face.

"It certainly couldn't hurt to have them," Ned chimed in. "But I get the feeling the pyramids are deadly if you don't, you know, pass the tests. At least, that's the impression I got from Magus Noka."

"Then we better make sure we pass them," Josh replied.

They continued to eat and discuss the pyramids for a good hour when Ned interrupted them. "Guys," he began, but they were so caught up in their conversation that they didn't pay him any attention. "Guys," he said a little louder, but they ignored him again. Ned slugged Scott's shoulder to get him to shut up.

"Ouch! What did you do that for?" Scott asked, rubbing his shoulder.

"Listen. Something isn't right," Ned said.

"I don't hear anything."

"Me neither," Eric added.

"That's my point. It's too quiet. When we first landed you could hear the birds and the insects. Now everything is silent."

"What are you saying, Ned?" Scott asked nervously.

"Well, I'm no expert, but usually when the birds stop their chatter it's because they don't want to be heard. Something's out there that they're afraid of."

"Ned, you're starting to give me the willies," Scott said looking around. He saw the frustrated look on Azinine's and proceeded to explain Ned's observation.

Azinine nodded and stood up, her wand out and ready in case it was needed. Josh had picked up a large log that, without the help of the gloves he was wearing, would have been impossible for him to lift.

"Maybe we should get out of here now, before whatever it is finds us," Josh suggested.

"We don't know what it is. If it's a dragon, taking off would be the worst thing we could do," Ned cautioned.

"Then maybe we should find a place to hide, instead of standing out here like sitting ducks," Scott suggested.

"Good idea. Let's grab our..." Ned began when Azinine interrupted him.

"Jump!" she screamed. The others saw it too. The creature was hurtling towards them from the tops of the trees with amazing speed. The five of them leaped any which way they could to avoid the beast. The animal attacked their MOC, where the food they had just been eating seconds before was demolished. The MOC was ripped to shreds by the creature's razor-sharp teeth.

"Lay still and nobody move," Azinine continued to instruct. "It hunts mostly by motion. If you sit still, it won't know you're there."

Scott's heart was thumping rapidly in his chest. He recognized this beast from the dreaming pond. It was a water dragon, only this time it was real. The creature, which looked like an overgrown alligator with short, fuzzy brown hair, had finished all the food they had brought, and was now trying to sniff them out for dessert.

Scott slowly turned to Azinine and whispered, "Is there some sort of spell you can use to stop it?"

"I don't know. I've never used magic on something like this before. I'm not sure how it will react."

"Well, there's no time like the present."

"Okay, here goes." She lifted her wand, and pointed it at the water dragon. "Ferret," she spoke. A thin stream of light shot from the wand and encompassed the animal. It froze and lay floating three feet above the ground. The water dragon was still alive but the spell had temporarily paralyzed it.

"Good going," Scott praised. "Now let's get out of here."

"Sounds good to me, but it looks like we're going to have to walk. The MOC isn't going to do us any good now."

"At least we still have all our other stuff," Josh commented.

"Yeah, including our lives," Azinine reminded him.

"Yeah," Scott said solemnly. He turned to the others, who were still standing motionless. "Come on, guys. Let's get out of here before that thing wakes up."

"Uh, Scott," Ned said hesitantly. "I think you're too late for that. It's already starting to wake up."

Scott and Azinine whirled around. The water dragon was moving towards them, still a little groggy, but definitely towards them. It extended its legs and pushed off the ground floating towards them. It pushed off again, this time faster. Azinine reached into her pocket for her wand, but was too late. The water dragon had pushed off one more time and was now at full strength. Scott dove, tackling Azinine to the ground, but the water dragon's lower jaw caught her robe and started dragging her along the ground. She screamed. Scott grabbed her ankle and held on as hard as he could, but only managed to pull her shoe off. The water dragon was now trying to shake her loose so it could get its jaws around her. Its sharp teeth were quickly tearing through the material and it wasn't long before Azinine fell to the ground. The water dragon whirled around, opened its jaws and was about to chomp when Scott leaped on its back and wrapped his arms around its belly.

It was just enough to annoy the water dragon and it quickly forgot about Azinine and concentrated on Scott. It whirled around and around like a dog chasing its tail. It shot high into the air and back down to the ground. Finally, it got smart and darted for some undergrowth hoping the branches would strip Scott from its back. But Scott, not about to be discarded so easily, held on for dear life. The bushes whipped at his face and arms stinging and cutting his skin. The water dragon bolted for a low hanging branch of a thick tree. The branch caught Scott on the shoulder, ripping him from the creature's back. He fell to the ground, clutching his shoulder in pain.

The creature stopped, turned and moved slowly towards Scott hissing its victory. Then, in one swift move, it pushed off and shot towards Scott, it's jaws open. He didn't have a chance to roll one way or the other, so he instinctively rolled up in a ball and threw his arms over his face. Scott was sure this was the end. Then he heard a crack and the water dragon fell on top of him. He opened his eyes and saw the beast lying there, lifeless. Standing above the water dragon was Josh holding the large log he had picked up earlier. He had cracked the log over the dragon's head and either knocked it out or killed it. Scott wasn't sure which one, but at this point, didn't care. Just as long as he, himself, was still alive.

"Ha! Get wrecked!" Josh exclaimed, standing over the water dragon. "You okay?" he asked Scott.

"I think so," Scott replied with a groan. "But I'm pretty sure I'm going to be sore for a while. Help me get this thing off me." Eric and Ned ran over and helped Josh roll the lifeless form off of Scott.

"Can you walk?" Eric asked.

"Yeah, my legs are fine. It's my shoulder and arm that hurt." He was about halfway up when Azinine ran over and tackled him to the ground. A sharp pain shot up his shoulder, but he did his best to ignore it.

She threw her arms around him. "Thank you, Scott! Thank you!" she cried. "That's twice now you've saved my life!" Then she kissed him. He lay there startled for a second, but pleasantly surprised, and then he winced.

"Oh, I'm sorry! Did that hurt you?" she asked.

"No, but could you please get off of me? My shoulder is killing me."

"Oh, sorry. I'm so sorry. I didn't mean to. I am just so grateful, I..."

"It's okay," he assured her. "I just need to get up."

Eric grabbed Scott under both shoulders and heaved him to his feet. "You are one crazy cowboy, little brother."

"Yippie ki yay," he said with a moan.

"Hey," Josh turned to Azinine. "I saved Scott's life. Doesn't that deserve anything?" he asked, closing his eyes and puckering his lips.

"Probably, but don't get your hopes up. I don't think Scott's going to kiss you," she said ruffling the hair on his head.

"No, but you could," Josh said hopefully.

"Like I said, don't get your hopes up."

"Oh! Get wrecked!" Scott laughed, using one of his little brother's own favorite phrases.

Chapter 17

Greymen

Scott checked all his limbs to make sure everything was still in working order. There were no broken bones, and with the exception of a few bruises and a sore shoulder, he seemed to be fine.

"So, what do we do now?" Ned asked.

"We'll have to make our way on foot," Eric replied. "Ask Azinine if she knows where we are and if there's anything near here."

"I believe we are about a day's walk from the pyramids," she answered after Ned had translated Eric's question.

"Okay then, we had better start walking. We don't have a whole day before it starts to get dark, so let's make as much progress as possible."

They had walked for most of the day, and the sun was just starting to set, when Azinine suddenly stopped.

"What wrong?" Scott asked.

"I don't know. Something just doesn't feel right. These just don't seem to be the right hills."

"Well, maybe we just haven't walked far enough," Scott suggested. The others stopped and sat down, taking this opportunity to rest.

"Maybe," she replied as she sat down to think. Scott explained her concerns to the rest of the group.

"We have to keep going," Eric declared. "Sitting here isn't going to get us anywhere." Scott nodded and wiped the sweat off his brow.

Ned looked over at Azinine. "Have you figured out where we are?"

She shook her head.

"Eric's right. We can't sit here. We need to keep going," Ned said nervously. Azinine nodded and slowly stood up. She didn't say anything, but she knew why Ned was getting nervous.

"Alright, let's keep going," she finally said to the others.

They gathered their stuff together and started walking again. Azinine and Scott took the lead, walking as fast as they could. The others kept up, but Josh wasn't too happy about the fast pace.

"Hey, up there. Where's the fire?" he yelled.

Azinine looked at Scott curiously. "Why is he asking about a fire? Is he cold?" she asked.

"No, it's just an expression we use on earth to ask why someone is moving so quickly. You know, if your house is on fire, you're going to quickly run away, right?"

"Oh, I guess that makes sense," she replied.

"It's going to be dark soon," Ned informed Josh.

"Are you telling me you're afraid of the dark?" Josh teased.

"I am not afraid of the dark. I am afraid of what's in the dark."

"What do you mean?" Josh asked cautiously.

"Besides creatures like that water dragon back there, there are other creatures, evil creatures, which only come out at night. Just to name a few, goblins, hags, trolls, draculas. Do you want me to continue? Your brother Scott ran into two womvampirs last time he was on Lumen. He knows firsthand about the things that come out at night. You can bet that's why he's moving so fast," Ned explained.

"Did you say draculas?"

"Yes. It's basically the same as a vampire. In fact, it was from our world that vampires were introduced into your world. They are one of the only creatures that succeeded in using magic in your world."

Eric had been listening to their conversation. "You're telling us that these forests are filled with these kinds of creatures?"

"I wouldn't say filled, but it's these forests where they live. So this is where you're most likely to run into them."

"Any sign of those pyramids?" Josh inquired nervously.

The group continued along their way, grateful the undergrowth was light, allowing them to make good progress. It was much darker now and they were getting more nervous by the minute. As they continued, Scott spotted a shadow moving to the right of them, but as he turned to look at it, it disappeared. Moments later, he noticed a similar shadow to the left of them. The shadows continued to appear and disappear here and there, moving silently through the woods. Whatever they were, they were following the kids.

"Have you noticed them?" Scott asked Azinine.

"Yes."

"What are they?"

"I'm not sure," she admitted. "But as long as they keep their distance, they can do whatever they want."

"How do you know they'll keep their distance?"

"I don't. That's what worries me. They're probably waiting for it to get even darker. We need to keep going as fast as possible." They had walked another minute when the slight sound of rustling branches a few yards off caused Azinine and the group to pause.

"What was that?" Ned asked. No one replied. They were all listening, trying to determine what had made the noise.

"Maybe it was just the wind. Let's keep going," Azinine said. The group started walking when they heard another slight rustling sound in another tree. They paused again, looking and listening for anything. On the ground, Josh noticed a shadow move a little way off in the forest.

"Uh, guys? I just saw something move over there," he said as he pointed into the forest.

"Yeah, we've noticed them also," Scott replied.

"What do we do if it gets dark and we still haven't reached the pyramids?" Josh asked.

"Normally we would climb a tree. They are usually safer than the ground. But there's something in these trees, so maybe that's not our best option," Azinine replied.

"We could build a fire," Scott suggested. "That might help keep us safe at least."

"No, that would just advertise to every creature in this forest where we are," Ned replied.

Scott shifted his backpack to his other shoulder. "Then let's keep going."

The shadows continued to appear and re-appear in the dark as the group proceeded. More movement in the trees, this time louder, and this time coming from several trees, caused the group to come to a complete stop.

"Something's up there," Ned said.

"I think we're in deep doggy doo doo," Josh replied slowly.

"Hello?" Scott called out, hoping to communicate with whatever it was. The unknown was killing him. If he had to fight, he at least wanted to know what it was he would have to fight. Unfortunately, there was no reply except for the rustling of branches in another tree behind them.

The group whirled around to see if they could see what it was, but it was getting so dark, it was pointless. Azinine backed up against a large tree, as more shadows moved silently off in the distance.

"It's too dark to keep going," Eric said. "We're more vulnerable walking. I say we stop here for the night and take up a defensive position. Scott translated for Azinine and the group found a cluster of trees that would at least protect their backs. They put down their packs and began looking for sticks they could use as weapons. Azinine pulled out her wand while the others searched. As she stood there, she noticed some markings on one of the trees.

"Freeze!" she cried out as quietly as she could, but loud enough that all could hear her.

"Why are we freezing?" Josh asked, expecting very large spiders to attack at any moment.

"Everyone move slowly back towards me. Okay, slowly," she instructed. The group didn't question her, and they all made their way back to her.

Once they were all clustered together, Scott whispered, "Okay, what's going on?"

"I know where we are." she said. "I know who's up in those trees."

A chill ran down Josh's spine. "Spiders?" he whispered.

"Greymen," she replied. "We are on the borders of their land."

"Greymen?" Scott repeated with a question in his voice.

"Yes."

"Do you think they might help us?" Scott asked.

Ned shook his head. "Not likely. They're not very friendly."

"That means Lardior's camp is just on the other side of these hills, right?" Scott asked.

"Yes, and he certainly isn't going to help us," Ned said.

"Well, then we'll just have to try the Greymen," Scott said.

"They won't help us," Ned said again.

"Those shadows that are following us. Are those Greymen?" Scott asked.

Azinine shook her head. "No, they are not."

"Then what are they?"

"I don't know, but they definitely are not Greymen. Greymen don't travel on the ground if they don't have to."

"Well, then our choices are to request help from the Greymen or face those shadows," declared Scott. "Lardior certainly isn't going to help us and there isn't another village for miles. The Greymen could certainly give us a safe place to sleep tonight."

"They won't help us. If anything, they'll do just the opposite," Ned said more adamantly.

Getting irritated at his friend's pessimistic attitude, Scott continued with his argument. "We don't have any other choice. Besides, we're kids. How threatening can we be?"

Ned shrugged and gave in. "I guess we can try," he said with a sigh. "But don't be surprised if it doesn't work."

The group stood in silence for a minute, then Azinine spoke again. "I have to warn you, Scott. If the Greymen don't help us, we could be in real trouble."

"They'll help us. They just have to," he replied with much more confidence than he actually felt.

"I hope you're right."

"The markings on the tree. What do they mean?"

"They are warnings. They obviously already know we're here, but they won't do anything until we actually trespass on their land."

"How do you know so much about the Greymen?" Scott asked.

"I used to come with my father when he served as an ambassador to them. He told me as much as he knew about them."

"Well, what's the best way to approach them?"

"I'm not sure. My father was always invited."

"Hmm," Scott mumbled.

"What do we do now?" Azinine asked.

"I'll try talking to them. Maybe they'll let us in when they see who we are," Scott suggested.

"Not likely, but it's worth a try," Ned said.

Scott stepped forward a few feet and called out, "Greetings, Greymen. We...come in peace. Please, we need to talk with you." Scott waited, but nothing happened.

"Please," he said a little louder. "We carry a message from Magus Polimar."

Azinine slugged him on the shoulder. "What are you doing? We don't have a message from my father," she whispered in his ear.

"What sort of message?" a voice not twenty feet away from them said. The group jumped back a bit, their hearts beating wildly in their chests. They had no idea a guard was so close to them.

"Uh..a message we need to give to your leader," Scott replied. The voice was silent for about a minute and Scott was beginning to wonder if he was still there.

"You may enter slowly, in a single file line. But your dogs are not welcome. They must stay behind. If we see any sign that this is a trick, you will all be executed."

"Dogs?" Scott asked. "We don't have any dogs."

Just then, three Greymen appeared out of nowhere and shoved spears at Scott's throat. "I told you no tricks," one of them growled. "Do you think we're stupid? For some time we have watched you and the dogs giving you escort. They are not welcome. Tell them to back off or you cannot enter."

Scott had no idea what he was talking about, but he wasn't about to argue. "Uh…dogs, we…no longer need your assistance," he said loudly.

The shadows they had been seeing appeared to move again. But this time they moved away deeper into the forest.

"Very good," the Greyman said. "Follow us." As they started to walk, they noticed several other Greymen appear as if from out of nowhere, and join the procession, some in back and some to the side.

"I hope you know what you're doing," Azinine whispered from behind Scott. Scott didn't say a word. He didn't dare. He was perspiring like crazy and his legs felt like Jello. He had no idea what he was doing or what he had just gotten them into.

They walked for what seemed like an eternity, but was probably only two or three miles, when they came to a city built in the trees. Iker trees stretched for miles in all directions. Within the Iker trees was a network of homes and walkways.

"Wow," Scott said, temporarily losing his fear. "Your city is beautiful."

The lead guard smiled for the first time. "Thank you. We are very proud of it." He then let out a whistle and a large float pad lowered to the ground.

He motioned for them to step onto it. Once they were all standing on the float pad, it began to rise into the trees. It stopped by a very large branch and the guard motioned for them to get off. He led them up a long staircase that made its way up a hill, moving from tree to tree. It was a long, arduous walk, and the kids were quickly wearing out, feeling the effects of their hike through the day. The guards must have noticed this and motioned for them to stop.

"We will rest here for a short while so you can catch your breath, but we cannot wait too long," the guard said. The group sat down for a couple of minutes. Then way too soon for the kids' comfort, the guard motioned for them to begin again. They climbed for another thirty minutes and were just about spent when they came to a large platform. The guard told them to wait while he entered a large structure. They gladly stopped and sat down on some benches that were positioned in a circular format. From where they were, they could look out over the whole valley. Tree after tree lit up with the glow of lights.

"Wow," Azinine commented more to herself than to anyone else.

"Yes, it's very romantic," Josh replied as he slowly put his arm around her. She looked at him with raised eyebrows. Slowly, she smiled and put her arm around him. "I like you, Josh. You're such a dreamer."

"Dreamer?" Josh exclaimed. He was about to say something more when they heard a soft whistle and a voice announce, "All stand and bow for the honorable Governor Adenha don Tolstrom."

"You must stand and bow as he enters. Remain bowing until he gives us permission to stand up," Azinine instructed the group. An older man with long flowing robes entered the platform. The group bowed and stayed that way until he sat down.

"Please, take your seats," Adenha instructed. The group sat down and the governor immediately focused on Azinine, having recognized her from past visits. He didn't look happy to be there. In fact, he looked rather annoyed. "Good evening, fair Azinine. What news do you bring and why did your father not come himself?"

Azinine hesitated. She had no idea what to say. It was Scott who said they had a message, not her.

"Excuse me, your honor," Scott interrupted, coming to Azinine's rescue. The governor turned and looked at Scott, even more annoyed. However, his expression turned into one of astonishment as he caught a glimpse of the young man sitting before him.

"Who...who are you?" he finally said after composing himself.

"My name is Scott Frontier. This is sort of an emotional time for Azinine. So if you don't mind, I would like to deliver the message, if that's okay?"

Adenha was silent for several seconds, still staring at Scott. Finally he spoke. "Where do you come from and who are your parents?" he asked. There was now a different look in his eye, one of greed or opportunity. At first, Scott wanted to tell him that he was the grandson of the late high king, hoping that might impress the governor and increase their status with him. However, his gut told him that wasn't a good idea.

"I am just a friend of Azinine, trying to help her in her time of need. My parents are common farmers, they hold no special status." The governor nodded as disappointment washed over his face.

"You may speak," he finally said.

"Magus Polimar and his wife have been abducted. They are heavily guarded and we need help rescuing them. Since you were a friend to Magus Polimar, we thought you might be willing to help."

Just then Azinine began to weep. Scott glanced at her. *Nice touch*, he thought, *those tears look real*. The governor looked over at her and for just an instant, an expression of sympathy crossed his face.

"Why do you come to me? Certainly, his friends on the Magi council would be better suited to handle this situation."

"You are correct, of course. But we don't know who we can trust," Scott replied.

The governor took in a deep breath. "I don't suppose your amulet has chosen a king yet?" he asked.

"No, unfortunately not," Scott replied.

"You understand we are a small nation that just wants to be left alone. If we helped you free Magus Polimar, it might be taken as an act of war."

"An act of war?" Scott said in astonishment. "You would be rescuing their leader. How could that be construed as an act of war?"

Scott could tell the governor wasn't pleased with his tone of voice, so as the older man spoke, he resolved to keep his voice calm. "Certainly you are aware of the civil unrest that has been brewing for some time. A king has not been chosen and it's rumored the amulet no longer works."

"What are you saying?" Scott asked.

"I'm saying," the governor started, his voice much colder now, "that it is our opinion that Magus Polimar will not be the leader for much longer. And that it would be...unwise...for us to antagonize the opposition." Azinine had stopped crying and was now looking at him in shock.

Scott stood up. "He is..." he began, but that's about as far as he got when the guards jumped forward and thrust their spears just inches away from his body.

"Sit down!" one of the guards commanded. "Nobody stands until the governor gives permission."

"Okay, okay, sorry. I'm new at this," Scott said as he slowly sat down. The spears retreated and he breathed a sigh of relief.

The governor did not look happy. "I will not sit here and be lectured by children, especially in my own land. Normally I would have you executed. But lucky for you, I'm in a good mood. So you may go." He then turned to the lead guard. "Take them and let them out the back door."

Scott could tell the phrase 'Back door' was code for something and he didn't like the sound of it. The governor rose and walked over to the lead guard and whispered something into his ear. The lead guard then whispered into the ear of another guard who left running. The lead guard commanded the group to rise and follow him.

"Excuse me, sir," Scott quickly said before the governor could leave. "Could we at least sleep here for the night under your protection?"

The governor hesitated for a few seconds. "I'm…I'm sorry, but we cannot allow that," he finally replied, keeping his eyes averted so he didn't have to look at them. He turned and quickly left the platform.

The group followed the guard, making their way down the same way they had come up. About halfway down, they turned in a different direction. They continued to move downward for another thirty minutes or so until they came to another float pad that lowered them back down to the ground into a large meadow. Once on the ground, the guard led them along a path for another thirty minutes until they came to a small stream with a foot bridge crossing it.

"This is our border. Follow this path until you come to a larger one." The guard shrugged his shoulders. "Where you go from there is your business, but do not come back or you will be executed." The group nodded and followed the path until they were sure they were outside the borders.

"So much for finding any safety with those people," Josh finally remarked, breaking the silence.

"Yeah, but the bigger question is, where are we?" Ned asked.

Chapter 18

Prisoners

The group looked around, trying to determine where they should go now. In the dark, it wasn't easy to see much of anything.

"Do you know where we are Azinine?" Scott asked.

"Not exactly, but I have a horrible suspicion."

"What's that?" Scott asked.

"If my sense of direction is correct, I think they dropped us off into the same area Lardior is camped," she replied.

"Out of the frying pan and into the fire," Scott mumbled.

"We'll just have to sneak past them," Ned replied.

"Yeah. If they catch us, Lardior might really torture and kill us this time," Scott said, only half joking.

"No, I don't think so," Ned commented. "If Lardior wanted to kill us, he would have the first time. Instead, he treated us like guests. I think Lardior is working for someone who wants us alive."

"Okay," Scott said, taking charge once more. "Unless anyone has any better ideas, we need to get out of here and avoid Lardior at all costs."

No one objected, so they started out once more. As they walked, Scott continued to scan the area for more shadows. The moon was just starting to make its ascent into the sky, but it was still difficult to see very far. They had walked for about fifteen minutes, when they saw firelight coming through the trees.

"Hold up," Scott whispered, putting up his hand. He could make out several fires with a good number of men encircling them. The men seemed to be playing some sort of game.

Ned leaned over to Scott. "It's Lardior alright. If he knew how careless they were being, he'd have them all hanged."

"Yeah. Good for us, bad for them." Looking around, Scott continued, "I guess we better do our best to slip past these guards as soon as possible. It looks like our best chance is over there in that grove of trees. What do you think, Eric?"

"It's as good as any place."

"Okay, let's try it," Scott said, leading the way.

They made their way slowly among the trees. They were very careful to stay in the cover of the trees and out of the moonlight that had now appeared. For the most part, there was plenty of cover, but they knew up ahead lay a clearing that offered no cover at all. That's where the danger would be the greatest until they actually reached Lardior's camp. When they came to the clearing, they stopped for a moment to scan the area for any guards they hadn't accounted for. When they were sure none of the guards were looking, they made a dash for it. They half expected to hear a warning horn blow at any moment, but to their relief no sound came. Once across the clearing, they looked back to check if they'd been seen. To their relief, the guards continued on with their game.

"This is going to be easier than I thought," Scott whispered to Eric.

"Don't count your chickens yet," his older brother cautioned. "We've only just started."

They could now see the moon reflecting off the lake where the portal back to CastleOne sat. Scott wondered if the golden rods, sitting in their backpacks, would work from this distance. If worse came to worst, they could use those to escape. They edged their way along the bottom of a cliff until they came to a small creek. Lardior's camp had been next to the creek, so they knew they had to be close, but they couldn't see it.

"Where is Lardior's camp? Scott asked Eric. "Shouldn't it be here?"

"I thought so, too," Eric replied.

"Listen," Ned quietly whispered. "The guards are no longer making all that noise."

"Everything is so quiet," Azinine whispered after they had paused for a moment.

"Maybe there's another water dragon," Josh suggested.

"If there was another water dragon, those guards would be making more noise now than before," Ned answered. "Something isn't right."

"Let's keep going. The sooner we get out of here, the better," Eric whispered. They moved forward, when right in front of them a bright light appeared. Then another, and another, until lighted poles, held by men, cloaked in black, surrounded them. The only way out was the way they had come. They had walked right into a trap. They heard something behind them and they whirled around to see what it was. Several more of Lardior's men were closing in on them, cutting off any chance of escape.

"Who are you and what do you want?" Ned asked.

"You don't know who I am?" a calm, but menacing voice called from out of the darkness. "Why, I'm insulted that you don't remember after the hospitality we provided and the insult you paid us when you so rudely left."

"We didn't mean to insult you. We…"

"Ned!" Scott whispered, digging an elbow into his friend's side. "He's being facetious."

Lardior continued, "I see you brought some extra guests with you this time. The young boy must be your brother. The resemblance is uncanny. And the young woman is obviously the fair Azinine."

"You know who I am?" Azinine replied, surprised.

"Yes, of course. I know your father quite well."

"If he's a friend of yours, then why don't you help us?" she asked.

Lardior walked into the light, his eyes cold. "I didn't say we were friends."

"Oh," she breathed. "What…do…you want with us?"

"With you? Nothing. But with Scott, I have a bone to pick. Besides, he has something I want and if he knows what's good for him, he'll give it to me."

"You've got to be kidding me," Scott said. "Let me guess. You want the Eigenholle."

Lardior narrowed his eyes and paused for only a second. "Do you have the Eigenholle?"

"No, for the last time. I don't even have a clue what it is!"

"I sec. Actually, it's not the Eigenholle I want. It's the sword. The golden sword. I know you know what that is."

Scott couldn't help chuckling. "I don't have the sword. The goblins have it."

"I don't believe you," Lardior spat out, his eyes flashing.

Scott just smiled. "If I had the sword," he said, "don't you think I'd have it with me?"

"Yeah," Josh said butting in. "Don't you think he'd be using it to cut off your arms and legs and gouging out your eyeballs, and…"

"Silence!" Lardior roared. "You are in no position to be joking."

"I wasn't joking," Josh said defensively. He turned to Scott, and asked, "Was I joking?"

"Be quiet, Josh," Ned warned. "You're going to get us all killed."

"Silence!" Lardior's voice thundered again. The leader of the outlaw band paused for several seconds, the disappointment clearly showing on his face. Finally, he turned to his guards. "Strip them of their gear and lock them up," he commanded.

The guards took their belongings and led them towards a holding cell. Josh was mortified as he and his backpack were taken in opposite directions. When they arrived at the holding cell, the guards attached a shackle to each of their arms just in case they tried to escape or decided to try anything else funny. Just as it had happened in the goblin mines, when the guard put the shackle on Scott, it came undone after several seconds and fell off. Scott had anticipated this and he quickly caught it before it attracted the attention of the guards. Once inside the cell, they were able to talk freely.

"Some back door," Scott remarked dryly. "That governor purposely handed us over to Lardior."

"What do we do now?" Ned asked.

"We try to find a way out of here," Scott replied.

"I don't suppose you have another one of those hair brained ideas, do you?" Ned asked.

"No, not at the moment," Scott admitted. "But I'll think of something."

"Well, do it quickly," Ned said tiredly. "I'm getting so sick of all the precarious situations we keep finding ourselves in. Not to mention that I'm sure Lardior isn't going to keep us here for long. In fact, if we're going to do something, it needs to be tonight."

"I agree," Eric said. "Lardior is going to be more careful this time."

"Look on the bright side," Josh joked, trying to lighten the mood. "At least we don't have to worry about those shadows now."

They sat down on the ground, silent for a while. Each was trying to come up with a plan to get them out of there. Josh had laid down and Scott, noticing Azinine in a corner by herself, walked over and sat down next to her. She gave him a faint smile and looked back down at the ground.

"Hi," he said.

"Hi, yourself," she replied.

"Are you okay?"

"I guess so."

"Is anything wrong?" Scott asked, realizing afterwards how dumb that sounded, considering the situation they were in.

"I just feel left out," Azinine sighed. "I can understand you and Josh, but Ned is always speaking in English, and my English isn't good enough to understand everything."

"Oh, sorry about that," Scott apologized. "It's just that Eric doesn't speak Lumen at all."

"I know. But it doesn't make me feel any better."

"Maybe you should get with Ned and Eric and arrange for some language lessons. They could teach you English and then you and Ned could teach Eric to speak Lumen."

"Why don't you teach me?" she asked, her eyes lighting up.

"I don't know Lumen, remember? When you speak to me it sounds like English. I speak to you in English, but you somehow hear Lumen. It would be hard for me to teach you."

"I guess that makes sense. I'll suggest it to them," she said, feeling better already. "I've always wanted to learn it. I guess now's as good a time as any."

"Plus, if you learn English," Scott pointed out, "we could take a trip back to earth when this is all over and check out all the cool places earth has to offer."

"I would like that," she said.

Scott squeezed her arm and then suggested, "For now, you had better get some sleep. Who knows what tomorrow will bring?"

Eric, Ned and Scott stayed up discussing different options of escape. They thought they had a pretty good plan when several guards showed up and entered the cell.

"That one, that one and that one," a guard spoke, pointing to Ned, Azinine and Josh. The other guards grabbed the three and hauled them outside.

"What are you doing?" Scott said, a trace of panic in his voice.

"Shut up!" the guard snapped back.

"Where are you taking them?" he persisted.

The guard slammed the door behind them.

"Scott, what are they doing?" Eric asked.

"I don't know," Scott replied, very concerned. "But we've got to find out. We have got to find out!"

"Scott, calm down," Eric said, placing his hand on his younger brother's shoulder. "We won't accomplish anything by freaking out."

"I'm not freaking out. I'm just…okay, fine I'm freaking out, but they've just taken our brother and our friends. We don't know why and there's nothing we can do about it. They..." his voice trailed off and he sat down putting his head between his hands.

Eric sat down next to him and put his arm on his back. "Scott, it's not your fault," he comforted. "We all knew the risks. What you and I need to do is think of a way out of here and go find them."

The guards led Azinine, Josh and Ned along a dark path. They walked for several miles it seemed until they came to a clearing where another camp had been set up. They were forced into another waiting cell. They could hear the guards outside talking about something, but couldn't quite make out what. After several minutes the guards left and the camp fell silent.

"What do you think they're going to do with us?" Azinine asked.

"I don't know," Ned replied.

"I still have the gloves. When those guards come, I'll smash their heads together like a bunch of rotten pumpkins," Josh threatened.

"Josh, don't be a fool. Those gloves make you strong, but they won't protect you from the shackles we're wearing. Nor will they protect you from magic or the weapons Lardior's men are carrying."

"Hmm, good point," Josh said.

The three of them had just laid down to sleep when the door opened. Four men dressed in scarlet robes walked in, accompanied by one of Lardior's guards and two servants holding staffs. Each staff had a crystal ball on top lit up like a light bulb. One of the robed men had a gold band around his forehead. Josh guessed he must be their leader.

"Stand up!" the guard barked. He sent a signal to the shackles they were wearing and all three cried out in pain. They stood up, keeping close to each other.

After several minutes the leader spoke. "The two boys are a bit shabby and the girl isn't much to look at. I'll give you thirty onin for them."

"Thirty onin!" the guard growled. "Those boys are healthy as can be. And the girl, although young, is the prettiest thing you've ever seen. Lardior will accept nothing less than a hundred onin."

The robed man spat. "Lardior is a fool. These are just kids that nobody else wants, and you know it. I'll give him fifty onin and nothing more. Take it or leave it."

"I'd leave it if I were you," Josh said butting into their conversation.

"Shut up!" one of the guards growled and set off their shackles for a brief second.

"Ouch!" Josh squealed. "Just saying, that's all. You don't have to get all…" Josh began to say, but all three shackles went off again.

"Ouch!" all three kids yelled.

"I told you to shut up," the guard yelled back. Ned gave Josh a look that said you better stop it or I'm going to kill you.

The guard glared at Josh while pondering the offer. "Fine, you may have them for fifty onin, but Lardior won't be happy."

"He'll get over it," the man replied and then turned to the others. "Replace their shackles with some of our own and put them on the MOC. I want to be back before sunlight."

The men did as they were told and the three of them were taken and placed on a large MOC. No sooner had they been seated than it took off and sped away. Josh and Azinine were amazingly calm, but Ned was very near panic.

"Where are they taking us?" Josh asked.

Azinine shrugged her shoulders. "I don't know. We've obviously been sold as slaves."

"Silence!" one of the guards commanded. "Do not speak or you will be punished."

For the rest of the trip no one spoke. They flew for several hours before they touched down in what appeared to be a barren wasteland, but it was so dark they couldn't really tell.

"Show them to their quarters," the lead guard shouted, "and brief them on their responsibilities. Then bring the girl to me." He turned around and walked away.

"If you so much as lay one hand on her, I'll rip you from limb to limb!" Josh shouted.

The man stopped walking and turned around. He had an incredulous look on his face and Ned thought he was going to break out in laughter, but he didn't. He only paused for a moment to look at Josh. Then he said, "You have spunk. I like that. Perhaps someday I'll give you that chance, but for now you will do as you're told or face severe consequences." He turned around and continued into the darkness.

They were led to a barracks, where the boys were told to enter. Josh felt like he was being put in prison.

"You had better get some sleep," one of the guards suggested. "The sun will be up in a few hours and then you will be expected to work." With that, they turned around, taking Azinine with them.

"Hey!" Josh yelled. "She stays here with us."

The guard turned and at the same time an excruciating shock coursed through Josh's body. He cried out in pain and fell to the ground.

"You will soon learn that you are a prisoner. Prisoners keep their mouths shut and do as they're told."

"I'll be okay," Azinine reassured them.

The guard grabbed her arm and warned, "Be quiet!"

As the door shut, Josh pulled himself up from the floor. It was then that he noticed numerous other prisoners now awake, glaring at him. Ned and Josh hurriedly changed into the clothes they had been given and found some empty beds. The beds stunk and the boys were sure the sheets hadn't been changed for months. But at this point they were both too exhausted to care.

Morning came much too quickly. Two guards entered, blowing a very shrill whistle to wake up the prisoners. The cooks entered and placed a measly piece of what looked like bread in front of each slave.

"What? No eggs and bacon?" Josh said to Ned jokingly. He turned back just in time to see a large man, whom he would later find out was named Tito, swipe his bread.

"Hey! That's mine!" he yelled.

"Exactly! It WAS yours and now it's mine," Tito replied, laughing as he walked back to his bed.

"You have to be careful around here," a prisoner sitting next to Josh whispered. "They'll take advantage of you if you let them."

"Here, you can have half of mine," Ned offered, tearing his piece in two. "I'm not really hungry."

"Thanks," Josh replied, still steaming.

Josh and Ned had just finished eating their bread when the guards returned ordering everyone to line up.

"You two," one of the guards yelled, pointing to Ned and Josh. "Come with me." The two boys walked toward the front of the line. On their way, Tito stuck out his foot and tripped Josh. The other men began to snicker, but the guards yelled for silence. Josh gave Tito a dirty look, but stood up and kept going. They followed the guard onto a MOC where they were flown to a rock quarry.

"Here are your hammers," the guard said, handing them each a tool. "Over there is a pile of rocks that must be smashed to pieces."

"Pile is an understatement," Ned muttered to himself. "Mountain is more like it."

"Within these rocks," the guard continued, "are small pieces of uhrielict. It's the small black pieces you can see throughout the rocks. You will sift through each rock and pull out what you can find. Place any uhrielict in those bins over there. Any questions?"

"What if we get thirsty? How do we get a drink?" Josh asked.

The guard let out a sardonic chuckle. "All you have to do is smash all those rocks and I'll gladly get you a drink," he said sarcastically.

"Promise?" Josh asked.

The guard gave him a dim smile. "I promise," he said mockingly knowing full well two boys could never finish off all those rocks by end of the day. He then turned to leave, but Josh had another question.

"What about lunch?"

"No lunch until all the rocks are smashed," he replied angrily this time. He turned around, but was once again interrupted.

"What if I have to use the bathroom?"

"Not," the guard yelled, "until you have smashed all those rocks!"

"Well, you don't have to get all huffy," Josh yelled back. The guard whirled around, glaring at Josh.

"Okay! Okay! We'll start smashing rocks," Josh said as he picked up his hammer. He studied it for a moment noticing it was a mixture between a sledgehammer and a meat tenderizer. The guard gave him a fake smile and walked away.

"Is there something in the Frontier blood that makes you all beg for trouble?" Ned asked.

"I just wanted to know," Josh replied defensively.

"No. No you didn't," Ned said exasperated. "I know you Frontiers. You said it because you thought it was funny. And you probably also did it just to annoy the guard. Well, I don't think he found it very funny and you probably succeeded in annoying him, which won't go well for us later on."

"You worry too much, Ned."

"Uggh! You're just like your brother Scott, except more psychotic." Ned said, exasperated. "At least Eric inherited some sense. Listen, Josh. You keep that kind of stuff up and they're not going to tolerate it. They're going to punish you. And guess what? I'll probably get punished too, just because I'm guilty by association. I'd rather not have that happen."

"I am not psychotic," Josh replied. "I just have a condition, that's all."

"A condition?" Ned asked warily.

"Yeah, my mother took me to the doctor and he said I have HDHD or something like that. He says it makes me hyperactive and makes it so I can't focus on things."

"Did the doctor say anything about this condition causing you to open your mouth at inopportune moments that could lead to death?"

"I don't know. I wasn't really listening at the time."

"Oh, brother. Did you, by chance, hear the doctor say there was a cure for this condition?"

Instead of answering, Josh turned to look at the mountain of rocks that stood before them, letting out a sigh. After a minute, he turned to Ned. "How about I smash and you find the uhrielict and put it in the bin?"

"Fine with me," Ned replied, knowing full well that smashing would be the hardest work. Josh walked over to the first rock, which was roughly the size of a large beach ball. He lifted his hammer and brought it down with all his might. It shattered into a hundred pieces.

Ned stared at him in amazement. "Wow, I forgot you had those gloves on."

"I never leave home without 'em." Josh replied with a big grin on his face.

They went to work smashing the rocks and sifting out uhrielict. Without the use of the gloves, this would have been an impossible task for the two of them to accomplish in a day. Most likely it would have taken them two or three days, which the guards surely knew. But after about six hours, they smashed their last rock and sat down to take a break.

"I can't wait to see the look on that guard's face when he sees this," Josh remarked. "In fact, I'm thirsty. I think I'll take him up on that drink." He started to stand up, but Ned pulled him back down.

"No. You can't do that."

"Why not?" Josh asked, puzzled. "We're done, aren't we?"

"Didn't we just have a conversation about six hours ago about you opening your mouth at inopportune times that could lead to death?"

"We might have. What's your point?"

"What's my point?" Ned threw his arms up in the air. "Josh, the guard isn't going to be happy."

Josh looked confused. "Why not? We did what he asked us to do."

"Yes," Ned agreed. "But first of all, they'll be very suspicious. They're going to be suspicious as it is that we even finished the task in one day. But they'll really wonder when they see how quickly we did it. They're going to think we've somehow tricked them, because there's no way two kids like us could have possibly taken care of all those rocks in this short amount of time. Is this making sense to you?"

"Yeah, I guess."

"We need to wait here as long as we can. When they show up, we'll act like we just finished. Oh, and there's another thing I hadn't considered. They'll probably double our load once they see how quickly we've done this."

Josh sat back down. "I guess you're right," he relented. "But it's going to get awfully boring just sitting here in this unbearable heat."

"Maybe not," Ned said. "See that hill over there? Let's see if these hammers can be used to dig a small alcove. If so, it will give us shade and we can sit there while we wait for them to come back."

Josh jumped back up. "Good idea! Maybe we could even tunnel our way out of here like the prisoners do in the movies."

"Josh, we'd have to tunnel for miles and miles. That's not going to happen."

"Ned," Josh said, turning very serious. "I know I joke a lot and seem reckless, but deep down inside I'm a little scared. These guys intend to keep us here the rest of our lives. We'll never see our parents, let alone, free them. We have to find a way out of here...with Azinine."

"Nice deduction, Einstein," Ned said shaking his head. Then in a more sympathetic voice, "We'll think of something."

The two of them went to work digging an alcove into the side of the hill. They barely had the place carved out when they noticed the guard returning. They quickly retreated from the entrance and sat down as though they were exhausted. The guard appeared and the look on his face showed his obvious surprise.

"Oh, there you are," Josh called out. "You're just in time. We just barely finished and I'm dying of thirst."

Ned elbowed him in the ribs. "Mouth shut!" he whispered out of the side of his mouth.

"Shut up!" the guard snapped. "Where are the rocks?"

"Excuse me?" Josh asked innocently. "We smashed them. Just as you asked."

"That's impossible! You couldn't have smashed so many in this amount of time."

"Maybe you gave us a soft batch," Josh suggested.

"Maybe," the guard replied hesitantly, still looking around in disbelief.

"You promised," Josh spoke up.

"Promised?" the guard repeated, caught by surprise.

"You said we could have a drink and lunch once the rocks were smashed."

The guard glared at him for a moment. He then looked around, trying to determine how the boys disposed of the rocks so easily, but he couldn't find any evidence. "Okay," he finally said. "Climb aboard."

Josh looked at Ned with a grin and climbed upon the MOC. The guard took them back to the barracks and dropped them off. Another guard brought them some water and a plate full of something that resembled mud. Hungry as they were, the boys dug in, deciding that it actually tasted pretty good. As Josh scraped up the last of his meal an idea occurred to him. Knowing it would be a while before the other slaves returned from their work, he took his empty plate outside and filled it with dirt. He then added water to make it look like the dinner he had just eaten. After getting it to just the right consistency he shoved his plate under his bed.

Ned watched him suspiciously. "What are you doing?" he asked.

"Nothing," Josh replied, knowing Ned wouldn't approve.

"Nothing, huh? You're up to something. You have that Frontier look that has trouble written all over it."

"I'm tired. I'm taking a nap," Josh replied, ignoring Ned.

It was several hours before the other prisoners returned, looking exhausted. They found Josh and Ned lying on their beds snoring. The noise woke the boys up, and they could tell, by the looks on their faces, that the other slaves didn't approve of them sleeping while they had been out working. However, most of the men were so tired, they simply grabbed their own dinner and plopped down on their beds to eat.

Tito and another man named Pip, were not about to sit down and let these newcomers have it so easy. Josh, who had anticipated this, quickly pulled his plate of mud out and placed it on his bed, randomly stirring it with his spoon. He started talking to Ned, acting as though he didn't know the two men were coming. Tito and Pip walked up to his bed and sat down, one on each side of him.

"Hello, friend," Tito began. "Did you have a nice day?"

"Oh, yes. Thank you. It was quite pleasant," Josh replied. "And your day? Did you also have a pleasant day too?"

Ned glared at Josh with warning in his eyes, but Josh just ignored him.

Tito smiled. "As a matter of fact, my day wasn't very pleasant," he said. "But now that I'm done and you're here, I'm sure it's going to get better."

"Really!" Josh exclaimed excitedly. "Sounds like a grand time. What should we do first?"

"First, I'm going to eat. Oh, what do we have here?" Tito said as he picked up Josh's plate. "My dinner!" He stood up to leave.

"Hey!" Josh exclaimed. "That's my dinner!"

"No, no, no. You mean, it WAS your dinner," Tito replied.

Josh jumped up. "Give it back!" he yelled. Pip turned around and placed a hand on his shoulder. "Unless you want to look like that dinner, you should probably just agree with him and sit down"

"That's not fair!"

"In case you haven't noticed, life isn't fair. Now sit…down!"

Josh nodded and sat down, but he didn't take his eyes off Tito. Tito had just reached his own bed and was now proceeding to combine the contents of Josh's plate with his own.

Ned, who had also been watching, whispered, "Now you've done it. You're dead meat."

Josh waved him off. "Shh!" he said snickering. "He's about to eat it."

By this time the whole room was silent. Everyone was looking at Tito. Tito took a large spoonful, but before eating it he glanced over at Josh and gave him a wink. He lifted the spoon up to show Josh what a tasty meal he was going to have and then he placed it slowly in his mouth and pulled out the spoon slowly. Keeping his eyes on Josh, he started to chew heartily for one or two seconds and then stopped. His face took on an expression of disgust and he spat the food out all over the floor.

The look on Tito's face was so horribly humorous that Josh couldn't hold his laughter in and he broke out in a fit of laughter and giggles. He laughed so hard, that tears started forming in his eyes. The problem was, he was the only one laughing. Everyone else was watching Tito. The men all knew his temper and that he would take out his anger on anyone in his way, regardless of fault.

Tito glanced over at Josh and snarled. His face had turned a shade of red, and his eyes were bulging from the sockets. Enraged that this boy and just tricked him, and not only that, but made him ruin his own dinner, he yelled, "Little boy!" not knowing Josh's name. "I'm going to mash you up into little bite sized pieces and then I'm going to eat *you* for dinner!"

Josh was still laughing, but he managed to squeak out, "Make sure you bring the salt and pepper." This brought a few snickers from the others, but they were quickly extinguished by the nasty look they received from Tito.

"Josh, stop it!" Ned warned, grabbing him by the shoulders and bringing him out of his laughter. "Why do you keep egging him on? He's twice your size."

"Have you forgotten already?" Josh asked, holding his hands up to his friend's face. "I have the gloves on."

"Those gloves won't stop his fist from smashing through your face," Ned whispered. "They have to make contact with something for them to work.

Even if you do succeed in beating him, they certainly won't stop a knife from entering your belly while you're sleeping."

Josh suddenly went serious. "Oh crap! I hadn't thought about that."

"Well, right now you'd better think about how you're going to deal with him," Ned responded pointing to Tito. Josh turned around to see Tito making his way down the aisle.

Chapter 19

Maulder

Eric and Scott woke the next morning from a very restless sleep. Neither spoke for some time, both trying to think of a way out of their situation. Scott's thoughts wandered back to Azinine as he wondered where she was and how she was doing. He thought about the fun they had playing tag in the clouds the first time he came to Lumen. His mind continued to wander over the different experiences he had while he was with her. He smiled as he thought back on how they had freed the unicorns. He then remembered flying over the animal showplace and seeing the blue bubble that kept the dragon from communicating with its own kind.

"That's it!" he cried out.

"What?" Eric asked.

"I have an idea, but I need silence."

"Silence?"

"I'll explain later."

Scott put his head down and concentrated hard, picturing Malmoth in his mind. "Malmoth," he spoke in his mind sending out his thoughts. "This is Scott. Can you hear me?" He waited for an answer, but none came. He took a deep breath and concentrated even harder. "Malmoth, can you hear me? This is Scott." Again, he waited, but no reply came. He raised his head and found Eric looking at him curiously.

"I take it whatever you're doing isn't working?"

"There must be a secret to it, but I don't know what it is," Scott said exasperated.

"Tell me what you're doing and maybe I can help," Eric offered.

"I'm trying to contact Malmoth, but I can't seem to get through."

"Who is Malmoth? And what are you actually doing to contact him?"

"Malmoth is a dragon," Scott explained. "Azinine said that since dragons don't communicate vocally, they are able to talk to each other from long distances."

Eric looked at Scott with raised eyebrows. "You're trying to contact a dragon. As in a very large lizard that breathes fire?" he asked.

"Yes. Don't tell me this makes my big brother, who's not scared of anything, nervous."

"I always get nervous when I meet animals that can eat me in one bite. I'm not sure, but I think I was born that way."

"Don't worry," Scott reassured him. "She's a friend of mine."

"She?" Eric asked.

"Yes, she."

"Okay. So, if dragons don't communicate vocally, then how do they communicate?"

"I'm not really sure. I know they can't read my mind, but when I speak to them, I speak to them through my mind. It's as if I send the thought or words to their mind and they pick it up. Does that even make any sense?"

"In a weird sort of way, sure," Eric replied. "When I speak to you close up, we speak in normal voices. But when we're far away, we shout. Maybe you have to do something similar."

"You want me to shout in my mind?" Scott asked.

"No, but maybe you have to broadcast on a different frequency. Like a radio station does when it broadcasts nationwide instead of locally to just one city."

"Okay, I can see where you're going with this, but how?"

"I don't know. You're the one with this language talent," Eric said. "Try concentrating on sending the message in all directions."

"It's worth a try." Scott put his head back down and imagined radio waves being broadcast in all directions. "Malmoth, it's Scott. Please respond if you can hear me." He waited for an answer, but none came. He tried again concentrating as hard as he could. "Malmoth, are you there?"

"It's no use," Scott sighed, lifting his head. "I can't get through."

"Try one more thing," urged Eric. "When I took my computer class, the instructor told us that when we send a message on a local area network, the message goes to every computer on the network. Each computer looks at the address on the message to see if it's addressed to it. If it's not, the computer throws the message away. Only the computer that it's addressed to keeps it. Basically, on the internet, the message is sent from computer to computer. Each computer looks at the address. If the message isn't for that computer, it passes it on until the message finally reaches its destination."

"So what are you saying?" Scott asked. "You want me to put an address on my message and ask each dragon that gets it to pass it on until it reaches Malmoth?"

Eric took a breath and patiently explained. "I'm just saying that perhaps there are some similarities. Look at it this way. If you were at a party and you yelled out, 'Where are you?' some people might look at you. But for the most part, they would assume you weren't speaking to them and they would ignore you. But... if you yelled, 'Malmoth, where are you?' then everyone but Malmoth would ignore you...I think."

"Eric," Scott said, exasperated. "I *am* calling her name and she's not answering."

"Maybe there are two Malmoths. Instead of sending out a name, trying sending out a picture of her or something like that."

"Alright. I'll try it," Scott promised. Once again, he envisioned the message going out in all directions. In addition, he pictured Malmoth in his mind. "Malmoth, where are you? It's Scott." As before, he waited, but nothing came back.

"Still nothing?" Eric asked.

"Nothing. I just can't seem to reach her."

Scott and Eric remained in their prison all day without anyone stopping by except a guard delivering food to them. They had discussed numerous ideas for escape, but nothing that they thought would actually work. Scott could tell by the amount of light in the enclosure that the sun was starting to dip below the horizon. Tired and depressed, both he and Eric laid down on their beds to rest, hoping something would come to mind. Scott was on the verge of dreamland when he heard it.

"Hi, Scott. I'm sorry it has taken me so long to reply. I heard you the first time, but I was busy and couldn't answer."

"Malmoth!" Scott shouted out, forgetting for a moment that he only needed to talk with his mind. Eric poked his head up, looking hopeful at Scott. Scott nodded his head indicating Malmoth was talking to him.

"How are you doing, my friend?" she asked.

"I'm doing fine, Malmoth, but I really could use your help."

"You want to fry some more goblins?"

"No. But I am being held prisoner by some evil men."

"Evil men are always my second choice," the dragon replied.

Scott laughed. "For a dragon, you sure are cool."

"And just what do you mean by that?"

"It's just that dragons are supposed to strike fear into the hearts of men," Scott hurriedly explained. "But when I speak with you, I have fun."

"We only strike fear in the hearts of those we don't like or want to eat. Now, what can I do for you?"

"I was hoping you could strike a little fear into the hearts of our captors and free us from this place."

"You sound far way. Where are you?"

"Do you know the kingdom of the Greymen?"

"You've been captured by the Greymen?" Malmoth asked with concern.

"No, by another group just north of the Greymen. Their leader is a man named Lardior."

"Lardior!" she growled.

"You know him?" Scott asked in surprise.

"It was Lardior that betrayed us into the hands of Cohar. I would relish the opportunity to free you from such vermin. In fact, I might bring a few friends along."

"That would be great! Thank you," Scott said gratefully.

"Thank you!" she replied. "I'll contact you when we get a little closer. In fact, I don't think we'll be there until morning, but don't despair. We will be there."

"I won't," Scott promised. He looked at Eric with a smile. "She's coming and she's bringing the whole armada."

Eric's eyes widened. "You mean she's bringing more man eating, giant, fire breathing lizards with her?" Eric asked dubiously.

"Yep! And she means business. It turns out that she already has a beef with Lardior."

"I trust you'll tell them all I'm a friend and I'm on the good side?"

"How much is it worth to you?" Scott asked with a gleam in his eye.

"That's not even funny."

Azinine sat in a room that was nicely decorated and had a plush bed for sleeping. The only thing that would give a person the idea she was a prisoner was the locked door, the shackle on her arm, and the guard stationed outside. She had slept all day and had just woken up when a knock came at her door. She didn't know whether to answer or not. As she sat there debating, the knock came again.

"Come in," she called out hesitantly. The door opened and in walked several female servants, or rather, slaves she presumed.

One of the servants approached, introducing herself as Sheldine. "We have been commanded to have you bathed and dressed in the finest attire," she spoke respectfully.

"Why?" Azinine asked.

Sheldine gave Azinine a slight smile. "He didn't say. But I'm sure it's to present you to Maulder."

"Who is Maulder?"

"He's the lord over this house."

"I won't do it," Azinine said defiantly.

"Please," Sheldine pleaded. "It's not my wish to make you do this, but if you don't, he'll punish us all."

Azinine could see the fear in the slave woman's eyes. She also saw compassion. "Oh, alright," she relented. "How long have you been here?"

Sheldine hesitated a moment before answering. "I think three years. I've honestly lost track of time."

Azinine nodded and said with confidence, "Well, you won't be here much longer. I have friends who are coming to rescue me. When they come, we'll take you and the others with us."

Sheldine smiled, but Azinine could tell she didn't believe her. "I, too, once thought my friends were coming," the older woman said wistfully. "They never did. I tried escaping, but it's hopeless with these shackles."

"My friends will come," Azinine persisted. "I know they will."

"And if they don't?"

"Then I'll just have to turn Maulder and all his goons into toads."

Sheldine laughed. "I'd like to see that! But for now, we need to turn you into a princess."

The women spent several hours grooming Azinine. Once she had bathed and they got her hair just right, they splashed perfume on her and dressed her in a sparkling purple dress. Sheldine looked at her with a frown, saying, "I'm afraid we've done too good of a job. He may ask you to marry him."

Azinine gave her a wink and said, "Unfortunately for him, he doesn't know what he's getting. I may be pretty on the outside, but I'm quite rotten on the inside."

"Be careful," Sheldine warned. "He's not a patient man and he certainly has no qualms about punishing or whipping anyone."

"Thanks for the warning. I'll be careful," Azinine promised.

"Then follow me and I'll show you the way."

Azinine was tempted to turn her hair gray and her dress brown, but she knew Sheldine would most likely bear the punishment for such actions, so she decided against it. They walked down a staircase and through a long hallway. At the end of the hall, there was a large wooden door with a man standing in front of it. When he saw the females approaching, he acted as though he were expecting them.

"Here she is, Thine," murmured Sheldine with a bow.

"It's about time. I'll take her from here," the man growled. Sheldine bowed again and left. Thine opened the door and motioned for Azinine to enter. As she did so, she purposely stumbled and grabbed onto his shoulder whispering an incantation. Suddenly, one of her specialties, an illusion of a large ugly spider appeared on his shoulder. It was far enough back that he didn't notice. Steadying herself, Azinine entered the dining hall where a large table covered with food stood in the middle. Thine motioned for her to sit down. At the sight of the food, Azinine's stomach growled and she sat down gratefully. She hadn't eaten for some time and was ravenous.

"You may eat as much as you want," Thine said as he turned to leave.

"Thank you," she replied. "By the way, you have something on your shoulder."

Thine looked over his shoulder and let out a yelp. He tried to whack the spider off his shoulder, but it jumped off before he had a chance, and crawled under the table. Thine quickly yanked off his shoe and dove under the table after it. He tried to smash the spider as it scampered back and forth avoiding his whacks. Azinine snickered inside as she controlled its movements. Just then, the door began to open and another idea entered her head. She quickly grabbed a pitcher filled with a green juice of some kind and spilled it on the bright purple dress she was wearing.

"Auhh!" she screamed, jumping up from her chair. She desperately dabbed at her dress with a napkin, trying to soak up the liquid.

"What is going on here?" Maulder roared as he entered.

Thine quickly crawled out from under the table and put his shoe on. "I'm sorry, my Lord, but there is a giant spider under the table. I was trying to get rid of it."

"Look what you've done to our guest's dress, you imbecile!"

"It's okay," Azinine spoke up. "I'll be all right. It was just a mistake."

Maulder ignored her comment. "Take her back to her quarters and get her another dress," he commanded.

"Right away, my lord," Thine replied. He took Azinine's arm and escorted her to her room where Sheldine helped her into a different dress. When she was once again presentable, Thine escorted her back to the dining hall where Maulder was waiting for her.

"Ah, you look much better, my dear. Please, come in and take a seat."

"Thank you," she replied.

"Were you able to get something to eat?"

"Not much."

"Well, after our conversation you'll have plenty of time to get whatever you like. I'll bet you're wondering why I've brought you here."

"I have to admit, I am curious."

"Yes… well… I would never think of taking a girl so young as yourself as my wife. However, you are quite attractive and I might do so if you were of the appropriate age."

Azinine grabbed a loaf of bread off the table, and not bothering to slice off a piece, bit into the whole loaf, taking off as large a chunk as possible. Then chewing with her mouth open, she grabbed her drink and slugged down a gulp, the liquid running out the sides of her mouth and dripping onto her dress. She looked over at Maulder, hoping to see disgust on his face. But instead, she saw amusement.

After she had gulped it all down, she said, "Excuse me. I haven't eaten in days and I'm starving."

Maulder smiled. "Do not think I am fooled by your charade. I can tell a cultured girl when I see one."

Azinine's jaw dropped. *Shoot!* she thought, and then said aloud, "I still have many more years until I'm able to marry." She then proceeded to pick up a bowl of salad and dish some onto her plate.

"Still, it would be a shame to make someone as pretty as yourself work like a slave. So, you will live here with me, as my friend and guest, until you are able to marry. We'll discuss the possibility of marriage then. In the meantime, you will have plenty to eat, nice clothes to wear and the freedom to do as you like as long as you follow my rules."

"There's only one problem," Azinine pointed out. "My father would never approve. He's very powerful and when he finds out I'm gone he'll come looking for me."

"That won't be a problem," Maulder said with a smile. "He may look, but he'll never find you here."

"He knows I was captured by Lardior," Azinine persisted. "He'll force Lardior to talk and he will come."

"Who is your father?" Maulder asked, his curiosity peaked.

"He...his...name...is...Artimi Noka," Azinine stammered.

"Artimi Noka? Do you mean Magus Noka of the magi council?"

"Yes, that's correct."

"I know Magus Noka, though I didn't know he had a daughter. I will have a talk with him. In the meantime, feel free to make yourself at home. And remember, life will be pleasant for you as long as you follow the rules."

"May I continue eating now?" she asked. "I really am starving."

"Of course, my dear. Help yourself."

Chapter 20

A Stroke of Good Luck

Tito made his way down the aisle. There really wasn't anywhere for Josh to go. He and Ned slept at the back of the barracks and the only door out of the place was at the front. As Tito slowly approached, he fixed his glaring eyes on Josh. Josh figured the bigger man's slow pace was a mental tactic he was using to instill as much fear as possible in Josh before he actually tore him apart. *On the contrary*, Josh thought, *it will give me more time to come up with a strategy*.

As Tito strode up to him, Josh stood calmly by the corner of his bed. "Get a move on it, will ya," Josh taunted. "I've got a long day tomorrow and I need to get some sleep." Some of the others in the room chuckled, but Josh didn't know if they were laughing at him or at what was about to happen to him.

"You'll have an even longer day by the time I get through with you," Tito snarled as he reached Josh's bed. Josh grabbed the corner of his blanket and threw it at Tito. Then with all his might he swung a fist into Tito's gut. All he hit was air. Tito had blocked the blanket and easily dodged his punch.

"Augh!" Josh let out, as Tito's foot slammed into his chest knocking him hard to the floor. His head hit hard and everything went fuzzy. Tito grabbed both of Josh's legs and hoisted him off the floor. Ned shot towards Tito in a desperate attempt to stop him from doing what was sure to seriously hurt, if not kill, Josh. However, before Ned was able to reach him, Tito let out a shrill cry and dropped Josh on the floor. Tito's shackle had been set off and Ned whirled to see a guard standing at the door.

"Tito!" the guard barked. "Back to your bed!" Tito hesitated, upset that the guard had denied him of his payback. "This isn't over, little boy," he threatened. As he turned to walk back to his bed, he gave Josh a slight, but unmistaken kick to the ribs. Josh grunted but didn't attempt to get up.

Ned knelt down by Josh. "Are you okay?" he asked.

Josh opened one eye and looked up at Ned. "Is he gone?"

"Yeah, he's gone."

"Then, I'm okay," Josh answered. "Just a little bruised."

"Well, you asked for it," Ned reprimanded as he helped Josh to his feet.

"I guess I thought I could take him with these gloves."

"Those gloves weren't made for fighting. They were made to handle a very special sword."

Josh didn't sleep well that night. He kept having nightmares of Tito and Pip with long daggers hovering over his bed. Of course, each time he awoke, no one was there, but it rattled him still the same. When morning finally arrived, a guard awoke everyone with a loud whistle. A cook brought them food that looked similar to what they had eaten the night before. Josh kept looking over his shoulder, expecting Tito, at any moment, to steal his food. But thankfully, it never happened. Josh guessed it was because a guard was standing in the room watching.

Josh and Ned ate their meal in silence, mostly because Josh wasn't in the mood to talk. He said it was because of his lack of sleep, but his chest still hurt and for the first time he wasn't as confident in himself. He was in real danger and he knew it. He realized there was a very strong probability he might never see his mother or father again. That thought got him thinking hard. They had to escape.

The guard who had escorted them the day before, again appeared in the doorway. "You two!" he barked, pointing at Josh and Ned. "Come with me."

They put their food down and walked towards the doorway. Knowing he would have to pass by Tito to exit the building, Josh kept his eyes on the bigger man. But Tito simply kept eating, making no attempt to look at Josh. Josh took comfort in this and approached with more confidence.

Once the three of them were settled on the MOC, the guard flew to the same quarry they had worked at the day before. Just as Ned had predicted, there was an even bigger mountain of rocks. The guard handed each of them a hammer. "All right, girls. You know what to do," he said pointing to the rocks.

Ned and Josh took the hammers and walked toward the pile. This time, however, the guard didn't fly away. He stayed to watch. Both boys began smashing rocks. Not wanting the guard to get any ideas, Josh hit the rocks soft. He tried hard to make it look like he was using a great amount of effort. After a half-hour or so, the guard got bored and flew off.

"Okay, Ned. Let's do what we did yesterday," Josh suggested.

"All right by me," Ned replied, already working up a sweat.

Josh went to work smashing the rocks. Rocks that usually would have taken several hits, he easily shattered in one stroke. Meanwhile, Ned grabbed what uhrielict he could find and placed it in the bins as he had the day before. The two of them worked hard for a period of about four hours and then decided to take a rest. They were headed over to the hideout they had dug, when their guard returned with another guard.

"See?" the first guard said, pointing at the pile of rocks. "Look how many they've already smashed. I'm telling you, the others aren't trying hard enough. If these two kids can smash all this, in this amount of time, imagine how much the others should be smashing."

"This is unbelievable!" the other guard barked out. "They've been fooling us all these years. They're going to pay for this. Double their loads and give them nothing until they're finished."

Ned raised his hand. "Uh, sir?" he asked hesitantly. "Um, could you not mention us to the others? They'll eat us for dinner if they find out we didn't work at the recommended slow pace."

"Yeah," Josh added. "Tito said he would kill us if we didn't work slower than he did. But we were determined to do our duty to your lord, so we kept working as hard as we could."

"Good work. You'll be rewarded for this," the second guard responded as he turned and walked back to the MOC with the other guard. They both climbed aboard and flew off.

Ned turned towards Josh shaking his head in disbelief. "Didn't you learn anything last night? If Tito finds out what you've done, he really will kill you! Especially if he's punished."

Josh shrugged his shoulders. "Maybe. But I'm guessing Tito will be so tired, he won't have the strength to bug me. Let's get back to work and finish off these rocks."

The two of them worked hard for another three hours and finished off all the rocks except one. They decided to leave that one until the guard came back so it would look like they were just finishing. They walked over and sat down in the alcove they created, away from the blazing sun.

"We've got to find a way to rescue Azinine and then get out of here," Josh mused as they rested in shade. "Who knows what they're doing to her?"

"I'm not too worried about Azinine," Ned replied. "She's a good witch and probably has a greater chance of escaping than we do. I'm more concerned about our parents. I have this sinking feeling they're in serious danger and we may already be too late."

Josh was silent for a moment. Then he asked, "Do you really think they would kill them?"

"I think they would do anything to get what they want."

Josh's mood turned sober. He thought about his mother being tortured and the very idea just caused his blood to boil. "Where's your police or army or whoever you use to uphold your law? Why aren't they out looking for them?"

"We have soldiers that are used to protect the people, but they answer to the Magi Council. Right now, many of the high-ranking council members are missing, including my father. I'm sure they're trying to do something. I just don't know what."

They rested for a while in silence before Ned stood up and turned to Josh saying, "We'd better head back. The guard is bound to return soon."

Without saying a word, Josh stood up and followed Ned. He couldn't get the thoughts of his mother out of his mind. His anger kept building while the desire to escape grew stronger and stronger.

The two boys stood by the stone, waiting for the guard to return. When he did, they acted as though they were very tired. Josh tried to hit the stone lightly to keep the guard from getting suspicious, but the anger building inside of him brought the hammer down hard and the rock cracked down the middle and split apart. Glancing furtively at the guard to see if he had noticed, Ned was glad the rock hadn't shattered completely the way they normally did when Josh really hit them hard. Figuring the guard was still too far away to have seen anything suspicious, they finished the rock off just as he landed. This time it was a guard they had never seen before. They grabbed what uhrielict they could find and put it in the bin and then wiped the sweat off their brow, trying to look tired.

"That was an impressive hit," the guard complimented Josh as he stepped off his MOC.

"Not really," Josh replied. "Once in a while we come across a rock that's soft. One that's already been knocked around enough to make it weak."

Not sure if the guard had bought his story, Josh was relieved when he changed the subject. "Since you two have finished your work here, I need your help rebuilding some of the stables."

As they climbed on the MOC, Ned asked, "What happened to your stables?"

"Maulder and a young girl went riding. When they returned, one of the beams suddenly cracked and almost fell on top of him."

"Sounds like he needs to maintain his stables a bit more frequently," Ned commented.

"That's the strange thing," the guard said. "Those stables are only three years old."

"Did you say he went riding with a young girl?" Josh asked.

"Yes. She arrived two nights ago. She's a pretty little thing."

Josh and Ned looked at each other. "That explains why the beam suddenly cracked," Ned whispered.

Josh gave him a questioning look. "Why? I don't understand."

"Azinine," Ned whispered back.

The house Maulder lived in was much farther away than Ned or Josh had anticipated. Their barracks were in the middle of a barren desert. Maulder's house, on the other hand, was nestled in a plush green valley surrounded by hills. As they settled down next to the stable, Josh noticed it looked like a lightning bolt had hit it. The roof was partially caved in and the stables inside were a mess. To the side, a large tree had been cut down, no doubt to replace the main beam that had cracked almost in half.

Josh turned and whispered to Ned, "Are you telling me this was Azinine's doing?"

"That's my guess," Ned replied. "I don't know what else would have done this."

"Could she really do this?"

"Azinine may look quite helpless on the outside, but she's a darn good witch. With the right combination of gravity and magic, she could pull this off."

"But how..." Josh started to ask but was cut off.

"Your job," the guard began, "is to strip this tree of all its bark using this bark stripping blade. Once that's complete, you will wipe this Junga oil completely over the wood." He pulled a bracelet out of his pocket and handed it to Ned. "Once you're finished, use this bracelet to contact me. Do you understand?"

"Yes, sir," Ned replied. Then on second thought, he asked, "We'll work our best, but are we expected to have all this done before dark?"

"No," the guard laughed. "I'm sure this job will take you at least until tomorrow night. You will sleep here tonight. When you're finished for the night, a servant will show you where to sleep."

"Uh, sir?" Josh asked politely. "Can we get some food and drink?"

"Again, the servant will provide you with that," came the reply.

"Thank you," Josh called out as the guard jumped on his MOC and flew away.

"Well, you're in luck. You won't have to deal with Tito tonight," Ned remarked.

"Yeah, I'm sure gonna miss him," Josh replied with a grin.

The two boys went to work stripping off the bark. The blade was fairly long and curved in the center. There were two large handles on each end, requiring each person on either side of the log to pull together. However, this proved to be quite awkward since Josh's strength was ten times that of Ned's with the gloves on. In the end, Josh had to take the gloves off to make it work. It wasn't easy work, but they slowly made progress. They had just begun working on a new strip of bark when Josh let go of the blade, sending the blade and Ned awkwardly to the ground.

"Josh! Why did you let…" he cried out, angry at Josh. Then he stopped, noticing Josh was looking at the sky. Glancing up, Ned saw a very large bird circling the area directly above them.

"What is that?" Josh asked.

"It's a dragon," Ned gasped. "Quick! Hide under the eaves of the house."

"It's too late for that," Josh said. "I'm sure he's already seen us."

"You're probably right, but what are you going to do? Stay out here like a sitting duck?"

The two boys moved towards the house. But before they reached it, the dragon was gone, so they went back to work. About an hour into their work, a servant arrived with water and food.

"I'm sure you two could use some of this," she commented as she placed the water and food on a nearby wooden table.

"That's an understatement," Josh replied as he once again let go of the blade without first warning Ned. Ned couldn't compensate and fell to the ground again.

"Josh!" Ned yelled in exasperation.

"Sorry," Josh replied as he walked over to the table. He grabbed the vessel of water and started to gulp it down like there was no tomorrow.

"Oh, dear," the woman chuckled. "I guess I'd better get another one of those."

"I would certainly appreciate that," Ned replied, irritated. "I don't think he realizes there are two of us here."

She laughed. "I'll be right back."

Meanwhile, Josh finally came up for air. "Sorry, Ned," he apologized. "I just couldn't help myself."

"Obviously!" Ned said in disgust. He got up and walked over to the table. "Can I have what's left?" Ned asked.

"Of course." Josh handed the vessel over to Ned and he drank what little was there. It was enough to tide him over, but he was afraid the food might make him thirsty again, so he didn't dare eat until she returned with more water. Josh, on the other hand, had plenty to drink and so he dove in. Ned, afraid that Josh would also eat all the food, grabbed some and stowed it away so there'd be some left when the servant returned with the water. He waited for a good hour and was beginning to think she wasn't coming back, when she finally appeared in the doorway with another vessel of water.

"I'm sorry it took so long," she apologized. "That blasted Maulder can't do anything for himself."

"That's quite okay. Thanks for bringing it out," Ned said.

"You're welcome. I'll be back shortly to show you to your quarters."

Ned took the vessel and started drinking. Once he had had enough, he put it down and picked up a chunk of bread. While Josh waited for Ned to eat, he sat down and rested his head against the side of the stable.

When Ned finished, he playfully kicked at Josh. "Come on, Josh. We had better get back to work. We've already lost a lot of time."

"Actually," Josh said, brushing off his pants as he stood up. "I was just thinking about that and about what an idiot I've been. I have two gloves. I'll give one to you and one to me. Even though we can only use one hand each, it should still be better than two hands without the gloves. We should still finish much faster."

"Not a bad idea," Ned replied.

Josh gave Ned one of the gloves and they began pulling the blade down the bark. With each of them wearing a glove, the work did go faster and within an hour all the bark was gone. Next, Ned grabbed the Junga oil and with a large paintbrush started spreading it all over the tree.

"What is that stuff?" Josh asked, wrinkling his nose. "It smells horrible."

"That's why they have *us* put it on, instead of doing it themselves," Ned explained. "It's our version of tar. When it hardens, it will protect the tree from the rain and other elements, making it very strong and durable."

"That may be, but the smell is hardly worth it," Josh said in disgust.

Ned shrugged his shoulders. "Once it dries, the smell goes away."

The boys were only about halfway done spreading the oil when the servant reappeared. "Wow!" she exclaimed. "You two work fast."

"It's amazing what a little water will do for you," Josh replied.

She laughed and motioned for them to follow her. "It's getting dark. You can finish in the morning. Let me show you to your quarters. They're not much, but at least it's a place to sleep."

They walked around the mansion and came to a small dwelling lit by lumenarty rocks. Inside there were three beds and a washroom, along with a lot of other junk that had obviously been placed in there for lack of a better place to store it.

The woman shook her head and said, "Like I said, it's not much but it's a place to sleep."

Ned and Josh grinned at each other. "Shoot," Josh said, "this is heaven compared to those barracks they keep us in."

"Pretty bad, are they?"

"Yeah!" both boys agreed emphatically.

"Well then, enjoy your night's sleep here. Someone will be by in the morning to wake you up."

"Thank you," Ned said as she was leaving.

"Wait!" Josh cried out. The woman turned around and came back inside. "Is there a new girl in the house with long blonde hair and dark eyes? Her name is Azinine."

The woman's face registered her surprise. "Yes," she answered. "You know her?"

"She's my girlfriend and he's her brother," Josh replied, pointing to Ned and giving him a smirk. "Is she okay?"

"Yes, she's fine," the woman reassured them. "But I worry about her."

"Why?" Ned asked anxiously.

"Maulder left for Lux this evening and she's been talking about trying to escape. If she gets caught, Maulder will treat her very badly. Believe me, I've seen what happens to those who try."

"Maybe we can convince her to stay. Can you send her out to us?" Josh asked.

"No, she's not allowed to leave the house without an escort."

"Why can't you escort her?" Josh asked.

"I'm a slave," the woman answered, as though Josh should have already known that.

"Can you take us to her?" Josh persisted.

"NO! If they caught you in the house, you would be severely punished."

"Where exactly is her room?" asked Josh, not about to give up.

The woman sighed. "It's on the east side, top floor. But I strongly advise you against trying anything," she warned. "I must be leaving now. They'll wonder where I am."

"Thanks again," Ned said.

"Wait!" Josh hollered. As she turned around once more, he asked, "What's your name?"

"Sheldine. Now I really must go."

"Wait!" he called out again.

"What?" she replied, exasperated.

"Will you at least tell her that we're down here, so she'll know we're okay."

"Yes, I will tell her. Now goodbye!" With that, she turned around and quickly left before Josh could stop her again.

Chapter 21

Malmoth

That next morning, Scott and Eric work up early, anxious for the arrival of Malmoth. She had said she would contact them when she was close, but so far nothing. The two paced back and forth for what seemed like an eternity. Finally, Scott sat back down on his bed and placed his hands over his head. The silence was killing him.

"Scott, are you listening?" Malmoth suddenly asked, sending her thoughts only to Scott so the other dragons couldn't hear.

"Malmoth!" Scott exclaimed, jumping up from his cot. "I was beginning to think you weren't coming. Where are you?"

"We're just over the Grey Hills Forest, but I don't see any sign of Lardior's camp."

"We're north-east of there. It might be hard to spot among the trees since they probably don't have any fires lit. They don't usually light any fires until after dark. That way no one sees their smoke."

"That's fine with us. We were hoping to get there in time to light their fires for them."

"Ha ha. Just make sure we're out of the way before you do," cautioned Scott.

"Who else is you with?" Malmoth asked.

"My brother Eric."

"Oh, I would love to eat him. I mean, meet him."

"Ha, ha, that's not funny," Scott jokingly scolded.

"You know I would never hurt any friend of yours," Malmoth assured him, "but I should tell you that Chinzar is with us. I don't think he'll hurt you. But ever since he rescued you from the goblins, he no longer feels any obligation to you, so consider yourself warned. I would be careful around him if I were you, and especially watch out for your brother."

"I thought that was you who rescued me from the goblins," Scott said in surprise.

"No. After I flew out of the goblin mountain door, and realized you had fallen off, I tried to turn around. But with your wolf friends on my back, I had to make the turn very carefully so they wouldn't fall off. By the time I had turned around, you were already running down the mountain. With the wolves on my back, I was in no position to attack. It was then that I noticed Chinzar. He must have also noticed my predicament, because he told me he would save you, which surprised me."

"That surprises me too," Scott replied.

"Actually, I think he was after your sword. He rescued you to repay his debt, but he also took the sword for his own."

"Chinzar has the sword?" Scott asked in astonishment.

"Yes," she replied.

"What would he want with the sword?" Scott asked.

"It's worth a lot. He already has a very valuable hoard, but the addition of the sword has probably made it one of the most valuable amongst dragons. I wouldn't ask for it back, either," Malmoth cautioned. "It would only offend him and give him greater reason to...eat you. In his mind, it belongs to him now."

Scott was dumbfounded. "I thought for sure the goblins had it."

"No. He has the sword alright," Malmoth confirmed.

"Does..." Scott began to ask, but the dragon cut him off.

"Scott, I think I see the camp. Where are you?"

"There are several green, dome shaped buildings down near the edge of the lake," Scott replied excitedly. "We are in one of those."

"I'll come rescue you, while Chinzar and the others go looking for Lardior."

"Try and keep at least one or two alive," Scott said. "I need them to tell me where they took my other brother and my friends."

"I'll let them know," acknowledged the dragon. "See you in a bit."

Scott went over and knocked on the door. The guard opened it. "What do you want?"

"Any minute now, a friend of mine is going to drop in. If you cooperate, she'll let you live. If not, she's going to eat you."

The guard laughed. "Ooooh, I'm shaking in my boots. What friend of yours could possibly be so horrible?"

"That one," Scott said, pointing behind the guard. Malmoth had just arrived and was lowering herself down. The guard turned around to see what Scott was pointing at and just about fell off his feet. By the sounds starting to erupt from the camp, Scott surmised the other dragons had also arrived. Scott and Eric could hear the whole area now in an uproar. Malmoth began to growl and bare her teeth at the guard.

"Call her off or I'll turn your shackle up full power," the guard demanded.

"You mean these?" Scott asked, holding both his and Eric's shackles in his hand.

"How did you...? That's impossible!" stammered the guard.

"Let's just say I have a little magic of my own."

Malmoth roared again and moved forward. The guard froze and was now literally shaking in his boots.

Eric grabbed the guard and threw him to the ground. "Ask him where they are," he said to Scott.

Scott knelt down by the guard. "Tell us where our friends are and we'll let you live."

Scott expected resistance, but the guard didn't waste any time spilling his guts. Apparently, the guard's life was more important to him than his loyalty to Lardior or Maulder. Scott was also able to find out where all their gear was being kept. They left the holding cell and ran in Lardior's direction. Malmoth followed them just in case one of the other dragons mistook them for one of Lardior's men. But at this point, there was nothing to worry about. All the men had fled, with Malmoth's friends chasing after them. The tent where their gear was kept had been badly burned. As they approached, they noticed that Lardior's personal dwelling was completely engulfed in flames.

Eric, who reached the supply tent first, ran inside to see what he could salvage. The supply tent had been partially burned, and was still smoking. As Scott entered, he found his brother rummaging through the debris. Three of the packs were completely melted and their paint guns destroyed, but Josh's and Scott's packs were untouched. They grabbed what was left and ran back out. They found Malmoth resting comfortably on the forest floor. Eric and Scott each put a pack on their back and walked over to Malmoth.

"Thanks, Malmoth." Scott said. "We really appreciate your help."

"It was our pleasure. I only…" she stopped and quickly stood up. "Chinzar, no!" she yelled, looking up. Scott and Eric turned their eyes sky-ward and saw a very large dragon diving towards them, fire belching from his mouth. Malmoth positioned herself between Chinzar and the two boys. Scott jumped underneath one of Malmoth's wings, but Eric was so enthralled by the scene that he just sat there watching. Scott grabbed his arm and quickly pulled him under. The big dragon landed on the ground next to Malmoth with a thunderous thud.

"Lardior escaped!" he told her, disgusted. Then he roared, belching more fire into the air. Soon two other large dragons appeared and landed. Eric's curiosity got the best of him and he couldn't resist a peek. One of the dragons had obviously just feasted, because Eric could see blood still on its lips.

"Are you going to share them with us, Malmoth?" one of the new dragons asked.

"No!" she replied.

"She's not even going to eat them. Are you, Malmoth?" Chinzar said butting in.

"What?" a dragon named Darmke blurted out. "If you're not hungry then hand them over to me."

"They're not for eating," Malmoth said, speaking calmly. "These Lumen are my friends. One of them saved my life. He also saved Volcar, Voxna and Chinzar's life," she added, giving Chinzar a nasty look as she spoke his name.

Chinzar didn't flinch. "The other one didn't save our lives," he pointed out. "Why do you protect him?"

"Because he's Scott's brother. He's family."

"We don't care whose brother he is," Chinzar roared. "We're hungry! Give them up!"

"Chinzar," Chaltor, the other dragon soothed, "we've had plenty to eat. We don't really need to eat them if Malmoth doesn't want us to."

Smoke curled from Chinzar's nostrils. "Because of this boy," he retorted, "my sister is dead and now he'll pay for it."

Malmoth looked Chinzar directly in the eyes and said, "Your sister didn't die because of him. She died because of that wicked warlock that entrapped us. If it hadn't been for Scott, we would all be dead!"

"If the boy saved your life, Chinzar, you owe him his life," Darmke chimed in.

"I also saved his life," Chinzar answered. "I owe him nothing."

"Chinzar," Scott spoke out using his mind to communicate like dragons. The other dragons, caught by surprise, looked to see if any other dragons were nearby. Scott walked out from under Malmoths wing. "If I could have saved your sister's life, I would have."

Chinzar roared and Scott jumped back under Malmoth's wing. "Not so tough anymore, are you, without your sword?" Chinzar growled.

"That sword belongs to me," Scott blurted out without thinking.

Chinzar roared again and began to stamp his feet. "Move out of the way, Malmoth. Friend or not, he will pay for his insolence."

"Scott, you and your brother stand on my feet and hold on to my legs," Malmoth whispered a direct thought to Scott so the others couldn't hear. Scott relayed the message to Eric while she continued to try and reason with the angry dragon. "Chinzar, he's not a dragon, he doesn't know our customs. He doesn't know what he's saying."

"Quit defending him and get out of the way."

"Chinzar, this is not a fair fight. Had another dragon made that comment, I would gladly stay out of the way, but he's Lumen."

"I don't care. He's insulted my dignity. Now move!" he roared.

"All right. I'll move," she agreed. "But this isn't right." Then, with Scott and Eric holding tightly to her legs, she leapt into the air and shot skyward. Chinzar roared and looked around for Scott and Eric. It didn't take him long to discover he'd been tricked. He leapt into the air and launched skyward like a rocket. Darmke and Chaltor followed, close on his heels. As Chinzar broke above the trees he looked around to find Malmoth. She was heading east towards the Clifaron hills, where there were several cliffs and tunnels to hide in.

"Malmoth!" Chinzar yelled for all to hear. "If you don't hand them over now, you too, will insult my dignity. I will be forced to kill you also."

"Maybe you should do as he says," Scott suggested, hearing what Chinzar had said.

"No, they're just threats," Malmoth assured him.

"You don't know that for sure."

"No. But I still think he's bluffing. A tactic to get me to stop."

"Maybe. But he seems to be gaining on us," Scott noticed, a little worried. "Can you fly any faster?"

"I am flying as fast as I can. Chinzar is much stronger than I am. We must get to the Clifaron hills before he catches us. There we have a chance of hiding from him or finding a place small enough where he can't follow you."

"Are they close by?" Scott asked.

"About twenty-five winglots," Malmoth replied.

"What's a winglot?"

"A winglot is a hundred wingflaps."

"So we're twenty five hundred wingflaps away?" Scott asked.

"Approximately."

"I don't think we're going to make it," Scott said, worried.

"Chinzar may be faster than I am, but I can easily out maneuver him. If it comes down to that," she warned, "you and your brother will need to hold on really tight."

"Sure thing," Scott replied.

"What's going on?" Eric asked.

"It seems that Chinzar, that dragon chasing us, still has a grudge against me and would like to see me dead."

Eric stared at him with disbelieving eyes. "You mean to say that dragon back there, that's rapidly approaching I might add, means to fry us?"

"That's right. Malmoth is doing what she can to keep us safe. It may come down to a dogfight, so hold on really tight just in case she makes any tight turns."

"Why is he so mad?" Eric asked.

"I guess I insulted his dignity."

"You insulted a giant fire breathing lizard?" Eric yelled. "Are you out of your mind?"

"I didn't mean to," Scott said, defending himself. "I simply told him the sword belonged to me and he got all upset and huffy."

"Well, tell him you're sorry," Eric said. "tell him he can have the sword. Tell him it belongs to him. Tell him anything to get him off our backs."

"But the sword doesn't belong to him. It belongs to me," Scott argued.

"The sword doesn't belong to you any more than it does to him. Besides, it won't do you any good if you're dead."

"Yes, but I… Whoa!" Scott yelled as Malmoth suddenly made a sharp right turn and bolted downward. In his conversation, Scott had relaxed his grip slightly and slipped a little. He was now desperately trying to climb back up. Chinzar had closed in while they were talking and was close enough to singe them with his fire if he chose to. Malmoth wasn't taking any chances and was now doing everything she could to avoid him. Chinzar followed her move and Malmoth counter moved by darting to the left and then upward. Scott and Eric almost lost their grip again and the sudden movements were starting to give Eric motion sickness. Malmoth quickly straightened out into a horizontal flight pattern. They both took this moment to wrap their legs around hers and tighten their grip.

A blast of hot air quickly brought their attention back to Chinzar, who was now shooting flames in their direction. If someone had been watching from the ground, it would have been quite a sight. The two dragons darted back and forth and up and down, the whole time Chinzar doing his best to roast the two boys like marshmallows on a stick. To make matters worse, Malmoth appeared to be tiring. She wasn't moving as fast as before and Chinzar's blasts were getting closer and closer.

"Are you okay, Malmoth?" Scott asked.

"For now, yes," she answered. "But I don't know how much longer I can keep this up. We may have to make a landing sooner than I had hoped. Maybe we can find a spot where you and your brother can find cover."

Scott scanned the area below looking for a possible hiding place. Spying one, he said, "Below to the right is a mountain with lots of trees. Let us down there and we'll make a run for it."

"Okay, but run in the opposite direction I fly. I'll try and make him believe we are all still traveling together."

"Thanks, Malmoth. You're the best."

Scott explained the plan to Eric as Malmoth made a sharp downward turn and shot for the ground. She aimed for a section of trees just barely wide enough for her to fit, and hopefully too small for Chinzar, who was much larger. Malmoth landed with a thud and both Eric and Scott fell to the ground from the impact. They quickly scrambled to their feet, and as they did, Scott could see Chinzar diving towards them.

"Malmoth!" Scott yelled. "Chinzar's coming in fast. Get out of here!" Malmoth tipped her head to look. There wasn't time for goodbyes. Scott and Eric ran into the forest and Malmoth shot forward and out of the trees, while Chinzar came crashing to the ground. Scott could hear several branching breaking from the impact of Chinzar's large body. Malmoth escaped just in time, and Eric and Scott were only thirty yards away when they heard Chinzar's horrible roar, followed by flames that licked at their heels. The fire didn't actually touch them, but they felt the heat and knew they had just barely escaped. Chinzar tried to chase after them, but only managed to get himself tangled in the thick forest. The two boys ran for about fifteen minutes when Eric stopped Scott.

"Scott, this is crazy. From the air he'll eventually spot us. We should climb one of these trees and just sit for as long as it takes. Eventually he'll give up and go home."

"Good idea," Scott agreed.

They found a large tree with plenty of cover, climbed up and settled in. Every now and again they would see the looming shape of Chinzar fly overhead. The large dragon had made his way back into the air, keeping a lookout for his prey. Thankfully, the boys noticed, it was just Chinzar. Malmoth and the other dragons weren't with him and Scott hoped that meant she was okay. Meanwhile, Eric peered into Josh's backpack and found a few cartons of pudding and several rolls. Realizing they were hungry, they broke them out and ate.

After several hours they decided it was safe to leave. However, just to be on the safe side, Scott climbed to the top of the tree to check things out. Scott was amazed to see Chinzar out in the distance still searching. They stayed put for several more hours, after which, Scott climbed to the top again. Chinzar was still out there searching for them. It wasn't until almost dusk that Chinzar finally gave up and left.

Eric and Scott climbed out of the tree. "Now what?" Scott asked.

"We have to find out where we are and then find a way to get to Josh, Ned and Azinine," Eric answered.

"While I was up there, I saw see a column of smoke rising out of the trees a couple of miles from here. Maybe someone there can help us," Scott suggested.

"Good idea. At the very least, they should be able to tell us where we are."

They walked for several hours as the moon rose into the sky. Using just the sun and the moon and Scott's sense of direction, they traveled in the direction of what they hoped would lead them to someone who could help them. After what seemed like an eternity, they came upon a house nestled at the foot of the mountain.

Chapter 22

Reunion

Azinine sat in her room feeling very glum. It wouldn't be long before Maulder returned from speaking with Magus Noka. He would know she had lied to him. On the other hand, she reasoned, maybe Magus Noka would realize she was in trouble and would come to her aid. As she sat on her bed, a knock came at her door.

"Enter," she spoke softly. Soon the knock came again. "Enter," she spoke a little louder, but still no one entered. Once more the knock sounded. "Enter!" she screamed. The door opened and in walked Sheldine.

"Well, that's a fine way to treat someone who's come to bring you good news," Sheldine said as she walked into the room.

Immediately contrite, Azinine apologized. "Sorry, but you must not have heard me the first two times."

"It's okay," Sheldine replied and she quickly walked over to Azinine with a big grin on her face. "Guess who's down in the garden house right now?"

"The prince of my dreams?" Azinine said, making a face.

"How did you know?"

"Give me a break, Sheldine. Maulder will be home tomorrow and he's going to know I lied to him."

"Well, that is an ugly thought," Sheldine agreed. "But I was serious about your prince."

Azinine's eyes grew wide. "Are you talking about a blonde haired, brown eyed, smile that would slay any girls heart, young man?"

"Yes! At least I think so," Sheldine said triumphantly. Then she added, "Although, I'm pretty sure his eyes are blue."

"Is Scott really down there?" Azinine asked, still not believing it.

"No," Sheldine paused, a little confused now. "I'm sure he said his name was Josh."

"Is Ned with him?" Azinine continued, not caring who it was, as long as it was a friend.

"Yes, he's also down there. I can get them a message if you'd like."

"I want to talk to them myself."

"You can't. If you're caught, you'll be punished."

"I'll just have to take my chances."

"Azinine," Sheldine warned, "I can't cover for you if you get caught."

"I know," Azinine said, grateful for the compassion this woman had given her. "You just go to bed. That way you'll have no involvement."

"Please be careful," Sheldine begged. "You certainly don't want to get caught."

"I'll be careful," Azinine promised. "Thank you for the warning."

Sheldine left and Azinine immediately began plotting how she could get out. She waited for an hour to let the house settle down. She knew there'd be several guards to get past, but she wasn't too worried about that, at least getting out. Getting back in might be a bigger problem. When she was ready, she opened the door and walked out. At the end of the hall was the first guard, just as she expected.

"Hello, Azinine. What do you need?" the guard asked.

"I need a drink," she replied. "I'm really thirsty."

"Go back to your room and I'll bring you one."

"Oh, thank you. You're so nice to me," she replied and gave him a hug. With a simple sleep spell, the guard immediately fell into a deep sleep. She would have preferred to use a stone spell so there would be less risk of the guard waking up before she got back to her room, but then the guard would know what she had done. This way she hoped it would simply look like he fell asleep and had dreamed the whole thing. She leaned him up against the wall and continued down the stairs. She expected another guard at the bottom of the stairs, but to her relief, no one was there. She headed down another hall, past the main dining room and towards the back door. Unfortunately, there was a guard at the back door who spotted her.

Thinking quickly, she ran towards him. "Help! Help!" she called out. "Something has happened."

"I can't leave this post," the man said. Looking around he asked, "Where are the other guards?"

"I don't know," she exclaimed. By this time she had reached him and had grabbed his hand. He tried to jerk it away, but was too late. He too became very tired, and now lay in a deep slumber. He fell back in his seat and she propped him against the wall to make it look like he was still dutifully at his post. With that, she opened the door and slipped out.

Josh and Ned had just covered the glowing lumenarty rock used to light their room and climbed into bed when they heard the door squeak open. They both looked towards the door, not saying a word. A figure slipped in and closed it again.

"Ned?" They heard a voice whisper. "Josh? Are you there?"

"Azinine? Is that you?" Ned called out.

"Yes! Oh, I'm so glad you guys are okay," she cried. "Where are you? It's so dark I can't see a thing."

"We're over here," Ned replied. Azinine walked in the direction of the voice. She stumbled on something, but caught herself before she made too much noise.

"Over here," a voice whispered, trying to give her some direction. She made her way closer and finally found Ned's hand. She gave him a big hug. "I was so worried about you!"

"I was worried about you too." The voice was not Ned's, but Josh's.

"Josh, you little stinker," she laughed, playfully slugging his chest. "I thought you were Ned."

"You mean you weren't worried about me?"

"Of course I was worried about you, but I thought you were Ned."

"I could tell," Josh went on. "That was a pretty pathetic hug for a girl to give her boyfriend."

"You're still a dreamer, Josh. But you are right, it was a pretty pathetic hug." She grabbed him in her arms and gave him a big bear hug.

"Now that's more like it!" he said.

"Now, where's my brother?"

"I'm over here." Ned reached out and grabbed her arm. She gave him a hug and sat down on his bed. They told her about their experience and she told them about Maulder and her predicament.

"We've got to find a way out of here tonight while we're all together," she told both of them.

"Yes, but how?" Ned asked.

"Let's just make a run for it now. If we get far enough away, maybe the shackles won't work?" Josh suggested. "They have horses in the stables, perhaps we could use those to make our escape."

"All they have to do is use their crystal balls, and they'll find us. They may not be able to view us, but I'm guessing they've spell rigged it so they can view all their shackles and that means all their prisoners," Ned said in response.

"I'm sure you're right," mused Azinine. "I've tried everything I can think of, but I just can't see a way out of this."

"Couldn't we find a tool and break these shackles off?" Josh asked.

"Of course," she said. "But as soon as you tried, it would go off, and I doubt you'd like that. Besides, if we actually managed to break it off, it would also set off an alarm."

"If we used the horses, we might get far enough away that the alarm wouldn't go off and we could break these shackles without them hurting us," Josh suggested.

"It would take them thirty minutes on a MOC to cover what it would take us all night on a horse, especially at night. It might work, but it would be very risky."

"Well, we can't stay here," Josh said in frustration. "We have to try. I'd rather chance it than stay here any longer."

"Me too," Azininc replied.

"What if we..." but Josh couldn't finish because Azinine quickly cupped her hand around his mouth.

"Shhh, someone's outside."

The door opened and in walked Sheldine. "Azinine?" she whispered trying to discern if she was in there.

"Sheldine?" Azinine replied. "What are you doing out here?"

"I came to warn you. The guards know you're gone. You've got to find a way back to your room without them seeing you."

"Thank you for the warning. Please leave now, so you don't get caught," Azinine said. Sheldine didn't say another word, but walked out. Moments later, she rushed back into the small dwelling.

"Sorry," she exclaimed in a frightened voice, "but there's something out there."

Eric and Scott made their way down the hill. The moon was out, but with all the trees, it was still difficult to see. It took them another thirty minutes to get to the bottom of the hill, but they finally made it.

"Who do you suppose lives here?" Scott asked.

"I have no idea," his brother answered. "But at this point, I don't see that we have a choice. Besides, I'm starving and maybe they have some food they could spare. Let's go knock."

"I'm not sure that's a good idea," cautioned Scott. "We don't know who they are. For all we know, that could be Lardior's home."

"Hmm. You could be right," Eric agreed. "Maybe we should look around a bit." They sneaked up to the house and peered into one of the windows. Inside was a lady folding linen. "She looks harmless enough," Eric whispered.

"Yeah, but she looks like a servant, not the owner," Scott argued. They walked around the house and peered into another window. A man with a spear sat on a stool talking with another man, who also carried a spear.

"They look like guards," Scott said.

"Yeah, I don't think we want to approach them."

As they continued around the area, they came upon a smaller dwelling that looked like it might be for storage.

"What do you think is in there?" Scott asked.

"Hmm, I don't know," Eric shrugged. "But it might be worth a look."

"Agreed, but let's be careful. It might be full of guard dogs or something."

"I think you're paranoid."

"Of course I'm paranoid! We have no idea what this place is. And if it has guards, don't you think there is a strong possibility that it also has guard dogs?"

Just then the door from the smaller house opened and out walked a figure, probably a lady, from what little they could see. Scott and Eric darted behind a large bush causing it to rustle a bit. The figure froze and stared. Eric and Scott held their breath, not making a move. The figure slowly crept forward trying to get a better look, but still kept her distance. She stopped again, searching the area.

"'Who's there?" she whispered. Scott and Eric looked at each other not knowing what to do.

Finally, Scott did the first thing that came to his mind. "Grrrr!" he growled. She let out a tiny scream and then quickly cupped her hand over her mouth to silence herself. She turned back around and flung open the door she had just emerged from and quickly ran back inside. From behind the bushes, the two boys could hear whispering going on inside, but couldn't make out what was being said.

"Why are they whispering?" wondered Scott. "It's like they're afraid *we'll* hear *them*."

"Most likely they're afraid someone else will hear them."

"What do you mean?"

"When the lady called out, 'who's there,' she did it in a whisper. She obviously didn't want to bring any attention to herself. Yet she wanted to know who or what was there. There's something else going on here we aren't seeing."

"Yes, but…" Scott was cut off by a loud gruff voice.

"Who goes there?" a man yelled.

"There's your answer," Scott whispered.

"Be very still," Eric warned. "We definitely don't want those guards finding us."

By now, four other men had joined the first one and they headed over to the small house, each one holding a lamp in one hand and a spear in the other. They opened the door and stepped inside, leaving the door open. "What's going on in here?" a man growled.

"Nothing! I just thought I felt a spider on me," Josh replied.

"Ha!" the man laughed. "Out here you'll probably feel more than just spiders."

"Sorry for the screaming," he apologized. "I just hate those little beasts."

"That sounds like Josh," Scott said, turning in amazement to Eric.

"It does kind of. Do you think it's him?" Before Scott could answer, the guard began to speak again.

"Have you seen a young girl out here? She's missing from her room."

"Nope," came the answer. "No one else in here, except us and the spiders."

"If you happen to see her, bring her to us," the guard commanded. The guards took a quick look around, but failed to see the figures hiding under the beds. "In the meantime, keep it down in here." Turning to one of the other guards, he ordered, "Let's go! We'll have to use the crystal ball to find her." The guards left and walked away.

"We've got to find out if that's Josh," Scott said after the guards were gone.

"I agree," Eric replied. "Let's go."

They crept up to the house. They were just about to open the door, when it suddenly opened and Eric and Scott came face to face with two other figures. One of the figures let out a startled cry while the smaller one lunged towards the boys, grabbing them both around the neck while muttering a spell. Eric immediately went stiff as a rock. The stone spell had no impact on Scott, who was still wearing the bodysuit. He grabbed the figure and tossed her effortlessly to the ground.

"Az...?" Scott started to ask as two other figures exited the small dwelling. One of them kicked Scott in the gut and pushed him onto the ground. Another figure jumped on top of him and was about to pummel him.

"Josh, stop!" Scott whispered loudly.

Josh pulled back. "Scott? Is that you?" he asked in amazement.

"Scott!" Azinine squealed, picking herself up off the ground from where Scott had tossed her. She threw herself towards him, knocking Josh over. "How in the world did you guys find us?" she asked.

"We didn't. Well, we did...but not really," Scott sheepishly replied. "We just sort of stumbled across you. How did you know it was me?"

"Because my spell didn't work on you," Azinine answered with a grin. "That's the second time it hasn't. And why is that?"

Scott shrugged. "I'm not completely sure why it doesn't work," he answered, thinking back to when the lady who had given him the bodysuit had warned him to tell no one about it.

"But you have an idea, right?" she questioned, noticing his evasive answer.

"Well, yes. But I'll have to explain later."

"Scott's right," Ned interrupted. "We've got a bigger problem on our hands and we don't have much time."

"What's the problem?" Scott asked.

Ned, with a few interjections here and there from Josh and Azinine, explained where they were and the predicament, they were in.

"So you see," he finished, "we've got to find a way out of here. The problem is we're not sure how."

"I've got a great plan," Scott answered.

"Really?" the others said in unison.

"Sure," he replied with confidence. "We tell the guard we saw Azinine run into the forest. We volunteer to help him find her. Once we get out a ways, we whack him, take the MOC and go."

"What about our shackles," Ned pointed out.

"Shackles?" Scott questioned innocently.

"Yes, shackles. You know, these metal things wrapped around our arms aren't for decoration," Ned said sarcastically.

"Oh, those! No problem. I can take care of them," Scott replied. "Come here."

"This isn't the time for jokes," Ned said.

"Wow! Aren't we a little grouchy today?" Scott spat back.

"I'm sorry," Ned said softly. "I'm just so sick of all the crap we've been through lately. I think the stress of it all is really getting to me."

"Yeah, I think it's getting to all of us. But in regards to the shackles, I wasn't joking," Scott said in earnest. "Come here and I'll prove it."

"Scott, I hope you know what you're doing," Ned warned.

"Don't worry," he said trying to calm Ned's fears.

Ned walked over to Scott. Scott reached up, touched the shackle and it fell to the ground.

Ned jumped back as the shackle fell off his arm. "Whoa!" he cried out. "That is freaky. How did you do that?"

"It's…a…gift I have," Scott finally said not knowing how to explain.

"A gift, huh?" Azinine questioned with raised eyebrows. "Besides being lingual, are you now going to tell us you're also immune to magic?"

"Immune to magic?" Scott repeated, not sure what she was getting at.

"Yes. For starters, none of my spells have worked on you. And now you're able to release shackles with the touch of a hand. I've never heard of *anyone* who can do that, Scott. What is going on?"

"Can we talk about this later?" Scott asked, trying to avoid the question.

"Scott, we're you're friends. Why can't you tell us now?" Ned asked.

"Because we don't have the time *and* I promised not to tell."

"Promised who?" Azinine asked.

Scott gave out an exasperated sigh. "Can we please drop this? Isn't it enough that I can do it? We've got to get out of here. I promise, when the time is right, I'll tell you."

Azinine took a deep breath. "Oh, all right," she relented.

"If you're done arguing, could you please release me?" a voice in the darkness called out.

"Josh!" Scott called out. "You're okay! I was worried about you."

"Why would you worry? I'm Hercules, remember?"

"Sure," Scott said with a grin. "But those gloves aren't all-powerful."

"Right. I learned that the hard way. But apparently you are. So would the all-powerful Scott Frontier please release my shackle?"

"I guess I could lower myself to help the common folk," Scott joked. He finished releasing everybody, including Sheldine, who had been standing just inside the door.

"Well, what are we waiting for? Let's grab a guard and get out of here," Ned said, anxious to get away from the place.

"We can't just leave," Scott replied. "What Maulder is doing here is wrong. We've got to find a way to stop this operation."

"Like what?" Ned asked incredulously.

"Well, we'll just have to go in there and kick some butt and release everyone."

"What do you mean, 'kick some butt?'" Ned asked cautiously.

"Just that. We have a witch, three guys trained in hand to hand combat and one miniature Hercules."

"I heard that," Josh said. Then pointing at Eric, he continued, "By the way, your best hand to hand combat dude isn't going to do anything unless you fix him."

"Oh, I forgot about him," Azinine gasped. She went over to Eric and reversed the spell.

"Uggh!" Eric cried out. "I really, really hate that spell."

"Scott," Ned continued to plead with his friend over the insanity of his plan. "We are outnumbered at least three to one."

"Have you learned nothing?" Scott asked. "We have the element of surprise and surprise them we will."

Ned groaned. "Why do I get the feeling I'm going to regret this?"

"Actually," Sheldine said, entering the conversation, "Maulder took several guards with him, so there aren't as many as there usually are."

"Even better," Scott said. Then turning to Azinine, ready to put his plan into action, he asked, "Can you create an illusion that will make it look like you still have your shackles on?"

"Yes."

Chapter 23

Freedom

Scott explained his plan. Once everyone understood, the group followed him to the back door where Ned and Josh knocked and the others hid by the MOCs.

The guard opened the door. "Sir," Ned began, "we just saw the young girl take a horse and head into the woods. If you want to take us with you on a MOC, I'm sure we could find her quite quickly."

"That would explain why the crystal ball still shows she's here. Good work," the guard replied. He blew a whistle and other guards came running. The door guard explained the situation and three guards immediately rushed over to the MOCs. Each guard took a separate MOC and Josh and Ned climbed on board the first guard's MOC. With everyone ready, the group took off.

"Which way did you say she went?" a guard yelled over to Ned.

"I believe that way," Ned said, pointing in a direction.

"That's funny," the guard hesitated, looking into a crystal ball. "I'm show-ing she's still back at the manor."

"Maybe it takes a little time to register?" the other guard suggested.

"Or maybe she only pretended to leave. You know, to trick everyone," Ned suggested.

The guard moved the MOC in several directions, but the crystal ball kept pointing back to the manor. He pulled up next to the other guards. "It shows she hasn't left. She might still be down there so I'm going to set back down and check it out. You two continue searching the area just in case this thing isn't working."

The other two guards nodded and swung away. The first guard set his MOC back down, but before he had a chance to lock it, Josh knocked him on the head with a rock. Josh and Ned each grabbed one of his arms and dragged him through the grass. Halfway there, they ran into another guard. They were just about to attack him when they realized it was Scott dressed like one. It was a little baggy on him, but it fit well enough.

"How did you get that uniform?" Josh asked.

"Courtesy of the door guard."

"Where's the door guard?"

"He's in the garden house waiting for this guy to join him," Scott said, pointing to the man they were dragging.

Once they had placed the second guard in the garden house, the five of them returned to the big house. As they entered, two other guards were waiting for them.

Scott grabbed Azinine by the arm. "I found her," he said gruffly. "Here she is."

"That was quick," one of the guards stated.

"How come her shackle isn't working?" another guard asked who was trying unsuccessfully to shock her.

"Hey! Who are you?" the first guard asked, just now realizing that he didn't recognize Scott's face. "You're not Akbar! Where's Akbar?"

"No," Scott answered. "He's taking a little rest. Perhaps you'd like to join him?"

"What…what's going on here?" the second guard asked, forgetting about Azinine's shackle for the moment. By this time, Josh, Ned and Eric had circled them and the guards began to get nervous. Azinine approached the first one, grabbed his arm and uttered a spell. The guard froze immediately. The second guard tried to back off and call for help, but Josh grabbed him while Azinine quickly took care of him too. They hauled the two guards out to the guesthouse and placed them next to the two that were already there.

"Well, four down," Scott said brushing his hands off. "Let's get the others," he continued as though it were one of his daily chores. "Ned and Josh, you wait here in case the other guards come back from searching for Azinine. The three of us will go find the others."

"Fine by me," Ned replied.

Eric, Scott and Azinine continued further into the house. They decided it would be best to free the other slaves as soon as possible, fearing the slaves might suffer repercussions for their actions. They found the guard at the top of the stairs still sleeping. Azinine reinforced her spell, making sure he stayed asleep, and they continued to the top of the stairs and down the hallway where they found the rest of the slaves. Sheldine had gone inside before all this commotion had happened and warned them. They were all gathered in Sheldine's quarters by the time Scott and the others found them. He quickly released each of their shackles and urged them to leave immediately. On their way back outside, Scott and Eric grabbed the sleeping guard and hauled him out with them.

"Sheldine," Azinine asked, "where are all the other guards?"

"Except for the two on the MOC's, I think that's it. As I mentioned earlier, all the others accompanied Maulder. If you didn't see any other guards, then my guess is the only other person left inside is Thine."

Azinine hit her forehead. "Thine!" she exclaimed. "I completely forgot about him."

"Who's Thine?" Scott asked.

"From what I can tell, he's Maulder's right hand man."

"We better get him out of here too."

Azinine and Scott walked back inside and headed over to Thine's quarters. They opened the door and walked inside.

"What do you think you're doing?" Thine bellowed as he jumped up from the chair he had been reclining in. "You're not supposed to be in here. Guard!" he yelled, addressing Scott, who was still wearing the uniform. "Take her out of here and don't bring her back unless I ask for her."

"Thine," Azinine said quietly, ignoring his outburst. "I'm going to have to ask you to leave. We're going to burn this place down."

The look on Thine's face was so incredulous that she almost burst out laughing

"What are you talking about, young lady? You will pay for your insolence," the big man replied vehemently. "Guard!" he yelled again. "Take her out of here and show her what happens to disobedient slaves."

"I'm afraid she's right," Scott said. "If you don't come with us, we'll be forced to burn this place with you inside."

Thine looked at Scott in disbelief. Then a look of comprehension crossed his face. "You're not one of my guards! Who are you?"

"Just a friend who helped release the slaves and capture the guards."

Thine's face went bleak at the thought. "Guard!" he yelled even louder, hoping one of the real guards would hear him.

"Haven't you been listening to what we've been telling you, Thine?" Azinine asked. "There are no guards. You can yell as loud as you want, but no one is coming."

Regaining his composure, Thine stood and walked out of the room. But instead of heading outside, he walked toward a closet where he opened the door and pulled out a sending bracelet. As he put it on his own arm, he smiled an evil grin. "Now you'll see who's going to burn," he snarled. He tried to use the bracelet to shock her, but nothing happened. Again and again he tried, but still nothing happened. "Why isn't this working?" he muttered to himself.

"It's not working because the shackle around my arm is really just an illusion," Azinine patiently replied.

"I don't believe it."

"I'll prove it to you. Watch. Now you see it," she pointed to the shackle and muttered the illusion spell. "Now you don't," she continued as the shackle disappeared.

"You're a witch!" he cried out.

"Surprise!" she said light heartedly. "Now, we're going to leave. You have until the flames start licking the soles of your feet to get out."

Azinine and Scott turned and headed for the exit. As they stepped outside they found two additional MOCs sitting by the first one. Josh and Eric were just returning from the direction of the garden house where Azinine and Scott assumed they had locked the last two guards. They, and the other slaves, had also stacked wood around most of the manor. Azinine picked up a stick, muttered a word and the stick broke out in flames.

"It's a shame to destroy such a beautiful home," Azinine said wistfully. "But we can't let this man continue to enslave people like this. I don't see any other way to stop him." The others nodded and she lit the fuel. The flames immediately jumped and the house began to burn. It didn't take long for Thine to join them outside. He didn't say anything at first, just watched the flames in disbelief as they got higher and higher.

"You will pay for this!" Thine finally yelled. "When Maulder finds out, he will hunt you down and you will all die a slow death!" He didn't have a weapon, so the kids didn't really fear anything from him, but they knew he was right. If Maulder ever caught them again, it wouldn't be pretty.

"Sorry, but it had to be done," Azinine replied.

Thine was now shaking his head back and forth, fear registering on his face. "Maulder will kill me when he gets back. He's going to literally kill me," he said out loud, more to himself than to the kids.

Azinine felt pity for the man. She knew he was right. Maulder really would kill him. "The other slaves are taking the MOCs," Azinine pointed out. "I'm sure I could convince them to take you with them and drop you off somewhere."

"I don't have anywhere else to go."

"Suit yourself." Azinine stood up, knowing she had done her best. "We've got to go."

"Where are you going?" Thine asked.

"To free the other slaves at the quarry. We don't want Maulder having any resources to rebuild his little paradise, now do we?"

"You better hope he never finds you," Thine warned again. "Because if he does, he'll show no mercy."

Azinine cocked her head to the side a little and in an innocent voice said, "And how do you suppose he's going to find out? Certainly you're not going to stick around and tell him, are you?" He didn't answer her this time, but turned his head and looked down at the ground.

The slaves at the house thanked the group, loaded onto two of the MOCs and flew away. The group of friends took the third MOC and flew towards the quarry. While Azinine flew the MOC, the others planned what they would do when they arrived. It took them most of the night, mostly because it was dark and they didn't exactly know the way. Through the process of trial and error, they finally found it, but by this time it was almost morning. The five of them climbed off the MOC and stretched a bit. Josh quickly donned the guard uniform that Scott had been wearing, including a sending bracelet he had taken from one of the sleeping guards. The uniform was way too big for him, but it was all they had.

They located the quarters where the cooks and the local guards slept. Surprisingly, all the guards were asleep. "Maulder would have their hides if he knew no one was watching the place," Ned remarked.

"Good for us, bad for them," Azinine said. She walked over and lightly touched each guard as she spoke the stone spell. She wanted to make sure none of them gave the group any trouble while they were there.

The cooks however, were awakened and were asked, or rather commanded, to start breakfast. While breakfast was being prepared, Ned and Josh went looking for their own clothes they had left behind when they were taken to Maulder's house. Ned changed into his, but Josh opted to keep the uniform on, and placed his own clothing on the MOC.

Once breakfast was ready, Josh was itching to get started on his part. "I'm going inside," he said.

"Josh," Ned cautioned, "don't get carried away. Remember, we do plan on releasing them, and when we do you won't have that bracelet to protect you."

"Don't worry, Scott and I already have that worked out," the youngest Frontier said.

"Yeah, that's what I'm afraid of," Ned replied.

"You worry too much," Josh remarked as he turned and walked inside. He grabbed a whistle hanging on the wall and blew it as hard as he could. He hadn't yet removed the covers from the lumenarty rocks, but he could hear the men jumping out of bed and standing to attention. Once they were all standing, he removed the covers, and the room lit up. The men stared at him, trying unsuccessfully not to laugh. Soon the room was full of snickers, including those of Tito. The men had expected one of the regular guards, but instead there stood a midget guard wearing clothes twice his size. Josh walked over to Tito and stood in front of him.

"Is there something funny?" he yelled as authoritatively as he could.

"No, sir!" Tito replied, not recognizing Josh, who was wearing a hat.

"What was that you said?"

"No, sir!" Tito yelled louder. "Nothing funny, sir!"

Josh turned to walk to the next slave. As he did, he stepped on his pant leg, pulling his pants off his waist. He tripped on them and fell to the floor. This was more than the slaves could handle and they all burst out in laughter. Josh jumped up as quickly as he could, pulled up his pants and turned back to Tito.

"You think that's funny?" he yelled.

"No..." he chortled a bit trying to get the words out. "No, sir. I..." he broke out into laughter again. Taking a deep breath, and doing his best to get his composure, he was finally able to get out, "No sir!"

Josh stared at him for a moment and then took off his hat. Tito and the rest of the slaves suddenly became very somber as they recognized who it was. They stared at him in disbelief.

"Well," Josh began, "I thought it was pretty funny," and began to laugh himself. The other slaves looked at each not knowing what to think. After Josh finished laughing, he looked at each one of them before speaking. "Today we're going to do something a little different," he barked out. He turned to Tito who was still in shock and a little worried. "Do you happen to know what that is, Tito?"

"No, sir," was all he could say.

"Outside these barracks, the cooks have food and water prepared for each of you. In a few minutes we're all going outside. Each of you will pick up as much food and water as you can carry. I will then release each of you from those nasty shackles. Once released, each of you are to run as fast as your legs can carry you away from this place. Do not, I repeat, DO NOT let Maulder catch you again. That's an order. All right, let's go." He turned and walked towards the door. He could hear the others whispering to each other, but no one moved.

"If you want to remain a slave, then be my guest and stay here. If you want freedom, then let's get going, I don't know how much time we have before Maulder returns and finds his house burned to the ground." They still hesitated until Tito grabbed a blanket off his bed and headed for the door. Outside, the cooks were waiting for them with sacks of food and flasks of water, just as Josh had told them. Eric and the others were already aboard the MOC. Josh walked over and climbed aboard. Azinine raised the MOC about fifteen feet into the air and then stopped. Josh waited until all the slaves had picked up their stuff before he spoke.

"I wish we could take you with us, but we don't have room. I hope you all find your way safely." With that said, he used the sender to release their shackles, which fell from each slave to the ground. The slaves cheered as Josh and the group rose higher into the air and disappeared.

Chapter 24

The Pyramids of Death

Their misadventure behind them, they flew directly to the pyramids, which took them a good part of the day. In the valley of a small mountain range stood four pyramids, each with a different colored point, rising high into the sky. Azinine set the MOC down between the two closest and everyone jumped off. The air was stifling hot and it was unusually quiet.

"These things are huge," Scott commented.

"Yes and twice as treacherous," Azinine replied.

"So, the book is in the pyramid with the black point, right?" Josh asked.

"That's my understanding," Azinine said. "But there's no door into it, or any of the others for that matter, except this one with the white tip, on our left. From what I've heard, you have to enter this pyramid and make your way through the others until you come to the pyramid with the black tip."

Ned now jumped in, "According to our school teacher, each pyramid requires a test, which if not passed, will turn deadly. If you pass the test, you get to move on to the next pyramid."

"Yeah, and if you don't pass, you don't get to move at all, forever," Josh said butting in.

"So, how do we proceed?" Azinine asked. Nobody answered. In fact, none of them wanted to proceed at all. The enormity of the task was beginning to dawn on them. It was practically a suicide mission. But they weren't about to turn back now. They had all worked so hard to get here, and it was the only way they could free their parents.

"I don't think we should all go in," Scott finally said. "We need some to stay out here in case those of us inside can't find our way out. Maybe those outside can find a way to get the others out."

"Well, we don't know what we will encounter inside, but Scott and Josh are lingual, and that's got to help," Ned said, trying push the responsibility to someone else besides him.

"There's also bound to be lots of spells or magic in there, and since Scott is exempt from spells, I vote he goes," Josh suggested. No one said anything, but they all turned to Scott to see what he had to say about it.

"Me?" Scott gulped, pointing to himself.

"He makes a good point," Eric said.

"But…but…I…I." Scott paused a moment and then finally let out a nervous breath. "Fine, I guess I am the best one to do this. Josh, give me your radios and camera."

"Whew! I'm sure glad I'm not the one going in there," Josh said with relief.

"I'm going with you," Eric said to Scott. "Two will be better than one."

"No way!" Scott replied. "I need you to find a way to get me out in case I can't find my own way out." Scott paused and then said quietly, "Besides, no use both of us dying."

"Do you really think you're going to die?" Josh asked.

"The statistics aren't exactly in my favor," Scott replied. "But what choice do we have?"

"That's true. But as we already mentioned, you'll have things going for you that the others who tried before you didn't."

"I guess," Scott replied.

"For instance," Josh continued, "you'll have the strength of ten men." Josh took off the gloves and handed them to Scott.

"Thanks," Scott replied with a wry grin.

The others in the group could tell he was still very nervous. "You can talk to any creatures you may encounter and you can read any of the ancient writings that may be inside," Azinine added.

"I hope so," Scott said with beads of sweat now forming on his forehead.

Josh pulled out the two-way radios. "You'll be able to communicate with us if you need help, and," he put his hand back in his pack and pulled out a flashlight, "you'll have light if you need it."

"And, as Josh has already pointed out," Azinine said again with emphasis, "for some unknown reason, which you refuse to tell your friends, "She said this with some spite, "you're not susceptible to spells. There are bound to be plenty of those inside."

"Hmm, that makes me feel a whole lot better," Scott said with a shake of his head. Knowing that his friends were just trying to help, he took a deep breath and said, "Thanks for trying to comfort me, but somehow I still think this isn't going to be easy."

"Oh, we didn't say it was going to be easy," Josh commented. "We're just inferring that your chances of success are better than all those who have tried before you, but never returned."

"Thanks, little brother. You sure know how to make a guy feel better."

Eric put his hand on his shoulder. "We'll be there for you. You're not alone."

Scott nodded and then asked, "Josh, what about your video equipment? Where's that?"

"Lardior's men must have taken it because it's not in my bag."

"Well, we'll just have to do without video then." Scott put the gloves on his hands and the radio in his pocket. With the flashlight in hand, he and the group walked toward the pyramid with the white tip.

Approaching the massive structure, they looked for a door, but to no avail. What they did find, however, were the words, 'nit forsikt ouf' written on the outside wall. Azinine studied the words carefully. "I can't read it," she declared. "It's written in the ancient tongue, I think."

"Enter with caution," Scott read.

Azinine smiled. "That is so cool you can read that."

"So how do we get in?" Ned asked.

"Well, you guys say 'af' in Lumen to open your doors. The same word in the ancient tongue for open is 'Ouf'," Scott replied.

No sooner had he spoken, than a section of the pyramid wall crumbled to the ground revealing a tunnel leading inside.

"Sweet," Josh breathed while he entered the pyramid.

"Ahh!" Azinine screamed and everyone froze, except Josh who kept on walking. Just inside the doorway about five feet away was a skeleton of someone who obviously didn't make it out. The others stood there looking at it.

"From the looks of it, he was a magus or a warlock. His staff is still resting against the wall," Ned said, pointing it out.

"I wonder who it was?" Josh said as he bent down over the bones.

"Don't touch him!" Azinine shouted. But she was too late. Josh had grabbed its robe and was trying to remove it when the skeleton came alive. At the same time, the doorway re-built itself, locking Josh on the inside and the rest of them on the outside.

"Ouf," Scott called out and, once again, the wall crumbled. To their astonishment, the skeleton had tackled Josh to the ground and had its bony hands around his neck. Ned grabbed the staff, hoping to use it against the skeleton. But it, too, was a trap and Ned was immediately turned to stone. Eric ran over to the skeleton and sent his foot slamming into the skeleton's ribs. The skeleton shattered, bones spraying everywhere, except its hands, which were still locked around Josh's neck, strangling him. Eric tried to free them, but they wouldn't budge. At this point, Josh started making a gurgling sound and his face was turning blue.

Scott ran over and with the gloves on his hands, he grabbed the skeleton hands, which immediately released their grip. He threw them to the side and helped Josh up. Josh was still trying to get his breath back when the skeleton came alive again, regrouping its bones until it was complete. It lunged again for Josh, but Scott caught it before it got a hold of him and the skeleton went limp and fell to the ground. Meanwhile, Azinine had reversed the spell on Ned and they all regrouped once again outside, where they felt safe.

Azinine turned on Scott. "Now are you going to tell us how you do that?"

"Do what?"

"Do what?" she mimicked. "That skeleton would still be attacking if you hadn't touched it. But as soon as you did, the spell controlling it stopped. I want to know how!"

Scott hesitated and then spoke calmly, "No, I'm not going to tell you… yet."

Not happy, Azinine gave a humpf. "Well, I guess that's a taste of what you'll be dealing with. Only I'm sure things are going to get a lot tougher as you make your way through each pyramid. Are you sure you still want to do this?"

"No, I don't want to do this!" Scott replied emphatically. He then continued with just as much emotion, "But I don't think we have a choice. It's the only way we'll get our parents back."

"Okay. But be careful and be alert. If you have questions, make sure you use those talking things," Azinine instructed him as she put her arms around him and gave him a hug.

Eric walked over to Scott. "I still feel like I should go with you."

"In our world, I would gladly have you along. In this world, I really don't think it's a good idea." The truth was, Scott really did want Eric along. However, Scott was sure he wasn't coming back out, and he couldn't bear to see his brother die with him. "Anyway, you'll be more useful back here," he finished.

Eric nodded. "Okay. Good luck and be very cautious."

"I will," Scott replied solemnly.

Eric handed Scott his backpack and gave him a hug, followed by Josh and then Ned. Azinine approached once again and gave him one last hug. She was shaking as she placed her arms around him and held him. She started to cry and held him even tighter.

"No, no, no. Do not start crying on me," Scott said as he released her, his own emotions started to build. "Everything is going to be okay. Understand?" he lied, trying to wipe away her tears. She nodded, but didn't say anything. He gave her one last hug. "I'll see you again once I've retrieved the book." She nodded and released him.

Scott turned towards the door, took in a deep breath and said, "Ouf." The door crumbled like it had before and he walked in. The others watched him walk down the tunnel. On the way down, he picked up the skeleton's cloak and the staff, but left the skeleton itself alone. He was almost to the end of the tunnel, when the door once again re-built itself, cutting Scott off from the others.

"I don't get it," Ned said, musing to himself. "How come Josh gets attacked by the skeleton when he touches it, but it dies when Scott touches it? How come I get turned to stone when I touch the staff, but Scott can carry it just fine?"

"There's only one answer," Azinine replied as though his questions were directed to her. "And the way Scott's been acting, it makes sense. But it's still hard to believe."

"What are you talking about?" Ned asked.

"He must be wearing the Shimmerall."

"Give me a break!" Ned scoffed. "The Shimmerall has been lost for hundreds of years. How would Scott get it?"

"How did Scott get the gloves? How did Scott know how to find the golden sword? How come the shackles don't work on Scott? How did Scott free all the slaves from Goblin Mountain? It's the only explanation I can come up with. For all we know, he could have found it in the goblin caves. But we're not going to find out, because he won't tell us, "She said with irritation, mixed with a bit envy. "And we're never going to see him again," she said as she placed her hands over her eyes and started to sob again.

Josh placed an arm around her. "What are you worried about? You, yourself, just pointed out how lucky he is. The guy should have already died several times, but he didn't. He'll be okay," he said, trying to console her.

"He does seem to be pretty lucky," Ned replied.

"He must be wearing it. It's the only explanation. But why wouldn't he tell us?"

"Azinine, didn't you learn anything in school? The Shimmerall was, or I guess still is, one of the most coveted magical items on Lumen. Men have killed for it. Naturally he would be cautious."

"I guess that makes sense, but we're his friends! We wouldn't do anything to him."

"I hope not," Ned said with a sigh. "But people have done stranger things for power. With that Shimmerall on, nothing magical on this planet can touch him. The only way someone will take him down is by brute force."

"I understand what you're saying, but it still bugs me," she replied.

"How well do either of you know this part of the woods?" Eric asked, interrupting their conversation, most of which he didn't understand. His Lumen was getting better, but he still had a long way to go.

"I've never been here before," Ned replied. "And Azinine has only been here once, a long time ago."

"Are there people who live around here?" Eric asked.

"Not that we know of. Others who have come back from here say the place is guarded by powerful magic."

"What do you mean?" Eric asked.

"Too many booby traps and magical spells to make it safe to live here I guess," Ned said. "For example, one guy said he was walking through the forest and several large bushes started chasing him."

"Bushes?"

"That's what he said. Another guy said a large piece of one of these hills came alive and tried to smash him with large boulders."

"Can't say I'd like to run into something like that," Josh replied, entering their conversation.

"They're probably just tall tales," Ned shrugged.

"Just in case they're not," Eric said, a little uneasily, "maybe we should raise the MOC twenty or thirty feet in the air and keep watch from there."

"That's a good idea." Ned explained their conversation to Azinine and the four of them climbed aboard and lifted into the air.

Eric picked up the radio and turned it on. "Scott, are you there?"

A few second went by before he received an answer. "Yes, I'm here."

"What's going on?"

"I'm in a large room. There was a doorway when I entered. Once I went through, it blocked itself backup, similar to the first doorway we entered. The room is well lit and there are several other skeletons in here. There's no exit that I can see, but there is a story on the wall along with a question. It looks like it's some sort of brainteaser or riddle, like the ones mom used to always give us. I assume I have to answer the question in order to move on."

"What's the question? Maybe we can help you."

"The questions is, 'Which owner eats fruit?'"

"What kind of question is that?" Eric asked.

"What happens if you answer the question wrong?" Josh asked.

"I'm not exactly sure. But none of these skeletons are intact, so I'd hate to find out."

"Well, I guess we better get it right then," replied Eric. "What other information do you have?"

"It gives several clues. Do you have anything to write on? It would probably help to write them down."

Ned turned to Azinine. "Do you know the spell to create a dynamic light board?"

"Of course," she replied.

"Okay, one second," Ned replied back to Scott.

He remained silent for several minutes while Azinine created a light board, which was really just another type of illusion. Its purpose was to allow a person to write things in a light bluish color. Ned took over and wrote things in English so Eric could participate. Azinine wasn't too thrilled with that, but she didn't make a fuss over it.

"Okay, we're ready," Ned spoke.

"Alright, listen carefully. There are five castles flying five different colored flags. The castles are lined up in a straight row. A different magical person lives in each of the castles. They each use a different magical tool. They each ride on a different mode of transportation and they each eat a different type of food. Did you get all that?"

"I think so, but that still doesn't tell us which owner eats fruit."

"Hold on, I haven't given you the clues yet. That was just some background. Here are the clues:

The witch lives in the castle flying the red flag.

The warlock eats bread.

The wizard uses a staff.

The castle flying the green flag is on the left of the castle flying the white flag."

"Whoa, slow down! You're going too fast," Ned yelled. "The castle flying the green flag what?"

"The castle flying the green flag is on the LEFT of the castle flying the white flag. Did you get that?"

"Yeah, I got it. Go on, but slower."

"Okay. The owner of the castle flying the green flag uses a magic ball." Scott waited for a moment and then continued. "The owner who rides a unicorn eats porridge. The owner of the castle flying the yellow flag rides a MOC." Scott waited again for a few seconds and then asked, "Did you get all that?"

"No," came the answer. "What does the owner of the castle with the yellow flag ride?"

"He rides a MOC," Scott replied.

"Okay, got it. Continue."

"The owner of the middle castle uses potions. The owner who rides a wagon lives next to the owner who eats meat. The owner who eats fowl lives next to the one who rides a MOC."

"Are you almost done?" Josh yelled into the radio.

"Almost," Scott responded. "Just a few more. Are you ready for me to continue?"

"Yes, go ahead."

"The owner who uses winged boots uses a wand. The Leppy rides on a column of light. The magician lives next to the castle flying the blue flag. The owner who rides a wagon has a neighbor who uses a cauldron. And the magician lives in the first castle. Ok, that's all of them. Did you get them written down?"

"I think so. Let me repeat them to just to make sure." Eric repeated each statement back to Scott who either confirmed he was right or corrected him when he wasn't.

"This isn't much different than some of the riddles we've done with Mother. I would suggest you create a grid and start with the last clue, since it's the most obvious," Scott suggested.

"I agree," Eric replied. Once the grid was completed, Ned plugged the magician into the slot titled 'Magical Person' and then waited for the next item.

"The castle next to the magician flies a blue flag. Mark that down," Eric motioned to Ned.

"The middle castle uses potions," Ned added.

"It looks like those are all the obvious ones," Josh commented.

"Ok, now comes the hard part," Scott said over the radio. No one said anything for several minutes. Each read the clues over and over trying to determine what else would bring them closer to the answer.

Finally, Ned spoke up. "The castle flying the green flag is on the left of the castle flying the white flag. That eliminates castles one and two. The fifth clue states that the castle flying the green flag uses a magic ball, eliminating castle three. Therefore, castle four must be flying the green flag and castle five must be flying the white flag."

"Good thinking, Ned," the others replied.

Josh now saw something. "The witch lives in the castle flying the red flag. So the witch must live in the middle castle."

"That's true!" Scott spoke. "Which means castle number one must be flying the yellow flag."

"Which means the magician rides a MOC!" Josh yelled with such excitement one would have thought he had just discovered gold.

"And the owner of the blue castle eats fowl," Eric added.

They all fell silent as they looked over the clues again and again.

After several minutes, Ned spoke up. "None of the clues gives us any information we can work with. I'm stumped."

"Me too," Josh agreed.

"Uh, guys," Scott said with just a hint of dread in his voice. "We really need to hurry and solve this."

"What's happening, Scott?" Eric asked in alarm.

"There's this black gas or something starting to enter the room. I really don't like the looks of this," he replied nervously.

"Okay, hold tight," Eric said.

"Easy for you to say," Scott replied.

Eric turned to the others. "The solution at this point is a simple matter of substitution," he began. "The warlock eats bread, which means he must own either castle four or five. The wizard uses a staff so he must own either castle two or five. In order to find the answer, let's plug the wizard into castle two and the warlock into castle four and see if the rest of the clues work."

The others, except for Azinine who hadn't understood what he said, agreed and Ned plugged in the answers as Eric had instructed.

"Okay, now that we've done that, the owner of castle five uses a wand and rides on winged boots. Put that in smaller letters so we know it's just a guess at this point," Eric instructed.

"And if the owner who rides a wagon has a neighbor who uses a cauldron, then the magician must use the cauldron!" Josh spoke up once again in his excited manner.

"I'm a little bit lost," Scott said, not being able to see the grid. "But wouldn't that mean the witch rides a unicorn and eats porridge?"

"That's correct. Very impressive," Eric replied.

"There's one problem," Ned said. "The Leppy rides on a column of light and that's impossible according to our current chart."

"True," Eric replied a bit disappointed. "Well, let's move the warlock down to castle five. You'll have to move the bread also since they belong together."

"Hey, that works!" Ned yelled out. The only square left is the food square belonging to the Leppy. That must mean the answer is that the Leppy eats fruit."

"I think we've done it, Scott," Eric shouted into the radio. "The Leppy eats fruit."

"Are you sure? I don't want to end up like one of these skeletons on the floor."

"Well, we're pretty sure. I mean, everything seems to fit."

"Pretty sure isn't good enough. We have to be positive," Scott said, perspiration forming on his forehead.

"Okay, hold on a second."

"Please hurry!" Scott said, watching the dark matter starting to form into something he had never seen before.

Eric and the others reviewed the chart, going over it again and again. Everything looked correct, so Eric got back on the radio. "Okay, we've reviewed everything and it looks correct."

"Are you sure?" Scott asked once again. Eric paused looking at the others for support.

Josh grabbed the radio. "Yes, we're sure."

Eric grabbed at the radio. "What are you doing?" he yelled at his youngest brother.

"Hey, we don't have all day. We've got to get this show on the road," Josh replied indignantly.

"Okay, here goes," Scott replied.

Scott took in a deep breath and was about to give his answer, when Josh grabbed the radio. "Wait!" he yelled.

"Ugh!" Scott breathed back. "Are you sure or aren't you?"

"We're sure, I think. But I was wondering if you could put the radio and maybe the gloves in a corner of the room, just in case we're wrong. Wouldn't want those getting damaged, right?"

"Give me that," Eric said, wrenching the radio back from Josh's hands.

"It was just a suggestion," Josh replied.

Eric pushed the talk button. "Go ahead, Scott."

Scott took in another deep breath and gave the answer. Nothing happened at first, and Scott wondered if the answer he had given was wrong. But soon another door appeared. Scott breathed a sigh of relief. "It looks like your answer was correct. I'm entering another room and the dark stuff is retreating."

Chapter 25

Mishopods and Tyranodites

Scott picked up the staff, the cape and a large stick pole he had seen lying next to one of the dead persons. Scott walked through cautiously, not knowing what might be inside. A staircase led him down into a tunnel and back up some stairs into another room. Scott guessed he must have passed into another pyramid. This next room was also well lit and once inside he could tell there was nothing inside.

"What sort of test do you have to pass in this room?" Eric asked.

"Well, it can't be too hard, there are no dead bodies in here. There's a picture of the pyramid with the moon directly overhead. Under the pyramid are three words, "Po Ta…""

Azinine grabbed the radio. "Don't say it!" she yelled.

"What?" Scott asked.

"Don't repeat those words! It's a moon spell," she explained. "In order for the spell to work, it must be said when the moon is directly overhead or something bad will happen."

"That doesn't seem very hard," Josh commented.

"No, it doesn't. Not unless there aren't any windows and you don't know when the moon is overhead," Azinine replied. "Those talking things will come in real handy for this test. Although we're going to have to wait for some time now."

Josh grabbed the radio again. "It's a good thing we didn't get here in the morning, Scott. I mean, it's not like those pyramids come with bathrooms."

"Oh man," Scott groaned. "I wish you hadn't said that. Now I have to go."

"Just number one I hope," Josh replied.

"Give that to me," Eric said, snatching the radio back. "See if you can find a hole or something. In the meantime, we're going to have to wait until the moon rises."

Several hours later, the moon began its ascent into the sky, and the temperatures started to fall. The four of them had been sitting on the MOC for over five hours. The first hour had been spent helping Scott pass the first test. The last four, waiting for the moon to rise, as well as taking a few bathroom breaks. They didn't use the radios anymore in an effort to save battery life.

"Guys, can we land this thing?" Josh asked. "It's getting cold and my legs are getting stiff. I need to stretch." The others agreed, so Azinine lowered the MOC back down. They all jumped off and stretched their cramped muscles.

Scott had nothing to do but sit against the wall and wait. He stood up and began pacing back and forth, wondering how this whole thing would turn out. As he did so, he noticed the walls starting to look different. Hours before, the stones glowed with a light blue tint, giving off plenty of light. Now the stones were spotted with black splotches, as though sections of the stones were losing their light. Scott figured this was part of the test and didn't pay much attention to it until he saw one of the spots move. As he studied the spots, Scott noticed they were becoming more and more numerous and they weren't only on the walls, but on the ceiling.

Scott picked up the stick pole and nudged one of them. It immediately grabbed onto the stick and began to consume it. He quickly smashed the pole against the floor, dislodging the creature.

Scott shuddered. "Um..guys?" he said, trying to get them on the radio. But there was no answer, so he put the radio in his pocket and stood very still while the little black creatures began to multiply, becoming more and more numerous.

After about twenty minutes, Scott heard Eric's voice on the radio. "Scott, you okay?"

Scott grabbed his radio. "Is the moon up yet? I'm starting to really hate this place."

"I'm guessing you still have about ten minutes. What's up?"

"Let's just say I've figured out why there aren't any skeleton's in here."

"Scott, are you in danger?" Eric asked.

"You could say that. My room is filling with land loving piranhas."

"Piranhas? As in the fish?"

"Well, of course they're not fish. But there are enough of them to consume my entire body in seconds if they decided to."

Ned whispered something in Eric's ear. "Ned says they're Mishopods. Very dangerous. He's guessing you probably have one chance at this. If you fail, they'll attack. So don't fail."

"Oh, great," Scott replied, his stomach starting to feel sick all of a sudden.

"The moon is just about there. You probably only have five to ten minutes, so hang in there. If you…what in the world?" Eric ended quizzically.

He still had the talk button pushed and Scott could hear Azinine yelling, "Run! We've got to enter the pyramid! It's our only chance!"

"What are they?" he heard Josh yell.

"Eric!" Scott yelled into the radio. But Eric still had the talk button pushed. "Eric!" he tried again, but still no reply. Then the radio went silent. "Eric! Eric! What's going on!" he yelled again and again, but Eric wasn't answering. His stomach lurched inside. He looked at his watch, which wasn't set for Lumen time, but estimated he had one minute to go. Without them to tell him where the moon was, he would just have to guess.

Scott looked at the walls, which were now almost completely covered with Mishopods. There were only a few spots of light now shining through the black mass of those nasty creatures, and as a result, the room had become very dark. He began to sweat profusely and he could feel his heart beating so fast he thought it might burst. If he waited too long, the Mishopods would eat him alive. If he didn't wait long enough, they would still eat him alive.

"Don't fail, he says. Easy for him to say. He's not the one about to be eaten alive," Scott muttered to himself. "There has got to be an answer to this task! There must be a way to know, but how?" He looked at the Mishopods, which were now beginning to get restless. There was now only one tiny gleam of light shining through the multitude of Mishopods on the walls and ceiling. Soon a Mishopod would take that spot and it would be pitch dark. Scott stopped suddenly, his eyes growing wider as a thought formed in his head. He looked over at the wall and watched as a Mishopod began to cover the last gleaming hole. The others were making a humming sound and the whole room seemed to be vibrating.

"Po Tay Olea," he spoke. The humming stopped and immediately the Mishopods disappeared back into the cracks of the walls. The wall in front of him began to crumble and an entranceway appeared. Scott gave a great sigh of relief, breathing heavily. His hunch had been right. He paused for a few seconds, then picked up the magi staff and the stick pole and entered. Behind him the wall began to brick itself back up again. Scott quickly grabbed the stick pole and shoved it in the doorway. This didn't stop the wall. It simply gathered itself around the stick pole until it was a rock wall again with a large pole sticking through both sides.

"Oh, well," Scott said. He still had the cape and staff. He walked down a hallway, down a flight of stairs, through another tunnel, and then up a flight of stairs and into a massively large room. A room much bigger than any of the others he had encountered so far. This room was dark and Scott hesitated before entering, straining his eyes to see what might be inside.

"If these tasks don't kill me, the stress will," he said to himself, hesitating to walk in the room. He took in a deep breath, picked up the magi staff, and holding it more like a baseball bat than a staff, crossed the threshold. The room lit up like a candle. The room was in the shape of a triangle and in each corner stood a statue of a creature Scott had only seen once before. It was the creature that Ned had taken the form of in the dreaming pond. Each one stood upright, resembling a very large ape. But unlike an ordinary ape, they had long, razor sharp claws, thin tan fur, and a head covered with a mane, like that of a lion.

Scott pulled out his radio. "Eric? Ned? Someone? Are you there?" he called. No one answered. He put the radio back in his pocket and sat down. He looked around, but could see nothing indicating what he needed to do. He stood up and walked over to one of the creatures. One of those claws would slice through him like a hot knife through butter, and he shivered at the thought of it. He turned around and noticed writing that had appeared on one of the walls. He walked over and read it.

> You've made it this far with brains, honorable and true. You join the ranks
> of only a few. But if you desire to pass through this door, you'll need your
> brains, and much, much more. The three in the corners must be defeated,
> before your task is truly completed.

Scott's face went pale and he thought he was going to be sick. How would he ever defeat these beasts? Only a true magus would know how to do that. Despair crept over him as he realized he had no choice. There was no way back. Even worse, there was still nothing to indicate what he had to do to start the battle. The three creatures remained silent and still. Perhaps he could destroy them before they came alive, but how? Then he had an idea. He took off his pack and pulled out some rope. He cut it up into three pieces and tied each of their legs together in hopes that it would at least slow them down. In the bag he also found a screw driver.

He pulled it out and laughed. "Why would Josh bring this?" he asked himself. Then a thought occurred to him, *this screwdriver could possibly be used as a sort of weapon.* He set the staff and the pack down and walked over to one of the beasts. He held the screwdriver tight in his hand and with all his might slammed the point of it into the beast's chest, hoping to kill it immediately. The beast jumped to life and roared out in anguish. Scott fell backwards in a mixture of astonishment and horror and landed on the ground with the screwdriver still in his hand. Even with the strength of the gloves, the screwdriver had only slightly penetrated the rock-hard surface, and the beast now stepped towards him. The rope held tight and the beast toppled to the ground.

Scott leapt to his feet, jumped onto the beast's back, and once again drove the screwdriver hard into the beast's back. This time it entered deep into its flesh causing it to roar even louder. It whirled over, swinging its arm towards Scott. The back of its fist connected with Scott's shoulder. Scott grunted as he was knocked off and thrown against the wall. Scott had wounded it deeply and the beast struggled to get up. Scott rose to his feet and was about to try and finish it when he noticed a second beast had now come alive. It immediately noticed the rope and snapped it like a string. It looked at Scott for only a moment, its anger glowing through its eyes and its claws extending like sharp daggers.

Scott froze. "I'm dead," he squeaked. The first beast was starting to rise. Acting with pure instinct, Scott leapt on top of it, knocking it to the ground. Once again, he drove the screwdriver deep into its back. Out of the corner of his eye, Scott caught a glimpse of the second beast leaping through the air towards him. He rolled off and jumped to his feet just as the second beast landed near the first, its claws scraping along the floor.

The screwdriver was still stuck inside the back of the first beast. Scott looked around for something to defend himself with. The staff he had taken from the skeleton lay at his feet. He picked it up and wielded it like a baseball bat. He knew hitting the beast would probably just make it angrier, but it was worth a try. The second beast had risen and was slowly moving towards him, growling lightly, its dagger-like claws outstretched. Scott moved along the wall hoping to give himself more room to fight. The beast made a sudden lunge towards him, its claws outstretched. Scott ducked and swung the staff hard into its gut. At first, the beast appeared to laugh at Scott's feeble attempt to wound it. But as it moved again, a startled look washed over its face. It stopped and looked down at its stomach where Scott had hit him. It took one of its claws and tapped it. A slight tinging sound rang out. It was not the sound of a claw hitting fur and flesh, but the sound of a claw hitting stone.

For a moment, Scott forgot they were fighting and curiously watched the beast. Suddenly it occurred to him the staff had been cursed to turn anyone to stone who held it. He himself was able to carry it because of the bodysuit he wore. The beast now looked up at Scott, its eyes flaming with extreme anger. It lunged awkwardly towards him. Scott once again dodged it and struck it in the leg and then in the back. Immediately its back and leg went hard as rock. The beast roared out in anguish as it tried to turn around for another attack, but it was slow and Scott knew he wouldn't have much trouble finishing this one. He took the staff and quickly cracked the beast over the head, turning its head to stone.

He was about to hit the beast again, when Scott heard the third beast land on the floor behind him. This beast hadn't noticed the rope tied around its ankles and had tripped in its attempt to attack Scott from behind. The rope had saved his life. However, it didn't take long for the beast to recover. The first beast was still on the ground, but seemed to be recovering. The third beast was now slowly and cautiously approaching Scott. The two circled each other, neither one daring to make the first move. This one seemed smarter and less angry, yet it had a confident look. As they circled, the beast took its claw and slammed it through the chest of the second one that Scott had partially turned to stone. This startled Scott and he jumped, but the two continued to circle until the beast came upon the first beast lying on the floor. Once again it slammed its claw through the downed animal's chest, killing it. The two crippled beasts quickly disintegrated into dust. Scott looked on in horror as the final beast began to mutate before his eyes.

The beast had stopped moving and its fur looked like a thousand bugs were running underneath it. It never took its eyes off Scott, but now it seemed as though it was smiling. Then Scott noticed that the beast was slowly growing larger and larger. Its claws growing longer and stronger. With horror, Scott realized it was taking on the strength of the others. At this rate, he wouldn't be able to get close enough to the beast to hit it with the staff. He grabbed the staff and charged the beast, hoping it might be vulnerable while transforming. He swung out with the staff, but the beast blocked it with one claw and smacked Scott with the back of the other. Scott fell hard to the floor, but still managed to keep hold of the staff. The beast had an evil grin on its face now. Scott backed off and waited to see what the beast had in mind. It roared in victory and then moved forward, slowly, as if to savor the moment. As it came within reach, Scott darted to the left to put additional space between himself and his impending doom. The beast struck out with its long arms, tripping Scott and sending him once again to the floor. Scott realized it was playing with him like a cat plays with a mouse. Twice now the beast could have finished him, but chose not to.

"What do you want from me?" Scott asked hoping to communicate with it. The beast stopped and gave Scott a puzzled look. It only paused momentarily before it began to advance towards him once again. As the beast came nearer, Scott had an idea. He took the staff, put it in his mouth and growled.

"Pretty cool, huh?" Scott said, once again hoping the beast could understand him. As before, the beast stopped momentarily and then once again continued towards him. This time Scott tossed the staff up in the air and tried to catch it in his mouth, but he missed and it hit him in the teeth.

"Ouch!" he said and he quickly picked it up and tried it once more. He missed again. This time the beast gave out a slight chuckle.

"Alright, let's see if you can do any better?" Scott replied and tossed the staff high into the air. The beast opened its mouth and easily caught the staff in its jaws. It looked down at Scott with a grin, which quickly froze as its whole body began hardening. It's eyes took on a look of surprise and it tried to spit out the staff, but it was too late and soon the beast was one large statue. This time is was Scott's turn to smile.

"It worked," Scott breathed a sigh of relief. "I did it. I did it! I beat all three of them!" he screamed out and leaped into the air again and again. "I did it!" His whole being was consumed with joy. He was still alive. A slight wave of disappointment washed over him at the loss of the staff, which was stuck in the mouth of the beast, but at least he was alive.

Chapter 26

Garlython

Eric and the others rushed for the pyramid door with a host of hostile creatures on their heels. "Ouf!" Azinine yelled, remembering what Scott had said. The door opened and they ran inside. However, the door didn't close behind them and several pygmy wyellits entered.

Each pygmy wyellits stood like a man, but was only about eighteen inches tall. They had fur covering their entire body, and their heads, which had large cat-like eyes and sharp jagged teeth, were too large for their bodies.

"Close the door," Eric yelled.

Azinine understood what he wanted, but didn't know how. She shook her head frantically back and forth.

Eric looked at Josh. "Josh, yell 'close' in the ancient language!"

Josh hesitated and then yelled, "oufsu!" The door closed, but not before several more pygmy wyellits entered. The small pygmy wyellits attacked with a ferocity that surprised them. Once of them bit Ned in the leg as he tried to kick it. One just about sunk its teeth into Josh's arm while he was fending off another, but it accidentally touched the skeleton and the skeleton instantly attacked the small wyellit.

None of them were any match for Eric, who easily cracked their skulls with each kick, but in the end, it was Azinine who saved the day with her wand. She rapidly began blasting each one with a paralysis spell that glued each wyellit's feet to the ground so they couldn't move. Despite their paralysis, they still screamed and howled making quite a ruckus.

"Josh," Azinine said, "ask them how they knew we were here and what they want?"

Josh walked over to them, acting very important. "Quiet!" he yelled as loud as he could. Surprisingly enough, they quieted down, most likely because they had heard him in their own language and were taken off guard by it.

"That's better," he stated when they were silent. "Who is your leader?" he asked. But none replied. He walked over to one of the smaller creatures and bent over, looking the pygmy wyellit directly in the eye as though he were some tough, Mafia type interrogator. He was about to speak when it spit in his eye. Josh jerked backwards trying to wipe the slimy stuff off. The other wyellits began to howl in delight, while even Eric and Ned let out a low chuckle.

"Silence!" Josh yelled once again after he had removed the spit. The noise died down and Josh approached the little wyellit with anger in his step and determination in his eyes. Once he was within striking range, he swung hard hoping to give the little bugger a good slap across the face. The wyellit, whose arms weren't paralyzed, grabbed his arm and tried to bite him. Luckily, Josh had good reflexes and pulled back quickly enough that it only nipped him a bit. It still drew blood and Josh began sucking on his finger. Again, the other pygmy wyellits broke out into howls of delight, with Eric and Ned joining in. Azinine, on the other hand, didn't find it amusing at all. She walked up to the little goblin and quick as lightning slammed her boot into its gut. It doubled over screaming in pain. The others stopped their howling to see what had happened.

"Tell him the next time he does something like that he'll get it in the head and that he'd better cooperate. We don't have much time."

Josh approached again. "Tell us what we want to know or she'll crack your skull open, rip out your guts and drink your fluids just for the fun of it." The little wyellit looked at Azinine in horror and nodded.

"How did you know we were here and what do you want with us?"

"We seek the Trouble Maker. He will make us rich. We were told he was here."

"Who is the Trouble Maker?"

"You! You are the Trouble Maker!" At this, the other wyellits started to scream and gnash their teeth.

"Silence!" Josh roared. "You are mistaken. I am not the Trouble Maker."

"You are the Trouble Maker!" it screamed out. "You have white hair and speak our language. Only the Trouble Maker can do that." The other pygmy wyellits continued with their screams and gnashing of teeth again. Many were trying desperately to free their feet and move.

"I am not the..." but he stopped when the wall to the outside began to crumble and hundreds of wyellits poured in.

"Run!" Azinine yelled. They ran down the hall, deeper into the pyramid and into the large room Scott had first encountered. Behind them the rest of the hoard of wyellits had just entered and were chasing after them. On the wall they could see the riddle they had solved with Scott.

"What was the answer?" Josh asked.

"I don't remember. Who eats the fruit?" Eric frantically cried out.

"It was the Leppy!" Ned yelled. Apparently, that was good enough for the spell and the door opened. They ran through just as the Pygmy Wyellits entered the room. Several tried to get past the second wall, but it closed too quickly and one got its legs caught in it, leaving its legs sticking out on one side and its body on the other side. Josh couldn't resist the temptation and started tickling its foot. He could hear it screaming on the other side.

"Come on, Josh! We've got to keep going," Eric said as he headed down the hall. Josh gave the little foot one more tickle and then followed the others. They walked down the staircase and into the second hall where Scott encountered the moon spell.

"Oh, great!" Ned muttered. "Do you think the wyellits will figure out the riddle before the moon rises again?"

"Uhh, that's like twenty-three hours and forty five minutes from now," Josh hesitantly pointed out.

"Even if they don't, how are we going to know when the moon has risen?" Ned replied.

"Somehow Scott figured it out," Eric chimed in. "Certainly we should be able to."

Just then, Scott's voice came over the radio. "Are you guys there?" he asked.

Eric still had the radio clutched tightly in his hand and answered, "We're here. How are you doing?"

"I'm still alive if that's what you mean."

"What's with this pole sticking out of the wall?" Eric asked.

"I put it there hoping to provide a way back, but the wall just closed up around it. Are you guys in the moon spell room?"

"Yep," Eric replied.

"I'm only in the next pyramid," Scott replied with excitement, which was followed by puzzlement. "Why did you enter the pyramids?" he asked.

"Because we were attacked by pygmy wyellits. We had no choice. They're in the other pyramid."

"What are they doing?" Scott asked, curious.

"I assume trying to figure out the riddle. That is, if they can read it."

"Oh," Scott replied. "Well, I apparently have another riddle to solve in order to enter this next room. Maybe you guys can help me out while you wait for the moon to rise again. Once we figure it out, I'll wait in this room so you don't have to fight these monsters like I did. Then we can all enter the next pyramid together."

"You had to fight some monsters?" Josh asked.

"Yeah. Ned," he addressed his friend, "they were the same things that you took the form of when we were in the dreaming pond. Right when we first started. You can tell the others about them."

"You fought a Tyranodite?" Ned asked, with awe in his voice.

"Not *a* Tyranodite, three Tyranodites. Two regular sized ones and one gigantic one.

"And you won?"

"I...got lucky."

"What's the riddle, Scott?" Eric interrupted, trying to get back to the task at hand.

"Okay, here it is," Scott began.

> *What's been around since the beginning of creation,*
>
> *Is as strong as a mountain with an uncertain formation.*
>
> *The only thing that dragons dread,*
>
> *But both together share a common thread.*
>
> *When morning comes it hides its face,*
>
> *When darkness falls, it offers no grace.*
>
> *Despite the terror when it's sighted,*
>
> *It only appears when it's invited.*
>
> *What is my name?*

"Did you guys get that?" Scott asked.

"Yes, I think so," Eric replied. "Give us a moment to think about it."

"I know what it is! I know its name!" Ned exclaimed, excited that he knew the answer. "Here, give me the radio," he said as he took the device from Eric. "Scott, are you there?"

"Yes, I'm here," Scott replied.

"The riddle is speaking of a Garglython."

"NO!" Azinine yelled. She ripped the radio out of Ned's hand. "Scott, DO NOT say its name!"

Scott didn't answer for a few seconds, then hesitantly added, "I think it's too late. Ned has apparently already done that for me."

"You idiot!" she yelled at her brother. "We've got to get past this room now. We've got to get in there and help him!"

"What's...a Garglython?" Josh asked hesitantly, spooked by the fear he saw in Azinine's face.

"You don't want to know and besides, there's no time to explain. I'm going to hit the wall with a shatter spell. When it hits, everyone grab onto that stick in the wall there and pull as hard as you can. Maybe we can break the wall." Ned translated the plan to Eric. They all turned and grabbed hold of the pole. Azinine pointed her wand at the wall and spoke, "Tsarshullen." A blast of red light flashed from her wand and the wall began to shudder. Eric and the others pulled as hard as they could. The wall began to budge, but quickly became solid again.

"Once more!" she urged, then spoke again, "Tsarshullen." As before, the blast of light shot from her wand and the wall began to tremble. The others pulled with all their might, but the wall still didn't break.

"Again!" Eric yelled. Azinine zapped the wall again. As it began to tremble, Eric grabbed the stick with both hands and with all his might lifted himself off the ground and slammed both feet into the wall. The wall began to shudder even more. "Keep zapping it," he yelled.

Scott was standing in the middle of the great hall waiting for a door to open, as had happened before. But this time, apparently, was going to be different. No door opened. Instead, what looked like a dark light began to appear and grow. He backed up and hid behind the giant Tyranodite he had turned to stone. What appeared before him resembled a very tall man without a face. It had long arms and legs and giant hands with claws in place of its fingernails. Scott kept as still as he could and watched as the man, or thing, formed. The room grew colder and an unreasonable fear crept into Scott's heart, as though he had breathed it in. It wore a black robe with the hood covering its head, but where a face should have been, there was only darkness.

Moments later, it stood in front of him very quiet, very still. It stood there for several seconds and then spoke.

"Come and stand before me," it said. It wasn't an audible voice, but nonetheless Scott heard it. However, he couldn't move. His legs were frozen in place. Fear gripped him unlike anything he had ever experienced. His heart was hammering in his chest. The thing stood there for several minutes, but to Scott it seemed an eternity. This time in an audible and thunderous voice, it ordered, "Come here now!" The voice shook Scott's whole body, but he still couldn't move.

Suddenly, a mouth appeared, which opened wide and out shot a blue ball of flame which engulfed the Tyranodite Scott was hiding behind. The flame was not hot, but it melted the stone Tyranodite as if it was made of ice. Scott still didn't move, even though he was now fully exposed to whatever powers the Garglython could unleash on him.

"What do you want here?" it asked.

"I…I have…come to get the book," Scott sputtered.

"You are not the High King!" it snapped back.

"True," Scott agreed. "But nevertheless, I need the book to save my mother."

"Hmmm. Your cause is noble enough, but I cannot make exceptions. Only the High King may retrieve the book."

"If I don't get the book there may never be another High King!"

"Why do you believe that?"

"There's this group called the Kingmongers, and they…"

"I know who the Kingmongers are," it said, interrupting Scott.

"Oh. Well, they're trying to overthrow the magi council and force a ruler into place. Without this book they might succeed."

"*With* this book they might succeed," the Garglython shot back. "Without it, they will not."

"I have to at least try and stop them," argued Scott.

"You have come this far, which is, indeed, impressive. Perhaps you might have been able to stop them."

"I still might be able to. Especially if I have the book," Scott replied, with a little more courage.

"Only the High King has permission to retrieve the book from the Pyramids. Anyone else must die."

"Well," Scott replied, trying to keep himself from being killed, "if you won't give me the book, perhaps you could show me a way out of here. Someone has to stop these magi!"

"No. We have wasted enough time." The Garglython opened its mouth again and another blue ball of flame began forming. Scott looked around for a place to hide, but with the Tyranodite gone, the room was empty. The blue ball, now as large as Scott, shot from its mouth and engulfed him. Scott braced himself for the worst, but nothing happened. The blue ball of fire simply evaporated.

Now, eyes appeared on the face of the Garglython. "Interesting. I have wondered where that was," it said, somewhat amused. "Where did you get it?"

"What?" Scott asked, still trying to recover.

"The Shimmerall."

"The Shimmerall?" Scott repeated.

The Garglython wondered at Scott's ignorance, but finally said, "The item you are wearing is called the Shimmerall. It makes the wearer immune to magic."

"Oh, that. It was given to me by an elderly lady."

"An elderly lady? Where was this elderly lady?"

"I'll tell you if you let me pass."

"YOU ARE NOT IN A POSITION TO BARGAIN!" it roared back.

"Sure I am. I have nothing to lose but my life, which you were going to take anyway."

"True," it said calmly. "It doesn't matter. I still cannot let you live. And if magic won't do it, then I'll have to use other means which are a bit messier, but more effective."

This time, its mouth opened wide and a blazing stream of hot fire shot from it. Scott leaped out of the way, but the flame followed him, scorching his hair and parts of his clothes. He rushed the Garglython, hoping it would stop the fire in order to save itself. Scott grabbed its legs, and using the gloves he still wore on his hands, pulled with all his might. The Garglython began to tip, but as it did, it changed shapes and took the form of large cat-like figure with wings.

It shook Scott off its leg and turned to face him. "Again, very impressive," it said in its smooth, silky voice. "Not only do you wear the Shimmerall, but you wear the gloves of Allendon. Do you also have his sword?"

"No. A dragon took it."

"You had the sword and you let a dragon take it from you?"

"No. I didn't *let* him. I was running from the goblins and I fell and blacked out. When I woke up, it was gone. The dragon who rescued me took it."

"A dragon rescued you?" the Garglython asked in surprise.

"Yes," Scott replied.

"Hmm," it mumbled. "Most curious."

Knowing he couldn't stall the inevitable attack much longer, Scott readied himself. But the Garglython sat still. After a moment it spoke again. "It seems a shame to kill you. You certainly show signs of promise."

"Well, there's no reason..." Scott began, but the large cat-like creature pounced as quick as lightning and pinned him to the floor before he could get out of the way. Scott lay on the ground, pinned under two large paws. Where the creature's mouth once appeared now protruded a large sword-like object that was certainly meant for Scott, but for some reason, the creature hesitated.

"Don't do this," Scott pleaded. "You are making a serious mistake."

Once again it spoke in an inaudible voice. "I believe you, but I have to do my duty. You do not meet the requirements."

The creature was about to kill him when all of a sudden, the large cat was knocked off balance and toppled onto its side. Scott looked over and saw Eric holding the stick pole. Behind him the others came running into the room. The large cat-like creature howled in anger and charged Eric with claws outstretched, the sword still protruding out of its mouth. Eric didn't budge. He held up the stick pole hoping to fend it off. Acting quickly, Scott grabbed its leg, but he no more slowed it down that a simple housefly would have. The cat made ready to strike and then, just before it did, it suddenly stopped.

"Get off my foot!" the Garglython growled at Scott. The giant creature shook him off, throwing him to the ground. It was staring past Eric, looking at Josh. Fear once again filled the room and everyone shrank backwards away from the creature, as if that might help. The Garglython didn't budge, but continued to stare at Josh.

"What?" Josh finally said, feeling really uncomfortable. "I'm just the hired help."

The Garglython continued staring at Josh a few seconds longer and then turned to Eric. "What is your name?" it asked.

Not understanding, Eric turned to Scott for help. "He wants to know your name," his brother supplied.

"Eric Frontier," Eric replied.

"He's not lingual?" the Garglython asked, turning to Scott.

"No, he's not."

"This is all very strange. You have the gloves of Allendon, but not the sword. Your hired help carries the Eigenholle and this brave boy isn't lingual." The Garglython sat silent, pondering for some time. It seemed to be contemplating something over and over again in its mind. To Scott it seemed like an eternity, but at least it wasn't trying to kill him.

Finally it spoke. "It is quite impressive you were able to get this far without the Eigenholle, and I do not say that lightly. The Eigenholle was meant to get a person this far, but it will not help you get the book. Just remember, things are not always as they seem."

"Does that mean you'll let us get the book?" Scott asked hopefully.

"I do this with much hesitancy, but since you now meet the requirements, although barely, you may proceed."

"Thank you!" Scott blurted out.

"Silence!" it shouted. "I am not finished. Before I let you go, you must understand the responsibility you are about to take upon yourselves." This latter part was spoken such that all of them somehow understood. "The book is very powerful. You seek it to free your parents, and in hopes of stopping the Kingmongers. But remember, this book doesn't play favorites. It will serve the Kingmongers just as it will serve you. Do not let it get into their hands. Once you are finished with it, there is a spell in the back that will automatically place it back in these pyramids. You must resist the temptation to keep it. You must return it as soon as you have accomplished your task. Do you understand?"

"Yes," they all replied in unison.

"All right, go," the Garglython said and then disappeared. In a small corner of the room a door appeared. They all walked towards it, but stopped at the entrance. Inside, it was pitch black. Azinine pulled out a glowing lumenarty rock which she always carried with her, stepped inside and held it up. The rock didn't make a dent in the darkness.

"We would be fools to enter this pyramid without light," she commented.

"I'm not sure we need light, do we, Joshua?" Scott replied a little anger touching his voice.

Josh looked at Scott quizzically. "Why are you looking at me? I'm just the hired help. Remember?"

"Give it to me," Scott ordered.

"Give you what?"

"The Eigenholle."

The others turned and looked at Josh in surprise.

"I don't have the Eigenholle. That garglthia, or whatever it was, must be mistaken."

"Put down your pack and pull everything out." Josh had picked up his pack when the group entered the room, and had been clutching it tightly to his chest.

"Okay," he replied hesitantly. Josh unzipped his pack and pulled out some squashed crackers, a sweatshirt, a pocketknife, a compass and small flashlight. He looked up at Scott. "I don't think any of these qualify as the Eigenholle."

"Is that everything?"

"Oh, alright," Josh replied begrudgingly. He pulled out the wooden box Scott's mother had given him and laid it on the ground.

"Josh! That's mine," Scott cried in dismay. "You took that out of my drawer without asking?"

"I'm sorry! But it looked cool and I wanted to check it out, but I didn't have time. I didn't think you'd get upset about a jewelry box."

"It's not a jewelry box. This was given to me by Mom. You shouldn't have taken it without asking me."

"I said I was sorry, didn't I?"

"Guys, guys! This isn't really the time to discuss this," Eric said interrupting them. "Is the Eigenholle in there or not?"

"That's everything in my pack. I swear," Josh said, crossing his heart.

"Are you guys blind?" Azinine asked in wonder. "That box has ancient Lumen writings on it. It must be the Eigenholle."

"You've got to be kidding me," Scott said in surprise.

Josh laughed. "Ha! Mom's pretty smart."

"If that's the Eigenholle, then how do we use it?" Eric asked.

Scott picked up the box. "Here's what the writing says. 'Place the box upon your head. If you're not worthy, you'll end up dead. To make it work, speak your name. Two crystals appear, both the same. The crystals will glow with magic light and then you'll have the needed sight.' Those are the instructions. Who wants to give it a try?"

"Not me," Ned immediately replied.

"Me neither," Josh commented.

Azinine walked over to Scott. "Since you have the Shimmerall, you are the best choice."

"Shimmerall?" Scott asked. "That's the same thing the Garglython said."

"The bodysuit you're wearing. It's called a Shimmerall. It's one of the most coveted magical items that exist. You must be wearing it. It's the only way you could have been immune to so many spells."

"Oh," Scott said, now understanding what they were talking about.

"Now place it on your head and let's see what happens?"

"Easy for you to say," Scott said fumbling with the box. "How come I always get stuck doing all the deadly chores? Why doesn't someone else take a turn for once?"

Azinine put her hands on her hips. "Sure, I'll take a turn, but hand over the Shimmerall first."

"You want me to take it off here? In front of you?" Scott asked, looking around the room in an effort to show Azinine it wasn't practical for him to do so. Besides the fact that he really did not want to part with it.

"Either give it up, or you have to try the Eigenholle."

"Okay, I'll try it." He took in a deep breath and placed the box upon his head. He waited to see if anything would happen, but nothing did.

"Well, speak your name," Eric suggested.

"I'm getting there," Scott replied. He took in another deep breath. "Scott Frontier."

The box began to glow and then it opened and began to form around his head. Two white rings appeared around his eyes and two lenses began to form inside the rings. It looked as though Scott was wearing a helmet with glasses attached to it.

"Whoa!" Scott whispered. He stood there looking around, his eyes wide with unbelief.

"What do you see?" Azinine asked impatiently.

"Everything. Man, I wish I had had these at the beginning. I can see every pyramid. The answer to the riddle is written on the wall. With these on, the pyramids are clear. I can see through all of them. That army of pygmy wyellits have surrounded all the pyramids. There's a group of them still inside the room with the riddle. They obviously can't read it, so they can't get out."

"What about the book? Can you see it?" Eric asked, trying to steer the group back to their goal.

Scott looked at the next pyramid. "Yes! At least I think so. There are several books, each resting inside a box at the top of the pyramid. Wow! It's a good thing we didn't enter that door. About five feet in, it drops off hundreds of feet. You have to take a sharp right once you enter. There's a small doorway that leads to a ramp. Then the ramp ends and drops off onto a round ledge that drops off on all sides except a long staircase that leads up to another room. That room has hundreds of swords sticking out of the walls and floor. There's only a small, winding path through it. Then.."

"Scott, we get the picture," Eric said interrupting him. "I don't think any of us are going to enter that pyramid without each of us having an Eigenholle of our own. Can you get the book and bring it back?"

"Sure," he said with confidence. "Piece of cake. One ancient book of magic coming up."

Chapter 27

The Ancient Book of Magic

Scott entered the last pyramid and followed the path indicated by the Eigenholle. When he reached the room containing the book, it was lit up by hundreds of tiny golden rocks set within the walls. It was one of the most beautiful things he had ever seen. He caught himself staring at them, mesmerized by the grandeur of it. Snapping out of it, he remembered his task and walked over to the shelf containing five identical metal boxes. Using the Eigenholle, he could see that each metal box contained a book similar in size. Even looking through the Eigenholle, he couldn't tell which one was The Ancient Book of Magic.

"Is there more than one book of magic?" he asked himself. "I thought there was only one. Otherwise Magus Noka would have said, 'The Ancient Books of Magic'. So why is there more than one? Was he mistaken?" Scott scratched his head and continued to reason with himself regarding the books. He finally decided to open one of the boxes and see what the book was called. Maybe he could tell by the title.

He unlocked the latch of the first one and slowly lifted the lid. The lid suddenly burst open and a black substance flowed out of the box and started to swirl around him. It made him feel sick inside, like death. It continued to swirl as though it were searching for something. Every once in a while it would try and penetrate his chest, but was repelled. He was quite sure that had he not been wearing the Shimmerall, this substance would have destroyed him or something to that effect.

"Get away from me," Scott finally said, trying to push the black mist away. The gas paused, and then slithered back into the box. The lid snapped shut with a loud clang. It was then that Scott realized that these boxes were also spell rigged. They were the last attempt to keep the book safe in the event that someone, like the Kingmongers, got their hands on the Eigenholle. It suddenly occurred to him that the Eigenholle wasn't going to help him here. He would have to figure this out on his own.

"There's got to be a way to know," he mused to himself. "But how?" He knew box number one wasn't correct, so he looked carefully at the other four, looking for any kind of clue. "Hmm," he muttered. "The first box was spell rigged. But what about someone like me who is immune to magic? I'm guessing that at least one of these boxes is booby trapped." He looked for any holes in the walls or the ceilings that might conceal a deadly spear or something like that. In his mind, he was picturing movies he had watched where darts or spears came shooting out of the walls.

"There has to be a simple solution to this. How would the high king know which was the correct box?" he asked himself. There was a small table in the room, but no chairs, so he sat on the table to rest while he thought about the solution. As he pondered the solution, he noticed the floor. On the floor, where a person might stand to open each of the boxes, were square shaped grooves, as if that portion of the floor could be removed. "But why would someone want to remove the floor?" he thought.

"Holy Hannah!" he exclaimed. "Those are trap doors." He stared at them for a moment more. "The trap door didn't open when I opened the lid on the first box, so maybe one is a trap door and the others are fake? If so, which one is real? Uggh! This is so frustrating." Then a thought struck him. He knew the first box wasn't the right one, and the trap door was fake. If he could open the second box while standing in front of the first box, then he wouldn't be standing on the trap door of the second box when he opened it.

"That's got to work," he said talking to himself again. He walked over and stood in front of the first box and carefully leaned over and undid the latches on the second box. Then with the tip of his finger, he slowly lifted the lid, but nothing happened. He lifted the lid all the way up and looked inside. As he did so, a ball of fire shot towards him. He ducked his face, but his hair wasn't so lucky. The ball of fire landed on his head and seemed to sit there.

"Ouch!" he yelled, as he flicked it off with his hand. He whirled around and to his astonishment, the ball of fire was bouncing off the wall and heading towards him. He dove to the floor to avoid it. He quickly turned over just in time to see the ball of flame bounce off the wall and start descending towards him. He turned over and tried to get up, but he wasn't quick enough and the ball slammed into his back.

"Ouch!" he yelled again and flicked it off with his hand. The ball hit the floor and rebounded back up, hitting him in the calf.

"Ouch!" He flicked it off again and noticed a hole had been burned in his pants. He looked up and noticed the ball moving towards him again. He dodged and it floated past him, hit the wall and started heading back towards him again.

"You have got to be kidding me," he muttered to himself. He dodged it again, and as before, it hit the wall and started after him. He noticed that it didn't burn anything else, just him. *I can't keep this up all day,* he thought as he once again dodged it. The fireball seemed to be picking up speed, and he knew dodging it wasn't going to be easy if it got any faster. Finally, he had an idea. He dodged it one more time and then pulled off his shirt. As the fireball headed towards him once again, he opened up his shirt like a baseball mitt, and caught it. Then he closed the shirt around it and crumpled the shirt up. His shirt was slightly warm, but not burning. He slowly opened the shirt up, and it was empty. He breathed a sigh of relief and silently thanked his father for teaching him that a fire needs oxygen to burn. Take away that oxygen, and the fire goes out.

As he put his shirt back on, he noticed a hole in the back where the fireball had hit him. Still, it was better than no shirt. He took in a deep breath and then walked over to the second box. As a precaution, he slowly placed his weight on the trap door to make sure it was safe. So far nothing had happened until he actually opened the lid of a box, so he figured the trap door probably wouldn't open until he did that. When nothing happened, he placed all his weight on it and stood in front of the second box. He leaned over and undid the latches of the third box. With his finger tip, he slowly cracked open the lid, but nothing happened. He lifted it a little higher, but as soon as he did, mishopods started pouring out. These were the same creatures Scott had seen in the pyramid with the moon spell. Scott quickly snapped the lid shut, but not before eight to ten of them escaped. He jumped backwards, as far away from the shelf as he could get. The mishopods wasted no time. Instead of crawling down the shelf they leaped and took off running as soon as they landed on the floor. They were headed for Scott. He moved around the room, but they changed course every time he did.

"Go away," he yelled, but to no avail. They had him backed into a corner and they spread out to ensure he couldn't run left or right. Scott let them get within a foot of him and then jumped over them. The little beasts turned and scurried after him. He looked around for any kind of weapon, but the room offered nothing. Finally, he climbed onto the table. The mishopods split up into smaller groups and each group headed for a table leg. They then proceeded to consume the legs, and little by little, the table was slowly getting nearer and nearer to the floor.

"Oh, you've got to be kidding me!" Scott complained. Then he had an idea. While the mishopods were busy consuming the table, he jumped off as quietly as he could, hoping they wouldn't notice. To his disappointment, they did and immediately stopped consuming the table and headed in his direction.

"Give me a break, will ya!" he screamed at them. He ran over to the doorway of the room and stepped out. The mishopods gathered at the doorway and stopped. As if they were guarding the room, they sat at the threshold making their vibrating sound. He had to get the book, but how? He didn't have anything to fend off these little beasts. "The table legs!" he whispered to himself. If he could break off one of the table legs, he could use it to smash them.

He counted to three and leaped over them. They immediately turned and headed towards him. He flipped the table over and pulled. Even with the gloves on, the legs were stubborn, and didn't give way immediately. He gave the table leg one really hard tug and the leg finally came free, sending Scott sprawling onto his back. He frantically pushed himself into a corner and then looked for the little beasts. He spotted them climbing over the upside-down table, headed in his direction. He quickly jumped to his feet and brought the table leg down hard on the first arriving mishopod. To his surprise the mishopod jumped to the side with lightning speed. He tried again, and it moved again. Each time he tried to smash it, it avoided the hit. The others were getting closer and panic was starting to set in.

He started to rapidly pound the floor, trying to hit any mishopod he could. One got so close to him that, in a panic, he brought the table leg down so hard that it broke in two and the other half bounced across the room.

"No, no, no, no, no, no!" he screamed. He had no choice but to jump again. He barely cleared the last one and headed over to the other side of the room. He found himself standing by box number one. Out of desperation, he lifted the lid, and the black mist of death flowed out. It swirled around him again, doing the same thing it did last time.

"Not me," he yelled as if the mist could understand him. "Them," he said pointing towards the mishopods, which were now making their way once again towards him. Scott ran to another corner of the room to buy himself some more time. The mist didn't follow him, but started attacking the mishopods. As it attacked each one, they turned to fine powder. Once they were all consumed, the mist returned to the box and the lid slammed shut.

Scott breathed another sigh of relief. After that adventure, he had no desire to open the fourth or the fifth box, but he knew he had to. He had a fifty percent chance of getting it right and with any luck he wouldn't have to open both of them.

He decided he was going to open the fifth box first, hoping the creator of the nasty room would have expected a person to start with book one and make their way down to the fifth book, assuming they made it that far. If that were the case, then the fifth book must be The Ancient Book of Magic. So far, nothing had happened until the lid of each box had been opened, so the plan was to first unlatch the fifth box, back away, and use part of the table leg to lift the lid. However, as soon as he stepped on the square in front of the fifth box, it gave way and Scott fell. It happened so fast, that he only had seconds to react. His three fingers on his left hand barely caught the edge of the floor, and he now hung there, a feat only made possible by the gloves he wore. He looked down and all he could see was darkness. He wanted to scream, he was so tired of this. With a ton of effort, he grabbed the floor with his other hand and lifted himself back up. He lay there panting, not wanting to get up. His heart was racing and he needed to let the adrenaline subside.

"Idiot," he said to himself. "You had to pick the wrong box, didn't you?"

Just then his radio crackled and Josh's voice came on. "Hey Bozo! What's taking you so long?"

Scott was exhausted. He hadn't slept in over twenty-four hours. He was pretty sure his body was out of adrenaline. Never in all his life, had he experienced so many emotions and been under more stress in such a short amount of time. He was starting to crack.

"What's taking me so long, he asks?" he repeated out loud. "What's taking me so long!?" he let out a chuckle, which quickly turned into a laugh. Soon he was laughing hysterically. However, abruptly his laughter died and he took in a deep breath. "I'm gonna kill him," he finally said. "But first I'm going to get that blasted book. There's one box left. Let's just get the book and get out of here."

Scott stood up and looked at the last box. He was about to approach it, when Eric's voice came over the radio.

"Scott, you okay?"

He pulled the radio out his pocket. "YES!" he screamed into it. "Now leave me alone!"

There was silence on the other end for several seconds and then Eric calmly replied. "That…doesn't sound like you're okay. Tell me what's going on."

Scott pushed the button. "Okay, you want to know the truth? No, I'm NOT okay. Do you know how many times I've almost died today? Well, I'll tell you. Three times down there and three times up here. That tends to mess with a guy a little bit, and I certainly don't want to go for a seventh time. So, leave me alone so I can concentrate."

He tossed the radio onto the floor, took in a deep breath and walked over to the fourth box. He gently placed his foot on the trap door area in front of the box and slowly applied pressure. It held. He let out a sigh of relief and stepped forward. He undid the latches and was about the open then lid, when he paused. The table leg he had broken off was lying on the floor about four feet away. He walked over and picked it up. He wasn't taking any chances. Once again, he approached the box. When he was close enough, he hooked the edge of the table leg to the edge of the box and lifted the lid.

Nothing jumped out of the box and the trap door didn't open, so he continued to lift the lid, expecting something to happen at any moment. Nothing happened. Once he was convinced it was safe, he stepped up and peered into the box. Inside he found a book, and written on the outside cover were the words, 'The Ancient Book of Magic.'

"Now we're talking," Scott mumbled and reached inside and pulled the book out of the box. He sat down on the floor and opened the front cover. But the first page inside was blank. He turned the page and noticed the second and third pages were blank also. He flipped page after page, but they were all blank. "You have got to be kidding me!" he cried. "The Ancient Book of Magic is a fake! Or maybe this book is just a decoy. But this wouldn't fool anyone," he said still talking to himself. "Unless, of course, the book is spell rigged and I'm just not feeling the effects of the spell." He breathed out a sigh of frustration.

"Where is the real book? Did we come all this way for nothing? Did I almost die six times today for nothing!" He slammed the fake book on the floor.

"Ahhhhhhhhhhhhhhhh!" he screamed as loud as he could and slammed his fist against the floor. He sat there breathing angrily. "This can't be happening!"

Eric's voice came across the radio. "Scott, are you okay? What's happening? We can hear you screaming all the way down here."

Scott looked over at the radio lying on the floor. He didn't want to answer it. He had failed and now they would never rescue their parents. A deep depression began setting in.

"Scott? Scott, answer me?" Eric asked over the radio. Scott ignored his pleas. Eric continued to call for his brother, but Scott wouldn't answer. He didn't want to talk to anyone.

"Scott," a voice came inside his head. It was Josh this time. "Tell us what's going on or I'm coming up there to get you."

Scott sat up. "No!" he said quickly. "That would be suicide. Do not come up here, Josh."

"Ha, I wasn't really going to. I just needed to get you to talk. Eric, Azinine and Ned are freaking out down here. You need to tell us what's going on."

Scott, almost on the verge of tears, said, "It's not here, Josh."

"What's not there?"

"The Easter Bunny, you numskull. What do you think?"

"Well, no wonder you're so frustrated. You're not supposed to be looking for the Easter Bunny. You're supposed to be looking for the book."

"Tell me you're not serious."

"Of course I'm not serious. I'm just trying to cheer you up. It's all part of my evil plan."

"Your evil plan?" Scott questioned.

"Yes, my evil plan to rule the world. And I need that book to do it."

Scott had to think about whether Josh was serious or not. Finally he said, "Well, you'll need to go to plan B to rule the world, because the book isn't here."

"What do you mean the book isn't there? Of course it's there."

"There are five boxes that, when looking through the Eigenholle, appear to have books in them. Every one of them is a trap. A death trap, I might add."

"Then the book has to be there," Josh said emphatically.

"It's NOT here, Josh! Believe me, I've looked. No, I've more than looked. I have gone through a living horror for it. It's not here!"

"If the book wasn't there, they wouldn't have gone through so much trouble to protect it."

"Hmm...I guess that kind of makes sense. But I don't know where to look now. The Eigenholle doesn't show anything else."

"Duffus brain! Are you telling me you're still wearing the Eigenholle?"

"Of course! It's the key, isn't it?" Scott replied.

"Didn't you hear what that Garglythia thing said before he disappeared?"

"What are you talking about, Josh?"

"It said the Eigenholle will not help you get the book."

"Yeah, I know that. It was useless against all five traps."

"You still don't get it. Take the Eigenholle off. Use your own eyes and ears to find it."

"Okay...but I can see the room just fine with it on."

"Just do it."

"Okay, whatever," Scott replied. He took the Eigenholle off his head and it folded itself back up into a box. He looked around the room, but nothing had changed. "It looks just the same, Josh. I don't see anything that's different."

"It's got to be there, big brother."

"Okay, don't talk to me for a while. I need to think."

"Fine, but don't take too long. We're getting kind of bored down here."

"Oh, well excuse me," Scott replied with a hint of sarcasm. "If you're bored, come on up. There's plenty of excitement up here. Now leave me alone."

Scott shook his head and leaned against the wall, closing his eyes. He didn't really need to think. He was pretty sure the book wasn't there, but he was so tired, he just needed to rest for a bit. As he sat there with his eyes closed, trying to relax, he heard something. It was a low ringing noise. Not an audible ringing noise, but an inaudible noise similar to the sound of the brace-let Azinine had given him. He listened more carefully, trying to determine where the noise was coming from. It sounded like it was coming from the wall. He stood up and listened again. Now he was sure it was coming from the wall. He placed his hands on the wall, slowly moving his fingers across the golden rocks. As his hand brushed over a particular stone, the sound sud-denly became louder. When he removed his hand the sound became softer. He placed his hand on the stone and once again the sound got louder. *With Azinine's bracelet, you push the stones to activate them,* he thought. He placed his palm on the stone and pushed. Nothing happened. Disappointment stabbed through him.

"This has to be something," he muttered to himself, scratching his head. He placed his hand on the stone again, and heard the sound get louder. He grabbed hold of the stone and tried pulling it out, but it didn't budge and still nothing happened. Next, he tried turning the stone. It turned. He heard a click, and the wall crumpled before him. Before him was a small room.

Inside the small room was a table, and on the table was an object that looked like a book. It was wrapped in a leather carrying case. Scott walked inside and approached the book. The case looked old, but it was still in good shape. He opened it up and inside was a book. He pulled it out and looked at it. It was beautiful. The book's cover had no writing on it, but it was in-tricately designed. He opened the book and turned the pages, discovering each one filled with various spells. He breathed a sigh of relief as joy flooded through him. He had found The Ancient Book of Magic.

He placed the book back in its carrying case and walked out of the small-er room. As soon as he stepped out, the wall bricked itself back up. He placed the Eigenholle back on his head and turned to join the others. He had just started down, when he realized a door had opened in the corner of the room. Glancing through it, he could see that it led to the outside. Now he wished the others had come with him. However, at this point he knew he would have to make his way back from the direction he had come and find some other way out, if there was one. He made his way back towards the group waiting for him and entered the room they were standing in.

The others were sitting against one of the walls. When he entered, they all jumped up and ran over.

Josh, noticing his burnt hair and the burned holes in his pant leg and shirt said, "Dude, you look like something out of a horror movie."

"Yeah, I kind of feel like I've been in a horror movie."

"Is that it?" Azinine asked, dying to get her hands on it.

"I think so," he shrugged.

"See? I told you it was there," Josh said.

Scott put the pack down, pulled out the book and handed it to Azinine. She reverently slid her fingers over the cover, tracing the designs etched into the leather cover. Ned did likewise while the others just peeked over their shoulders to get a look. Opening the book, Azinine took one glance at the first page and disappointment washed over her as she discovered the book was written in the ancient language.

"Batwings!" she blurted out in frustration.

"What? Where?" Josh asked, looking around.

"It's just an expression," Ned told him. "She's mad because she can't read it." Playing the role of the gallant gentleman, Josh offered to read the pages for her. He took it in his hands and read the first page. "The Book of Ancient Magic, written by Zandor Allendon."

"Oh my freak," Scott blurted out. "The Garglython called my gloves the gloves of Allendon. That must mean that Zandor also created these gloves and the sword."

"He also created the Shimmerall," Azinine pointed out.

"Really? He made all these items?"

"They didn't call him 'Zandor the Magnificent' for nothing," Azinine said smiling. "He was a pretty amazing magus."

"How did you find the book?" Josh asked.

"I heard it."

"What do you mean, you heard it?" Azinine asked.

"It's similar to the noise your bracelet makes when you signal you're coming to CastleOne," Scott replied.

"Huh?" she asked in confusion. "Those bracelets don't make any noises."

"Yes, they do. It's sort of an inaudible ringing noise. That's how I always knew you had signaled the bracelet."

"Really?" she replied. "I have never heard those make any noises."

"Scott," Josh butted in, "you said it was an inaudible noise. Maybe it's like the way we can talk in our heads. Maybe you have to be lingual to hear it."

"Oh, I hadn't thought about that, but maybe you're right."

"Okay, let's read the book," Azinine said with enthusiasm.

"Good idea," Josh replied. "I'll read it out loud so everyone can hear."

"I know it would be fun to read the book," Eric said, "but time is of the essence. We really need to get the book back to Magus Noka as soon as possible."

Scott could see that Azinine really wanted to read it. "How about we let Josh and Azinine look at the book, while the three of us," he pointed to Eric and Ned, "figure out how to get out of here and what to do next."

"Good idea," Eric agreed. Ned was a little disappointed. He wanted to look at the book also, but knew Eric was right.

Josh and Azinine thumbed through the pages, while the three boys discussed how they were going to get out. Scott was hopeful, with the use of the Eigenholle, they could leave the same way they came in, so their conversation turned to how they would get past the wyellits outside waiting for them.

The two boys were so busy discussing things that they didn't notice a small black cloud forming overhead. Boom! A miniature bolt of lightning struck about four feet from Ned with a deafening crack. The three boys just about jumped out of their skin.

"Wow!" Josh exclaimed.

"Oops! Sorry," Azinine said before she and Josh broke out into an uncontrollable fit of laughter. Ned had been slightly singed by the lightning and his hair was sticking straight up in the air. Once Scott and Eric had gained their composure, they too, began to chuckle. Ned, on the other hand, didn't think it was funny.

"Sorry, Ned," Azinine said again as she tried in vain to flatten his hair. "I didn't realize it would do that. Good thing I only tried the practice spell, I can only imagine what would have happened if we tried the real one."

"Azinine," Eric said, a thought forming in his head. Speaking very slowly in English, he continued, "Can…you…do…that…bigger?"

"Don't ask her that!" Ned shot back. "She might kill us all."

"I don't mean in here. I mean outside. If we could create a large enough storm, maybe we could scare them away." Ned translated his remarks to Azinine.

"Maybe, but I'm not sure I would be successful. I may need some sort of magic conductor like a staff or something if we want it on a scale that big," Azinine replied.

"Why don't you at least try?" Scott asked.

With a smile, Azinine looked back in the book and with Josh's assistance she performed a spell called, 'Fire From Heaven.' With the Eigenholle on, Scott could see outside that the clouds were gathering and the sky was getting darker. Soon a single lightning bolt fell from the sky and cracked the air. The wyellits jumped, but stayed in their place. A moment later another bolt of lightning cracked and in the seconds following, another one hit. Scott could see the wyellits were visibly shaken, but still not moving.

"Keep it up, Azinine. I think it's working. Can you produce more?"

"I'm trying, but I can't seem to keep then coming fast enough. Maybe if Josh and I did it together, we could produce more."

"Huh?" Josh asked, looking up from the book he had been studying.

"I need you to help with the spell. We need to produce more lightning bolts."

"Oh! Sweet," Josh replied. Then turning to Scott he said with mock superiority, "You see? She recognizes a true magician when she sees one."

The two of them started chanting the spell. Azinine's lightning bolts continued, but as Josh recited the spell, a large cloud started to form inside.

"Run," Scott yelled. The group ran down the stairs and through the tunnel that led to the previous pyramid. Boom!!! The sound of thunder roared through the pyramid.

"Josh, are you trying to kill us all?" Scott cried out, turning on him.

"Sorry," he replied.

"It's not his fault," Azinine said. "We just haven't trained him. He doesn't know how the magic works."

"So...what did I do wrong?"

"You said the spell without thinking about where you wanted it to take place, so it defaulted to your location. If you want it to take place outside, you need to concentrate on the outside."

"And the spell knows what I'm thinking?" Josh asked in amazement.

"Yes, it's how a lot of things work on this world," she explained.

"Okay, I think I can do that."

"You two go back into the pyramid to do it. We'll wait here just in case Josh messes up again," Scott suggested. "I've had enough excitement for one day. I don't need anymore."

Josh and Azinine nodded and headed back into the pyramid. They both started chanting the spell. This time Josh said it correctly. Lightning bolts began to fall more frequently, but still not enough to scare the wyellits away. Azinine and Josh soon grew tired and the lightning bolts slowly stopped coming. Scott and the others made their way back into the pyramid where Josh and Azinine were.

"It's no use," Azinine said as they walked in. "We really need a staff if we're going to do this on a scale large enough to scare them away."

"Scott, there must be another way out," Eric said turning to his brother. "Certainly the Eigenholle should show you that."

"There is only one other way out that I can see and that's near the room where I found the book."

"That's too dangerous," Eric said shaking his head. "You can't see any other way?"

"Well," Scott paused, "in the tunnel we were just in, there is another tunnel that looks like it leads out of the pyramids. In fact, I think it leads into the forest. The only problem is that it's blocked off by the wall."

"If there's a tunnel there," Eric surmised, "then there must be a door. It's worth a try."

The group found their way back down the stairs and into the tunnel that led to the previous pyramid.

After a few minutes Scott said, "Stop. It's right here."

"I don't see any other tunnel," Josh commented, looking around.

"You're not wearing the Eigenholle."

"No, but I can see this whole wall is made of rock."

"That's what I told you before. But behind this rock wall is a tunnel. We just have to find out how to get to it."

"Maybe there used to be a tunnel and someone blocked it off," Eric suggested.

"I don't think so. Now that I think about it, the walls in all the other pyramids crumpled to allow access, but only when a certain event or word triggered it," Scott replied. "We just need to figure out how it opens."

Eric ran his fingers along the wall, searching for any indication of a hidden door of some type. "Scott," he asked, "do you see anything that would trigger the door?"

"No, it just looks like a wall."

"Maybe we could just break it down," Josh offered.

"I doubt it. It's at least two feet thick," Scott replied.

"Try the word for open in the ancient tongue," Ned suggested.

"Okay, 'Ouf'" Scott said, but nothing happened.

"Stand back," Josh ordered the others. "Let the master do his job."

"You're not going to create more lightning bolts, are you?" Ned asked.

"Of course not," Josh retorted.

"Don't break anything, Josh. I'm not going to carry you out of here," Eric warned.

"Don't worry. I think I got the hang of this now."

"Oh, great," Ned blurted out. "I suggest we all take cover."

Josh ignored the others as they all flattened themselves against the tunnel wall. He stretched his hands out in front of him. "Kenig muga ammr ver ouf dur ans terch," is what most of the group heard. Scott, on the other hand, heard, "Kings magic, always true, open the door and let us through." The wall crumpled and behind it lay the tunnel.

"Josh! You did it!" Azinine squealed, getting up and putting her arms around him.

"No way! For once, one of your magic tricks actually worked. How did you know how to do that?" Scott asked.

Josh took in a deep breath and puffed out his chest. "Well, real magicians just know these things."

Eric patted him on the shoulder. "Well, meister magician, grab your pack and let's get out of here."

Josh put the book back in its cover and then kissed it. "I love you," he whispered.

The group entered the tunnel and one minute later they all turned at the sound of the wall putting itself back together again. They made their way along the damp, clammy walls. The tunnel went on for several miles it seemed before they came to another wall, but this one opened as they approached.

"Well, at least we don't have to worry about getting out," Josh commented.

"No, but we do have to worry about getting home," Eric said. "Does any-one know where we are and which way is home?"

"The pyramids are southeast of Lux. So based on the position of the moon, we need to go that direction," Azinine pointed, after Ned translated what Eric had said.

"That's good enough for me," Eric said. "Let's get going."

"Eric," Azinine spoke in broken English. "Too dark. Too dangerous. We stay, sleep, wait for light."

"She's right," Scott agreed. "We don't know what's out here. We're better off staying here and waiting for morning. We probably only have a few hours anyway."

"Okay," Eric said, nodding his head. "Let's rest."

Chapter 28

Alon

The kids sat down on the forest floor next to the entrance of the cave they had just exited. It wasn't comfortable, but it felt good to finally rest. Scott removed the Eigenholle from his head, and as he did so, it folded back into its original jewelry box shape. He placed it in the pack and sat down next to a large rock where Azinine joined him. She laid her head on his lap and instantly fell asleep. Scott smiled and rested his arm on her shoulder. He had been so caught up in everything that he had forgotten about his feelings for this girl.

Josh sat down next to Eric, who was whispering something to Ned. For a while he just sat there looking up into the sky. "Eric?" he said after a moment. "Do you think Mom is still alive?"

"Yes, of course she's still alive," his older brother replied with as much conviction as he could muster.

"What are we going to do once we get back? Even though we have the book, how will we use it to free her?"

"I don't know. We'll leave that up to Magus Noka. He said he would help us."

"I guess so."

Scott was right. It wasn't much longer than two hours before the moon finally disappeared and the sun began to rise. The group, however, was so exhausted that they didn't wake up until around noon.

Eric was awakened by the sound of loud birds chasing each other in the forest. He stood up, stretched and then walked over to Scott, who was still fast asleep. Nudging him with his foot, he said, "Wake up you two love birds. We've got to get going."

Scott and Azinine slowly woke. She looked up at him and smiled. "Thanks for being my pillow."

"Any time," he replied with a big a grin on his face.

The group packed up their stuff. "Do you think those wyellits are still guarding the pyramids?" Azinine asked. "It would sure be faster if we could take our MOC, or I guess technically it's Maulder's MOC."

"Only one way to find out," Scott said. The others nodded and they headed back towards the Pyramids, which ended up being further than they thought. When they finally got there, the pygmy wyellits were gone.

"Yes!" Azinine squealed in delight. "Let's grab the MOC and get out of here." The group ran to the first pyramid, but to their utter disappointment, the MOC was gone.

"Curse those little buggers," Josh remarked.

"I guess we're on our feet again," Scott wearily sighed.

They walked through the forest all day long without seeing any sign of civilization on the ground or in the air. It was tiring, but they didn't have much choice and the thought of their parents drove them on. They continued to walk, even when the sun went down and darkness began to fall.

Knowing how tired everyone was and how unpredictable things could be on this world they knew so little about, Eric urged the group on. "I know it's getting dark, guys, but we've got to keep going regardless of the dangers. Our parents lives are at stake here. We'll just have to stay alert."

Josh caught up to Eric, and with a worried note in his voice, said, "Speaking of being alert, they're back."

"Who's back?"

"Those shadows we saw the night Lardior's men caught us."

"I've seen them too," Ned said, joining in on the conversation. "They're like ghosts moving in and out of the trees. I first spotted them around dusk, far off in the distance, but I couldn't make them out. Since then, they've come much closer."

"What are they?" Scott asked.

"I don't know," Ned replied.

"Eric," Azinine spoke up again, "we stop, okay?"

Eric hesitated, but finally gave in. "Okay, but where? There isn't really a good place to rest."

"Let's try over there. Look at that patch of grass, it's perfect," Josh said pointing to a lush patch of grass.

"Really?" Ned said.

"Sure," Josh replied. He walked over and stood on the grass turning himself around as though it was paradise.

"JOSH!" Scott screamed. "Get off that grass!"

Josh looked at Scott like he was some sort of lunatic. "Hey, I have just as much right to this grass as you do," he yelled back. Scott took off running as fast as he could and tackled Josh into the brush. Both of them picking up their fair share of scratches.

"What did you do that for? There's enough room for all of us!" Josh asked angrily.

"Get off it!" Scott screamed at Ned and Eric, who had now just entered the grassy area. Eric jumped off and grabbed Ned with him.

"Okay, we're off," Eric said with confusion. "Now would you mind explaining why you're so paranoid?"

"It's a trap!" Scott yelled as he and Josh got back on their feet. "We've got to get out of here fast!"

"What kind of trap?" Ned asked.

"No time to explain," he said as he pulled Josh further away from the grassy area and motioned for the others to follow.

"Hurry!" he yelled when the others were slow to follow him.

Just then, the ground, where the grass lay, suddenly opened up and numerous goblins poured out with swords in hand. This did the job and the others started running the best they could in the dark. But they were no match for the goblins, whose eyes could see in the dark very well. Still, they ran about fifty yards before the goblins caught up to them. Josh and Ned were the first to be captured. Azinine had her wand out and had used the stone spell on several, but there were too many and she, too, was eventually disarmed and captured.

Scott and Eric heard the cries of their friends and stopped. The goblins reached Eric first and several tried to lay hands on him, but not before he took down four or five. Everybody but Scott had been captured. The goblins stopped for just a second to assess the situation.

"Seize him and the pack he's carrying," a large, ugly goblin commanded, pointing to Scott. Two goblins approached Scott. When the first one reached him, Scott struck the goblin with the palm of his hand directly against its chest. The force of the hit, combined with the magic of the gloves, sent the goblin flying and landed him flat on his back, writhing in agony. This was enough to make the second one think twice before approaching. He drew his sword and pointed it at Scott, motioning to the other goblins for backup.

"We want the book. Hand over the pack and we may let you live!" the goblin demanded.

Scott knew he couldn't do that. "Come and get it," he replied, trying to sound as threatening as he possibly could.

The goblin snarled at him. "Nothing would give me greater pleasure." It slowly approached with the point of the sword aimed at Scott's chest. Scott was trying hard to think of what he could do, but his mind was blank. The goblins holding Eric had relaxed their grip slightly, believing he wouldn't try anything with so many other goblins around. Before they had a chance to react, Eric flipped both arms upwards, grabbed the back of both goblins necks and slammed their heads together. The two goblins crumpled to the ground and Eric bolted towards Scott. A goblin jumped out in front to block his way, but Eric knocked it aside with a strong blow to its jaw and kept going. Two other goblins tackled Eric to the ground and a third had to jump on him to keep him down.

"Make a run for it!" Eric yelled.

Scott looked around to see where the best escape route might lie, but in his heart he knew he couldn't leave his friends. One of the goblins, noticing Scott's distraction, leapt at him and knocked him to the ground. The goblin with the sword pounced and placed the blade up to Scott's neck.

It gave Scott an evil grin. "Now you will pay for all the trouble you have caused us," it growled. The goblin was just about to shove the blade through Scott's neck when a terrible cry pierced the night and a shadow from behind leapt through the air and caught the goblin by the neck pulling it to the ground. Several more shadows appeared and then even more came, growling and howling. They attacked the goblins with an intense ferocity. The goblins were forced to release their prisoners as they tried to protect themselves. They put up a fight, but the shadows were just too quick for them. Scott and the others sat there in amazement watching the attack.

Eric crawled over to Scott and asked in bewilderment, "What are they?"

"They sound like wolves."

"Do you think these are what we've been seeing? The shadows that have been following us?"

"I don't know for sure, but it's a good possibility."

"Will they attack us next?"

"Well, they haven't attacked any of us yet, so I'll take that as a good sign."

"I agree, but why are they helping us?"

"I don't know," Scott shrugged. "But I think we're about to find out."

The fight was over rather quickly and those goblins who had survived the attacked were now all retreating back into the mountain, leaving the small group alone with their rescuers. The group could only see the eyes of the creatures, but it was enough to tell that they were beginning to encircle the kids. Out of the darkness, another set of eyes appeared before Eric and Scott.

The creature was huge. If it was a wolf, it was the largest wolf Eric had ever seen. It yapped, and to Eric it sounded like a dog or a wolf growling, but to Scott it was much different.

"Hello, son of Valar."

"Alon?" Scott spoke with some hesitancy and disbelief. "Is that you?"

"Yes, it is I, my good friend."

"Alon!" Scott cried in relief. "How did you know it was us?"

"We have been following you, when we could, that is."

"Why?"

"In the beginning, just to make sure nothing happened to you. I owe you a great deal. And when word came to me that five 'stupid' Lumen children were walking the woods alone and it was about to become dark. I knew I had to make sure nothing happened to you. Then you entered the Greymen domain and we lost you. It wasn't until the ancient book had been taken that I knew where you were."

"How did you know we have that?" Scott asked in surprise, now wondering how the goblins had also known they had it.

"You used it. You spoke the ancient language to command nature and we felt it. We weren't one hundred percent sure, but we felt pretty certain it was you. In any case, we knew that someone had taken the book and came to investigate."

"Thanks, Alon," Scott said with sincere gratitude.

"Scott," the old wolf warned, "we're not the only ones that felt it. I am sure of that. Others, like these goblins, will also come looking for it. They will try to take it from you, even if they have to combine forces to do it. You and your friends are in grave danger. Where is your sword?"

"I don't have it," Scott replied sheepishly.

"What? You don't have it?" Alon growled. "Are you crazy? You took the book without the sword?"

"We had to get it," Scott tried to explain. "Our parents are being held captive. We have to try and save them. The book is the only way."

"Do you know how to use the book to save your parents?"

"No," again Scott answered a bit reluctantly. "But Magus Noka does and he said he'd help us if we were able to retrieve it."

The old wolf pondered that for a moment. "Hmm," he finally spoke. "Okay, we will continue to accompany you for as long as we're able. We must get you to Magus Noka as soon as possible. We surprised the goblins, but they'll be back in stronger numbers, and they're probably not the only ones. I am sure there will be others. The sooner we get moving the better."

"I understand. Again, thank you for your help."

Alon sent up a howl, letting the other wolves know it was time to go. Scott picked up his pack and turned around just in time to see a blur out of the darkness knock him to the ground. Scott thrashed about trying to knock over his assailant.

"Can we eat him? Can we? Please, please!" Scott heard a wolf growl.

"Carakaz?" Scott asked.

"I'm so hungry! Let me eat him," the wolf growled some more and then began licking Scott.

"Carakaz!" Scott laughed. "You old fool. I could have killed you."

"Killed me? I just heard you say you don't have your sword."

"No, but I could have hit you pretty hard."

"I'm too quick for you. You couldn't have..."

"Carakaz!" Alon snapped. "We don't have time to play."

"Yes, sir," Carakaz replied and moved back into the dark.

Eric picked Scott up. "I take it you're friends?" he asked with relief.

"Yeah, friends of mine from the goblin mines."

"Uh, good friends to have."

The grouped decided to keep walking even though they were extremely tired. The moon was finally making its ascent into the sky. This would make it easier to travel, but also easier to be spotted. They moved in and out of trees and brush. Scott could feel Alon walking next to him like some ghostly bodyguard. Azinine had found her way over to Scott and slipped her hand in his, but didn't say anything. Scott was glad to have her near him.

They continued to walk for several miles. The air was fresh and smelled heavenly. Scott couldn't help feeling what a shame it was to be here under these circumstances. It would be so nice to just sit and relax. He had had very few moments on Lumen where he could just relax and he looked forward to the day when peace would once more be restored. This thought gave him renewed vigor and he began to walk faster. Azinine glanced at him quizzically, but kept quiet, matching her pace with his. The wolves turned to the left and led them down into a ravine, up a small canyon and into a cave.

Alon turned to Scott, saying, "Here, you and your friends can rest. It will be safer during the night. Take advantage of this time because you will all need your strength tomorrow. We will keep guard."

"Thank you, Alon," Scott sincerely replied.

Scott informed the others and they gladly laid down to rest. Even though the ground was hard and rocky, none of them had any problems falling asleep. Sometime during the night, Scott thought he could hear wolves fighting outside. He tried to rouse himself, but his exhaustion overcame him as he once again fell back into a deep sleep. Sometime later, he was jerked out of his sleep by someone shaking him.

"Wake up, Scott! Wake up."

Scott opened his eyes and even though the face peering down at him was a blur, he could tell it was Eric. "Is it time to go already?" he asked drowsily. "I'm still so tired."

"We're all tired," Eric replied. "But we have to go."

Scott sat up, rubbed his eyes and then he heard it. The noise he had heard earlier that night, but it hadn't registered in his brain until now what it was.

"What's happening?" Scott asked.

"The wolves are doing their best to fend them off, but they won't be able to keep them off for long. We've got to slip away while they still think we're in here."

"You want to leave the protection of the wolves?"

"There won't be any more protection pretty soon. If we stay here, we'll be sitting ducks."

"But if we leave, they'll have a better chance of getting to us."

"Scott, Josh has been talking with some of the other wolves. It's not just goblins they're fighting out there. They've brought trolls. I can't even imagine what those are like, but I know they can't be good. And they have some other creatures called womvampirs. We have to get out of here! If not for our sakes, then for the sake of the wolves. I know they said they would protect us, and that's what they've been doing. But do you want them to fight to the death? Are their lives worth risking?"

"They've brought womvampirs and trolls?" Scott asked, still in a daze.

"Yes, now get up," Eric replied emphatically, pulling Scott to his feet. "A few of the wolves have agreed to accompany us, so we won't be completely without protection."

"Okay, okay! I'm coming," Scott agreed.

With everyone awake, the group grabbed their stuff and slowly crept out of the cave. The moon was still up and they could see a battle raging beneath them in the canyon. The only way out was up the canyon, which became steeper as they went. The wolves accompanying them, however, knew the way, and led them along a steep, narrow path. As they neared the top, they looked down and could see a brigade of goblins and several larger figures pursuing them.

"Are those trolls?" Scott asked Ned

"I'm not an expert on trolls. I've never even seen one in real life, just pictures. But by the size of them and the clubs they're carrying, I'd say yes, those are trolls."

"Wow, those things are huge." Scott said in amazement.

The lead wolf turned to Scott, saying, "You won't be able to outrun them. Go the opposite direction of the moon. You will soon come to a meadow with long grass. Your best bet is to hide there until morning. We'll lead the goblins in the opposite direction if we can. Good luck."

With that, the wolves turned and strode away. Scott led the others in the direction he had been instructed. They ran for about ten minutes before they came upon the large meadow. The grass was about five feet tall and the group was glad to have the cover.

"We should probably split up," Eric instructed. "If, by chance, they do look for us here, at least they won't find all of us together. In the morning, we'll meet up by that large tree over there," he said, pointing to a tree. The others agreed and split up. Ned went with Eric while Josh went with Scott and Azinine. This perturbed Scott since he was hoping to be alone with her, but Azinine seemed to be glad to have him.

"Scott," Josh whispered.

"What?"

"Beat it."

"You beat it," Scott said in not so soft tones. "Go sit with Eric."

"No, I want to be with my girlfriend."

"She's not your girlfriend," Scott piped back much louder.

"Well, she sure kisses like it."

"What!" Scott blurted out.

Josh was about to answer, enjoying how easily he could provoke his brother, when Eric came flying through the grass and tackled both of them to the ground. "Are you two crazy!" he whispered menacingly. "There is a whole army of goblins and who knows what else out there looking to fry us for dinner and you guys are doing your best to give us away! Josh, I want you to come with me, now!"

A bit chagrined, Josh walked over to Azinine, who was still very amused over the whole incident. He picked up her hand and held it in his. "I guess you'll have to spend the night without me. But be brave, my love," he whispered, looking in her eyes. He walked slowly away still holding her hand, only letting it fall when he was too far away to hold it any longer and then he winked.

Scott, on the other hand, wasn't amused, but he kept quiet. Josh walked over to where Ned and Eric were standing and the three of them found a spot to hide.

"What was that all about?" Eric asked once they had settled down.

"I just told him I wanted to be with my girlfriend."

"You don't really believe she's your girlfriend, do you?" Ned asked, incredulously.

"Of course not. But Scott doesn't know that," Josh replied with a grin.

"Next time you decide to entertain yourself, do it when our lives aren't at stake," Eric warned.

"Sorry," Josh replied. They made themselves comfortable and try as they may to stay awake, exhaustion overcame them and they fell asleep.

Chapter 29

Kliandro

The morning came quickly and relief filled them as they realized the plan must have worked with the goblins following the trail of the wolves. They worried about their four-legged friends, but knowing there wasn't anything they could do about that, they readied themselves for a new day. With the arrival of the sun, they felt a little safer knowing that the night creatures such as the goblins, the trolls and the Womvampirs were held at bay for the moment. However, they were also very aware that the day might also bring other dangers.

Azinine found some berries, which were sour to the taste, but at least edible. They ate what they could, although it wasn't enough to satisfy their intense hunger. Just as they finished, Josh hailed them from on top of a small hill.

"Hey, guys! There's a small pond over here."

"Oh, that sounds great!" Scott replied. "I haven't bathed in days."

"Me neither," Ned said as he started into a trot towards the hill.

"I'll…just stay here," Azinine replied.

"Come with us, Azinine," Eric said putting his arm around her and prodding her towards the pond. "We all need to stay together. We'll let you go first and the rest of us will turn our backs, standing guard. Then Ned and I will go while Scott and Josh stay with you. When we're done, Scott and Josh will go. What do you say?"

Azinine hadn't understood every word of what Eric said, but between the few words she had managed to grasp, hand gestures and Ned, she got the gist of it. "Okay," she replied with a smile. The group headed for the pond. Eric explained the plan to the rest of the group and they all agreed.

"Scott, before I get in, would you put on the Eigenholle and make sure there aren't any water nymphs or any other dangerous creatures lurking in that water?" Azinine asked.

"Sure," Scott replied. He hadn't thought of the Eigenholle as a tool for such things, but why not? He put the Eigenholle on his head and looked about. It was amazing. It was as though the water in the pond had disappeared, but the fish were still swimming. He could see everything.

"Well? What do you see?" she asked after waiting for about a minute.

Scott was so fascinated by the scene in front of him that he had forgotten why he was looking in the first place. "It looks fine. I can't see anything unusual, except for one large fish with unusually sharp teeth."

"Ha, ha! Very funny. Now take that thing off and turn your head," she demanded. They all turned around and while Azinine took her bath, the boys discussed plans for the day. The water was cold, but it felt good to get clean and seemed to lift everyone's spirits. Scott and Josh were the last ones to bathe. They put their clothes back on and went to find the others, who had gone looking for more berries. After searching for several minutes, they found them arguing about something.

"I'm telling you it was Morgan, queen of the fairies, and she's up to something," Ned said.

"No, it wasn't. Morgan only lives upon the waters, she wouldn't travel this far just to find us," Azinine replied.

"Who are you guys talking about?" Scott asked.

Ned ignored his friend. "She would, if it meant getting the book."

"Her powers aren't that strong here. She would need the help of other fairies. Have you seen any other fairies?"

"No, but that doesn't mean there aren't any."

Azinine turned to Scott, exasperated. "Would you please put on the Eigenholle and tell us if there are any fairies lurking about?" she snapped at him.

"Sure, I guess," he replied, disturbed at Azinine's intensity. Scott put on the Eigenholle and looked about. The world definitely looked different with it on, but he couldn't see any fairies. "Nope. I don't see any."

"I rest my case," Azinine said, glaring at her brother. "You were either imagining things, which is most likely the case since you haven't slept much, or something else created the illusion."

"I wasn't imagining it," Ned snapped back.

"Who are you talking about?" Scott asked again.

"Morgan, an evil fairy we don't want to run into. She travels in a ship and Ned claims he saw it."

"Well, either way, I suggest we keep our wits about us." Scott suggested.

"Is there a round-about way back home?" Eric asked, surprised at how much he had understood and how easy he seemed to be learning this new language. "The more direct route is most likely being watched. Does anyone have an idea where we are?"

"Home is northwest of the pyramids. Assuming we haven't veered too far off course, home should be that way," Ned said while pointing in a south east direction.

"Good. Then we'll travel east for several miles and then head south. Does everyone agree?"

"As long as it keeps us away from those goblins," Josh replied.

The group set off walking with high spirits. They had walked for several hours when Scott turned to Azinine. "Tell me more about Morgan."

"Morgan is a fairy sorceress. She calls herself the queen of the fairies. She lives in an underwater palace and has magical powers, which she uses to cause a great deal of trouble. Let's hope we never run into her. She's nothing but trouble and her magic is quite powerful. Morgan's been around since the beginning of time and it wouldn't surprise me to learn she has visited your world a time or two."

"Do fairies live that long?"

"Fairies are immortal, in that, they don't get old. But they can be killed. Although," she added as an afterthought, "it's very bad luck to kill a fairy."

"What do you mean?"

"I'm not sure exactly. Most fairies are good and are very important to the balance of life on Lumen. Killing one might upset that balance, not to mention all the upset fairies you'd have to deal with."

"How come we don't ever see them?"

"Fairies..." Azinine began to reply when Ned interrupted her.

"There!" Ned cried out. "See? I told you I wasn't imagining things."

"What are you talking about?" Azinine blurted back, annoyed that Ned had disrupted their conversation.

"There," he said pointing. "In the glen behind those trees. Don't you see it?"

Azinine squinted, the sun in her eyes. "I don't see any...wow!" she slowly breathed out, finally seeing it.

"What is it?" Josh asked.

"Looks kind of like a ship," Scott replied. "But how did it get out here? There aren't any rivers big enough around here for a boat that size."

"It's a Gord," Azinine whispered. "They're round on the bottom like an egg, but flat on top. They can fly through the air or dive under the sea."

"Do you think it's Morgan's?" Scott asked.

"Hmm...It guess it could be. It looks like something she would use, though I'm no expert. I'm sorry for doubting you, Ned."

"It's okay, but what do we do now?" Ned asked, shaking off her apology.

"You come eat with us," a voice from behind them said.

The group whirled around. There behind them, on top of a fallen log was a man. He wore brown pants, a brown shirt and a golden cape. A thought flitted through Scott's mind that he looked like something out of a comic book. However, they were all so shocked that no one said a word.

"How rude of me," the man smiled. "I forgot to introduce myself. My name is Kliandro and that Gord belongs to me and my family. We spent the night here while we gathered a few supplies. Before we left, we were going to have lunch. You are welcome to join us if you like and perhaps you could help us at the same time.

"What sort of help do you need?" Ned asked.

"We are not from these parts. We come from across the sea and are traveling to a city called Lux. Have you heard of it?"

"Heard of it? We live in Lux!" Ned blurted out, astonished at this coincidence. "We're headed there right now."

"Good. Then we'll have lunch and you shall accompany us to Lux. Unless, of course, you'd prefer to walk."

"Nooo, no, no! We prefer to fly," Josh said, speaking up before anyone had a chance. "And we could use some food. We're starving."

"Then that settles it," Kliandro nodded in satisfaction. "You're coming with us. Follow me and I'll introduce you to my family."

After introducing themselves, the group followed Kliandro through the trees to where the Gord rested. Ned and Scott couldn't believe their luck and Josh couldn't wait to get something to eat. Eric was willing to go, but went cautiously, wondering if this man could be trusted. Azinine was the most suspicious of them all, but she also went along.

"Hello," Kliandro called up. "I've brought some guests."

The head of a kindly looking older woman peered over the edge, followed by the heads of two other young ladies. They were quite beautiful and Azinine noticed the boys gawking at them, giving her even more reason to dislike them.

"Kliandro," the lady yelled down, "we don't even know these people. How do you know if it's safe? No offense," she said looking down at the group.

"Because I watched them for some time and I don't think they have any ill intentions. Besides, they're from Lux and can show us the way."

"You're from Lux, are you?" she asked the group.

"Yes," Ned replied. "We've lived there all our lives."

"Do you know a Magus McDougal?" asked the lady.

"Yeeees," Ned answered, drawing out the word. "Do you know him?"

"Not well. He visited our city a long time ago and was very kind to us. We were hoping to drop in and say hello."

Ned hesitated and looked at the others. They just looked back at him with blank looks on their faces. No one gave him any suggestions on what to say.

"Well, uh…uh..sure, we can show you where he lives, but he may not be home. He travels quite extensively."

"That's always a risk when you pop in unannounced," Kliandro replied, smacking Ned on the back. "But we'll take our chances. If not, it'll give us a chance to see the city."

"The city is a nice place. At least, it was when we left."

"Is it no longer a nice place?" Kliandro asked with a concerned tone.

"Well, I don't think it will be dangerous for you, but it's just going through a little unrest right now."

"Oh," the man replied. "You mean the demonstrations against the magi council, don't you?"

"Yes," Ned said.

"Have you been away from Lux for long?" he asked.

"No! My brother is just rambling," interrupted Azinine. "He hasn't had much sleep or food for that matter. Maybe we could eat?" Even Azinine was hungry, but the sooner they could get away from the ship the better, in her opinion.

Blelano, the older lady, let down a device similar to the disks they had stolen from Lardior's men, but large enough to fit them all. They climbed aboard and rose to the top. Blelano eyed them suspiciously and her two daughters moved, positioning themselves on the other side of the ship. Far enough away to flee if they needed to, but close enough to get a look at their visitors. Blelano showed them to the table where four settings were placed. She brought additional settings while Kliandro rounded up additional chairs.

"Please, sit down. You are my guests. Don't mind my family as they are only being cautious. These days you have to be cautious. But I believe myself to be a good judge of character, and I think you are not the bad sort."

Blelano brought some appetizers and a drink that had a little fizz to it, but tasted quite good. They all gulped it down like there was no tomorrow. She filled their glasses a second time and left to bring out the rest of the dinner. When she returned with the main course their glasses were empty again.

"Thirsty are you? Well, I hope you don't down this food like you did your drink. You'll give yourselves a terrible stomach ache." The girls giggled from their spots and the others laughed.

"We'll try to control ourselves," Scott replied.

She placed the food on the table and called the girls to come over. They slowly walked over and once again the boys stared at them, enchanted by their grace and beauty.

Scott put his hand on Azinine's shoulder and whispered in her ear, "They don't hold a candle to you."

"A candle?" she asked quizzically.

"It's just an expression to say that you are far better than they are."

She smiled. "Thank you, but I noticed you looking also."

"They are beautiful, but not as beautiful as you are. Plus, beauty is only skin deep. I like you because of your inner beauty."

"Oh, brother!" Josh said, overhearing their conversation. "It's a good thing I don't have much food in me or I think I'd throw it all up."

"Mind your own business, little brother."

When the group finished eating their meal, Kliandro announced they'd be leaving soon. He took a small glowing crystal ball from his pocket and placed it in a socket that was obviously made just for that purpose. He mumbled a few words and the ship began to rise slowly above the trees. It was a beautiful sunny day and the group was grateful they didn't have to walk. Scott wondered if they should tell their hosts about the possible danger they might be in, but then decided against it. He realized he would have tell them about the book and he definitely didn't want to do that. He was pretty sure those who were seeking the book wouldn't suspect them in a flying ship. He was also very hopeful they might get home undetected. The girls seemed to lose their shyness and were now freely conversing with Ned and Josh. Eric stumbled through much of the conversation, but Scott was impressed with how much he could actually speak and understand.

"Beauty may only be skin deep, but your brothers and mine don't seem to mind. Look at them gawking at those girls," Azinine remarked.

"Are you jealous?" Scott asked.

"No, but don't you think they ought to get to know them first?"

"Azinine, they are getting to know them."

"But look at them! It's as though they were enchanted or something. How could two girls, regardless of how beautiful they are, cause that kind of attraction? Sure, they're just talking, but they can't take their eyes off them."

"I think you're jealous," Scott said with a grin.

"I am not jealous."

"Azinine, if you haven't forgotten, boys like girls. Especially ones that are easy on the eyes. They…" Scott lost his words as he was suddenly caught by a sharp pain in his stomach and doubled over.

"Scott, are you okay?" Azinine asked with concern.

"Yes, I think so. It's just…my stomach doesn't feel so well."

"Maybe you ate too fast…uhh!" Azinine moaned, grabbing her stomach.

"Are you having pains too?" Scott asked softly.

"Yes," Azinine replied, her eyes showing apprehension. "Skin deep," she spoke out loud, but more to herself. "Scott, put the Eigenholle on, quickly."

"Why?"

"Just do it. Tell me what our hosts look like."

Scott awkwardly pulled out the Eigenholle and placed it on his head. "Oh my," he whispered. "They look old. Even the girls look like old hags."

"I thought so," Azinine said. "This is not some family we accidentally stumbled onto. They are hags and they've fed us some sort of potion."

Scott and Azinine were both hit with another set of attacks and their stomachs were now starting to swirl. They noticed the others beginning to have the same problems, while their hosts did nothing but stand by and watch.

"Josh!" Scott yelled. "Come here!" Josh looked at Scott and could immediately tell something was wrong, but didn't know what. As he stood up, one of the girls tried to get him to sit down, but he shrugged her off and walked over to Scott.

"What's going on?" he asked.

"We've been poisoned by our hosts. You've got to do something! You're the only one who can save the book now."

Azinine gave Scott a quizzical look.

"I let him wear the Shimmerall when we got out of the pond," Scott replied to the question he could see forming in her eyes.

"Why would they poison us?" Josh asked.

"Look," Scott said pointing towards them. The hags had just finished drinking out of a small green bottle, and were in the process of turning back into their regular selves. Josh looked at them in horror. Kliandro on the other hand still looked like Kliandro. He was obviously a warlock of sorts.

"Scott, what do I do?" Josh asked with a pleading look.

"You have to find a way to stop them from taking the book. You must..." but those were the last words he spoke as his body twisted and turned until he transformed into a turtle-like creature. Josh gasped as he saw Azinine do the same. He glanced toward Ned and Eric and saw they were also morphing.

"Scott!" he yelled. But the turtle just looked up at him.

Chapter 30

Magus Frontier

The hags were now cackling amongst each other. One of the hags moved toward him and pulled out a wand.

"What's this?" she spoke in a high squeaky voice. "Didn't you drink? How very naughty of you. I guess I'll have to show you what happens to naughty children who don't eat their dinner."

Josh panicked. "What should I do?" he asked himself.

The hag walked closer with her wand raised above her head. "Won't drink my drink, won't eat my bread, make this boy as good as dead!" she yelled out. A purple light danced from her wand and struck Josh in the chest. His heart was pounding, expecting any moment to be struck down. Surprise slowly spread over his face as he realized nothing had happened to him.

Meanwhile, the other hags fell into a fit of laughter. "You always were incompetent, Nila," one of the hags spoke as she approached Josh with her wand held high. "Let me do the job. Witches brew, warlocks tea, shrink this boy to the size of a pea." Once again, a purple light flew from the wand and struck Josh in the chest, but as before, nothing happened. Kliandro sat at the other end of the ship watching and chuckling to himself, amused that these hags couldn't even handle a boy.

"It works," Josh whispered in wonder to himself. "They can't touch me with their magic." His fear began to dissipate. Josh had been obsessed with magic all his life and because of this interest, he had taken every opportunity he could to study the ancient book of magic. The book, which at this moment, lay next to the animal that was Scott. As the third hag now approached, a plan began to form in his head.

"I will take care of this boy," she spoke as she now raised her wand with an ugly look in her eye. Josh, now confident that no magic could touch him, stood there and waited with a smirk on face.

This only made the hag angrier. "Midnight sky, goblins rage, put this boy inside a cage." Immediately a cage formed around him, taking him by surprise, but only for a moment. He knew the cage couldn't hold him nor stop him from casting the spell he had in mind.

The other witches clapped with utter delight. "Very good! Very good!" the others chanted, but their laughing was soon interrupted by Josh's laughter.

"What are you laughing at?" the third hag asked menacingly.

"You celebrate, yet you have no idea who I am," he spoke, beginning softly, but with each word raising his voice little by little. "This cage is but a simple trick. I am not some little boy you can easily capture." He now brought his voice down to a soft whisper. "I drank your potion. But as you can see, it had no effect on me. Your silly spells can't touch me." He paused for a second, wanting to create a dramatic effect while also thoroughly enjoying the moment. Then, putting on the most serious, but defiant face he could, he continued, "And this cage cannot hold me!" he cried out loudly for effect. He grabbed hold of the bars and spoke a single word, not in English, not in Lumen, but in the ancient tongue. "Hrumdrihn." The cage immediately disappeared and reappeared around the hag who had originally cast the spell. Kliandro flew to his feet and the hags shrieked in horror and retreated towards Kliandro to hide behind him like little children. Kliandro, startled at the boy's power, now began to take the situation very seriously.

"Abtu," Kliandro whispered and his staff flew from its resting place and into his hands. He raised it high while chanting, "Power of darkness, power of night, combine together and make black light." The crystal on his staff began to turn black as he continued, "Staff of mine that coils and rips, consume this boy and shut his lips." A dark misty cloud shot from his staff and enveloped Josh. It didn't harm him, nor did it shut his lips, but it did stink something fierce. Josh waved the mist away, coughing a few times to remove the nasty stuff from his lungs. When the small black cloud finally dissipated, he looked back at Kliandro who waited silently to observe whether his spell had worked.

Josh also waited silently for a second, repeating the spell he had read in the book over and over again in his mind to make sure he had the words right. He was a little concerned the spell might not work since he didn't have a staff, but figured it was worth a try. After several seconds had gone by, the witches broke out in a cheer and Kliandro let a smile steal across his face. They mistook Josh's silence as a sign that he could no longer speak.

Kliandro walked over to Josh, taunting him. "Not so tough, are you? Now that you can't speak."

Suddenly, an idea flashed into Josh's head. He grabbed the staff Kliandro was holding and kicked him in the groin. Kliandro let go of the staff and buckled to his knees. With the staff in hand, Josh began his spell. "Fugul ni vudnr, hinml ne bihrschn, hurr ahl mui indr andr rifen. Veghr vidnen ahnr tou, cunmen hol ahlr wegnen vew." Which interpreted means, "Birds of wonder who rule the sky, listen all and hear my cry. Four enemies I have here at bay, come pick them up and take them away."

Even though Kliandro couldn't understand what Josh had said, he knew it was in the ancient tongue. "Who are you?" he asked as he staggered to his feet.

"Magus Frontier is my name," Josh replied, rather liking the sound of that.

"I've never heard of you before. Where do you come from?"

"Some people around here know me as Zandor the Magnificent," he winked at Kliandro. "Does that ring a bell?"

"You are not Zandor the Magnificent," the older man growled, and lunged towards Josh.

"Keep your distance or I'll blast you," Josh threatened while pointing the staff at Kliandro. Kliandro stopped, not because of Josh's threat, but more because of the wailing and shrieking that suddenly came from the hags. A black cloud was beginning to develop all around them. It was getting bigger and bigger and a horrific sound bellowed from it. The hags ran to Kliandro. "What is it?" they cried.

"It...looks...like thousands of birds," the warlock said in wonder.

"Save us! What do we do?" they all shrieked.

"We'll have to take cover below deck. Hurry, before they get here."

"What about me?" the hag in the cage cried.

"We can't help you," Kliandro yelled back. The hag shrieked again and again. "Help me! You can't leave me here! Help me!" It was too late, as her companions had already disappeared below deck.

"I can help you," Josh said. But first, you have to tell me how to turn my friends back to normal."

"You mean you don't know?" she said, mocking him. "I thought you had great powers."

"Perhaps," he shrugged. "But I don't have time to figure it out. But more importantly, you don't either. Tell me how to restore them or I'll leave you here for the birds to peck out your eyeballs."

Noticing the black cloud of birds quickly closing the space between them and the ship, the hag quickly came to the conclusion there was no point in holding out and hurriedly answered his request. "There's a bottle with a purple potion in the cabinet over there," she said pointing to a set of cabinets. "Pour one drop on each of them and they'll turn back to normal."

"Thank you."

"Now let me out!" she screamed.

"Not until my friends are back to normal," Josh replied.

The hag screamed and cursed Josh, but he paid no attention to her. He walked over to the cabinet and pulled out the bottle with the purple fluid.

He turned back to the hag. "If this doesn't work, I'll have the birds first pluck out your eyes, before they pluck off your toes and fingers."

The hag looked at him, her eyes filling with terror. The squawking of the birds was getting louder, as they came closer. "Okay, okay," she relented. "You must pour three drops on them. Three drops."

"Three drops?" Josh asked, raising his eyebrows. "You better be right. If anything happens to my friends, I'll have those birds peck at you for days while you're still alive."

"It's three drops! I promise! I promise!" she shrieked.

Josh nodded and walked over to Eric. He uncorked the lid and was about to pour it on Eric when the hag shrieked again. "Stop! Stop! You're using the wrong bottle. You need the bottle with the green potion!"

"The bottle with the green potion? Get your story straight, will ya!" he yelled back at her. "Tell me exactly what needs to happen or I won't give you another chance." The screaming of the birds was so loud now that he could barely hear her.

"I promise," she cried. "Take the green bottle and pour three drops on them. That will do it."

Josh grabbed the bottle with the green fluid and poured three drops on each of his friends. Each of them began to jiggle and jerk and grow. It suddenly dawned on Josh that their clothes had fallen off them when they morphed into the turtle like animals, and now that they were growing, and their clothes were not growing with them. Embarrassed, he turned his head so he wouldn't see Azinine when she had returned to her normal self. She was the first to turn back into herself since Josh had poured the three drops of liquid on her first. She quickly grabbed her robe and her clothes and turned her back to dress while the others were morphing back. The others quickly dressed also. There really was no time to be embarrassed since the birds were about to land. Josh was tempted to leave the hag where she was, but a promise was a promise. He let her out and she quickly climbed below deck with the others.

"Josh! You were amazing!" Azinine cried as she threw her arms around him and give him a hug. "You may just make a great magus someday."

"Yeah, but why do I get the feeling we've just come from the frying pan and into the fire?" Scott remarked as the cloud of birds had arrived and started landing on the ship.

"Maybe we should get below deck like the others," Ned suggested.

"Not yet!" Scott yelled as he frantically searched the deck on his hands and knees.

"What are you looking for?" Azinine asked.

"My gloves and the Eigenholle! I lost them when I changed into that animal."

"We really need to get below deck," Ned said more urgently this time.

"No, the spell was directed towards the hags. The birds shouldn't touch us," Josh said, not all too sure of himself.

"Well, I'm not sure I want to stay here and test that theory," Ned cried out as the second wave of birds reached the ship. There were birds of all kinds. Big ones, small ones, fat ones, skinny ones, ones with sharp beaks, claws, etc. As it turned out, Josh was correct. The birds paid no attention to them, but went straight to work trying to get at those below. They began to scratch at the wood and peck away at it with their beaks. The whole ship began to rumble and rock.

"We've got to get off this ship!" Eric yelled. "These birds are going to tear it apart with us on it."

"Yes, but how?" Ned replied.

"Maybe Josh could...aah!" Ned screamed as the boat rolled wildly to one side throwing all of them to the ground. A very large bird had just landed on the edge of the ship, tipping it considerably. The group had just righted themselves when another large bird landed on the ship tipping it the other way throwing them again to the floor. The contents of the upper deck were starting to spill out of the cupboards and onto the deck. Bottles were breaking everywhere, creating an awful stench.

"Josh, you've got to call them off or we're all going to die," Azinine yelled to Josh.

"I can't! I don't have the book," he said helplessly.

"Ah! The book!" Scott cried out in desperation, thinking of all they had gone through to get the book. "Where is it?"

The others searched frantically for the book. The deck was so full of displaced items that it was hard to see, but Josh finally spotted it amongst several brooms and cloaks that had fallen out of a cabinet.

"I see it!" he yelled to the others.

"Good going," Scott shouted back, crawling over to get it. As he reached it, he also noticed the Eigenholle sitting next to it.

"You're a genius!" Azinine yelled. The others looked at her strangely.

"I wouldn't give him that much credit," Scott replied. "After all, any of us could have spotted it."

Azinine furrowed her eyebrows. "I wasn't referring to the book. I was referring to the broomsticks."

"Broomsticks?"

"That's right!" Ned screamed out. "Those broomsticks belong to the hags. They're our ticket out of here."

"Don't tell me those things fly?" Eric asked with uncertainty.

"Yes, they do. A lot of witches fly broomsticks," Ned replied.

"How come you don't use one?" Scott asked Azinine.

"I have a broomstick, but I don't ride it much because it's very uncomfortable," she replied.

"Basically, she's spoiled," Ned cut in. "Most hags don't have their own MOC, so they use brooms. It's sort of the difference between a car and a bicycle."

"I don't..." she began to say, but was interrupted by one of the large birds who had just smashed its beak through the deck, creating a large gaping hole.

"This is probably not the time for this conversation. We need to get out of here!" Scott yelled. He grabbed the Eigenholle and the book. As he lifted the book, he spotted the gloves underneath it. He grabbed them and jumped up.

There were only four brooms, so Eric and Azinine doubled up while Josh, Scott and Ned each left with their own brooms. Azinine had no problem with her broom and Ned, who had ridden one before, got the hang of his fairly quickly. However, Josh and Scott struggled. The brooms would sway back and forth and then up and down. They almost fell off several times, but were able to recover and finally get the hang of it, for the most part. With Azinine leading, the group flew from the ship as it began to rock uncontrollably.

They flew for a good part of the day. They hadn't had a good night's sleep for several days and now they were so exhausted they could hardly fly their brooms.

"Guys, if what Ned has told me is correct, we are closer to the portal back to CastleOne than we are to Lux," Eric spoke out. "I know we can't really afford to do this, but we need to get some sleep or we'll be useless. At CastleOne we can sleep without fear of someone or something trying to kill us. A little food wouldn't hurt either. We are in no condition to take on the Kingmongers in our current state. I recommend we head back to CaslteOne to get some sleep, some decent food and a change of clothes."

"How are we going to find the entrance?" Ned asked.

"Josh still has a golden rod in his backpack," Eric explained. "I'll use it to locate the entrance and the rest of you can enter on your brooms." The others whole heartedly agreed with this change of course and they headed for the entrance of the Kirtsvag Roum.

Chapter 31

The Switch-a-Roo

When the group arrived at the portal, they approached with caution, keeping an eye out for any of Lardior's men. Thankfully, there were none to be seen. They supposed the dragons must have run the outlaws off for good. With the use of the golden rod from Josh's backpack, they easily found the portal door and entered.

"Oh, my butt and my back are killing me!" Scott commented, once he had dismounted his broomstick.

Ned nodded. "Mine too. Those brooms are murder."

"Now see why I no go on mine," Azinine commented with a wry grin in her broken English.

As the group of friends walked through the halls of the castle, it slowly began to dawn on them that it was empty. There were no teachers in any of the classrooms, no staff roaming the halls and none of the cooks were in the kitchen. In fact, they could see that locks and chains had been placed on the doors to keep trespassers from entering.

"Where is everyone?" Ned wondered.

"Once they realized Headmaster McDougal was missing, they must have closed the school and all gone home," Eric replied.

Holding his stomach, Josh asked, "Do you think there's any food left? I'm starving."

Scott put his arm around him. "Only one way to find out, little brother."

Eric nodded in agreement. "Okay, let's get something to eat and a good night's rest. Tomorrow is going to be a big day."

The kids were able to find plenty to eat. The refrigerators were still running and they were packed. The bread was a little old, but still edible. They ate until their guts ached and then, even though it was still early in the evening, they headed up to the boys' dorm. It felt good to shower and put on clean clothes. Scott demanded that Josh give back the Shimmerall. He decided he didn't like going to Lumen unprotected.

Each found a bed, dropped into it, and immediately fell asleep. All except Josh, that is. Even sleep wasn't going to keep this budding apprentice from becoming the greatest magician alive. Once he knew everyone was sound asleep, he grabbed the book out of Scott's backpack and headed off to the library where he could study it some more. He was fascinated by the fact that this book was written in the ancient tongue, the language that was used to create Lumen, and even more so that he could understand it. He especially loved that the magic contained in its pages could control the elements of nature. It was powerful and Josh knew it. He could feel it. By studying the words in this book, he would become the most powerful magus on Lumen.

It was late morning when the kids awoke, and Eric was furious they had slept so long. He began to tap everyone on the shoulders, urging them, "Get up! Get up! We've got to go. It's getting way too late."

The others struggled to pull themselves out of their dreams, and were all successful except Josh. He had stayed up all night with the book and had barely gone to bed a couple of hours before Eric woke him and his body refused to move. Eric and the others tried to get him moving, but it was no use. They decided they had no choice but to leave him. Scott picked up his backpack and looked inside to make sure the ancient book was still there. The last thing the group needed was to lose it.

They entered the Kirtsvag Roum and found their brooms sitting in the corner where they had left them. Eric picked up one of the golden rods, saying, "We had better take one of these just in case."

They were about to board their brooms when Josh leapt into the room and fell to the floor. He lay there for several seconds without attempting to get up.

"Is he dead?" Ned asked, only half joking.

"No, he probably just fell asleep again," Scott replied.

"I'm okay," Josh responded from the floor. "I just need a moment, that's all."

"We don't have a moment," Eric said impatiently, perturbed they hadn't already left.

"I can't believe you were going to leave me," Josh barked back.

"Well, you wouldn't wake up! And if you don't get up now, we're still going to leave you," he threatened.

"All right! I'm coming." Josh slowly rose, his body complaining all the way up. Finally, when he was standing completely vertical, he adjusted his backpack tight around his shoulders and grabbed a broom.

The group headed towards Lux in search of Magus Noka. The trip was a long and painful one. They were forced to stop many times to rest in order to keep a certain part of their body from falling asleep. In Josh's case, it was to keep every part of his body from falling asleep.

They had just risen above the treetops after taking one of their rests, when Josh, who was in the rear, sped up to the others. "Uh…guys? We have company!" he yelled. The others looked behind them and saw eight MOC's flying towards them at high speed.

"Who are they?" Scott asked.

"I don't know," Ned replied. "Just act like we're out for a joy ride."

"Oh, no!" Azinine shouted more to herself than the others.

"What?" Scott asked.

"That's Maulder! He's found us," she cried out.

"You mean the guy whose house we burned down?"

"Yes!"

"Really?" Josh moaned. "Can't we catch even one break around here?"

"Are you sure it's him?" Scott asked.

"Positive. I'd recognize that red robe he wears anywhere."

"Everyone split up!" Scott yelled. "Head down into the trees. Maybe we can lose them in the forest. If we lose each other, find your way to Lux and meet at the potions factory."

The group split off just as the MOCs arrived. Eric and Azinine, who were on the same broom, dropped into the trees and Eric had to wrap his arms around her to keep from falling off. Ned and Scott split off in the opposite direction and dove into the trees.

Josh did exactly the opposite of the others. He turned his broomstick and shot skyward. "Yee haw!" he screamed as his broomstick shot like a rocket toward the clouds.

Maulder and his men hesitated only for a second, then they also split up. Two chased Josh into the sky, three chased Eric and Azinine and the other three went after Ned and Scott.

Azinine dropped to almost ground level and then zipped along the forest floor, weaving in and out of trees and bushes. The men on the MOCs tried to keep up, but the flying carpets were much bigger and couldn't maneuver quite as well as a broomstick. It didn't take long for Azinine to ditch them, and so they gave up and headed to the tops of the trees to see how the others were doing.

Scott and Ned weren't so fortunate. They dipped below the trees, but they didn't know how to maneuver a broomstick quite like Azinine did. Scott was almost decapitated by a tree branch. He was fortunate to duck just in time, but in the process sent his broom careening into a bush, throwing him from his broom. One of the MOCs stopped and at spear point, the guard commanded him to get on the MOC. Having no choice, he climbed aboard. One of the guards tried to pull his backpack off him, but Scott held on tight. Two other guards came over and held him tight while the other unzipped the backpack and looked inside. He looked up at the others and nodded while he zipped the backpack up.

The other two MOCs pursued Ned. He gave them a pretty good chase, and even lost one of the MOCs as it crashed sideways into a tree, ricocheted into another tree and finally landed inside a thicket of thorns. However, the two that had originally chased Azinine spotted Ned flying below and sped up ahead of him and then dropped down into the trees just in front of him, heading him off. Ned finally spotted them, tried to put on the brakes, but it was too late. They caught him before he had a chance to maneuver to a different direction.

As their captors rose above the trees, both Scott and Ned looked up just in time to see Josh penetrate the first layer of clouds, with the two remaining MOCs close on his tail. It wasn't that Josh was trying to be different or even that he thought heading into the trees like the others was a bad idea. That wasn't it at all. Josh had stayed up all night reading the Ancient Book of Magic. He had spent a good deal of time memorizing a number of his favorite spells. He had been successful with some, but the harder ones he had finally resorted to photocopying, using the school's copy machine. He knew he'd get in big trouble if anyone found out, but in his mind, no one was going to find out and what they didn't know wouldn't hurt them. There was one spell he really wanted to try, and the clouds, along with the two MOCs chasing him, gave him the perfect opportunity.

Once inside the clouds, he leveled off his broom and came to a stop. The two other MOCs came up beside him, one on each side. The guards on the MOCs weren't magi so they didn't have staffs to cast spells. However, they did have long spears, which they now pointed at him.

"You cannot escape," one of the guards said to Josh. "Come with us willingly and you won't be harmed."

Josh, feeling quite confident in himself, gave out a little laugh, but it didn't have quite the dramatic effect he had hoped for.

"You find this amusing?" the guard asked coldly.

"You have no idea who you're dealing with, do you?" Josh asked with confidence. "I am Zandor the Magnificent! Ruler of the sky and earth," Josh proclaimed.

The guards gave each other quirky looks, not sure if they should take this kid serious or not.

One of the guards replied mockingly, "Zandor the Magnificent, ruler of the sky and earth, rides a broom?" The others laughed, causing Josh more than a little embarrassment.

The lead guard finally spoke again. "We don't have time for your little games. Get on our MOC willingly or we'll take you by force."

This time Josh let out the most evil, mad scientist laugh he could muster. "Ha, ha, ha! You! Puny little…little…uh, oh yeah, little peons! You think you can take me by force?" he yelled out. Now was his moment, his moment of glory. He raised his hands high in the air and in the ancient tongue spoke, "Clouds of wonder, clouds of might, gather round these men so tight. Within your spheres, and with all your tears, create a storm and raise their fears."

The clouds swirled and gathered about the two MOCs until the men upon them were completely surrounded by dark clouds that began to thunder and pour down rain upon them. "Get us out of here!" the lead guard yelled. The guards driving the two MOCs, began to move, but the clouds followed. They darted this way and that, but wherever they went, the clouds followed. The clouds were so dark, and rain was coming down so hard they couldn't see outside the cloud and they were now flying blind.

"Ha ha ha haaa!" Josh cackled again as loud as he could so they could hear him. "Try and take me now, you ninnies!"

"Descend!" a guard yelled. "Get us out of these clouds!" The drivers switched course and headed towards the ground.

Meanwhile, back closer to the ground, Scott and Ned, along with the guards who were holding them captive looked up curiously. They could hear loud booms, like thunder, but the clouds above weren't thunder clouds. They continued to stare, and soon two very small, dark clouds, emerged from the cloud cover diving towards the ground at a rapid pace.

Maulder's eyes grew wide with astonishment. "I don't know who that kid is, but I think we'd better leave," he commanded. Then in a more animated voice, he barked out, "Get us out of here now! We have the book. We don't need the others." The six remaining MOCs turned and shot off towards the north as fast as they could, leaving their companions to deal with their circumstances by themselves.

Josh dipped below the clouds to see what was happening. The fleeing MOCs, with Scott and Ned, were moving away. Josh knew he had to follow them, so he took off on his broom chasing after them as fast as he could. He had only been flying for about twenty seconds when he noticed another broom emerge from the trees, heading in the same direction. He grinned, though they looked very small, he knew it had to be Azinine and Eric. They, too, were pursuing the MOCs just above the treetops. Josh pointed his broomstick down and quickly descended towards them.

Josh pulled up beside them, giving them both a little start. "Josh!" Eric yelled. "That was incredible! How in the world did you do you that?"

"Have you forgotten?" Josh yelled back. "I am Zandor the Magnificent."

"Oh, right. I forgot," Eric chimed back with a smile.

"Can these things fly any faster?" Josh yelled. "We're losing them."

"This is as fast as they go," Azinine shouted back. "Just keep your eyes on them for as long as you can."

"In that case," Josh replied, "let's fly higher. We'll be able to watch them for a longer period of time."

"Good idea," she called back and they each pointed their broomstick towards the clouds. Eric wasn't thrilled with the idea. He didn't like the idea of flying on a broomstick in the first place, but they hadn't failed him yet, so he gritted his teeth and held on.

Scott and Ned were being held on different MOCs flying side by side. Scott clutched his backpack like it was gold. He didn't know how he would accomplish it, but he knew he had to somehow keep these thugs from getting their hands on the book. They flew for at least an hour before the MOCs descended into a clearing. There was a large dwelling with multiple terraces and a large pool that Scott figured must be for swimming, since the water was too clear to be anything else. They landed by a smaller dwelling, that at first glance, looked like it might be stables. But when they landed and got a closer look, he noticed with a sudden sinking feeling that it had bars -- like cages.

Several guards approached Scott as he tried to get up to make a run for it, but the MOC still held him tight. They reached for the backpack and tried to remove it, but Scott held on and wouldn't let go. Several guards approached. They released the boys from the MOCs and dragged both Scott and Ned over to the cages and placed them inside, but not before forcibly removing the book from Scott's backpack.

"No! That's mine!" Scott yelled, all the while knowing it was useless. The men ignored him and handed the book to Maulder, who had just arrived. Maulder was about to pull the book out of its holding case, when he heard a voice coming from someone who had just exited the house.

"So, I see you were successful," the voice exclaimed. Scott and Ned looked in that direction and saw two magi walking towards Maulder. Ned recognized one of them as magus Mitle, but he didn't know the other one. As the two approached Maulder, they nodded at Scott and Ned.

"Well, hello, Axtar," Magus Mitle said in very polite tones. "So nice of you and your friends to get this book for us," he said with an evil grin.

"Traitor," Ned spat back. "Wait until I tell my father about you."

"I'm afraid your father is…a bit tied up at the moment. I don't think he's going to be a problem." The other magus chuckled, but didn't say anything.

Magus Mitle turned to Maulder. "You will be highly compensated for your trouble," he said as he held out his hands for Maulder to give him the book. Maulder, however, made no move to hand it over.

"You are correct. I will be. I've decided to give it to the highest bidder."

"What?" Magus Mitle roared. "We had a deal!"

"I wouldn't call it a deal," Maulder said calmly. "You simply said you would pay a high price for it if I were to somehow come by it. I never said I would sell it to you and you never told me how much you would pay for it. So, you see, an auction seems to be the best way to ensure I am getting an appropriate price."

Magus Mitle smoldered, but then quickly got a hold of his emotions. "Okay, I suppose that's fair. Who else is bidding?"

"Hard to say. Once word gets out, who knows who will show up?" Maulder replied.

Magus Mitle's eyes became incredulous. "Are you mad?" he asked, trying to calm himself. "You will attract all kinds of riffraff. For that matter, if word even gets out that you have it, what's to say whole armies don't show up to take it from you?"

"They can try, but I will take precautions," Maulder replied.

"Fine," Magus Mitle agreed. "Can I at least look at the book to make sure it's legitimate?"

"I suppose there's no harm in that. But," Maulder paused for effect, "you may not open it. In fact, you may not remove it from its covering. You may only lift the covering slightly to look inside. I don't want you getting spell happy."

"Deal," Magus Mitle replied. Maulder gave him the book and several soldiers took up positions with their spears pointed at Magus Mitle. The other Magus backed away, not liking the looks of those spears. Magus Mitle turned and handed his staff to the other magus, then knelt down on one knee and placed the book upon it.

"You may not pull it out!" Maulder said in a much firmer voice this time.

Magus Mitle looked up. "I understand. I just need my knee to balance it while I take a peek. That is all."

As Magus Mitle opened the covering to reveal the book, the other magus spoke a spell and both staffs lit up, firing a stone spell. One hitting Maulder square in the chest and the other hitting the guard nearest him. Both turned rock hard. The other guards instantly raised their spears, but the magus jumped behind the guard he had just hit. The other guards hesitated, not wanting to hurt or even kill their friend. The magus wrapped both staffs around the stone-like guard and fired again hitting two other guards, turning them to stone also. Several of the men guarding Ned and Scott took up positions behind trees or anything else they could use to shield themselves. Some were able to make their way around the magus going from tree to rock to tree and so forth until they actually had a good shot at the magus. They just needed to make sure they did so without getting hit themselves. The magus was now surrounded, and Scott could see he was getting nervous.

Because the guards had focused all their attention on this magus, Magus Mitle took the opportunity to slowly move away, until he was able to sneak over to his own MOC, where he jumped on.

"Guards!" Ned yelled. "He's getting away!" One of the guards turned and saw Magus Mitle lifting into the sky. He pulled back his spear and was about to throw it when the other magus jumped out from behind the stone guard and hit him with a stone spell, turning the unfortunate man to stone. However, this now left the magus in a vulnerable position, and another guard, taking advantage of the situation, threw his spear, killing the magus. Scott and Ned both grimaced and looked away.

Despite their efforts, Magus Mitle escaped with the book. One of the remaining guards walked over to Maulder and placed his hand in his leader's shoulder, "Yederharstal," which Scott recognized as the word used to reverse spells.

Maulder came to life with a groan. "I hate that spell!" he spat. He noticed the magus laying on the ground and looked back at the guard. "Mitle? The book? Where are they?"

The guard shook his head. "He just barely escaped before we could stop him," he replied.

Maulder let out a string of curses and kicked the dead magus' body. "Quickly! Get on the MOCs! We must catch him!" he yelled. His men immediately sprang to action, all jumping back on their MOCs in pursuit of Magus

Mitle, leaving their companions who were still under the stone spell to wait until a future time to be released.

Josh, Azinine and Eric were only about a hundred yards away when they saw two MOCs shoot out of the trees chasing after another MOC that had appeared just minutes before.

"What we do?" Azinine yelled in her best English. "Follow or look Ned and Scott?"

"They most likely have the book," Eric reasoned. "One of us has to follow them while the other tries to free Ned and Scott."

"I'm not so sure that's a good idea," Josh replied. "I think we're all better off trying to find Scott and Ned."

"We can't let them have the book!" Eric yelled back. "If we lose them now, we may never find them."

"Have you forgotten so quickly that I am Zandor the Magnificent?" Josh replied with a big grin. "I'll take care of everything."

Azinine understood a little of what Eric had said, but she could understand Josh perfectly and so she resorted back to speaking in Lumen. "Josh, this is no time to play games. We have to get that book back."

"We will. We will. I promise," Josh replied.

"Can we trust him?" she yelled back in Lumen to Eric.

Eric looked at Josh. "She wants to know if you can trust me," Josh interpreted.

"I'm not sure when to take you seriously and when not to," Eric shot back. "I need you to be serious. Can you really get the book back?"

"Yes! I told you I could."

"Alright, Zandor, you better not screw this up," he warned. "Let's go get Scott and Ned."

They approached the approximate place the MOCs had emerged from the trees and soon saw the dwelling below. They flew down to the ground to discover several guards standing very still and Scott and Ned sitting in a cage.

"Are you guys okay?" Azinine asked as they landed. Both looked very glum. She walked over and let them out.

"Yeah, we're okay. But they got away with the book. This is exactly what we were warned against," Scott said glumly, "and I failed!"

"Well, Zandor the Magnificent there," Eric said pointing to Josh, "says he knows of a way to get it back."

They all looked at Josh who was dismounting his broom very gingerly, as though he'd been riding a horse for months. Josh didn't say anything. He just walked around stretching his legs.

"Well?" Scott said impatiently. "Can you really get the book back?"

Josh looked up at his older brother. "Seriously, after all the times I've saved your butt, and you still doubt me. I am Zandor the.." he started to say, but was cut off by Scott.

"Josh! Quit playing games! We need to get that book back!" he said in a panic.

"Okay, okay, put your shorts back on," Josh replied as he pulled his back-pack off his shoulders and unzipped it. Holding the pack with one hand, he waved his other hand around and around over the backpack, while chanting, "Ancient Book of Magic, hear my voice. I, Zandor the Magnificent, command you to appear in my backpack." Then, as if someone had dropped a heavy rock in his backpack, he pretended to almost drop it. He then reached inside and pulled out the Ancient Book of Magic. The others stared at him in shocked disbelief.

"Where?...Why?... But I saw them pull the book out of my backpack and take it," Scott finally blurted out. "How did you do that?"

Josh hesitated a second before answering. "It...was...magic of course," he said as convincingly as possible, trying to convince them, knowing full well they would be angry with him if they knew the truth.

"That wasn't any kind of spell," Azinine pointed out. "It wasn't even in any kind of magical language. Really, how did you do that?"

"I...I'm Zandor the Magnificent?" Josh said weakly.

"I can't believe it! You took it out of my backpack while I was sleeping, didn't you?" Scott accused him.

Josh hesitated. "Maybe."

"You had no right to do that!" Scott yelled back.

"Maybe not. But you have to agree it's a good thing I did," Josh replied defending himself.

Scott opened his mouth to continue berating his little brother, but then shut it again, as he realized his little brother was right.

Azinine had just gotten over her shock as relief flooded over her. They still had the book! She ran over to Josh and threw her arms around him. "Josh, you impetuous, wonderful boy, you. I could just kiss you!" she cried out joyfully.

As she pulled away, Josh puckered up. "Go ahead! Lay one on me baby," he said.

"I said I *could* kiss you, not that I *would* kiss you." Then she leaned over and kissed him on the forehead, leaving him grinning from ear to ear.

"Wait a second," Scott said interrupting their affections. "If that's the Ancient Book of Magic, then what was that book in my backpack?"

"Oh," Josh replied, "that was some old encyclopedia I found in the library back at the school."

"Ha, ha," Ned began to chuckle softly, but he soon broke out into hysterical laughter.

"What's so funny?" Josh asked. The others were looking at him curiously too.

When he finally got control of himself, Ned answered, "Can you imagine the look on Magus Mitle's face when he pulls the book out and finds he risked his life for an encyclopedia?" He let out another hoot, and the others joined in with him.

"Yeah, and imagine how stupid he's going to look when he meets up with the other Kingmongers and tells them he finally has The Ancient Book of Magic, and it turns out to be an encyclopedia," added Josh.

"I think we had better get out of here before Maulder returns or his guards here wake up," Azinine suggested.

"Good idea," Scott said pulling the book out of Josh's hands and placing it in his backpack.

"Hey," Josh argued, "don't you think we should keep that in my backpack where it will be safe?"

Scott glared at him, but didn't reply. The others gathered their stuff and grabbed their brooms.

"Why don't we skip the brooms this time," Eric suggested, "and borrow one of these other MOCs?"

"Now you're talking," Josh replied. Nobody was going to complain about that, so they loaded up their gear, along with their broomsticks, just in case, and took off towards Lux.

Chapter 32

Rescue Mission

After several hours they finally reached Lux. It seemed so strange to them how normal and busy the city appeared after all they had been through. On the other hand, because of all they had been through, they weren't taking any chances. Lux was a big city and they were sure it held spies looking out for them. They landed just inside the gates of the city and hid MOC and their brooms.

"Let's hurry, guys," Eric urged. "We have to find Magus Noka as soon as possible. Ned, why don't you lead the way since you know this place best?"

The others agreed and even though they were sore from their travel and events of the past several days, they made pretty good time. The door to the potions factory was open, like always, and they carefully crept inside. This time the cauldrons were dry and the place certainly felt deserted. Still, they crept slowly along being careful not to be seen by anyone who might still be there. They crept past several shelves that contained all kinds of ghoulish things. Josh was fascinated by the contents and several times he found himself lagging behind the rest because he stopped to take a look. Azinine had to keep coming back to get him. Josh grabbed several flasks containing potions and shoved them into his pack before leaving the room and heading up to Magus Noka's private quarters. They carefully walked inside and found Magus Noka resting on his bed.

Before any of them had a chance to utter a word, they heard him say, "Please be quiet. I think everyone's gone, but I can't be sure." The older man sat up and climbed off the bed. "I'm so glad to see you. I thought for sure you had gone after the book and I'd never see you again. It's good to see you're safe." Then with an almost hesitant pause, he continued, "Unfortunately, the Kingmongers have been torturing their captives, including your parents." At this last part, he glanced toward Azinine and Ned. "I'm so sorry. They're convinced one of them knows where the Eigenholle is. But if they do, they're not telling, despite the terrible pain being inflicted upon them. We have to try something to free them now or I don't think they'll last much longer. But I have to admit, I'm not sure what to try."

"We have the book," Scott said, pulling the book out and showing it to Magus Noka.

Magus Noka stared at the book, his face expressing surprise. "How... how did you get it?" he asked reverently.

"It turns out we had the Eigenholle all along. We just didn't know it."

"Really?" he replied, even more surprised.

"May I?" he asked, reaching for the book.

"No!" Azinine said more passionately than she meant to. "The book stays with us until our parents are free."

"Azinine!" Scott said, looking at her incredulously. "What is up with you? Magus Noka is on our side."

"No, she's right," agreed the magus. "I shouldn't have the book. It's far too great a temptation for me. You keep it and when I need the spells, I'll ask you for them."

"So, what do we do next?" Scott asked impatiently.

"The next step is to travel to Cohar's gorge. However, before we go, I have to warn you that this will still be very dangerous. If we approach Cohar's gorge from above, we will certainly be spotted. In which case, we would certainly have to fight or retreat. Even with the book, I can't guarantee we'll win. We haven't had enough time to study the writings contained within."

"Then what do you suggest?" Ned asked.

"We should approach through the canyons. This would make it harder for anyone to spot us. However, if we are seen, which the chances are pretty high, we'll still have to fight, and there may not be much room, if any, for retreat."

"Do you have any weapons we could use?" Scott asked.

"No," Magus Noka said shaking his head, suddenly looking old and weary. "I'm not a warrior. I only have my staff."

"Do you have any extra staffs?" Scott asked.

Magus Noka eyed him warily while at the same time Ned was shaking his head at Scott. "Yes," replied Noka, "I do have extras. But why do you ask?"

"I...Well," Scott paused, not sure why Ned would have objections, but decided to just blurt it out. "Azinine is pretty good with magic and Ned knows a little. Why not give them each a staff also?"

Magus Noka chuckled. "I keep forgetting you are not from this world. No one, who hasn't achieved Magi status is allowed to carry a staff."

"Under normal conditions I would agree," Scott countered. "But these are desperate times and desperate times call for desperate measures. I think we should make an exception here."

"Scott, staffs are not trivial toys to play with. Without proper training, someone could hurt themselves or someone else."

"Oh poohaha," Azinine blurted. "Ned doesn't know enough to hurt anything and I've used a staff many times. We'll be fine."

Now it was Magus Noka who was taken off guard. He wasn't used to being spoken to like that from a witch, and a young one at that. "Well..I guess.. it would be acceptable considering the circumstances."

"My father has a few swords hanging on the wall at home. I'm sure he wouldn't mind us using those, considering the circumstances," Ned offered.

"Very well, then. Let's retrieve the staffs and the swords and be on our way," Scott said.

The journey to Cohar's gorge took them in a direction that Scott had never been before and he could certainly see why. There was little vegetation, mostly rocks, with a few small plants here and there; it was like a desert. The ground was relatively flat, which made flying low to the ground easy. The journey took them about a half a day. As they approached Cohar's gorge, the hills began to rise before them, until they found themselves blocked by a wall of black and red rock cliffs shooting hundreds of feet into the sky. They entered a large crack in the wall, which opened up into a passageway with cliffs rising hundreds of feet on both sides of them.

Eric looked over at Scott. "Now I know what Noka meant. If we get caught in here, we're trapped," he whispered.

"Yea, we definitely need to keep our wits about us," Scott murmured.

The MOC made its way in and out of curves until the walls around them gave way slightly to an oasis of sorts. Magus Noka came to a stop to contemplate which direction they should continue. Their canyon ran into another canyon running perpendicular. There was a stream meandering through it with trees growing all around. The only options were to fly upstream or downstream and Noka didn't seem to know which.

"What's wrong?" Ned asked. "Are we lost?"

"No, but something doesn't seem quite right," Magus Noka said.

"What is it?"

"I don't know. Let's set down and look around a bit."

"Okay, what are we looking for?" Azinine asked.

"I'm not sure. Anything out of the ordinary," Magus Noka replied.

Magus Noka began to lower the MOC to the ground and was nearly there when Scott screamed, "Stop! Stop! Take us back up! Take us back up!" He yelled over and over again.

Scott had put on the Eigenholle and could now see they were surrounded by water and tree nymphs. Magus Noka appeared confused and placed the MOC on the ground anyways. Several tree nymphs took on physical forms and leaped for the MOC, attacking its passengers. Before Eric could draw his sword, one had landed on him reaching for his neck. Eric dodged and shoved the nymph sideways right into Magus Noka knocking him from the MOC.

Josh, who had traded his sword for Ned's staff, smashed another one over the head with the staff, but was immediately grabbed by another nymph, which attempted to drag him from the MOC. Ned reacted quickly by drawing his sword and whacking the nymph with the flat side of the blade. The nymph whimpered, but held on. Ned hit it again and again until it let go.

While the others fought off their assailants, Azinine took control of the MOC and flew them out of reach as Eric thrust the last of the nymphs off the MOC to the ground below. The group looked desperately for Magus Noka, but he was nowhere to be seen. The nymphs had dragged him off, but from their vantage point, they couldn't see where. Scott watched the nymphs below as they gnashed their teeth and shook their fists at the group. Azinine flew the MOC downstream and then upstream trying to find Magus Noka, but to no avail.

"I don't get it. Where could they have taken him in such a short amount of time? Certainly we would have seen him if they had dragged him to a tree or into the stream," Ned said with frustration.

"I wasn't even looking," Scott said. "I was too busy trying to save my own neck."

"Me too," Josh replied, exasperated. "And next time, Ned, try using the sharp side of the blade. It tends to work a lot better."

"I'm sorry. I didn't have time to think about it."

"You shouldn't have to think about it. It's a sword!" Josh replied.

"Why didn't you use...," Ned was started to snap back, but was cut off by Eric.

"It doesn't matter. You are both here and you are both safe. We have to stick together now. Especially since Magus Noka is no longer with us. We're going to have to figure this out ourselves."

"I don't know how we'll do this without Magus Noka," Ned replied.

"We'll just have to do the best we can," Eric said, trying to take control of the situation. "I would suggest we fly back the way we came and find a place where we are safe and give Josh and Azinine time to study the book some more. Maybe they can find some spells that will help us. We have the book; we might as well use it to our advantage."

The others agreed and Azinine flew the MOC back to the flat lands. Scott used the Eigenholle to make sure they were safe and when he motioned that the coast was clear they set down. The group spent several hours going over spell after spell. Josh would read the spell so the others knew what it said, and then they would discuss how it could be used. Many of the spells were fairly complex and they had to be spoken in the ancient tongue, word for word, in order to work. This meant memorizing them if you wanted to use them at a moment's notice. This was even more difficult for someone who didn't speak the ancient tongue or wasn't lingual. They decided to keep their arsenal simple and stick to a few well-memorized spells.

Once prepared, they headed back the way they came. They flew low, in and around each bend, until they came to the river where they had en-countered the nymphs. Scott, who was still wearing the Eigenholle, noted that their numbers had increased. "I hope this works," he said, taking a deep breath. "There are now three times the number here than before."

Josh stepped forward holding his staff high, repeating the words, "Light of dawn and light of being, light that's been here since the beginning, reverse your power of creations and make these creatures rock formations."

A bright light erupted from his staff and lit up the walls within the can-yon and then left as quickly as it came. Scott looked around to see what had happened. The nymphs were still there, but they stood stone still.

"What do you see, Scott? What happened?" Eric asked.

"They're all still there, but none of them are moving. It looks as though it worked, but I can't be sure."

Eric turned to Azinine. "Lower the MOC to the ground. Scott, watch them carefully. If you see any of them move, let Azinine know so she can get us out of here." Azinine lowered the MOC to the ground and Scott began to scan the area for any movement. When they touched down, Eric slowly crept off with sword in hand.

"Hold it!" Scott yelled. Azinine, in a knee jerk-like reaction, shot skyward almost giving all those on-board whiplash, while at the same time, leaving Eric on the ground.

Eric frantically searched the area for movement, wielding his sword this way and that. "What?" Eric shouted, his heart racing. "What is it?"

"I think I know how Magus Noka disappeared."

"That's it? That's it!" Azinine yelled at Scott. "You could have got one of us killed."

"What are you talking about?"

"When you yelled, I panicked. It sounded like we were under attack or something."

"I didn't yell. I simply asked everyone to hold it. You were the one who panicked."

"Listen, guys. It's all right," Ned butted in. "We're all just a little jumpy right now."

"Hello up there!" Eric yelled. "We don't have time for this."

Azinine glared first at Ned and then back at Scott.

"I'm sorry," Scott said. "I guess I got a little excited about my discovery."

"Humpf," she breathed and turned around to lower the MOC. When the MOC reached the ground, the group looked at Scott who gave them the okay to get off.

Eric turned to Scott. "Did you say you know where they've taken Magus Noka?"

"I think so, but I can't be sure. There's an invisible door in the cliff just over here," he said, pointing.

"Really?" Ned asked. "Maybe, if we can get in, we can find Magus Noka. This may even be a back door into their stronghold."

"Maybe," Scott replied with caution. "But we might also be walking into a hornet's nest."

"A hornet's nest?" Azinine asked, having never heard that before.

"It's pretty much the same as us saying dragon's lair," Ned replied.

"Oh," she replied, nodding her head in understanding, "I would like to see these hornets someday, they must be fierce."

"In any case, I don't see that we have much choice. We really need Magus Noka to help us. We've got to try and find him," Scott said.

"I agree," Azinine said. "His understanding of magic and of this place is far better than ours. Our chances of success will be much greater with him."

Scott nodded. "Okay, we'll proceed, but with a lot of caution. Josh, you've been awfully quiet, what's on your mind?"

Josh looked up, and with some trepidation in his voice, asked, "What if we die?"

"Whoa!" Ned blurted out. "Did I just hear that from a Frontier? I didn't think the Frontier's even thought dying was possible for them. At least, not Scott. He thinks he's invincible."

"You're not going to die," Scott reassured his younger brother while patting his shoulder. "You're with me and as Ned just pointed out, I'm invincible."

"Oh. Okay, well in that case, let's go get him," Josh replied, confidence flowing from him.

"I don't believe it!" Ned said, throwing his hands in the air. Josh and Scott looked at each other and gave each other knuckles. Together, they walked over to where Scott said the door existed.

"Open," Scott spoke in the ancient language. The door, however, didn't budge. Scott turned to Azinine and asked, "It looks like it's protected. Any ideas?"

"They could have used anything," she replied, shrugging her shoulders. "Even a word from their own language which I don't speak."

"How about we just break it down," Josh said as he thrust himself against the cliff. To everyone's utter surprise, Josh disappeared.

"Ha! That's not a door at all," Ned observed. "It's just an illusion. All you have to do is walk through it."

The group walked inside and found Josh wiping the dirt off his pants. The 'door' had obviously taken him by surprise. "See," Josh said. "all it takes is a little muscle."

"Good thing we have you along then, runt," Eric said punching him in the shoulder.

The group made their way down the path, which banked to the right and then began heading down hill. The deeper they went inside the mountain, the damper the path and the air became. It was obvious they were following the same route as the stream above. The path quickly bottomed out and soon began to rise again. It was lit by what looked like crystal balls fixed atop large wooden posts. It was obvious this path was used quite frequently and the group began to get nervous they would run into more nymphs, or worse, be ambushed by them. As a precaution, Scott led the group, wearing the Eigenholle and keeping an eye out for any sign of danger.

They walked for another ten minutes until they came to a large room that was decorated quite handsomely for a cave. In one corner was a large wooden table and several couches. On another side of the cave were several large maps hanging on the wall. At the opposite end, there was a doorway leading out of the cave, which was what Eric was looking for.

He didn't like being in this room, as it was obviously some sort of workroom that was frequently used. There was also a small holding cell, which at the moment was empty. They needed to find Noka, rescue him, and get out as soon as possible. The longer it took, the greater chance they had of getting caught.

The others, on the other hand, didn't seem to be in such a hurry. Josh and Azinine had made their way over to the table to examine a crystal ball sitting on top of it. Ned and Scott were studying the maps trying to figure out what they represented. Josh pulled out The Ancient Book of Magic and placed it on the table.

Azinine put her hands on the ball and began searching for her parents. The gray gas inside began to swirl momentarily and then cleared. Both Azinine and Josh gave out a gasp. There, in the ball, were her parents, the boys' mother, Magus McDougal, and several others on the Magi council. Their faces were ragged and bruised. They had obviously been tortured and they looked terrible. The others in the group, noticing what was happening, ran over and peered into the ball. Their hearts sank as they saw the horrible scene, yet they also became even more determined to succeed in their attempt to rescue their parents.

"We've got to find Magus Noka. He's our only hope now," Eric said, urging the others to leave the ball and be on their way. The group slowly pulled themselves away and turned towards the door leading further into the mountain, but were stopped in their tracks. Standing in the doorway was Magus Mitle, with several goblins behind him blocking any chance of escape. Several other goblins were blocking the way they had come in. Azinine grabbed her staff and tried to zap the magus, but he easily blocked the spell. Before she could react, he spoke another spell that ripped the staff from her hand.

"Nice of you to join us," he laughed. "We're grateful you've come. Obtaining that book ourselves would have proved quite wearisome."

"Did you enjoy the encyclopedia," Josh asked with a snicker. He looked over at Ned, thinking their friend would be laughing too, but Ned was scowling at him, shaking his head.

Magus Mitle's face went red with rage. Eric and Scott pulled out their swords ready to fight any who came near them. Josh grabbed for his staff, but Magus Mitle ripped it from his hands as easily as he had Azinine's. He then spoke another spell, which trapped each one inside a glass cage. Eric and Scott were so confined, that they couldn't get enough force with their swords to break the glass. Ned hadn't even bothered to pull his out. Magus Mitle walked over to Josh, trying to compose himself. "Now we'll see how who has the last laugh," he said venomously. He removed the glass cage, took the book, and once again placed the young boy back inside the glass cage.

"No!" Josh yelled. He pounded on the glass, and to everyone's surprise, it shattered into a thousand pieces. Josh had given the Shimmerall back to Scott at CastleOne in exchange for the gloves. He charged the magus, but he was intercepted by three large goblins, who held him tight.

Desperation came over them all. They had worked so hard for that book and had come so far. It hardly seemed fair. And their parents? Their parents needed them. If they didn't free them soon, they might never see them alive again.

"Place him in the holding cell," Magus Mitle barked.

"Let our parents go!" Ned demanded.

Magus Mitle looked at him pathetically. "Young Polimar, did you really think you could walk in here and rescue your parents with a couple of swords and a few inexperienced staffs? You are in no position to make demands right now, so I'd be a good little boy and cooperate if I were you. Otherwise, something dreadful might happen to you and your parents."

The group looked at each other, each trying to think of what they could do to get themselves out of this mess. Magus Mitle took the book over to the table, reverently placing it on the wooden surface. He stared at it for a long moment until one of the goblins approached him.

"The book is to be brought to him immediately upon capture. I'll deliver it," the goblin said in perfect Lumen.

"Get your greedy paws off it," Magus Mitle growled. "I'll take it to him, after I have a chance to study it first."

"That is not acceptable. Give me the book!" the goblin growled back.

"Unless you want to end up like our friends over there, I suggest you wait until I'm finished."

"We shall see about this," the goblin warned as it stomped away. Magus Mitle picked up his staff and a bolt of light struck the goblin in the back turning it to stone. The other goblins shrieked and ran from the room.

"Filthy tunnel dwellers," Mitle grumbled to himself. "Nothing but trouble."

Mitle took a sip of a drink he had nearby and began perusing the book. It didn't take long however, for him to realize he couldn't read the text. He cursed the old language the book was written in and pulled out another book which he used to translate some of the words. "This will take forever," he muttered.

Meanwhile, Josh pulled one of the flasks he had taken from the potions factory out of his pack. It read 'toad.' "Ugh!" Josh whispered to himself. He put it back and pulled out another one that read 'Fobus,' which Josh knew was a sparrow-like bird. "Aha, I could possibly use this," he whispered to himself. He was about to pop the cork and drink it when Magus Mitle turned to Josh, obviously very frustrated.

"You are lingual, are you not?" he asked.

"Yes," Josh replied.

"If you ever want to see your parents again, then I expect you to cooperate," he barked, as he let Josh out of the holding cell. "I need you to translate this for me."

"Sure, no problem," Josh replied.

"Josh! Don't do it!" Ned yelled. "He's never going to let our parents go."

"Maybe not," Josh agreed, "but if I don't help, he really won't let our parents go. It's a chance I'll just have to take." As he walked over to the table where Magus Mitle was now waiting for him, a plan began to form in his mind, but he needed a distraction.

He and Scott had once communicated with their minds, like the way Scott had communicated with the unicorns, by sending thought waves to each other. On a whim, he glanced at Scott, and then thrust his thoughts out to him. "Scott, can you hear me?"

Scott suddenly went rigid and looked around. "Who's talking to me?" he asked in his mind.

"It's me, Josh. You numskull."

Scott stared at Josh with surprise. "You?" he asked, still using just his thoughts.

"Yes, and I have a plan but I need a distraction. Can you cause some sort of commotion?"

"Yeah, I guess," Scott replied. "But be careful, Josh. This is a very dangerous man."

"I know. I'll be careful."

As Josh reached the table, Scott began to scream as though his stomach was turning inside out and there was no air to breathe. Everyone, including

Magus Mitle, turned to see what the matter was. Magus Mitle walked over to Scott. "Halt your sputtering or I'll give you something to really scream about! Such tricks will not work on me." Scott stopped, and with that, the magus turned around and walked back to Josh who was waiting patiently to begin his translation services.

"Really," Josh said dryly to Magus Mitle, "sometimes I wonder if we're truly brothers."

Magus Mitle looked at Josh. "You seem to have more sense than your brother. We might just get along yet." He took another drink and then, turning back to the book, he commanded, "Tell me what this says."

"Oh, you don't want to waste your time on that one. It's really quite stupid."

"I'll be the judge of what is stupid and what is not. What does it say?"

"It says, 'Heavy burden, heavy load, turn this magus into a toad.'"

Rage crept over the magus' face and he roared at Josh, "Don't play with me! You know very well it doesn't ..." but his voice cut off and he was no longer able to speak. His body began to twist and convulse and then, *poof*, he turned into a toad.

"I told you it was stupid, but noooo, wouldn't listen to me," Josh said with a huge grin on his face. He quickly scooped him up and placed him in a large clay pot standing next to the table. He then grabbed his staff and ran over to Azinine. "How do I get you out of this?" he asked.

"The command is Glaster Yederharstal."

Josh held up the staff, concentrated on Azinine and spoke the command. Her glass container disappeared.

"How did you do that?"

"I just did what you told me," Josh replied.

"No. I mean, how did you turn Magus Mitle into a toad? You're not supposed to be able to perform any of those spells without a staff or with a staff for that matter. In school, we were told that there isn't a spell that exists that can turn someone into another creature; only potions can do that. That was amazing!"

"Yeah, I am quite amazing. I have to admit."

"You're a natural born magus," she said with a touch of awe.

"Baloney!" Scott scoffed, interrupting them. "Maybe you could let *us* out and then you could show Azinine the flask containing the potion you poured into his drink."

"You had a potion?" she asked.

"Yeah, well, I guess I did have a little help."

"Where did you get it?" she asked, and then before he could answer, she hit her forehead with her hand. "The potions factory! Duh!" she groaned.

"Never mind that," Scott said. "We've got to get out of here now, before we get caught again."

"Okay," Josh said. He performed the same command on the others until they were all free. He then placed a glass cage around the pot that held Magus Mitle so he'd be held captive once he returned to his normal self. "There, that you should make you feel more at home."

Chapter 33

Noka and Josh

The group headed for the door that lead further into the mountain and they were just about to enter when Josh halted everyone. "Wait! What do we do if we run into a band of goblins or another magus?"

"First off," Eric began, "we need to be more careful and keep better watch. Second, we'll probably have to fight. If they capture us again, we may not get so lucky. I liked the way you turned all those nymphs into stone. Maybe you could keep that spell handy."

"Um, I don't think that one will work. That particular spell takes a long time to speak and it only works on magical creatures. It won't work on real creatures like goblins." Josh then turned to Azinine and asked, "Azinine, maybe you could teach us that stone spell. Everyone seems to know that one. It can't be too hard."

"I could, but it only works on one person at a time and you have to be very careful. If there are a lot of people fighting, it's possible you might hit the wrong person. If we have to fight, let me cast the spell. I'm pretty quick and until you've had more practice, it's probably better I do it."

"Still, it could come in handy," Josh commented.

"Okay, the command is 'Wertistene.' But when you do it, make sure you are concentrating on the intended target."

"Gotcha. Wertistene," he repeated. A light began to glow within the crystal ball on his staff.

"Duck!" Azinine yelled to everyone. A small light shot from the staff he was holding, but it quickly fizzled out.

"Are you crazy?" she yelled at him.

"I was just trying to remember the command."

"Then try and remember it without the staff in your hand."

"Well, how come it didn't work?"

"Probably because you didn't give the command with any real conviction and there wasn't an intended target."

"Sorry, everyone," Josh apologized.

The group proceeded down the tunnel. There were several forks in the road, but they always stayed on the path that seemed to be the main one. It wound back and forth for some time and then headed upward and upward and upward. It seemed as though it would go on forever and Josh was sure this was some conduit leading into the clouds or something. However, it eventually leveled out and they found themselves looking out a doorway onto a flat plateau. The door itself was carved out of a cliff that overhung part of the plateau and made a slight horseshoe. The entrance was heavily guarded by at least ten men. The actual door was obviously an illusion also, because the men outside couldn't see them.

"Whatever it is, it's got to be something quick! I think I hear footsteps behind us," Ned replied. Everyone listened intently, and sure enough, they could hear several sets of footsteps heading in their direction.

"Do you think Magus Mitle got free?"

"Maybe," Scott said. "It looks like we're going to have to fight and I'd rather fight the men at the door first before we attempt Magus Mitle. They, at least, aren't magi."

"There's no time like the present. Let's go!" Eric said, leading the charge through the door. The kids poured to the outside, and without waiting for a reaction, charged the guards. The guards, caught by surprise were slow to react, and it was only after Azinine had turned two of them to stone that they realized they were under attack. The men drew their swords and the boys began to fight, but it was over before it really began. Azinine was quick enough with her stone spell that they were all turned to stone before any serious damage happened to the boys. Now that the immediate danger was over, they glanced around to get their bearings and see where they were. The scene was most discouraging. The guards they had just fought were only the tip of the iceberg. Now, as they looked around, they could see on top of the cliff, overlooking the plateau, that they were surrounded by at least two hundred-foot soldiers and at least fifty soldiers on MOCs. The armed men all looked down upon the small group, but made no attempt to approach them. Most likely, they were too surprised by the unexpected entrance of the little band. The two groups simply stared at each other in awkward silence. A moment later, however, a single MOC approached and the young friends could see that each of the men held a staff, indicating they were trained as magi.

"We're doomed," Scott said softly to Eric.

"Maybe. What do you think Josh is doing?" Eric asked, hoping his brother had another card up his sleeve and would be able to somehow get them out of this predicament. Although he couldn't, for the life of him, think of how he could possibly do that.

Josh hadn't participated in the little attack, but had instead stayed behind, just outside the doorway. He was fumbling through the pages of the book, obviously searching for a spell.

The MOC approached the group of teens, and landed with their backs to Josh. The MOC contained four magi, one of which was Magus Noka, in chains. The other three, Azinine recognized as Magus Mordi, Magus Timpka and Magus Himnal, all friends of her father, or so she had thought. As they landed, a blast from each of their staffs disarmed Eric, Scott and Ned. Another blast of light ripped the staff Azinine was carrying from her grasp. The magi looked at the group for several seconds before speaking.

"Well, Scott. I'm especially glad to see you here," Magus Mordi spoke.

"Me? Why me?" Scott asked in confusion.

"Last time we met, it was on a dark street in the middle of the night. Somehow, you managed to give me a very large bump on my head that took some time to heal. Does any of this ring a bell for you?" The magus' voice became colder as he spoke. "I have vowed from that day to pay you back, not only for the bump but for the embarrassment you caused me."

Scott's memory flashed back to the time when he was attacked while staying at Magus Polimar's house. He had escaped, but found himself wandering the streets of Lux in the middle of the night. He had run into a magus on a dark street who had tried to take him by force using the death grip. Fortunately for Scott, another young man, who later became his friend, happened to be hiding in the area and overheard their conversation. Believing Scott to be someone of importance, the young man had decided to whack the magus over the head in order to capture Scott for himself. His objective had been to trade him for services to rescue his own parents who were slaves in the goblin mines. As the memory flashed through Scott's mind, he remained quiet as he stared silently at the magus standing before him.

"I have to admit, I'm very impressed with your determination," Mordi continued, speaking to the group as a whole. "I would never have guessed that such a group of kids would have given us so much trouble. However, your little adventure is over. So, if you would be so kind as to hand me the book, we might find it in our hearts to go easy on you."

The group of friends just stood there and again said nothing. Technically, they didn't have the book. Josh, who was still standing behind the magi, was continuing his frantic search through it.

"Don't make me get nasty!" Magus Mordi said in a cold voice.

Scott knew that Josh had something in mind so he tried to stall as long as he could, giving his brother time to find what it was he was looking for. "I'm sorry about the bump on your head, but it wasn't me at all who did it to you."

"No?" the magus asked, raising an eyebrow. "Then who was it?"

"It was some city rat who thought I might be of more value to him than to you. He wanted to capture me for his own reasons so he whacked you over the head. So you see? There really is no reason for you to be embarrassed."

"A city rat? I don't believe it. I checked out the area myself, making sure there was no one else around."

"It's not my fault you weren't very thorough."

"Are you..." Magus Mordi began, his face turning a deep shade of red.

He was interrupted by Magus Timpka. "Magus Mordi, we have more important issues right now than to debate who hit you over the head that night."

"Of course. You are right," he replied, calming himself down. "Okay then, the book please."

"If I give you the book, will you let our parents go?" Scott asked.

"No," laughed Magus Mordi. "Why would I do that? They have been terribly uncooperative. What I can promise you though, is if you don't hand over the book, you will suffer their same fate."

"I don't think so," Scott replied calmly, noticing that Josh was now standing, holding his staff ready. "We didn't come this far just to be stopped by a little rodent like yourself."

"Why you impudent, little brat!" Magus Mordi roared, surprised at Scott's brashness. He raised his staff high in the air and said with disdain, "I will show you what happens to disrespectful children."

Scott glanced back over to Josh, who was once again kneeling down, stooped over the book. Scott had thought his younger brother had found what he was looking for and was about to let Mordi and the others have it. He now realized he was mistaken since Josh was still poring over the pages. Knowing he had riled the magus' temper and that he needed to buy more time, he continued, "Okay, okay. I'm sorry. You're right. I should be more respectful when addressing such a great magus."

Scott was wearing the Shimmerall, so he knew Magus Mordi's magic couldn't hurt him. But he also knew it wouldn't protect him from swords and spears, which was exactly what the army above the magus on the cliff were wielding.

Magus Mordi eyed him warily. "If you mean it, then show it. Kneel down before me."

Josh, by this time, was once again standing on his feet. Hoping he was reading the situation correctly this time and that Josh had some spell that would zap him, Scott spoke again to Magus Mordi. "Well, on second thought, you're not *that* great of a magus."

"Kneel before me or else!" Magus Mordi demanded.

"Or else what? I'm not scared of a two-bit magus like you." Just then, Josh bent back over the book and continued reading again. Scott gulped.

"I have heard enough!" Magus Mordi roared. Then he mumbled something Scott couldn't quite make out, which was followed by a blast of light which shot from his staff. Instinctively, Scott put a hand out in front of him as though to block it. The spell hit him square in the chest, but just as he had expected, it had no effect on him.

"Really?" Scott chuckled, trying to give Josh more time. "Is that the best you got? You really shouldn't try such difficult spells. You're just going to embarrass yourself again."

"Impossible!" Magus Mordi screamed. He raised his staff and once again hit Scott with a spell. As before, Scott remained unharmed. He tried a third time and again, nothing happened.

"Arrrrgh!" Magus Mordi screamed. His face turned a deep shade of purple and his eyes looked as though they were going to explode from their sockets. Scott could see admiration in the eyes of Magus' Timpka and Himnal, but Magus Mordi was beside himself.

"Guards! Seize this boy!" the enraged magus screamed. At his command, several guards hovering nearby on a MOC, flew down and headed in Scott's direction.

"Stop!" Scott commanded. "Or I'll send you all to your death." The guards, not sure about what was going on, hesitated momentarily.

"What are you stopping for?" barked Magus Mordi. "He's only a boy. He has no staff. He has no great magic. If he did, he would have used it by now. Seize him!" The guards once again, headed in Scott's direction, but after another second, they halted again. This time, however, it was not because of Scott, but because they had just spotted Josh. The young boy was holding a staff while muttering something. Their gaze alerted the magi to Josh's presence. The three men whirled around to see what he was doing.

"Star and sky, earth and lumber, cause all here to sleep and slumber."

Magus Mordi lifted his staff to counteract the spell, but as he did so, he suddenly became very tired. In fact, everyone except Josh and Scott became instantly tired, fell down and went to sleep.

Josh walked over to his brothers and friends. They were all fast asleep. On top of the cliff, the whole army was sleeping. It was an eerie feeling to be there on the plateau. It was as though they were all dead and he and Scott were the only ones left alive.

"I did it! I can't believe I did it! I really did it!" Josh cried out in exuberance.

"Wow! That's some spell," Scott said while looking around.

"Yeah. You know, it reminds me of that movie where the princess gets a spell cast on her and all the people in the kingdom fall asleep. How cool is this, that we're actually living that scene. In real life." Josh siad excitedly.

"Really?" Scott quirked back. "After all we have been through…"

"Hey," Josh asked, realization dawning on him. "How come it didn't work on you?"

"Did you forget? I'm wearing the Shimmerall."

"Oh, yeah. So what do we do now?"

"How long will they stay asleep?"

"I don't know. I guess until we wake them up."

"I think I remember how to do that," Scott replied. He walked over to Azinine and took her by the hand, and said, "yederharstal."

Her eyes opened and she slowly came to. "I feel so drowsy. Have I been sleeping?" she asked.

"Yes," Scott replied with a smile. "But not for very long."

Azinine looked around in amazement at the scene before her. "Josh! You did this?" she squealed.

"Did you doubt me? I am Zandor the Magnificent!" he roared.

Rolling his eyes, Scott said, "We can talk about how wonderful Zandor is later. Right now, we need to hurry and wake the others, find our parents and get out of here before Magus Mordi and his army wake up."

"Of course," Azinine replied. They woke up Eric and Ned first and then Magus Noka. It took them several attempts at different spells to get the chains off him, but they finally managed. They lifted the other Magi off the MOC and following Magus Noka's instructions, flew to where their parents were being held.

Once there, they peered over the edge of the MOC, looking down into the gorge. It was deep and a little scary just looking into it. It was triangular in shape and about half-way down they could see the platform where their parents were being kept. Three polar light beams held it suspended in the air.

Scott turned to Magus Noka and asked "How do we get them out of there safely?"

Magus Noka nodded toward Josh. "There should be a command in the book that will undo the locks without needing to know the password. I'm not sure what it would be called, but look for the word lock. Hopefully, it exists. We'll need it to unlock and remove all three polar light beams at the same time. Then you'll need to find the command that allows levitation of large objects. Since that's a more difficult task, I'll perform that."

"Okay, give me one second," Josh said as he leafed through the pages. Having come so close and yet, still feeling so helpless at this point, the others in the group were getting a little impatient. After several minutes of nerve-wracking silence, Josh found the levitation command but still no sign of the command to break the lock.

"Please hurry, Josh. It may take some time to perform the spells and we need to get out of here before they all wake up," Magus Noka pleaded.

"Won't they just sleep until we wake them up?" Scott asked.

"No, those type of spells are rarely permanent."

"I'm hurrying as fast as I can, but I can't find it," Josh explained. Then a second later he blurted out, "Wait! There's a spell here for releasing objects. Would that be it?"

"Well, it certainly sounds like it could be the correct spell," Magus Noka said. "Let's try it."

"Whoa," Scott said, intervening. "Wait a minute here. If this spell doesn't work, will we be putting our parents in danger?"

"Scott, we're putting your parents in danger by simply trying this. None of us have ever done this before. This is not normally how it's done. I just don't really see any other choice."

"Ugh!" Scott screamed in frustration.

"However, my gut tells me it will work," Magus Noka said convincingly.

"Okay," Scott said with a sigh. "We're trusting you know what you're doing."

Josh read the levitation command to Magus Noka who memorized it, while he concentrated on the command for releasing objects.

"Okay. On three, we must say the commands at the same time," Magus Noka instructed. "Josh, you'll need to concentrate on all three polar beams at the same time. Do you think you can do that?"

"I think so," Josh said, taking a deep breath. He wasn't sure of this plan himself.

"Josh," Scott warned him, "our parent's lives are at stake here. Can you or can't you focus on all three at the same time?"

"You're not exactly making this any easier, big brother."

"All right, let's do it," Magus Noka said encouragingly. "On three. Ready? One, two..."

"Wait!" Josh yelled. "What if we don't do it exactly at the same time? What if you finish yours before I do? Or I finish mine before you finish yours? What happens?"

"Josh," Magus Noka said calmly, "they don't have to be said *exactly* at the same time. It would just be better if they were said pretty close to each other."

"Oh. Okay."

"Ready? One, two..."

"Wait!" he yelled again. "So, what happens if I mess up on mine or you mess up on yours?"

Magus Noka let out an exasperated breath. Yet knowing it was difficult for Josh to bear this responsibility, he explained the consequences as far as he understood them. "Well, if I said mine and you didn't say yours or you goofed up, then the spell would try to lift the platform, but the polar beams would keep it from rising. On the other hand, if you completed yours, but I didn't say mine or I goofed up, then the polar beams would release and everyone on the platform would plummet to the bottom of the gorge. So you see, it's really important that I do the levitation command, because I won't mess up."

"Well, I…I'm not going to mess up either," Josh replied, with much more confidence than he felt.

"Then what are you worried about?" Scott asked.

"I'm not worried. I just wanted to know."

"Uhg," Scott groaned. "Then let's get this show on the road."

"Okay, okay."

"All right then, on three," Magus Noka said once again. "One, two, three."

They both said the commands at the same time. but nothing seemed to be happening. Magus Noka continued to concentrate on the platform, using his hands to give him focus. It took several minutes, as the others in the group just watched in silence, not wanting to break the older man's concentration. Suddenly, the platform appeared and the group let out a loud cheer. Still concentrating, Magus Noka moved the platform and set it down on the plateau. The teens could see their parents lying down on the floor.

"Are they okay?" Josh asked.

"They're not in very good shape," admitted Magus Noka, "but they're also probably just asleep. I'm sure your sleeping spell affected them also."

Josh handed the book to Magus Noka, and the young kids ran over to the platform. To their relief, they found their parents sleeping. They were a little beat up, but other than that okay. Azinine quickly woke them up, using the reverse spell and they all carefully hugged each other with tears of joy running down their cheeks.

"Am I dreaming?" Valar asked, as all three of her sons hugged her tenderly.

"No mother," said Eric, trying to hold back his sobs of relief. "It's not a dream. How are you doing?"

"I've known better days," she whispered.

"Can you walk?"

"I think so. I may need some help, but I think so," she answered weakly.

It broke the boys' hearts to see their mother like this. If only they had reached her sooner, she might have been spared much of the torture inflicted upon her.

Ned and Azinine had similar conversations with their parents. The men seemed to have been tortured more than the women, but they were all able to walk to some degree or another. The children wanted to take more time, enjoying their reunion, but they knew they couldn't hang around very long without taking a risk of the others waking up and capturing all of them. On the way out, they explained the situation and how they had used the Ancient Book of Magic to rescue them.

"You used The Ancient Book of Magic?" Magus Polimar said, half in wonderment and half in despair."

"Yes, it was the only way we could rescue you," Ned replied.

They also explained how Magus Noka had helped them. At the mention of Magus Noka, both Magus Polimar and Magus McDougal stopped in their tracks, but it was Magus Polimar who spoke.

"Did you say Magus Noka helped you?"

"Yes, he's right over there..." Ned answered, pointing at the spot they had cast their spells from. "Or at least he *was*," Ned said with concern, as he searched the area for the magus who had helped them. "Where did he go?"

"The book! Where is the book!?" Magus Polimar asked, all of a sudden finding it hard to breath.

By now, they had reached the spot where they had last seen Magus Noka and Josh looked around for the book. "I left it with Magus Noka, but I don't see him or the book." His face turned pale as he muttered, "He must have taken it." Then, turning to Magus Polimar, he asked, "Is...that a bad thing?"

Magus Polimar crumpled to his knees as he struggled for breath. Magus McDougal stayed on his feet, but he was also struggling. For the longest time, they said nothing, leaving the group of young teens to wonder what was going on.

"Are you okay, Father?" Azinine asked him. But Magus Polimar couldn't find his voice to answer his daughter's question.

It was Valar that now spoke. "Kids, it was Magus Noka that put us here. It was he who tortured us. And it was he who planned the murder of my father. He has been after that book for a long, long time and now it looks like he has it. It's just a matter of time before he wages war against us and forces himself as king upon this land."

Josh's eyes went wide with fear. "I'm so sorry," he said in a whisper. "I didn't know. He was chained up, we thought by the other magi. He helped us rescue you! How were we supposed to know?"

"You couldn't," Magus Polimar finally spoke, not wanting these young kids to feel the responsibility of Magus Noka's actions. "He's very cunning. He also tricked us. It has been years, and we have always believed him to be on our side."

A thought entered Josh's head at that moment. "The book is in the ancient language. Maybe he won't be able to read it," he said hopefully.

His mother gave a quick sigh and then explained, "Magus Noka is my uncle, my father's brother. He is also lingual, like you and Scott. He won't have any trouble reading the book."

With a sigh of resignation, Magus Polimar now took control of the situation. "We have to get out of here and prepare the best we can. Even with the book, it will take him some time to prepare a large enough army. What you children have accomplished is incredible. We are deeply grateful for your bravery and your persistence. For now, we are tired and hungry. Let's go home and get some rest," he said as he grabbed Ned and Azinine's hands. "Tomorrow we will make plans and face whatever comes."

The end…for now

www.ingramcontent.com/pod-product-compliance
Lightning Source LLC
Chambersburg PA
CBHW020329180626
46812CB00001B/113